Where Are All The
MAGPIES

A Memoir

Patty Atcheson Melton

"Where Are All the Magpies"

Another book from Patty Atcheson Melton

Copyright © 2012, By Patty Atcheson Melton

Holy Wow Publishing

Melton, Patty Atcheson

1.   Biographies 2. International policies

ISBN: 978-0-9838149-4-8
Editor's Note: This is a true story. For privacy reasons, some names have
been changed, or on occasions certain individuals have been eliminated
from this story altogether.

Dedication

To my: son, Chris Atcheson; daughter, Zoë Atcheson;
Grandchildren, Eva, Mickey, and Hannah;
ex-husband, Fred Atcheson; and husband, Wayne Rollan Melton

Table of Contests

Chapter 1

Millions of lush, green leaves stirred on the branches above me.

An 11-year-old girl, I sat on a rock and looked straight up, appreciating how the branches of the many trees all around embroidered the sky into one huge canopy.

To say that the bossy light breeze tickled my senses would have been an understatement. That day Mother Nature decided to avoid any arguments with me, assuring clear and sunny skies when thunderstorms might otherwise have prevailed.

A simple, good-hearted and kind child, in 1958 I lacked first-hand knowledge of the world's many wretched and eternally wicked natural events such as deadly tornadoes.

If anyone had told me at the time flat-out that "Patty, you are poor," I probably would have failed to fully grasp the gravity of my family's precarious financial condition.

All I knew for sure on that particular day was that I had found my own secret place, a small wetlands area. I wasn't about to tell a single person of this discovery.

Until stumbling upon this private sanctuary, during that phase in life I lacked a bedroom, a bathroom or any personal space to call my own. During my pre-teen years, I felt ugly and goofy looking, unlike the vast majority of my attractive classmates.

Most of them hailed from middle-class or wealthy families, unlike my parents who barely generated enough income for us to survive. I owned only two or three dresses at most. Like each of my parents, everything that I owned was kept in my own, pre-designated individual drawer in our 23-foot-long trailer.

Whenever mother and father were away at work, I worked dutifully to keep our modest accommodations sparkly clean in the Home Gardens Trailer Park in Reno, Nevada. Along with this run-down facility's other low-income residents, we shared the same puny, rancid restroom and shower. Hardly bigger than a common chicken coop, this commode mandated outdoor excursions whenever restroom chores became necessary at all times of day, whether during cruel snowstorms, blistering summer heat, or extremely rare thunderstorms.

"Hello, my friends," as I told a handful of birds, while sitting alone in my secret private place.

The vast majority of my winged buddies were magpies, black and white creatures that usually answered by singing: "Caw-cawww. Caa!"

Their friendly, peaceful, vibrant and lively phrasing would permeate my soul, infecting my heart with boundless love. For one day those magpies became my closest friends in the entire world—except for Susie, a frog so big that she took all of my attention and both arms to carry. Eager for a close, permanent pet of my own, one afternoon I had scooped Susie up from a stream that flowed through the heart of my secret place. For a period of several days, although slimy to the touch, Susie became my best buddy while staying in my family's cramped trailer home. Within a week or so after adopting her from nature, the grim reality emerged that we were all packed together like sardines in a tin can. Common sense motivated me to lug Susie back to my secret place and summarily return her back to nature.

"Goodbye, Susie," I told her, as she bounded head-first back into the water as Mother Nature commands.

I smiled as my friend disappeared from sight, knowing full well without any reservation whatsoever that letting her go had been the best and only decision.

During my occasional explorations, I had discovered my secret place less than 100 yards from our trailer. The blessed find came while walking to and from Baker Stables. The owners, Henry and Barbara Baker sometimes allowed me to ride their horses in exchange for cleaning stalls and helping to bathe the animals. This arrangement proved delightful, since my parents lacked enough income to pay for such activities.

An expansive, lush, green and quaint meadow along a soothing, relaxed stream close to the stables emitted an exquisite atmosphere suitable for any picture post card. To the west, a labyrinth of upward sloping hills poised toward the high Sierra range. At least some of those who could afford day long rides must have passed many a tempting creek while approaching the pine trees at much higher elevations 12 miles in the distance.

To the southwest, some 17 miles away, the peaks of Mount Rose and Slide Mountain perched high on the Truckee Meadows horizon, monuments to some of the earth's most spectacular high-elevation splendor. The Home Gardens Trailer Park nestled like a misplaced hen's egg, tucked onto the west side of Virginia Street, five miles south of downtown Reno.

At the time we perceived the community as a quaint, out-of-the-way little town, almost all of us unaware of the evil underbelly upon which mobsters had once latched their tentacles.

Oblivious to such horrors as a little girl, I made a consistent habit of scurrying alone at least a couple of days a week to my secret place. Rather than a meadow in the common sense of the term, my hideaway lacked grassy spaces or expansive dry strolling areas such as those enjoyed at nearby Baker Stables.

Instead, my private space consisted of a microscopic wetlands area, a circular or oblong curved space of about 50 yards in circumference surrounded by a healthy maze of dozens of trees. I never knew the precise species. All I could say for sure was that the sky overhead became a virtual canopy comprised of spectacularly fashioned, glorious leaves and branches. To me, this seemed like nature's way of concocting a massive green envelope, nature's way of imitating pre-fabricated canopies that extremely wealthy people erect for garden parties.

Exquisite. Delightful. Fun.

Lacking eloquence at the time, all that I would have been able to tell myself as a little girl when describing this scene was "this is pretty." With each passing week, common sense continued ordering me to sneak away to this wonderfully lonely site as often as possible. Every human soul craves inner reflection. All of us deeply yearn for quiet time, a chance to reflect on ourselves. The essence of who we are can engulf the spirit with pure light, particularly when ensconced in a serene, tranquil setting.

"Hello, birds," speaking to the magpies, as if they understood me, convincing myself that they were some of my best friends ever. "How are you today?"

Invariably, their answer came in the much-appreciated form of their own unique whistling, cawing and distinctive phrasing that only magpies communicate. To me, their answers seemed to say that these creatures appreciated me, liked me and somehow fully recognized the great potential of love within my heart. Of course, at the time, I never would have been able to express all these reflections with such eloquence. Looking back now several decades later—in my senior years—I fully realize without any question whatsoever that my thoughts would have honestly conveyed such a message, if indeed I boasted any eloquent expressiveness at the time.

More than five decades later, I still remember that afternoon as if it had occurred yesterday. Following my usual practice, still at 11 years old, I ambled alone into my secret place and sat on my favorite rock. The sight of many hundreds of magpies, all in the branches directly overhead, sculpted my little heart into the essence of love. I spent what seemed like an eternity, listening to these birds singing. Their sounds sprang forth like cooling, soothing streams coming down from the nearby mountains. By their own sheer will, they crisscrossed from branch to branch, wholly putting on a world-class show for me as the only human spectator. No amount of teasing among them could possibly have enabled those perfectly pitched high tones and marvelously generous low notes to match the fervor of Mother Nature's song, that soothing wind that rustled the branches and leaves together just ever so. Lapsing over and under each other, soaring from branch to branch like finely woven threads of denim, through their songs and motions on that afternoon these birds allowed me to peek into the heavens. Whirling, swirling and chafing for position, literally hundreds of them converged—all for my benefit and for my benefit alone. Gripped in my own silence, I could only smile—and immediately I began to consider what it would be like to live as just such a bird. From where they came, and to whence they would go, I never knew for sure. All that really mattered to me was, at that very moment, my new feathered friends kept dashing and singing as if to reassure the essence of my spirit that life would always somehow be okay for all of us—me and those reliable, faithful birds.

As if sensing and appreciating their own God-given talents, the birds individually and collectively tended to increase the vibrancy of their song. *Magical.*

One of them swooped down toward me. She among them became their primary messenger. She landed on my shoulder, as if to signify that all of us were indeed one within this universe. Like the others, she sang without letup.

I remained wide awake, unafraid and delighted that my friends cared so much about me, a mere poor little girl who now recognized and fully appreciated this, their animal kingdom. For perhaps a full minute or two, this messenger walked to and fro along my shoulder, occasionally hop-hopping as if to keep right along with the beat of her many singing friends.

"Hello," I said, careful not to make any sudden moves that might startle this special messenger. Oh, God, I wanted her to stay at least for a little while longer. Oh, God, I wanted her to stay, at least until the very end of their collective orchestral song.

As such situations invariably dictate, the messenger took flight, shooting her way through the air with the same grace and confidence of a swan gliding atop a secluded pond. Sure enough, seven or eight ducks waded through the nearby waters, their feet as reliable as Mississippi paddle wheelers. Without having to be told, I knew that this was a place made by nature over time, untouched by people. The wilderness had offered me this secret, untarnished spot and in return I gave my silent promise to appreciate such amenities for a lifetime, however infrequent they might appear.

Then, suddenly without warning in one massive, all-encompassing, one-fell swoop, all my hundreds the magpies took flight. Standing alone at the center of my secret spot, I waved up at them: "Goodbye."

While they steadily disappeared from view, I smiled—happier than I had ever been, fully unaware that this would mark the last time that I would see such birds for at least the next half of a century.

Fifty-three years after seeing those birds in my secret place, instinct motivated me to return to that precise spot.

At age 64, I still possessed my lifelong skill of intuitively knowing precise directions. Letting my senses take command, I drove on a hellishly hot early summer day in late June 2011 to the back of a Raley's Shopping center.

I parked my 8-year-old, root-beer colored Saturn Vue beside a chain-link fence at the rear of the shopping complex's paved back parking lot. Arm-in-arm with my husband, Wayne, I walked to the same precise location as my secret spot from childhood.

We stood on a massive swatch of pavement. At our feet, the wickedly hot asphalt marked a sharp contrast from the wet cool earth that had soothed my toes as a child. Mindless and uncaring, oblivious of any need to preserve and protect our environment, the developers had literally paved over my secret little spot.

This time, nearby—just 35 yards away at the back edge of the mall stores—food delivery trucks were parked in a single row. Like giant metal elephants preserved in molten ash, these potato chip and beverage company vehicles singed the eyes at the very sight of them. Gone were the many trees that had once provided much-needed shade for my lonely childhood soul. Gone was any hint of the delicate nature that had once permeated this location. Modern technology had brought economic priorities upon this place, bringing this location to what developers call its "best use."

The former nearby meadows, once the site of Baker Stables, had long ago been transformed into a ratty apartment building. From the pavement at the center of my former secret spot with Wayne, I could see chipping paint peeling from the old apartments—absent any evidence whatsoever of the blessed, charming stables.

Hoping to find at least some signs of the miraculous past, I led Wayne through the scorching back parking lot to the edge of the chain-link fence. Together, we looked at plastic trash bags floating carelessly along a ditch that had once been the delicate stream gently caressing through my secret place. This time, crumpled aluminum cans and beer bottles dotted the muddy banks, which failed to give any signal whatsoever into this location's once-vibrant past. A few confused looking ducks wandered amid the errant trash. Each bird looked as if on a miniaturized cruise ship mindful of the urgent need to avoid colliding with chemical-laden icebergs that came in the form of plastic bags.

"Ohhhh," Wayne said, sadly, looking down to the soles of his finely polished business shoes. He had inadvertently stepped smack-dab into a pile of steamy dog poop, which I surmised had been summarily swept by people to the back edge of the parking lot beside the fence.

No, this was not funny at all. It was not funny what people had done to our environment. It was not funny, the callous, cold and heartless actions of America's uncaring and money-hungry corporations.

And, where were the magpies, my friends from so long ago? Where had they gone, those black and white winged creatures who had once sung so brilliantly for me?

Nowhere to be seen, they had disappeared from the heavens, their songs by now only a distant memory. Unable to control my emotions, I got into the passenger seat while Wayne started the car and shifted into reverse. I burst into tears.

My husband shifted to park and gently, comfortingly placed an arm around my neck as I wept.

"People are so cruel to Mother Nature," I said, tears spilling onto Wayne's arm. "How could developers have done this, and where are the magpies?"

A half hour after leaving my former secret spot, Wayne and I arrived home in old northwest Reno having traveled through the heart of downtown while en route.

The hectic work schedules of our independent businesses kept us both busy. He promptly went straight upstairs to his home office computer. Meantime, I checked emails in my ground-level office, eager for an update on my latest graphic design project.

Unexpectedly, I found myself reading an email from the Historic Reno Preservation Society. The organization wanted to know if I would give permission to have the public tour my classic old home three months later in September.

I answered "yes," right away. The proceeds would go to a fantastic cause, a "Neighborhood Preservation Fund." These mini-grants would offer community improvement projects, inspired by similar efforts in other communities.

As soon as I clicked the "send" button giving my initial authorization, a flood of compelling thoughts began to overwhelm my senses.

At age 64, I had just given the initial okay for hundreds of people to tour my home. What a remarkable change this had been, considering the fact that as a child I essentially had grown up in the front seat of a pickup truck.

During World War II and for the first year or so afterward, auto-body repairmen such as my father often earned more money than some doctors. Rather than getting cash, many physicians received payments in the form of commodities such as pigs and cows. By contrast, dad earned tons of cold, hard cash in Las Vegas in the mid-1940s.

There he met a woman who would become my mother, Stockton, California, native Audrey Patricia Chisholm. My mother selected my name upon my birth in Twin Falls, Idaho, in January 1947. Mother always had liked "Patricia" because when in Stockton she knew a student with that name who reigned as her school's most beautiful girl. The name seemed natural, since my mother hoped I would have her qualities.

My mom devoted her full-time hours as a housewife while pregnant with me at their new residence in Twin Falls Idaho, where they had moved shortly after eloping in Sin City. She must have realized that challenging times lay ahead because my father continued drinking during the months, weeks and days prior to my birth. He often spent time drinking with his buddies, occasionally returning home in the wee hours of the morning. Naturally, amid that final trimester of mother's pregnancy, she realized her mistake in marrying him—and for at least a brief time she threatened to leave him.

As a young woman, mother yearned to return home to Las Vegas to be with her mother and step-father. Stuck in her challenging predicament, mom felt as if locked in an inescapable situation. Eager for friendship, mother spent time with another housewife who lived in an adjacent home. This new girlfriend taught my mother to smoke cigarettes, soon developing a debilitating habit that would eventually lead to mom's death at the young age of 64 nearly four decades later.

During the early phase of their marriage, normally a sacred time for sharing, bonding and romance, dad often returned to their rented Twin Falls home so drunk that just being near him became challenging for her. Invariably, the next morning dad always ended up apologizing to mom, vowing to mend his ways.

"I'm so sorry," he would say, always giving her one of his charming smiles. "Please forgive me, honey."

A sucker for his sugary apologies, mom always took him back. Surely his charms, manliness, good looks and sweetness ruled her gullible heart. Although a bright woman, her logical mind took a back seat to the dream of potential happiness that he might provide.

Thankfully, at least somewhat on the positive side, when in the domestic environment he avoided evolving into a mean drunk. Nonetheless, she detested the mere thought of living with an alcoholic.

"I need to be with my buddies," dad would say. "I need that in my life. I work all day, and I need to go out and visit with my friends. We're planning our fishing trips."

Sure enough, during the last half of 1946 as my parents awaited my birth dad went on plenty of fishing excursions with his many pals. Since mom loved to go fishing, too, she accompanied them as much as possible until late-stage pregnancy prevented her from enjoying such activities.

During the initial months after my birth, parenting chores and household responsibilities prevented her from joining dad and his fishing pals in the outdoor fun. Almost every weekend whenever weather permitted father enjoyed fly-fishing on Idaho's scenic Snake River, either alone or with friends.

Perhaps dad chose to drink during these excursions and during frequent nighttime outings with buddies because he still lacked a specific vision of what he wanted to do in life. From what I surmise, he likely pondered taking up a new profession, rather than spending his entire career as a body-and-fender man.

As a guy who literally swam through bookcases full of adventure books, he must have yearned to live just such a life for himself and for his new family in the so-called "real world." He felt young, lucky to have survived the war, and by God if anything he was going to live his life to the fullest.

Topping this off, he had always been a drinker since the 1930s while attending high school in Filer Idaho, just eight miles from Twin Falls. Exacerbating the problem, dad had enjoyed boozing and carousing with his Army buddies as much as possible during World War II in England, their escape from misery at any available drinking establishment.

Without realizing he had evolved into an alcoholic, dad must have felt in a sense that drinking somehow made him a bigger person. Alcohol lubricated the proverbial engines of my dad's heart and spirit, enabling him to talk more with people, to explain whatever he wanted in a no-holds-barred manner.

Enticed by dad's keen storytelling abilities, charisma and good looks, just about everyone that he interacted with during initial stages of these drinking excursions must have been mesmerized by his vibrant, interesting tales—until alcohol got the better of him. When his words became garbled and his behavior became rambunctious, everyone's perceptions must have changed in an instant. All bets were off.

Past the point of sensibility, he lacked any notion of when to stop drinking. Largely as a result, his penchant for booze often sparked rowdy bar fights. Lord only knows at that point what specific conversations led to these violent altercations. The only evidence my mother saw always arrived home in the form of cuts and horrible bruises across his face and body.

Much of the problem came down to the simple fact that my father liked fighting.

Determined to excel in her duties as a new mother and housewife, mom took tremendous delight and pride in taking care of me as an infant. Desperately missing her own mother, my mom increasingly felt that she had made a major mistake in failing to marry another man whom she had been engaged to in Las Vegas.

Emotionally torn and financially dependent on my father, she continued her pattern of continually caving in to his persistent, shallow apologies.

"I love you so much, with all my heart," dad would tell her. "Don't you worry yourself one bit. Things will get better. Our life is going to be full."

I have little doubt that my father must have struggled to convince mother to stay. After all, the same pattern would continue through my childhood and for several decades beyond.

Throughout 1947, the year of my birth, my mother lacked any idea whatsoever that her universe would evolve into that of a "gypsy person," a non-stop life on the road.

All these many years later, every fiber of my being tells me that she would have carried out her threat to leave my father without hesitation that year had she known of their future life, which eventually would evolve into living in the front seat of a pickup truck while wandering like nomads from town to town as he hunted for work. Like just about every other woman of her age during that era, my mother envisioned a stable life with a working, sober husband who returned home straight from work, cared for his family and maintained a suitable home.

Sadly, she never sensed what was about to happen, her heart ruled by love. Thank God, she stayed with him. Otherwise, I wouldn't have evolved into the person that I had become by July 2011 when Sharon Honig-Bear contacted me for the second time about the possibility of allowing the public to tour my Reno home.

Several decades after my parents died, Sharon visited my classic 1920s-era house with other committee members from the Reno Historic Preservation Society. They expressed their delight at seeing the inside of my home, the creative and vibrant way that an artist can furnish a cottage-style dwelling.

As I gave these women a tour of the residence, they openly expressed interest in the fact that my house was graced with artwork that I created plus the works of others that I personally knew.

Like many visitors have through the years, these highly appreciative women noticed vibrant old black-and-white photographs of my family. The frames and photo scenes captured the essence of the long-lost '30s-, '40s-, and '50s-era that countless nostalgia buffs still yearned to re-enact.

Every step of the way, I kept telling these visitors compelling, colorful stories. Just as I had hoped, they openly expressed their desire to share the glorious beauty from inside my home.

From my perspective, an overriding hope began to swell, the possibility that these distinct, heart-touching features would soon enable visitors to experience feelings about their own childhoods. Relaxed and eager to share these sensations, I told the committee about a couple who had walked past my home every autumn for the past 21 years.

"We walk here, because this house brings back memories," said the woman, arm-in-arm with her male companion of a similar age. "We lived on the East Coast, and your house brings back warm emotional feelings for us. This home brings us back to another time when we were younger."

The front of my cottage-like home evokes thoughts of a fairy tale. Lots of vibrant flowers and natural green colors embosse the front of the structure, the primary color a light pumpkin. The appearance from the street generates a distinctly positive curb appeal, giving passers-by a comfortable yearning and desire to see what everything looks like behind the entrance of my home."

The outside emits an inviting, relaxing sensation, the only such home in all of Reno. Just four steps up the stairs inside the main entrance, visitors see a vibrant photograph of my parents when they first married. Right away guests notice the deep romantic love emanating from them, the image evoking an aura of attractive Hollywood movie stars from the classic 1940s film era.

During their years together, my parents would probably never have imagined that many hundreds of people might someday adore face-to-face close-ups with this classic photograph. My mother never had a home of her own throughout her entire adult life, other than living in the front seat of a pickup truck, a maze of successive hotel rooms, a few rented homes and small trailers.

My mother died yearning for a house of her own, perhaps a dwelling such as mine, which I purchased four years after her death.

This home emerged as a blessing in my life, long after my own experience living with my parents almost as if homeless nomads always on a quest of a permanent dwelling. Adding vibrant spice from my perspective, my house emits an aura of the 1930s and 1940s, my favorite styles. Naturally as a result, every nook and cranny of the structure features authentic furniture from those eras.

I also appreciate and find myself attracted to amenities that prevailed throughout the United States during the post-Victorian era during the first 60 years of the 20th Century. Many of my preferences stem from watching old movies during my early childhood.

Such features emboss my home with distinct, memorable features, a sharp contrast to cookie-cutter, everything-looks-the-same homes that fail to spark my emotions. Genuine early-American structures stand tall, like sparkly stars across the Milky Way, far more vibrant and shiny than today's boring malls and tiresome, repetitive housing developments.

Here, within my yard and inside the comforting walls of my home, I feel like I'm far away from modern selfish corporate America where every house on a new street looks almost exactly like every other dwelling in the same neighborhood.

I feel relaxed, whole and complete in my serene, tranquil home, generating calm and enchanting feelings similar to the magical place that I sometimes visited alone as a curious, innocent little girl. Here, just as I did when visiting those magpies, I can relax and enjoy nature and comforting sensations. I can close the doors, sit in my beautiful home, and read a book or talk to God, have joyous dinners with my family, and spend quality time with my husband.

I feel safe here. Connected.

My living situation today sparkles with warmth, color, and comfort.

For one thing, my dining room is wider than a succession of trailers that I lived in through childhood, and my living room is bigger than most little crackerjack-sized homes that my parents occasionally rented. Every place that we lived in while I was little was nondescript.

Each room of my home today features multiple windows, overlooking my garden or across to spectacular early-1900s homes across the street. My old neighborhood attracts people who enjoy an escape from today's fast-paced, difficult-to-reach, far-flung communities.

Contrary to what many people think, I earned and paid for my home on my own before my husband waltzed into my life.

On my own, I left the so-called nomad, gypsy lifestyle far in the past. To that point, while preparing for the much-anticipated tour of my house, I realized that a lot of my longtime friends and plenty of people who had heard about me lacked any inkling of my unique and challenging past.

"Nobody understands my story, because no one ever asks," I told my husband as we began preparing for the tour. "No one ever talks about how I got here. And as you know, you don't tell people of your past. Neither of us do that. No one talks about it."

Yet as the final weeks prior to the tour kicked into full gear, I began experiencing more feelings than usual about my past. Even during the limited tour with the Preservation Society committee, such questions never arose.

Every time I took committee members into a different room, these visitors would say things such as: "Ah-hahh. This is wonderful. People are going to love this home. They're going to really feel like they're stepping back in time, and that's what we want people to feel—to get them to see something that makes them feel great. And, Patty, this house really makes a person feel good."

After taking them through my home, I sat and talked with committee members in the living room. They asked me about all the paintings, plus whether I had intimate stories about the home's history. Coincidental tales kept popping up.

While leaving, these women admitted to their excitement because by touring my home people were going to get a feeling of being taken back in time.

"This is going to be a hit," one of them said.

Within 10 minutes after the committee left, I got into my Saturn Vue to run much-needed errands to prepare for the tour.

I always felt safe in this car because my late father's ashes remained securely in a box tucked under the back seat. While some people might consider this a bit bizarre, he remained there for a very good reason. You see, my dad liked to have wheels under his feet, always on the move, rarely staying in one place very long. With dad's remains hidden, I had a sense that he took care of me without fail amid my many road travels.

In late 1947 shortly before my first birthday, my parents set out from Twin Falls, Idaho, to move back to Las Vegas. My dad yearned to return to work with his friend and partner Ray Bandle. The men had worked together as partners there immediately after World War II.

This time dad worked for Ray, rather than as a partner. Although just a toddler, I had already begun developing a keen memory that would serve me well much later in life. Just barely old enough to walk, shortly after my first birthday in early 1948 dad and Ray got me all dressed up to go with them to the Flamingo Hotel.

Keep in mind that this occurred more than 12 years before Las Vegas surged into the national mind-set. When we lived there the town was essentially a tiny speck in the sprawling, seemingly endless Southern Nevada desert.

Like almost every tourist visiting "Sin City" during that era, my dad and Ray lacked even a hint that the mob legend Bugsy Siegel controlled the Flamingo during at least part of our brief time there. Historians insist that an assassin shot Siegel multiple times on June 20, 1947, with an M1 military carbine in the Beverly Hills, California, home of Virginia Hill, a woman described as a courier for the Chicago mob's Genevese crime family.

Less than a few months after Siegel's murder, or shortly before the slaying, Ray and my dad used me as cute little, adorable "bait," perfect for striking up conversations with the Flamingo's drop-dead-gorgeous cocktail waitresses. Both these handsome men would go out on the town, Ray a single man always on the prowl for enticing women.

"Oh, isn't she cute," several of these women told the men. The ladies invariably cuddled me, essentially swallowing the proverbial hooks that these guys had set.

My dad loved having me around anyway. To this day, I have no idea what was in these gentlemen's heads at the time, their motivations for taking me along. What were these guys doing with this little girl who was so cute, taking me around to bars? Why did they keep giving me yummy alcohol-free pinky-winky drinks that made me happy? Also, remember that through this period my mom remained a full-time housewife.

Around this time, Ray told my dad while the two worked at his auto-body shop: "Hey, Larry, do you want to get some property?"

"Land? You want to buy land, out here in the middle of this God-forsaken desert?"

"But think of it, Larry. We can get it for only one-dollar an acre."

For a reason that I have never been told, my dad apparently scoffed at this suggestion. Imagine if he had felt otherwise. Much of that land eventually became the core of the Las Vegas Strip and a huge section of Sin City's McCarran International Airport. Such properties now sell for many millions of dollars per acre.

Ray's body shop stood out on Las Vegas Boulevard. I'm unsure what this man called his establishment, but undoubtedly the place must have been just large enough that the guys could simultaneously work on two or three cars. They ran the only auto-body shop in town, smack-dab in the middle of the community where everyone would have seen the shop's sign. The place made good money at a hectic pace thanks indirectly to the city's mob-induced economic boom—which enabled Ray to recruit my dad back.

Without a doubt these fellows must have enjoyed plenty of fun, each youthful, handsome, vibrant and energetic. They worked hard all day and played non-stop all night, drinking and carousing while my mother stayed home caring for me.

Ray evolved into a certified, full-time, and avowed "playboy," several years before that term became embossed in the common American vernacular.

By this point, my parents had been together less than two years. They first met while my mother worked at Sears in Las Vegas. She often walked past the body shop. One day she spotted my father working in the garage, her spirit energized by his lean muscular body and super-handsome face, so masculine—I'm sure—that a world-famous Hollywood movie starlet would have swooned at the mere sight of him.

By this point, my mother already knew that her good friend Josie, another Sears employee, had been dating Ray. Before long, Ray and Josie cooked up a plan to fix mom and dad up on a blind date. My parents became a hot number, sticking together right from the evening of their first meal.

This emerged as a surprise to my Grandma Geneva, my mom's mother. At the time of her initial tryst with my dad, my mother had been engaged to an illustrator of Western art. Stephen Cartwright adored mom, an attractive and athletic Heldoraho Days rodeo princess.

A cowboy who owned numerous quarter horses, Cartwright bought my mom a horse and an engagement ring before she met my dad. The illustrator's apparent good luck in meeting my mom took a turn for the worse when he went on business to illustrate a book in Texas, clearing the way for my dad to win my mother's naïve heart.

My dad's smooth-talking ways won out over common sense. Unable to help herself, mother fell madly in love with my father during that double-date with Ray and Josie. The mere sight of my dad must have made mother tremble with anticipation. The universe left her with no other option than to throw common sense to the wind.

An excellent horsewoman from her days at Angel's Camp, California, during the summer before my mother met my father she had blossomed into a sensation at the Las Vegas Helldorado Days Rodeo and Western extravaganza. Long before Las Vegas became a world-renowned entertainment Mecca, she catapulted into star status there, at least among fans of true-to-life, authentic and entertaining wild-West shows.

Until snared by my father's inescapable and magnetic charisma, she had dreamed of spending the rest of her life on a ranch. At such a rustic setting, as her heart dictated, she would have been able to live in a comfortable home and rear as many children as her heart desired.

A native of Stockton, California, my mother moved to Las Vegas with my grandmother Geneva Hedman and Grandma's husband, Oscar. The pair each landed jobs at a new Sears in Las Vegas. Grandpa managed the men's department, while Grandma oversaw the women's section. Using their new positions and connections, they had helped mom at age 20 to land a job at the same store.

Adventure, the promise of more money and a yearning to grasp a new opportunity served as the primary motivation for leaving Central California.

Thanks largely to mom's winning personality and eye-popping physical beauty, she had numerous boyfriends in Stockton. All of them had struggled to win her heart and soul, particularly Peter Buchelante, who would later become one of the wealthiest people in the San Joaquin

Valley. Peter's widely acclaimed fish market lured eager buyers from many miles in every direction.

Throughout her subsequent years in a low-income family, my mother had to look back on her many blown opportunities when she easily could have married prosperous men. Sure, the old saying goes, "money cannot buy you love," but when you're with a spouse who drinks alcohol like a fish goes through water and keeps you just above the poverty level, true love can become fleeting.

Mom always told me, "You could have ended up as Patty Buchelante, and you would have ended up a short little Italian girl with lots of fish and lots of money."

Shortly after returning to the United States from Europe at the end of his military service in World War II, my father had heard that Las Vegas would soon evolve into a boomtown, an ideal place to get a great, fresh new start. Before war erupted, while living in Idaho and Southern California he already had learned and honed his skills as a highly talented auto-body repair expert.

Initially upon dad's return to the U.S., he went to see his mother, Mamie Edwards, a widow living in the Los Angeles area. Dad's late father, Jesse, had worked as a building contractor in Idaho, doing quite well until the Great Depression. Before moving to the Potato State, where my father was born in 1918, Mamie and Jesse had labored in a casket production factory in Texas.

Prior to moving to Texas and then Idaho, the couple had lived in Oklahoma, where their daughter, Audrey, was born in 1916, two years before my dad. But his older sister died of influenza during the great worldwide flu pandemic of 1918 that killed millions of people worldwide.

Dad's parents made the goofy and perplexing decision to officially name him on his birth certificate, "J. Lawrence Edwards," using only an initial for his first name. Needless to say, this caused dad endless confusion throughout his adult life. He always became upset upon recalling the many times when U.S. Army officers told him: "You cannot do that. You need to have a name. You can have 'Lawrence J;' but you cannot have 'J-period Lawrence.'" This always irked him. But at least he had a nickname, "Larry," which people used most of the time.

Tensions swelled between my parents as a young married couple in Las Vegas in late 1948, when my dad kept drinking, carousing and running around "Sin City" to his heart's content.

As a small child within several months before my second birthday, I remained oblivious to their growing rift. Even so, to this day I carry a vivid memory of my time alone with my father on the evening before mother took me away from him.

Even now, more than 62 years later, I recall sitting with my dad having fun at night on a Ferris wheel. I loved being high, overlooking the lights of the little town of Las Vegas as my dad pointed below, and said: "Look around at everything, honey." Cradling me in his arms, he kept telling me stories, and I felt comfortable and protected. Father remained big and strong, as if he could take care of me for all eternity. From our perch we took delight looking down at everything.

To this day, I remain unaware of whether my dad knew of my mother's plan to take me the following day.

Feeling squeezed and without any option other than to escape his selfish behavior, my mother packed our suitcases and took me, apparently while dad worked at his job. We got on a Greyhound bus headed for Reno, at the time a nine-hour drive clear across Nevada, the nation's seventh largest state in geographic area.

"We're going to go see Grandma," mother said, holding my hand as I sat on her lap. That temporary feeling of safety soon disappeared when a sudden heavy snowstorm forced the bus to stop in the isolated high-desert town of Tonopah, half-way between Las Vegas and Reno. The crush of stranded travelers forced mother to sleep with me on the floor of the Mizpah Hotel. The excursion resumed the following morning after inclement weather subsided.

"Where is my daddy?" I kept asking my mother, the first time I had ever been away from him for an extended period. "I love my daddy. Where are we going?"

Mother gave no response, perhaps because parents during that era often made a habit of telling their children as little as possible. To that point, I had never seen my parents argue, unaware of any rift between them.

My mother must have been thinking, "What is going to become of us? How in the world are we going to survive?"

As a mature adult in my mid-60s, I felt pretty mellow, not even close to high-maintenance. A happy soul, I realized that the upcoming tour of my home had nothing to do with ego. I viewed the event as an opportunity to give people a glimpse of what I have, the opportunity to walk into a neat old house unlike thousands of look-a-like homes.

This was nothing about bragging. Simply stated, I loved the house, a nice feel for our entire community. A humble, loving person, and a simple woman, my mother would never have permitted a tour of any home that she might have owned. Non-material to the core, all she cared about was me. She never had many friends; her life focused on her child. She never bought herself a dress, but instead spent any available funds on purchasing garments for her daughter.

Humble to the core, this upcoming tour would have struck her as a nice thing to do, but nothing she ever would have considered allowing if she owned such a residence.

Nonetheless, my home and the upcoming tour carried great meaning for me, largely because of my difficult, challenging and unpredictable childhood.

"I have this amazing home," I told myself. "And, I deserve it. This house and tour mean so much to my heart, one of the gifts that I can share. I fully appreciate such gifts from life, largely because of the lifestyle that I endured as a child.

This home represents all the glorious dreams of my childhood—such as the time when many hundreds of magpies perched in those trees high above me—long ago in my secret place."

Chapter 2

Focused more than ever on making necessary preparations, I cruised the streets of Reno while running necessary errands for the upcoming public tour of my home. As always I felt at least some comfort in knowing that my late father's ashes—technically his "remains"—remained safely ensconced under my vehicle's back seat.

Dad had wanted to be buried in Arlington National Cemetery. But the facility's administrators had so many problems keeping track of remains that my family became reluctant to risk having that facility lose his remains. For the time being, I knew where he belonged, protecting me on my driving excursions.

Thanks to his presence, I managed to avoid serious auto accidents. My car escaped damage amid two horrific wrecks during the previous year, one at a busy intersection of multiple boulevards, and the other at a freeway off-ramp.

Dead-set on accomplishing many essential tasks, I visited a variety of hardware stores and garden shops to buy flowers, fertilizer and yard tools. I knew that while this event had nothing to do with my ego, people would be talking about the tour. I yearned to make a great impression.

Shortly after I agreed to open up my home for the tour, Sharon gave me and the other selected homeowners interesting news: "We estimate that up to 500 people will visit your home."

So, imagine the responsibility.

"I want the first impression to be welcoming for everyone," I had told Wayne, who offered his much-welcomed encouragement. Although blessed with skill-sets that put him on the cutting edge of the writing, publishing, technical and marketing world, my husband admittedly lacked any sense or know-how in maintaining a home and a yard.

Preferring to focus on the positives, throughout the previous spring and well into that summer we hired a creative and energetic Native-American to handle our yard-work chores. This man, Pan, was what I openly and unashamedly call "that Big Indian Guy," part of a spiritual group that I participated in. Although a tall naturally blonde woman, I have verifiable American Indian blood thanks to my matriarchal heritage.

Pan played a vital role in helping me improve my yard throughout the summer, especially after I received the invitation to participate in the tour.

Pan's life was such that if I said something such as "Will you do this for thirteen dollars an hour?" He would say: "Of course." Sometimes I ended up paying this strong but gentle man more than that, while he commented: "It's not about the money. Pay me what I'm worth. Pay me whatever you feel like."

Invariably I ended up willing and eager to give him more money than originally agreed to, because this man worked as hard as four men combined—all while adding unique creativity. Sure enough as his work in my yard progressed and the date for the late-September tour rapidly approached, by early August long-time acquaintances who saw the yard were asking me: "How in the world did just one man accomplish this, in such a short period of time? Where in the world did you find this guy?

Like me and my husband, Pan believes in a loving and a caring God. While Wayne kept busy working on our book publishing business, Pan and I spent hours outside talking about love and nature, and the essence of the important things our universe provides. We spoke about Pan's family, what had been happening in his life. Then, all this heart-felt stuff started erupting, emerging from my past.

I started telling Pan of my trying childhood. We sat under the mid-day August sun, working with the earth, planting flowers and moving huge boulders. As the hours ticked past, we continued our non-stop work while also chatting about my many struggles throughout childhood.

My soul reflected where I grew up, and where I came from, while learning from Pan that racists had murdered Pan's Indian father at age 29, when Pan was just 5 years old. My Indian friend's wise, peaceful words brought back so many memories that had long been hidden deep within my soul. Yes, I considered myself a loving, spiritual person, fully aware that God has a plan for everyone, that we're all graced with the opportunity to evolve into truly kind, good, giving and loving individuals.

As we talked, Pan began to tell me: "Yes, the spirit has sent you to this house."

Ever since Pan had first visited my property several years earlier, he had started loving the home and gardens. He became so pleased that we had begun together—the two of us—to make this eye-popping yard even more spectacular. As this Big Indian Man and I continued chatting, we started to discuss the spirit that brings us here. We realized, fully and with complete acceptance that nothing occurs by accident. All the universe brings us to precisely where we are today.

Mindful, we accepted this work flow. He's a handsome, strong man blessed with the "most-Indian features" that you can imagine. Embossed with a continual sparkle in his eyes, he kept a smile on his face, mindful of the need to remain positive. Like Pan, I realized that the spirit leads us in all we do—every single minute.

When Pan worked, he could accomplish during one hour what any other person would take four or five hours to do. At age 50, this man's strength, endurance and spirit always shined as nothing less than amazing. Wayne and I realized that's exactly what we needed to get the job done in a creative and highly skilled manner in time for the upcoming tour.

Working with Pan, I began to realize and to think that: "The best place to go to church is right here in my garden."

Sadly, however, Pan soon broke the news that he would be leaving with his beautiful wife and toddler to move to her home state of New York. Working diligently to create an enticing, pristine and almost heavenly pathway through the back of my garden, this Giant Indian Man labored hard to leave a positive part of his spirit for my family and for the people who would stroll the garden.

As an unexpected gift, adding a sparkle that surely would catch the eyes of September's tour-goers, Pan erected a wooden Indian statue that he carved at the entrance to the pathway. Rather than one of those cheap-looking artifacts sold at roadside stops across the American West, his unique, lifelike statue emitted character and charisma.

Adding additional vibrancy, during the previous several years members of my spiritual group who had converged on my property left Native American gifts and artifacts hanging from the trees. These included wind chimes and carved artifacts, helping to keep bad spirits away from my house, and making the home a spiritual place.

The urgency to get my home in proper order increased in mid-summer, as my 43-year-old son Chris made final arrangements to bring his two kids—my grandchildren—to this home for the first time in more than six years. At that point I had not seen them for four years, since visiting them at their home in the Czech Republic.

With their much-anticipated arrival just a few days away, as the scheduled day for Pan's pending departure for New York approached, he worked with me on a daily basis to increase the pace of my various yard- and home-improvement projects.

Working with the focus and diligence of 25 beavers, Pan moved tons of rocks, cleared pathways, removed overgrown trees, and tore out unsightly bushes. He cleared out all unnecessary vegetation including huge swaths of weeds. Just a few days before my grandchildren's scheduled arrival, Pan's vision for the yard had begun to meld with mine.

Yet the pressure intensified, since much more work needed completion, prior to this Big Indian Man's scheduled departure.

My mother would have adored my grandchildren, whom she never met. My late parents were agnostic, a sharp contrast to the loving spirit that helps guide me today. My mother's mom, Grandma Eve, had been agnostic as well until the day she died at age 104. Grandma mirrored the feelings of my parents, saying: "When you die, you die. There is nothing else left."

Unlike my mother, who stayed away from all types of organized community activities, my Grandma Eve became a Grand Matron of the Eastern Star. This might have struck some people as paradoxical, since that fraternal organization is based on Bible teachings; Grandma remained a secret agnostic within the organization.

Perhaps Grandma joined in order to widen her network of professional contacts, or, maybe she had signed up in order to satisfy my Grandpa Oscar, a devout member of the freemasons throughout his adult life. Freemasons believe in a Supreme Being, a loving God as described in the King James Version of the Bible.

My mother and Grandma got along great all the time. These women loved, adored and devoted their lives to one another. Always close, they shared non-materialistic tendencies—my grandmother more-so. Grandma liked fine dining and going out with people, yearnings that my mother lacked.

Grandmother also worked in management jobs, the type of responsibilities that my mother shunned. Eventually, my grandmother became very well liked by loads of people while managing high-end motel lodging facilities, while mother remained a loner for the most part—dedicating her life to me.

Unlike her future daughter who avoided large social functions, as a teenager my Grandma Eve liked to attend formals, and she dressed up in fancy dresses for special public occasions. My mother never cared about dressing up, always mostly in Levis with her informal shirts. As an adult my mother wore dresses to work, but only because that's what employers required women to wear on the job.

My mother never paid keen attention to her appearance, while my Grandma Eve cared much more about her own. Yet mom's physical beauty permeated any need to dress fancy or to wear make-up; she always glowed with a movie-star quality whatever she wore. I remember seeing magnetic photos of my mother during her childhood and teen years, exceedingly beautiful and emitting a happy aura.

At the height of World War II, mother joined the "Waves," formally known as the Women Accepted for Volunteer Emergency Service organization. A division of the U.S. Navy, the Waves trained young adult females for acceptance in the U.S. Naval Reserve. The organization's commanders had no option other than to release mom from their system when she became terribly homesick in New York during the early 1940s.

Before joining Sears as a manager in the Stockton California store, my Grandma had owned Eve's Beauty Shop, before leaving for Las Vegas; she and Grandpa Oscar went there to manage a sister department store. All along, Grandma Eve showed absolutely no interest in horses, which had emerged as my mother's consuming passion during the 1940s.

Born in French Camp, California, my mother's father was William Chisholm, my Grandma Eve's first husband. During the 1930s, when my mother was a pre-teen and in her early teens, their family had moved from the Stockton area to Washington State, where William worked as a Depression-era electrician. His unique skills enabled my mother's family to escape the type of financial hardship that plagued many Americans of that era.

Mother had a great childhood in Washington State, where the family enjoyed their pet collie and cherished vibrant fishing excursions.

The happiness faded when Grandpa William died of a heart attack while only in his 40s. Medical technicians would have been able to save my grandfather using technology prevalent in the 1990s and beyond. But no such medicines existed then. The emergency occurred while he worked up on a power pole. After suffering his initial chest pains, Grandpa William came home where he died within six hours, frustrated physicians unable to help him.

Their family dog, Laddie, stayed out on their porch, wailing like a lonely coyote, mourning the whole time as Grandpa William lay dying inside the home. When recounting this tale to me many years later, mother referred to this incident in an almost spiritual sense—although, as an agnostic, she never spoke of God or Jesus. Mom avoided mentioning things that were not of this earth.

Grandpa William's death devastated my mother, partly because they would go camping and fishing, activities that she would later desperately miss. Worsening matters, this Grandpa's death forced mother and the rest of their family to leave the beautiful Washington state town where they had enjoyed life.

Heartbroken, my mother disliked the notion of moving back to Stockton, but their family's only option was to return to the region of their roots in order to establish a solid economic base. That's when Grandma Eve launched her beauty shop, "Eve's Salon." The prevalent '40s hair-styles for women undoubtedly forced Grandma to generate pin-curls and permanents for her clients.

For the most part, the women from generation to generation in my family lacked serious conflict. They always got along.

This marked a sharp difference from many families I have met or learned about through the years. While growing up, I saw or heard about many instances where teenage girls disliked or fought with their mothers. By contrast, I never fought with my mother, and she never exchanged a cross word with her mom.

Grandma Eve met my Grandpa Oscar Hedman when she had given up her beauty salon business, becoming a women's department manager at the Stockton Sears Roebuck store. Grandpa managed the men's department.

The only weird thing about Grandpa Oscar became evident when on occasion he used his right hand to continuously swat at his own right ear. This apparent nervous condition might have seemed like an irritant to anyone who failed to know the man well. Once you learned of his intense kindness, this irritating habit became at least somewhat easy to overlook, but only for awhile. His persistent ear slapping sometimes became so intense that the noise bugged me to no end.

With such irritation aside, I'll have to admit the man beamed as a fairly good looking fellow when Grandma Eve first met him—thin and nicely dressed, perhaps thanks to his extensive experience at the Sears men's department. His charm melded well with Grandma's appropriately alluring outfits and her infectious smile.

My mom disliked Grandpa Oscar, thinking of him as what she would call "not a real man." To her, this kind and handsome gentleman could never come even close to being a manly fellow such as her own late biological father, my late Grandpa William. That strong and strapping guy who provided well for his family doing manly work contrasted sharply to what my mother perceived as a "fancy man."

Mother never related at all to Grandpa Oscar, although he tried to make their relationship work. The sudden death of my mom's father had occurred as she entered her difficult teenage years. This probably hailed as among primary reasons why she never got along with Grandma's new husband.

By contrast, I adored the man.

Sweet and kind to the core, he often made my favorite dunk-eggs, toast and bacon. Grandpa Oscar would do nice things for me whenever he could. During my early childhood, he often took me to the Reno airport, a small facility at the time.

We sat together enjoying the view as we watched commercial airliners take off and land. Our camaraderie intensified when seeing in-bound visitors deplane. We enjoyed watching everyone's clothing styles and demeanor, or looking with our wondrous eyes as out-bound passengers departed for a wide variety of different places. All those scenes were visible from outside airports in those days, when passengers boarded and deplaned via stairs rather than terminals.

Adding to the luster, as a member of the Shriners Grandpa Oscar had different ways to get us into the Circus. None of these attributes impressed my mother in the least, but these same characteristics made the man shine within my very young eyes.

So, upon heading with me to Reno from Las Vegas, after leaving my father, my mother was essentially en route to live at least for a while with her own mother and grandpa Bud that she never totally liked. At least mother never hated the man. She needed a place to stay, deeply attached to Grandma Eve, her best friend.

Grandma carried a worldly aura, a natural expert in the social graces. This woman's longtime membership in the Eastern Star had enabled her to become more sophisticated. But in other ways, Grandma remained very bigoted, calling blacks "colored people." Although she and I had been very close, to this day I'm unaware of whether Grandma graduated from high school; she never shared those details.

Highly skilled at writing and memorization, Grandma Eve could easily learn things. To me she seemed self-educated, although she never attended college. A ferocious reader, she raced through many books—primarily romance novels—until shortly before her death at age 104 in the summer of 2008. Her reading preferences never seemed to focus on any desire to learn.

Upon leaving my father behind in Las Vegas, my mother became the first woman in her family ever to separate from her husband. This failed to spark any angst from Grandma Eve, since she had never liked my dad.

"I told you so," my Grandma Eve probably said to my mother.

Shortly after first meeting my father, Grandma voiced her clear, concise opinion that the man seemed unstable, lacking the ability to care for his new wife and family.

More than anything, I'm sure Grandma felt happy to welcome my mother and me while dad remained many hundreds of miles away in Las Vegas. While graciously welcoming us with open arms, Grandma expressed her sincere and loving hope that my dad would avoid any attempt to return to my mother's life.

Good.

That's precisely how my grandmother felt, increasingly hopeful that my mother would find a better man capable and willing to support a family. Grandma knew of my dad's wretched penchant for carousing and alcohol. This made her distrustful of him, since people with such propensities rarely change their wicked ways. As a toddler, I never picked up on these tensions. Oblivious to such worries, I felt great delight in enjoying time with my Grandparents—who each spoiled me rotten, both loving me fully and without reservation. Although I missed my daddy terribly, along with my mother they made my life comfortable in an small three-bedroom house with a nice yard they owned on Bartlett Street. Three months after my second birthday, I scurried around the small lawn and garden to collect Easter eggs. My mother and Grandparents felt great delight upon seeing my unstoppable, rambunctious, energetic behavior.

Sensations of warmth and inviting aromas surrounded the house.

But happy times were about to end for my Grandparents, because around that time my dad announced his intention to move to Reno for the first time. His plan focused on getting a good auto-body shop job while winning mommy's heart and getting me back as well. Although Grandma and my mother continued to get along, tensions increased as joyful sensations engulfed my mom, delighted that dad wanted to re-enter her life.

Eager to retrieve his wife and daughter, my dad arrived at my Grandparents' home to pick up mommy and me. Conflict immediately reached the boiling point, as my Grandpa Oscar essentially read my father the riot act.

"You need to do a better job of caring for your family," Grandpa told my dad, dead set on making his feelings known.

As a seasoned war veteran, my dad imposed a lightning-fast reaction, the type of unexpected response that today's military experts refer to as "shock and awe."

"Don't you ever tell me what to do!" My father yelled at Grandpa. My tall, muscular, thin dad yanked the short, small-framed man by the collar, picked him up, and shouted face-to-face at his adversary. "This is my family! Whether you like what I do with my family or not, it's none of your concern. It's not your family, and you shut up. I'm taking my family, and I don't care what you think."

Many years later my dad would admit to me, without making any attempt whatsoever to censor details that the confrontation marked "the end of Bud ever telling me what to do."

Bud.

That was my dad's nickname for my Grandpa. Hardly anyone else referred to Oscar by that term. Once my dad decided to dislike a person, such adversarial sensations stuck like glue for a lifetime.

"That man never told me what to do ever again after that," my father would later tell me. Dad seemed to take delight in winning that battle, for he always hailed as a man who refused to allow anyone to tell him what to do. Refusing to let their grudge fall by the wayside, my father disliked sweet Grandpa Oscar until the day that senior gentleman died from natural causes three decades later.

Keep in mind that several years earlier my mother had threatened to leave my father just a few months before my birth. Like before, shortly after our arrival in Reno he sweet-talked mom, insisting that things had changed thanks to his decision to stop drinking and to get a stable, steady, long-term job.

To my father's great credit, he loved my mother with all his heart. Goodness knows he must have called her countless times, saying: "I'm sorry. I miss you and Patty. I want us all to be a family. You need me. I'm going to straighten up. I'm coming to get you guys, and I'm going to go to the university in Reno. I'm going to be somebody. I'm going to take advantage of the GI bill, and I'm going to take care of us; we're a family."

"Well, I hope you mean this," mom probably said. "The university will provide a perfect opportunity for you to seek a new career. I can get a little job, and you can work part-time while attending classes."

Desperate to resume their passion and to return to each other's arms for good, my parents promptly took this path. Within several weeks, mom and dad rented us a small apartment at Victory Heights overlooking the University of Nevada campus.

Dad worked part-time at Scott Motors, a high-end vehicle sales and repair business in downtown Reno at the time. Mother landed work at a box factory less than a mile east of our new residence. Every day, they took me to a baby-sitting service in an old Victorian-style house on South Virginia Street just south of town. My memory from those early years remains vivid to this day. I still can clearly and vividly recall the nice, old day care home. Even in the high-desert community, bright, colorful flowers surrounded the house framed by a massive, finely-mowed yard.

The residence gave me sensations of comfort, and my loving young soul adored the plain-looking woman who cared for me.

Lenses big enough to use for telescopes made her eyeglasses look larger than binoculars. But other than that the woman appeared fairly normal, not quite beautiful but also far from ugly.

"Hello, sweet Patty," my kind baby-sitter would say upon my daily arrival, her voice soothing and comforting although raspy, almost as deep as a man's. Somehow, don't ask me why, but her curious eyes seemed to smile even more than her mouth. She always made me feel good and protected, far from the type of witch that my father might have perceived my Grandma as being. On occasional days this woman even snuck me a yummy chocolate chip cookie on the sly shortly before my mother showed up to get me.

This arrangement enabled my father to concentrate on his studies in forestry and agriculture. Dad carried loads of textbooks for his general courses into our tiny apartment, plus numerous publications that focused on grammar and journalism.

During those classes my dad befriended a kind-hearted, industrious student, Bill McCabe. As his own graduation approached, Bill and his wife, Franny, each became close pals with my parents. Yet their positive-minded activities and collective plans for a good future soon came to a sudden, screeching halt—at least for my parents.

Unable to handle the pressures of school and work, my father began drinking again.

But mom stuck with him.

The new Reno operations of a taxi business that my Grandparents left Vegas for fizzled due to administration hassles at their bosses' Las Vegas headquarters. The partnership disintegrated.

Yet thanks largely to Grandpa Oscar's connections with the Shriners my Grandparents landed new jobs co-managing the high-end Hill & Sons Motel in Reno.

Selling their small Bartlett Street house, Grandma Eve and Grandpa Oscar enjoyed staying in their latest home, the motel's management headquarters.

Far from a flop house or a quickie-stop along a busy highway, Hill & Sons gained a well-deserved reputation as one of the nicest motels in Northern Nevada. My Grandparents' second-floor apartment afforded a clear view of an adjoining outdoor movie theater, The Midway Drive-In. After sundown on spring, summer and autumn nights, from my Grandparents' living quarters we enjoyed watching new films popular in the late 1940s and early 1950s, such as the legendary Gary Cooper classic "High Noon."

In a sense, at least in my heart, my dad was like the sheriff in that film. Faced with a moral dilemma and striving to make difficult yet righteous decisions, my father behaved like a heroic character striving to make the best choices that he knew how.

Looking back, I suppose that many people would have been a bit envious of my Grandparents' comfortable situation. With their general living area upstairs, Grandma and Grandpa also benefited from a spiffy first-floor kitchen behind the general office check-in and check-out desk. Lacking such comforts for himself and for his own family, my father's resumption of his boozing lifestyle emerged for a reason that I'll never specifically understand. Perhaps father considered alcohol as a way to cope with conflict.

Rather than deal with his in-laws face-to-face, dad always stayed home alone in our apartment whenever mother took me to spend quality time with Grandma and Grandpa. My father strived to steer clear from my Grandparents, whom he knew were always hoping to get my mom away from him.

Did dad's loneliness intensify on holidays such as Thanksgiving, Christmas and Easter? Did apparent failures at work and school motivate him to resume drinking full-fledge? Did father feel any sort of shame or envy, due to Grandpa Oscar's reputation as a sober, successful role model throughout the community?

Unbeknownst to my dad, at the time Grandpa excelled at being what I call "a sneaky drinker." Even Grandma failed to sense that her husband sometimes drank just as much or perhaps even more than my father. On the sly, Grandpa would buy tiny liquor bottles, hiding them from grandmother and taking quick gulps in private.

In fact, as I would learn many decades later, Grandpa Oscar successfully pulled off his own boozing behavior throughout his entire life. As sneaky as a field mouse, Grandpa would buy loads of tiny pocket-size liquor bottles, cleverly storing them in hiding places that he knew Grandma would never check.

Whenever Grandpa's burning inner craving for booze struck, he would guzzle an entire miniature bottle of liquor in one-fell swoop without ever bothering to pour his drinks. All along, at least as far as I can surmise, whenever the mood struck amid private conversation with my Grandma or my mother, Grandpa roundly criticized my father's boozing ways and "dead-end profession."

Somehow Grandpa must have managed to hide his penchant for booze from the motel's many high-end clients as well. Increasingly popular among visitors from throughout the nation, particularly the West, the facility lured numerous high-income clientele including sports car owners. Collectors of classic automobiles organized glitzy, fun and uproarious rallies, each held on the Hill & Sons spacious grounds.

While my mother and father struggled to make ends meet in relative obscurity, my Grandparents' popularity soared among Reno's tourists. Some of the most popular annual car rallies featured 1930s and 1940s sports vehicles taken on one-mile drives around Virginia Lake, at the time several miles south of Reno's primary city core.

At the insistence of these guests, Grandma and Grandpa received the honor of being the first people to ride the tram at the new Mount Rose Ski Resort 17 miles southwest of Reno, ideal for winter sports enthusiasts. The moment Grandma Eve exited the new ski lift atop the mountain, the device broke. Dozens or perhaps scores of people got stuck in their seats on the device behind her, trapped high above the snow.

Scenes such as these provided ample fodder for lively stories that my Grandparents and their delighted motel guests enjoyed telling for many years.

Hailed since the 1910s as "The Biggest Little City in the World," during the late 1940s and early 1950s Reno reigned as Nevada's largest city by far. At the time, Reno hailed as the world's capital for legalized casino gambling. This notoriety or prestige only served to focus the spotlight even more on my Grandparents, who seemed to benefit from their steadily increasing popularity and growing cadre of classy business connections.

Just as important, at least at the time, Reno gained what I considered a well-deserved reputation as one of the most beautiful cities in the United States and probably the world. It wasn't until several decades later that the town gained an undeserved status as the low-end, greasy capital of trailer trash and slimy neighborhoods.

To the contrary, especially during my early childhood Reno glistened both day and night, nestled at the cusp of the glorious eastern Sierra range. Mount Rose, Slide Mountain and other eye-catching peaks command the horizon immediately to the west and southwest, while brown, curvaceous and mysterious desert peaks caress the south, east and north edges of the valley-like region called the Truckee Meadows.

Without exaggeration, since the mid-1800s through the middle of the 20th Century and even up until today, many people have instantly decided to spend the rest of their lives here as soon as they first see the community.

Characters played by the world's most popular film stars mentioned Reno in countless movies in the decades before and immediately after my Grandparents' heyday here. "I'm going to get a divorce in Reno," some characters would say. In reality, streams of soon-to-be divorcees flocked to the region due to the state's divorce laws, ultra-liberal for that era on a worldwide scale.

Streams of women, many of them mega-wealthy, stayed at facilities labeled as "dude ranches" throughout the region, in order to fulfill a required six-week residency obligation necessary to qualify for a "quickie divorce." Super-wealthy husbands and wives, many of them on the outs, flocked like excited geese to the Hill & Sons, where many of them eagerly befriended my Grandparents.

If this grated against my father's soul and his heart, he never mentioned that fact, at least in front of me. Always filled with pride and determined to behave his way, he must have brushed off my Grandparents' growing acclaim with ease.

Although their names never reached the national superstar level, my Grandparents achieved "notable personality" status in Reno during an ideal time. Many of today's nostalgia buffs still yearn for that era, when I surmise that my dad might have felt at least some inkling of contempt for the well-deserved acclaim that his in-laws had earned.

Perhaps these conflicts played a major role in the fact that my immediate family's Reno stay lasted just a couple of years. Around my fourth birthday, mother and father packed their suitcases and left with me for Idaho. If you were to ask me today, I'd guess that my father's decision to high-tail it out of Reno and to give up other potential professions must have bothered him for the rest of his life.

Rather than striving to struggle his way through college my father took the easy route, falling back on the only profession he knew—fixing cars. Little did any of us know that this departure from Reno marked the start of a non-stop, on-the-road pattern that would last without letup for many years.

Without question my father took the wrong route, and from that point forward there would be absolutely no opportunity to turn back.

Chapter 3

While making the path along the garden of my Reno home, Pan walked up to me: "Patty, look what I found."

"What is that?" I asked, perplexed, studying a flat, palm-sized, sharp-edged stone that the Indian held in his outstretched hands.

"Patty, this is a wonderful omen for you—a spectacular sign," Pan said.

I sat on a bench while accepting the stone from him, mesmerized and still uncertain of its meaning. The object's touch felt cool to my skin, sending shivers up my arms and down my spine. The broad muscular man sat beside me, and the enticing smell of his light perspiration brought thoughts of a wild, untamed forest.

"Patty, if you unexpectedly find an Indian relic like this on your property, the Creator is giving a sign that good things are headed your way," Pan said. "You and your family are indeed blessed, due to this discovery."

"But what is this?" I said, gently moving the tips of my fingers across the stone's long flat portion. "Something seems so powerful, Pan ."

"To find an Indian relic like this is a truly remarkable event." Pan said, his smile as genuine and true as the placid waters of nearby Lake Tahoe. "This was used for important Indian work, such as carving wood, or the cutting of animals for vital food. Feel how sharp this is, and then admire its craftsmanship."

I sat still, my heart pumping steady and true while gazing at the gardens of my home, by this point much different and far more glorious than just a few days earlier when we first started our diligent work. Seeming to sense my genuine awe and my respect for this unexpected discovery, Pan explained that while scraping the ground he found this stone smack-dab in the center of the new pathway that we had been busy creating.

"This is yours, Patty," Pan said. "This is not my gift to you, but rather a positive sign from the universe."

As an avid reader of history and an amateur lover of the age-old Indian culture, I realized that the Washoe Indian Tribe and the Northern Paiute people have lived throughout Northwest Nevada for many hundreds or perhaps thousands of years. Discoveries of such relics had become increasingly rare in the metropolitan Reno area, especially in the wake of massive, sprawling and poorly planned developments.

This stone made me think of my dad, who had told numerous old-West stories during my childhood. Just as important, I started to feel a steadily increasing sense of pride, since Indian heritage flows in my blood thanks to my great great-grandmother, Francis Bean, a full-blooded Cherokee on my mom's side of the family.

This discovery made me feel as if I remained on the right path despite my difficult childhood and certain challenging situations since then. More than ever, I began to sense that everything I had done throughout life took me on the path toward this home.

Although a natural blonde due to European heritage, I hail directly from a female line sired by a powerful Cherokee Indian chief. Grandmother Francis Bean's mother, had married a white man in the American Southeast. This woman's new husband brought her with him in 1848 to Sutter's Mill in California. They were with James W. Marshall when he discovered gold there, sparking the 1849 California Gold Rush.

As the new territory's white population boomed, Francis gave birth to my Grandmother Eve's father, my great-grandfather. Shortly after William Smith was born, an appendicitis attack killed her at age 25.

Relishing the discovery of this magical, powerful stone and cutting tool, Pan and I began to chat about our separate and diverging paths in life. Pan spoke of his ongoing plans to go with his new wife and child to New York State, their departure scheduled for late August—just one month before the scheduled Historic Preservation tour of my home.

"It's all about the paths—both the paths we build in our gardens and the routes we build in life," I told Pan; these words somehow spilling forth as if cascading from the essence of my eternal soul. "There are no accidents."

During the previous several years Pan had developed into one of my very good friends. At the same time, the two of us developed a solid platonic attachment. Side-by-side on my garden bench, Pan admitted his concern stemming from pre-set plans to leave me amid the final stretch of efforts to get my property spruced up in time for the home tour. With increased intensity, this wise and powerful Indian and I began to discuss why and how every person chooses his or her own distinct path in life.

This made me think of my late father. Yes, dad had taken the wrong path. Or, am I wrong in saying this? Was my dad's choice the incorrect route?

I don't know. Certainly, looking back on what occurred, at first glance just about anyone would swear right away that dad made an awful decision to leave Reno. But in recent months, my senses had started telling me that perhaps such assumptions were dead wrong.

If all went as planned, by mid-August, just several days away, my grandchildren from the Czech Republic in the heart of Europe would walk along this garden path that I just created with Pan. Yes, all of a sudden, now I had become the grandmother, the much older woman who yearned for love and quality time from her children's offspring.

The many lessons that I learned during the first half of that summer, especially in building the path and finding the Indian stone, told me that "there is meaning to life, and in carrying your positive message forward."

Long after my parents had passed away, I felt a burning need to carry on, continuing to convey a positive message for my grandchildren. Hopefully, they would choose to pass this spiritual message on to their own grandkids.

Meantime, amid the ongoing chores to prepare for the tour, I still needed to accept the past for what it was, making me who I had become. My difficult early years continued to touch me in many regards, despite the spiritual messages still flowing my way.

Fully packed and on the road straight from Reno, we zipped eastbound on old U.S. Highway 40 in a 1940s Plymouth that my dad had repaired after buying the vehicle.

I sat alone in the back seat, feeling comfortable at age four. Obviously lacking a brand-new-car smell by that point, the vehicle emitted a musky, old-car odor—far from offensive or nose curdling, but far from a spit-polished aroma. A rusty essence pinched the air, coupled with the brisk, musty odor from unique fabric on the ceiling.

My parents must have enjoyed themselves in this large, expansive vehicle, which afforded lots of leg room. I benefited from similar comfort on the back-seat, my inquisitive eyes gazing at the endless Nevada desert.

Keep in mind that during that era new cars lacked seat belts, and the mere notion of possible air conditioning seemed like something that you would see in a science fiction movie. At the end of 1951 while approaching my fifth birthday, I depended on my parents for vocal entertainment during this excursion—partly because the vehicle lacked a radio. Mom and dad talked up a storm, chatting non-stop about their dreams for a better life. Although I fail to recall specifics of that conversation, I'm sure that my mother must have expressed her desire for a suitable house while dad spoke of work endeavors.

"Since we're headed to my old stomping grounds in Idaho, I feel great because the territory and the land suit me well," dad must have said. "Maybe I can get a job doing what my brother is doing there now, a bureaucratic government position visiting bars to determine if the proprietors hold certified licenses for their businesses."

By this point, mother must have grasped and appreciated father's promise that Idaho would provide an excellent place to rear a family.

Undoubtedly mother spoke of her burning, unending desire to have and enjoy horses again such as those she had owned as a teenager in Central California. At age 27, she still looked stunning enough to hire as a cover model for "Vogue Magazine."

Despite mother's penchant for chain-smoking and the tiresome work in a box-production factory the previous several years, she still emitted a distinct aura of vibrant, youthful health. Without a doubt, my father must have told her that "Once we get settled in Idaho, I'll start looking for a ranch—a perfect spread for all of us to enjoy."

For the next three or four years straight, as we scurried aimlessly from town to town, he always uttered this phrase, continually promising a bright future: "We're going to have a great, comfortable house, lots of land, and plenty of horses."

Mother always latched on to these pitches from dad. The promise of a safe, worry-free environment always rested around every upcoming corner, although we never saw or enjoyed such a place—at least one that we could call home.

Filled with hope, mom mesmerized people with her stunning looks as soon as they met her. Blessed with the most beautiful teeth that anyone ever saw, she often graced long-time friends and even strangers with a smile so loving that she immediately became impossible for them to forget.

Her mere presence captured the imaginations of everyone around her, from the very young to people well along in years. Rather than make a big deal about her many positive attributes, however, mother pretty much kept to herself. Always a practical woman, she liked things plain and simple, rather than gaudy or filled with excessive amounts of spice.

Yes, for the most part, I would have to say that mom was pretty much a "meat-and-potatoes" woman. Her stunning looks and winning personality easily could have earned her a place among Hollywood's elite or opened many doors for her.

Instead, she chose to latch on to my father at least for the time being, due largely to what I can only assume must have been her overpowering, passionate and dedicated love for him.

At this point, the fact that they already had essentially failed to fulfill their dreams during the earlier foray into Idaho seemed far from a primary concern. Like my father, mother enjoyed reading and studying as many books as possible, particularly anything that involved history.

Biographies and autobiographies also grabbed her attention, I would guess some of them real-life rags-to-riches stories. As a genuine tried-and-true native of the American West, she believed that a person should play the leading role in making his or her own way in life. A few decades before the women's liberation movement kicked into full gear, for the most part she must have felt that a lady's true place was to stand by her man.

She also adored historical stories about the loves of true royalty, the dalliances and commitments of blue-blooded families—particularly kings, queens, princes and especially beautiful princesses. Igniting just as much spark, she also enjoyed well-written romance novels. Looking back, I realize these reading preferences seemed a perfect fit for mother, since after all she had lived with a guy who kept romancing her in whatever way he could. No matter how harrowing and difficult their trials and tribulations seemed at any particular time, my father always showered her with a sense of hope.

Mother genuinely loved my father despite their many difficulties, and I'm sure that although by that point they already had been together for about five years dad still did whatever he could to continue sweeping my mom off her feet.

Despite whatever his many promises and expressions of hope might have entailed, her unbending vision of a perfect man must have been that of a handsome, strong guy—industrious in work and taking good care of his family, providing a nice home.

Just as she had hoped, my dad fulfilled many of those attributes, handsome, energetic and industrious. Yet he failed miserably when it came to the category of providing for his family, maintaining a nice home and generating an adequate income.

Although a man's-man in almost every regard, my father fell flat on his face whenever stability and a necessary income became the focus of their concern. Worsening matters, his penchant for alcohol essentially served as a baseball bat that walloped any chance of true happiness clear out of the proverbial ballpark that came in the form of domestic life.

During that excursion we cruised across Northern Nevada, which would eventually fill a generous, loving place within my soul.

The heart-pumping high-desert mountains spill across every new horizon. The musky aroma of sagebrush soothes the senses, while the rolling scenery gives the eyes plenty of delights. Always another surprise around every curve, this state's great outdoors enables a person to envision the essence of the American West's romantic era.

At age 64 I failed to remember specifics of what we saw that day six decades earlier. But subsequent experience during childhood had taught me that each new bend in the road generates ample reason for appreciation. Back then at age four I must have perched my little head against the old Plymouth's back-seat window. A perennially positive, highly inquisitive child such as I must have asked far more questions than my parents could possibly have answered.

Why are the clouds so puffy, white and multi-tinged in this region? Why does everything I see here seem so pretty, when there is actually very little to look at?

Of course, a small child likely would have had difficulty expressing such queries with such eloquence. Still I know without any reservation whatsoever that this particular car ride must have latched my little heart, generating a deep-felt, eternal appreciation for the Silver State.

We often went for many miles, perhaps 100 or more without seeing another car. Nearly a decade before the advent of our nation's interstate freeway system, we floated like a carefree eagle atop wandering two-lane highways.

On blustery, stormy or windy days in the high desert, especially during the spring and fall, the mischievous clouds perform a well-choreographed dance across the many valleys and curiously shaped mountaintops. As if dancers in a Broadway musical directed by the famed Bob Fosse, the clouds float to and fro to the step of Mother Nature's whispering wind. Each new crest, downward slope and upward crawl along the lonely highways generates another unique, much-anticipated "ah-ha" moment.

My parents must have adored these settings, having grown up in the American West shortly before the Industrial Revolution reached its crescendo, scarring much of the land. In a sense, the high desert mirrored the route that the three of us would take together during the trying, difficult adventures that would soon follow.

Just like he had this time, on virtually all of those treks dad would stop at small gasoline stations, well before the advent of large vehicle service facilities. Gas stations at the time lacked convenience stores. If my mom wanted a soda, she would give the station attendant a few coins before pouring an ice-cold Coke from a rickety beverage machine.

His mind perennially focused on a much different beverage, dad always grabbed himself a beer. Many stations that featured old-style, tall, curious-looking gas pumps were adjacent to small, unique, fun mom-and-pop stores. We grabbed snacks, instilling my life-long love for potato chips.

My parents started hunting for a suitable place to rent as soon as we arrived in Idaho, initially staying with relatives in the small town of Filer amid the property hunt.

I cherish memories of those first weeks, preferring to concentrate on the many positives of the period rather than the huge obstacles that subsequently smashed into our family. That brief stay with my Uncle Lehman and his wife, Aunt Marita, captured my heart forever despite the coming tribulations.

At the time Filer was a small, untainted community. As corny as this might seem, the God's-honest truth dictates a description similar to the quaint, peaceful town of Mayberry made famous by the 1960s CBS-TV sitcom, "The Andy Griffith Show." Unlike Otis, the lovable town drunk from that program, my dad soon became what I now call an "icky alcoholic." Instead of behaving in an adorable, goofy and comical state of inebriation the way Otis had, dad would come home in a loud, boisterous and obnoxious state. Thankfully, dad's cravings for the so-called magic elixir of life initially stayed in the background after our arrival. Our new life got off to a rousing start at least in my mind as soon as we pulled into Filer.

My little jaw hung wide open, my spirit filled with awe, upon the sight of a classic brick community school that my dad's father, Jesse Edwards, built using his own funds in the 1930s at the height of the Great Depression. Nestled against the community's main road, the schoolhouse dwarfed most Filer business establishments, including a grocery store where everyone in town shopped as if members of one big family. To their credit, residents kept any hateful feelings or prejudices against minorities behind closed doors, out of sight and out of mind.

An expansive field at the edge of town served as a community gathering place, ideal for county fairs where residents enjoyed family-oriented activities. Mirroring the trend from other small American towns, on the sly rowdy young men undoubtedly went on the prowl for any gals willing to enjoy illicit trysts.

Like just about every small, isolated American community in the mid-1900s, Filer undoubtedly held plenty of secrets close to the vest. What outsiders failed to realize never hurt them, at least most of the time anyway. Rivers of moonshine must have flowed there throughout the Prohibition Era, only in a much different way than at the former speakeasies of Reno 450 miles to the southwest.

Most everyone in Idaho struck me as behaving more sober than a judge, a far cry from the likes of my father. Thanks to his teenage years there, surely he knew more of the region's deep, dark secrets than my mother could possibly have imagined.

Always careful to dole out the sugary details while holding back any distasteful information, the moment we cruised into town my father began telling mother and me about the community's clean, vibrant and proud heritage.

"This community—especially the town of Twin Falls just seven miles away—are the perfect place for us," dad proclaimed.

Mother never said otherwise, at least in my presence. Looking back, I feel no reason to fault her for being tight-lipped, especially since in a flash Filer seemed like an ideal town to make our family's fresh, clean start. Every time we walked down any of the streets, people would say "hi" to us, smiling and friendlier than anyone we had ever encountered before. Although Reno had gained a reputation for its burgeoning kind-hearted population, maybe our immediate family had always been looked upon as outsiders there. So this transition marked a positive change, at least judging by my mom's unusually delightful demeanor.

Within a few days after our arrival, my parents took me to the Filer home of Uncle Leyman and Aunt Marita. At a necessary afternoon nap time due to my tender age, I sat alone in a tiny bedroom. A comforting breeze swept over me through an open window. While drowsiness began to overcome me, I stared at the wallpaper and began imagining many different things. For the first time, I started to naturally meditate, engulfed in a soothing sense of comfort. This must have been summer, long before today's widespread use of air conditioning. With each passing minute I relished feeling the breeze, which made the opened pull-up blinds gently beat against the wall.

Click-click.

Vertical curtains lining the sides of every window moved in perfect concert with the breeze, as if each were a flower in pristine wetlands. In my mind the bedroom became a blessed, sacred place. This marked the first time in my life that I felt protected, engulfed in a sensation of solitude. My innocent, girlish imagination must have played an integral role. For the first time in my life, I saw everything around me fully and completely, my internal soul sensing everything of vital importance. For the moment, my immediate universe was that bedroom.

Although alone, and without any person telling me to do so, I suddenly realized instinctively that the best advice that any of us can ever receive comes from deep within our placid, peaceful and all-knowing hearts.

Maybe the essence of my spirit had gently and lovingly taken charge, somehow giving me the onset of a steadily growing ability to cope with trying times that were still to come. My senses of smell, sight and hearing became intensified at the onset of that nap period. Alone, I could hear birds singing outside, perhaps from many miles away.

Without anyone telling me the answers, I felt this way: at one with the universe; an integral part of nature; a vital cog in God's great eternal plan; and a loving, kind and generous spirit. Despite my tender years, I had unexpectedly discovered within my own soul what some of the world's great masters throughout history have essentially called "The Higher Unlimited Self."

This is an inner sense, an instinctive knowledge differentiating the opposing elements of "right and wrong." Then and there, I knew without any reservation whatsoever that each of us is unique, each of us is special, and each of us is here for one primary purpose—to understand, appreciate and spread the message of love.

Well, if you're now wondering if I suddenly became a preacher and told others of this experience, the blessed, simple answer is "No."

To be sure, "no," I did not tell other people about what rested within my heart, the pulsation of purity. And no, I avoided pontificating about my opinions of how people should treat each other. Never once as a child did I speak harshly or all-knowingly to other people, seizing the audacity to tell others what to do or how to behave.

Instead, in keeping with our Creator's plan, I merely accepted my position as a typical little girl, lucky enough to be alive and healthy with a family that loved me as if I were the world's most precious princess.

Fully awake and laying on my back atop the bed, I listened carefully at every voice as people strolled down nearby streets. I picked up and fully sensed each and every unique sound within the engine of a passing car.

To this day in my mid-60s, I vividly recall each of these spirited sensations as if they were happening at this very moment. My heart, mind, body, spirit and soul became sensual in every blessed, innocent way imaginable. This kind, forgiving, eternally loving and sharing essence filled my aura, making me shine in a way that sparkles even to this day. While starting out a new life with my parents, everything about this universe told me to avoid judging other people, to always keep the focus on positive possibilities. Even more amazing, without anyone telling me so, I fully realized that, yes, my body will die someday. But after that occurs, as every fiber of my being teaches, every sparkle of our souls shall live on for all eternity.

Instinctively cognizant of these unchangeable pillars of every spirit, my job would be to endure and to learn from the many trials and lessons that life throws toward all of us. Partly because our Creator blesses each of us with "free-will" in order to discover our own paths and lessons, at the time I failed to realize or to envision the many hardships that would soon engulf my entire family.

We made countless seven-mile excursions between Filer and Twin Falls amid my parents' hunt for a suitable residence.

Expansive fields spread as far as the eye could see in every direction as viewed from the roadway. I often poked my head out of our Plymouth's back window, looking up at pheasants soaring high overhead. The pheasants occasionally landed atop posts or atop distant trees.

The various excursions between Filer and Twin Falls gave me an ever-increasing appreciation for Mother Nature. Compelling sunsets in those flat lands across potato fields gave me just as much joy as the spectacular dusks from our times a short while earlier amid the rolling hills and mountains of Northern Nevada's high desert.

The summer heat forced us to keep our car windows down during these many Filer-to-Twin Falls excursions. Sweet, aromatic and pleasing aromas filled my senses with a steadily increasing appreciation for the great outdoors. The visual sensations swelled me full, packed solid with a keen sense of farming, the magnetism of seeing life-giving plants as they steadily grew from day to day.

Earth. Sun. Air.

Nature's beauty, her promise, and her kindness all swept into my tender young heart during those several weeks. With each new day, I loved my parents more than ever, fully unaware of the underlying current that had riddled their shared past.

Whenever Twin Falls came into view, I momentarily lost my breath. The mere sight of that town's unique old houses made me sit up straight with anticipation. Similar sensations would engulf me more than sixty years later, whenever I would come upon a unique, classic old house—a far cry from today's everything-looks-the-same dwellings.

At the time, in Twin Falls lots of unforgettable homes were Victorian Era-style structures reminiscent of the late 1800s and early 1900s. Other dwellings were just as precious, such as houses erected in the '20s, '30s and '40s. For the time being, I never saw construction crews building new homes in Idaho in the early 1950s; such sprawling projects may have started in that region then, but I never saw them.

Imagine my uncensored delight and my mother's joy when my parents finally managed to rent a small, sturdy, comfortable home in Twin Falls where dad landed a job at an auto-body repair shop. This simple dwelling served as the first and only house that I had ever lived in to that point with my immediate family.

Small even by 1950s standards, the house had two tiny windows in the front and a miniscule three-step porch only large enough to accommodate just a few people. A small steeple-like feature adorned the top front of this nondescript structure.

For the first time, we had a living room where we could sit and listen to the radio, several years before TVs spread to mainstream America outside major metropolitan areas. The two bedrooms lacked even a hint of flare, yet this potential setback never seemed to bother mother since we finally had a home to call our own.

With a bigger, more modern kitchen than we had enjoyed before, this home also had a quaint, small and useful basement. Much more important, for the first time ever I sensed a growing happiness swell within my mother.

Before diving full-force back into alcohol, dad went pheasant hunting on weekends, one of his favorite activities by far besides fly-fishing. On lots of weekends mother and I accompanied him on these refreshing and vibrant excursions. She loved to fish as much as possible with father, although parenting duties often required her to stay at home with me. Eventually, my parents discovered their favorite fishing hole in the nearby Snake River. Mother often took me to a safe, secure place near the shore, commanding: "Patty, you stay in this spot without going anywhere, and don't you dare leave." Then, she went fishing side-by-side with dad, keeping her eyes glued to me every second to ensure that I remained safe.

Dad also maintained firearms at home, necessary for his many hunting trips. He took great pride in his gun collection, which he kept in a rack in our rented home.

"You see those guns over there," he told me several times. "*Don't you ever touch them.* They're always loaded, and they will blow your head off!"

Needless to say, I never touched those guns in all my life.

At any rate, I could feel that we had found a fantastic place to live. Twin Falls had grabbed a huge part of my heart, a spectacular town. Making matters even more delightful, I developed a close friendship with a little girl my age, Kathy, who lived just down the same street in a house similar to ours.

Kathy's pip-squeak mom, Penny, looked as tiny as a mouse and she talked like one, too. Even so, the woman somehow managed to become close friends with my mother. The ladies bonded, often enjoying coffee and smoking cigarettes together.

Kathy and I were about the same size, her hair brown and mine blonde. Almost every child my age looked far chubbier than me, probably because I happened to be super-skinny. Shortly after we bonded, my Aunt Iva from Kansas, avid at her sowing hobby, started sending me unexpected gifts via the U.S. Postal Service. These handmade dresses included a ballerina costume and a Snow White outfit suitable for a princess.

Delighted, I invited Kathy to my family's home right away. For the first time, I got a distinct, devilish feeling of being better than another little girl. After all, I had these cool garments. My feelings of superiority intensified when Kathy started hollering: "Patty, I want to wear the ballerina outfit." Of course, as soon as she uttered that request I wanted to wear the ballerina garment, allowing her to put on the princess costume.

I thought at that time that "I'm just the cutest little girl in the world. I have these things that she doesn't."

At five years old, for the first time ever I got a sense of being better than someone else. I lack any notion of where my new-found snooty attitude came from, but at the time I'll have to admit that I thought of myself as pretty cool.

Yet my feelings of superiority would end soon.

You see, Kathy attended a dancing school for young children, and one day I went there with this little friend after being invited by the child and her mother. Finally, I realized why Kathy had yearned to wear the ballerina dress, perfectly suitable for these lessons. The memories of that single visit to Kathy's school have stayed with me for a lifetime.

I vividly recall two songs that I heard just one time during that brief visit. And ever since then, I have remembered the lyrics. Just repeating them and singing the songs makes me cry now in my mid-60s. You see, the tunes had a major impact on my life, although I heard each of them only once. One lively tune went like this:

> *"Trinka goes to dancing school, dancing school, dancing school, Trinka goes to dancing school, in her white gown. With eyes of blue, cheeks of red, neat white cap on her head, Trinka goes to dancing school in her white gown. Trinka goes to dancing school in her white gown."*

When singing these lively, unforgettable words, I danced along with the other little students although not yet enrolled as a pupil. Now, once every several years while telling this story to some of my closest adult girlfriends, I break out in tears. The other song stayed with me as well:

> *"Kookaburra sat on the old gum tree, eating all the gum drops he could see. Stop, Kookaburra stop, Kookaburra. Save some there for me."*

The joy of remembering those songs continues because I loved being a little girl, I loved my life, and our house. Finally, I could feel a sense of place, a deep inner message that finally we belonged. Finally, I had started developing good, close friends of my own age. I thought I would be going to dancing school, and the children in the neighborhood had started to accept me.

The neighborhood impressed my soul as perfect. This blossomed in my heart as the ideal neighborhood where any child would want to grow up. Literally and without exaggeration, we lived—at least during that brief period—in the perfect place for a youngster. We often visited my cousins in Filer, enjoyed the first Fourth of July that I remember, and cherished our precious outdoor activities.

Just a few days before my fifth birthday of January 6, 1952, my Grandma Eve traveled 450 miles by Greyhound bus from Reno to Twin Falls.

My life changed for the better, indirectly paving the way for my future career throughout most of my adult life as an award-winning graphic designer.

The moment we arrived at the bus depot to pick up Grandma, I noticed stunning illustrations on compelling, eye-grabbing posters throughout the facility. Images promoting unique places throughout the United States grabbed my attention.

Always a highly visual person, I gravitated toward these magnetic illustrations. Vibrant colorful scenes captured my imagination. The graphic, stunning images depicted Greyhound buses traveling through diverse regions from New Mexico to Vermont.

Remember that all visual advertisements in those days were illustrations rather than photographs. The artwork captured my soul at the very time that as a small child I had just begun to start fine-tuning and honing my initial drawing skills.

To me the bus depot became a virtual museum, a place where even a child could enjoy alluring images of many kinds. This marked the beginning of a lengthy period when I would see full-scale posters and billboards clear across the Western United States. Everything from signs promoting Coca-Cola to Wrigley's Chewing Gum made my imagination go wild with clear, distinct images of the apparent joys such products could bring. At this point in life, I had not yet visited a museum or a full-scale library crammed with images of the outside world.

Compelling advertisements in magazines, on billboards and via posters sent my mind into these other realms. All this had started in the Greyhound facility. Before long I began noticing such advertisements embossed to the walls of supermarkets. During the holiday season, huge Santa Claus posters lured consumers to everything from cola products to department stores.

Even before entering the first grade, I had come to love illustrations—fully unaware at the time that beginning as a young adult I would start playing a significant role in that industry. As a child, these images enabled me to see a huge part of the world far away from my regular home environment. This generated an important impact on my life.

Energized and increasingly filled with boundless curiosity, at home I would flip through all major magazines that my parents purchased. My favorites included "Look," "Life," "True," and any publication such as the "Saturday Evening Post" featuring covers drawn by the famed, legendary illustrator Norman Rockwell.

Except for a limited number of photographs promoting women's fashions, all newspaper and magazine advertisements needed hand-drawn illustrations. These ranged from drawings of men holding cigarettes to images of the latest automobiles.

Around this time, because my mother loved horses, she occasionally drew them. From a professional artist's viewpoint, her artwork would have been deemed as amateurish. But at least she could draw them.

"That's cool—she can do that," I thought. Starting in those early years mother would show me how to draw these animals. Before long, quite early in life I also started creating drawings based on images inspired by magazine illustrations.

These budding skills gradually improved, starting to play an increasingly important role in making me feel like a whole and complete person. My joyful emotions soon increased when mother started teaching me how to color.

The only problem came when she insisted that I "stay in the lines." Later on this would strike me as interesting, when as an art teacher I told people *not to stay in the lines.*

"An artist should go off and color any way he or she wants to," I would tell my students later in life. "You need to express your own creativity, which can open your world in an effort to see and capture all-new possibilities."

Throughout my childhood, teens, early adult years and much later in life my drawing skills always gave me something useful to accomplish. Boredom became impossible. Before my art skills started picking up speed during childhood, on numerous occasions I could have told my parents "I'm bored." But as a good, respectful and loving child who wanted to please her mother and father I never could have made such comments.

I probably would have gone nuts without having a pencil and paper during our non-stop travels during subsequent years. So, my love for art emerged as a saving grace.

Throughout the ensuing decades my drawing abilities opened up many doors for me, leading the way to lucrative jobs, high-end commissions and a continually growing armada of strong, life-long friendships.

Within several months before my fifth birthday, my mother took me to a downtown Twin Falls photography studio that offered a discount price.

The store's staff told her, "If you just want the photos, you can buy them. But if you dislike the images, there is no obligation to purchase whatsoever." My mom thought, "Okay," and so she got me all fixed up.

The chief photographer snapped several shots. My mother felt that she could never afford to buy the images, perhaps one at most.

During subsequent weeks, my father strolled past the photo shop every day while walking to and from lunch. Each time, he saw the photograph of his beautiful little girl in the studio's front display window he became overwhelmed with emotion. He decided to spend probably half his entire paycheck to purchase the photographs, three separate images of me. Every time someone saw the primary image framed at my home in later years, even well into my 60s, people often told me: "You looked like a little Shirley Temple," the iconic child movie star who catapulted to international fame in the 1930s.

"You were the cutest little girl," people often proclaim, and well I was, I'll have to admit that—little Patty was adorable.

During my 30s in the late 1970s and early 1980s, I started doing lots of watercolor portraits of various people as part of a nostalgia series. While undergoing extensive self-training to hone my portraiture skills, I chose to paint an image of that old photo—largely because of my appreciation and adoration of the style photographers used in the 1940s and 1950s. I loved what photographers did with portraits in those days.

Shortly after Grandma Eve's arrival by bus, I clearly remember her taking mother and me shopping—my first such experience.

We went to a Twin Falls department store where Grandma bought me a little watch, and a dress. This made me excited because the grandmother that I loved so very much had traveled all this way partly for the purpose of buying me these presents.

The three of us had a fabulous time, especially when Grandma took us to dinner. Seeing Grandma filled my spirit with gratitude. The store's high-end ambiance, being with my pretty grandmother and holding my gorgeous mother's hand allowed me to begin enjoying "female-bonding" for the first time.

Memory tells me that my father and Grandma got along okay during her visit, a far cry from his earlier attempts to avoid her as much as possible in Reno.

For the first time I discovered the joys of sharing experiences just with women. These early excursions taught me that females can evolve into super-cool friends, soft, nice and cuddly—talking "girl stuff," and just having simple fun. These joys came into clear focus for me upon watching my mom become so happy when with her own mother. The bonding, caring and unbendable interaction between these women gave me a comfortable feeling. I sensed undeniable love between all three of us, nothing equal ever by comparison. In subsequent years, both separately and individually my mother and grandmother told me that they intentionally spoiled me rotten. They loved and cherished me with all their hearts.

This permeated whenever we got together. When first seeing Grandma upon her arrival at the bus station, for instance, I became so excited to see her that I began jumping up and down with more energy than a yo-yo. A lot of times, my mother would tell me later on, "Patty, you're way too exuberant. Settle down."

Indeed, upon seeing Grandma I started yelling out to her so that everyone at the bus depot could hear: "Hi! Grandma, we're here!"

Needless to say those behaviors made my grandmother feel great. My mother's observations about my boisterous behavior hit the mark. I never had any inhibitions. Whenever a vibrant, compelling emotion struck I soon made my feelings known for everyone present to hear, even strangers.

During a family vacation several years later Grandpa Oscar took a home movie of me dancing down the street near Yosemite National Forest. Those images captured the essence of my personality.

In fact, seven years later during my middle-school years when I never got any boyfriends, my mother would say: "It's probably because you're too exuberant. You've got to settle down. Be a little not-so-excited."

Despite such gentle admonitions, throughout early childhood and well into my teens I often made no attempt whatsoever to censor my super-energized zest for life.

I was probably just a goofy little girl. Each of us certainly has his or her unique personality traits. Well into my senior years, my distinct attributes remain a perennially positive attitude, a trait that has enabled me to generate some close friendships.

"Aren't you going to come to dancing school with me?" My friend Kathy asked one day.

"Well, my mom said that I can't go."

"But why?" Kathy asked, energized by a steadily increasing sense of curiosity.

"I don't know," I said honestly, perplexed.

Confused and wanting a more concise answer, within a few days I approached my mother, inquiring: "Why can't I go to dancing school?"

"Because your teacher says that you have two left feet," mother replied matter-of-factly, as if there should be no additional reason for discussion.

That statement always stuck with me, leaving my heart to wonder for many years why the instructor would have said such a thing. As a child, I refrained from complaining, because in those days when your mother said "No," that was the end of any discussion. Needless to say, I never returned to the dancing school, having only attended that one time. Looking back, I realize the actual reason probably stemmed from the fact that my parents lacked enough income to pay the school.

Children simply fail to realize such things because they happen to be "just kids."

On the positive side, although my parents' budget remained meager, they loved me with all their hearts. Such commitment and devotion can eventually twinkle, literally more precious than all of the world's gold combined.

Around this time I enjoyed sitting on my father's lap more than ever. Whenever possible we spent lazy evenings listening to "Amos and Andy" radio shows, situation comedies featuring two lovable African-American characters. We often broke out in laughter at these uproarious programs. While nestled snuggly on my daddy's lap, he would let me fiddle with his hair. This became one of my most fun activities since he used loads of "Dapper Dan" brand men's hair product. This substance enabled father to slick his hair back; the product also enabled me to twist his hair into little curls.

Because my father's love swelled for his only daughter, he would allow me to sit there the whole time and keep fiddling with his hair—fixing it funny—as we listened to these programs. Dad often let me do this to my heart's content.

He always kept telling me stories about life and just things that I should know, the lessons necessary to become a good person. He told me of many incidents from his childhood, such as fishing trips with his brother in Idaho and what he experienced growing up. Perhaps most of all, I adored his compelling stories about cowboys and Indians in the Old West. These never involved tales about killing people but rather compelling yarns, struggles in settling the wild country this side of the Mississippi River. He described the difficulties early settlers were forced to endure when traveling.

Most stories involved intricate yarns about the trials and tribulations of how the earliest Americans had to overcome extreme difficulties in their quest for happiness. Little did I realize at the time that in a sense my immediate family struggled in a similar quest, except with vastly different technology.

Strangely, however, he never told me about the world, anything outside of the United States. To him, at least from my perspective at the time, it seemed as if the USA hailed as the earth's only country. It wasn't until much later during school that I learned that other nations existed, a revelation that left me both stunned and delighted.

For my first Fourth of July celebration we walked to an enchanting park near our little rented home. Full of fabulous big trees and picnic tables, the park attracted swarms of people who enjoyed meeting friends and relatives. Children played, scurrying all about as their parents sat on blankets.

This also marked the first time I remember eating watermelon after my mother said: "Now, don't eat one of those watermelon seeds, because if you do you'll get a watermelon growing in your little belly."

So, needless to say, I didn't want that to happen so I ate the fruit as carefully as possible. Even so, with a sense of horror and pure fright I suddenly realized that I had just accidentally swallowed a seed. Soon putting that out of my mind, I enjoyed a lovely day playing to my heart's content with other children. But that night when I went to bed, I thought for sure that a huge watermelon would grow in my stomach.

The next morning, I felt happy that my tummy had not bloated to the size of a pregnant woman. Remember that in those days, many children believed exactly what adults told them.

Another major milestone occurred one day when dad returned to our Twin Falls home from one of his fall weekend pheasant hunting excursions. At age five, my little eyes opened as wide as glass coasters upon seeing the birds he had shot. Dad wore a red Pendleton brand shirt. In that moment he made my spirit twinkle, upon the sudden, first-time revelation that he was by far the most handsome, strongest man that I had ever seen.

I just remember he was so magnetic, and to this day every time I see a Pendleton shirt that look attracts me. I must have hustled back upstairs, rather than watching him handle initial meal-preparation chores such as pulling feathers from the carcasses.

About this time I started begging my parents to let me go to school. During that era many other states had kindergarten classes for 5-year-olds, but no such courses existed then in that section of Idaho. So, the following summer at age 6 my mother went with me to sign up for classes. Mom made this a vibrant, special, unforgettable summer day for me. First, we went to see the school that I would soon attend—or so we all hoped. Other children and their parents did the same. Afterward, the two of us visited a dime store for a sandwich. I sat at the counter, always exuberant.

"I'm going to go to school next year!" I hollered to everyone who passed by the dining area. A bubbly, energetic, happy child, I felt excited to tell everybody of my upcoming adventures. All older, they would ask me numerous questions, and much of the time I would answer: "Yes, I'm going to be in the first grade!"

Never shy, I made no attempt to censor my excitement. My delight intensified even more about the same time my friend Kathy told me, "There's a circus coming to town. My mom is going to take us today. Would you like to come with us?"

"Yes! Oh, yes! I want to go so badly."

I ran home and asked my mother, saying: "Can I go to the circus with Kathy? They're even going to pay for me."

"Okay."

Kathy's mom took us two little girls to the circus. Keep in mind that I didn't even know what a circus was, so this evolved into a huge event for me. Right away I noticed a giant tent. We walked inside, and for the first time I saw elephants and horses upon which gorgeous women stood while wearing colorful costumes. The funniest characters of all were the clowns, especially the antics that they performed. At that time I didn't even know what a clown was, and I had never heard of them before. I laughed so hard, by far the neatest thing that I had ever seen. To put this into perspective, keep in mind that at that point I had not even seen a movie or watched TV. This emerged as the most amazing show, magical in every way. I sat in awe, my spirit and little soul glued to virtually everything that happened before my delighted eyes. Simultaneous shows tickled my senses, striking my funny bone and inspiring innocent curiosity.

Everyone under the big top, perhaps hundreds of people, smiled and laughed in unison.

Suddenly a bear appeared.

Then, my gaze became glued on the elephants, my brain magnetized since I had never seen a picture of such a creature, previously unaware that they existed.

In those days people, especially young children far from big cities, never had visuals constantly coming at them from every direction as in the current era. When I was very little through age four and beyond, my mother would read me "Mother Goose" books filled with interesting, colorful images. Energized and highly creative, I memorized as many of those tales as possible.

As if my spirit had not already been cranked up enough, the circus performers launched aerial acts where athletic entertainers seemed to fly among various contraptions high above. One visual stimulus after another gave me enough happy memories to last for a lifetime. Energized and delighted by this new adventure, afterward I scurried home and told my mother all the details.

"Oh, I'm so excited that you had fun," mother told me, shortly before my dad came home.

Moments after coming through the front door, he motioned for me to jump into his arms, saying: "Patty, I want to take you to the circus."

"Well, I already went."

"But I wanted to take you to that," he said, frowning and hugging me. "That wasn't as exciting for you, because I would have gotten you cotton candy and hot dogs, and lots of toys if you would have waited until I got home."

From that point forward, I felt bad for having gone that day. The wish emerged that I had never gone with Kathy and her family, instead waiting to go with my dad.

So, that became my first "Hooray!" moment, intermixed with a downer sensation that "This could have been much better." Instead of my dad coming home and saying, "Wow, what did you experience? Tell me what happened. What did you see?" I heard nothing but his strong declarations that the show would have been much better with him.

Looking back, I realize that my heart felt friction from our continually growing, unseen, unspoken household tension. Those brief years in Twin Falls had become a very happy time in my life, and my exuberance faded somewhat upon our sudden, unexpected departure for a non-stop, multi-year trek.

Keep in mind that before moving to Twin Falls, my father had promised mom that he would get her a horse and a dog.

Finally, when mom began to feel settled after about a year there, she purchased an adorable puppy, a collie similar to an animal mother had owned during her early teens in Washington State. This played such a pivotal role in mother's heart that she gave her new Potato State dog a name similar to the animal she had owned in the Evergreen State— Laddie. My mother had suffered a broken heart in her early teens when a farmer living next to her family's Washington property killed her initial pet for chasing his chickens.

So, now, once again she had her own Laddie, which we loved. This new pet became the most beautiful, lovable and faithful animal that I had ever known to that point.

The new dog in Twin Falls loved my mother seemingly beyond belief.

But whenever Laddie went outside, he chased cars down the street. Although we lived on a small, out-of-the-way road with very little traffic, Laddie always chased every car that passed our small rented home. Finally my dad said, "We just can't have that."

For some reason, my mother agreed. They decided to take our pet to a spectacular ranch ten miles outside of town where Laddie would have a wonderful home. I remember going with them to the ranch so that I would understand: "Look, Laddie is going to have a nice home."

So, we gave this beloved pet to the rancher's family, who told us: "Don't worry. We'll take good care of Laddie. We're so very happy to have him."

My family felt delighted by this arrangement, convinced that Laddie would be okay. But about three days later the dog ended up back on our porch.

"What's that?" We all asked that morning, after hearing a noise outside. We opened the door, surprised to discover our beloved little friend.

Soon afterward, we got a call from the rancher who said: "Laddie took off. We don't know what happened."

Naturally, this time we decided to keep the pet, mesmerized by the fact the dog had found its way home. What else could we have done? Any attempt to give the animal away again likely would have generated similar results. So, Laddie resumed his dangerous habit of chasing every car that passed our residence.

My heart soon got shattered during the period when I started becoming increasingly excited, eagerly anticipating my entrance into the first grade.

Suddenly one morning mother started packing up all our possessions and stuffing them into the trunk of our car. Confused and failing to understand, I somehow knew that we were in the process of leaving.

My parents never gave me the opportunity to say goodbye to my friends. The change came in a flash. Although my memory of my childhood years remains vivid for the most part, to this day I fail to recall us talking about the move beforehand.

Adding to the growing mystery within my heart, we made no attempt to take any of the furniture that we owned. We only took suitcases packed with clothes.

I became increasingly puzzled when my parents made no attempt to take our dog, Laddie.

"What are we going to do?" I asked my parents. "Why can't Laddie come with us?"

"No, Laddie cannot come," my father said, while helping mother stuff the suitcases into the trunk. "We've got to go, and we must leave now."

Momentarily, with dad behind the wheel of the Chrysler we took off down the street. Right away Laddie started chasing after us.

We turned at a corner onto another road, and I looked out the back window hollering to my parents: "Look, Laddie is chasing after us! She loves us! She wants us to take her!"

Undaunted in his task of leaving as soon as possible, my father started driving through downtown Twin Falls. Running faster than a heroic dog from the movies, our loyal, beloved pet kept following us. The determined animal darted through numerous intersections, nearly getting hit by lots of cars several times and never stopping or slowing down at all. Refusing to give up, and eternally loyal, Laddie scurried right behind us, always going as fast as he could.

"Dad, please stop for Laddie!" I begged, my little face perched at the back window. Endless rivers of tears streamed down my cheeks, as my parents sat in the front seat. I began to wail as if a close relative had just suddenly died. "Dad, won't you please stop!"

My mom kept looking straight ahead.

"Mom, another car just almost hit him!" I hollered, by this point my tears forming puddles on the back seat. As we progressed, Laddie was finally further back.

Then, I didn't see Laddie any more.

And, we were off.

To this day, I lack any specific notion of why our departure came with such sudden, unstoppable force.

Perhaps father and mother lacked rent money.

Put into our past forever were the radio that we had listened to almost every night, the kitchen table where we ate many fun breakfasts as I listened to the Kellogg's cereal characters say "Snap, Crackle, and Pop" talk to me, and the bed where I had slept comfortably. We took nothing. Bedding. Pillows. Everything.

I never even got a chance to say goodbye to cousins that I loved in Filer.

From this point forward, my immediate family's emotional pain, heartache and wandering lifestyle would continue for many years to come.

Chapter 4

Five weeks before the scheduled September 24th tour of my Reno house, I returned to the residence with a trunk full of supplies necessary for yard improvements.

As usual for this time of year in the early evening streaks of determined sunlight beamed across the yard. Exhausted from a full day of hard work, I sat on a bench beside my husband Wayne. As we do on most summer evenings, we fully enjoyed these silent, tranquil and reflective moments.

The non-stop pressures of everyday life always seemed to fizzle away in those late-summer evening hours. Without uttering a single word, we conveyed similar thoughts.

Yes, these were the peaceful moments. While the sun began to say its final "good-night," the two of us listened as birds chirped their final delightful songs for the day. Robins lazily pecked at the plush, deep-green, finely mowed lawn. The birds insisted on scooping up worms, tricked by our sprinklers into venturing to the surface.

Our sweet dog, Diva, a 16-month-old snorkie—a mix between a schnauzer and a Yorkshire terrier—hopped onto my lap. Wayne petted our little friend as the animal began licking my face. I smiled and giggled. We chose the name Diva in honor of our late grandmothers. Wayne's Grandma Dorothy Royle died at age 102 in the spring of 2009, and my Grandma Eva died at age 104 in the summer of 2008.

These women had met for the first and only time in this same yard when both ladies were only in their 90s or early 100s, at our Fourth of July celebration for close friends and family in 2004. The women spoke with each other only briefly, each hailing from unrelated pioneer families that played integral roles in settling the American West.

On this day, while sitting alone with Wayne, I looked up at the branches directly above. The 100-year-old pine tree provided soothing, much-welcomed shade and comfort for this home, particularly during summer. Super-tall trees of numerous varieties lined every edge of the property comprised of two adjoining lots.

Together these parcels covered nearly eight-tenths of an acre. Twenty-four pots filled with flowers, many of them geraniums, adorned a cozy cottage within the property directly behind the main house. A massive, well-appointed flower garden buffered a quaint, old-style area nestled between the lawn and a long, comfortable wood porch behind the cottage. As if sent as a gift from God, in the early 1990s numerous flower species had started growing here on their own without ever being planted.

Some of my favorites included hollyhocks, long-stemmed varieties that disappear during the occasionally harsh winters, before insisting on glorious re-appearances by late spring. My garden generated a cornucopia of diversely colored flowers, whites, purples, pinks, light-blues and other teasing sensations.

Eager to keep the natural fun in full motion, timid hummingbirds crisscrossed the yard, tickling the hollyhocks, roses, geraniums, daisies and a vast smattering of wildflowers. Mother Nature's delightful dance had continued throughout the season, a crescendo of natural growth that would have made classical music virtuoso composer Mozart proud.

While this day's generous sun made its final two-minute bow, Wayne lobbed a softball across the yard. Diva, about 20 pounds and 15 inches long, jumped off my lap and hopped like an energized Easter bunny across the lawn.

With the orb firmly affixed within her jaw, our beloved pet raced back toward us. Forever a "puppy" in my eyes, this little girl dropped her favorite ball near my feet. Summarily, I obliged, picking it up and hoisting the ball toward the center of the yard.

Oops.

Off target, the ball tumbled through an area of mid-size trees, before cascading onto the rock-lined path that Pan and I had just built along the back fence.

Exceedingly loyal and always playful, Diva scurried past a Japanese maple near the back door, its auburn leaves as vibrant and welcoming as ever.

A fun, delightful labyrinth of sparkly blue long-stemmed flowers popped up early every September, lasting only a few weeks. I feared that these delightful eye pleasers would sadly have come and gone before the upcoming house tour.

Other flowers, all determined on retiring before the event, included these hollyhocks, each already bending down in preparation for a well-deserved seven-month sleep. Although disappointed by this predictable turn of events, the usual gang of placid bumble bees already started focusing on new sensations nestled along the yard side of the main house.

Once again, Wayne tossed the ball for Diva as neighborhood residents enjoyed a cool evening stroll along the 4-foot-tall picket fence that lined the front section of the yard.

"You have a beautiful home," some of them stopped briefly to tell us.

As darkness threw a cozy blanket all around us, crickets started to sing their soothing tune that we enjoyed every August evening. Wayne lighted a candle in the middle of our black metal table close to the front fence. We offered a toast to each other, sipping delightful, icy, lime-laced summer rum beverages.

The sight of Wayne's face made me feel warm and protected. I wrapped my arm around his as we hugged, continuing our usual practice for that time of year.

Nearly 10 years my junior, at age 55 he possessed youthful energy that enabled him to work non-stop at our book publishing and ghostwriting business.

"I've never been happier in my whole life than I am at this very moment," I told Wayne, fully and honestly after our dinner that evening outside. "I feel great, we are healthy and look at this place. The weather is perfect."

Looking deeply into Wayne's hazel eyes illuminated by this soft candlelight, I sensed that he felt my words ring true. He poured more of our favorite summer drink for me.

Toasting our good fortune.

Wayne made no apologies about the fact that he lacked many of my late father's positive attributes. Dad died of natural causes at age 73 in 1991. Four years later I met my husband, who lacked many of what I consider the manly skills that enabled my father to earn a paycheck even amid those many difficult times in the 1950s and 1960s.

Although every fiber of my being loved, appreciated and adored Wayne, he lacked any perception of how a hammer works. If you asked my spouse to change a light bulb, he would invariably end up breaking the burned-out unit, leaving the impossible-to-turn screws stuck inside the socket for someone else to fix. For my hubby, sweeping the outside walkway became a formidable task. Wayne's idea of hard labor entailed sipping a diet soda before leaving peanut shells strewn across the floor of his office—striving to sweep them away just in the nick of time before my expected arrivals.

Is it true that up to 500 people, will soon be tromping through our home?

My God, what have I done in saying "yes?" There is so much to do around the house. Is it too late to turn back, to cancel my participation in this event?

For many years, Wayne never lifted a hand to help out around the house. Despite my persistent and relentless nagging over a period of years for him to change his ways and step up to the plate in matters of housekeeping and home maintenance, Wayne had continued to stand tall among our nation's super-lazy house-husbands.

Pushed to the limits, I actually considered booting him out at one point. Other factors helped push me over the edge—lots of them, far too numerous to list.

Just in time for much needed work around the house, a mysterious, unspoken and inexplicable change in him kicked into full gear. At first I failed to notice.

Within recent months, his office had begun to sparkle, something that never even came close to happening before. On Wayne's own initiative, his closet became so clean that I would even allow the public to view it.

Consider this additional surprise. My arduous journeys to haul loads of dishes from Wayne's office to the kitchen had become far less frequent and often unnecessary. These totally unexpected changes almost made me break out in tears of happiness.

Needless to say, these many mysterious, unexpected and much-welcomed changes had left me stunned, puzzled, mesmerized and often totally confused.

As to why this great transition happened, I haven't got a clue. The threat of a divorce had failed to do the trick, because that happened many years ago. Pumping even more delight into my body and heart, Wayne summarily dumped his losing efforts to make a living via entrepreneurial Internet endeavors. Always high-energy, focused and determined to achieve greater success, during the previous decade he had ghost-written many dozens of books, perhaps more than sixty voluminous publications. At least one celebrity that he indirectly wrote for had a book soar to the top of the New York Times Best seller list.

Wayne's perennially positive attitude, sparked by a burning desire to generate much-deserved recognition for his clients, motivated him to write a whopping three full books during a mere six-week period. All this happened amid the initial phase of my urgent, fast-paced efforts to prepare the house for the upcoming tour.

As Wayne's closest business partner, I thoroughly read all books that he wrote secretively for a wide variety of clients. I always remained my husband's "worst critic," telling him first hand, point-blank whenever one of his book drafts stunk. As an avid reader myself, I'll have to admit that my guy sparkled high above most others within his profession. How and why he accomplished all this, especially at such a voluminous and eloquent pace, I'll never know or fully understand.

All I can say with any certainty is that this man had changed because he loved me, because he carried a passion for life, a yearning to convey vibrant, distinct messages through his writing.

For the most part, my man had definitely changed, significantly for the better. Although I fully doubted that he would ever evolve into certifiable butler-quality status, I'll have to admit that I liked and even admired the transitions that had occurred so far and I could only pray that such improvements would continue at least somewhat.

"I've never felt richer or more perfect in my life than I do right now," I told Wayne once again, as our meal came to an end that evening.

"Patty, you really should write a book about this!" Wayne said, out of the blue.

"About me? But, I'm not a celebrity."

"Yes, honey," he paused to slowly sip his summer rum drink. "Patty, your story is compelling—the lessons you've learned, and the message that you can convey."

I sat up straight, stunned. I looked at Wayne for a few seconds before realizing that my husband had never been more serious.

"Think about it," Wayne persisted. "Your natural experiences should be written about."

Flabbergasted and internally honored by the mere notion of such a suggestion, I took a long, deep breath and thought about his proposal for several moments. The mere notion made my mind spin, particularly Wayne's observation about a "message."

"You know, Wayne, I'll have to admit that you're right on track. My intuition, a gut-feeling tells me this right away."

Wayne continued, "Start talking right now as much as you feel like. There's nothing more important than letting our soul spill forth, uncensored."

"Alright, Wayne, the story is this—that a little girl can have a vision, and that vision can come true. And, it might not be the way that you think the path is going to take. But, it'll happen if you stay in that vision, and you stay true to the flow, and you have that in your heart and soul— that this is where you belong, the path that you've chosen. And, if you realize it, that's such a gift."

"Keep talking."

"What I'm trying to tell people is that you have to pay attention. You have to take time to smell the roses, you have to go back in your life, and see where your path led you. And, maybe if that path led you on a different direction than originally intended, explore what could have happened. But perhaps people can sit down and look at things. Get away from the TV, get away from everyday life, and look at your own life—see where you've gone, who you are, who your family was, the history of your life, and analyze it—take everything in, and embrace your experiences. Take in the good, take in the bad, but also say 'Why am I here now?'

"And I'll tell people, Wayne, that there is a reason why I'm sitting here with you this very moment. Nobody else got me here. Yes, my parents led the way for awhile, and they made plenty of mistakes, because I took those trips with them on their journey. But then you take your own journey. So, here I am at 64 years old, and I'm thinking about it, I'm looking at it, I'm taking it all in, and that's the lesson."

Inspired and suddenly deciding a short-term path that I needed to take, I then proclaimed: "Yes, I am going to write this book about my life. It's the only decision for me to make. We all have to take time to look at ourselves. We don't, we're in a hurry. People are not bothering to take time to really look at themselves."

My incredible conversation with Wayne continued unabated, full-bore for the next half hour. This exchange stuck each of us as natural and necessary; for the previous several years we had devoted our professions to writing and publishing books for people. Chronicling the lives of others in a passionate, compelling way had long since become our obsession. And, now, here for the first time, our own separate but co-mingled pathways in life and compatible professions motivated us to tell the story about my interesting life—plus integral details of the upcoming tour along with how those efforts suddenly started to commingle while impacting our lives.

"We're seeing that everybody has a story—some people maybe not as compelling as others," I eventually said, Wayne's ears obviously glued to my every word. "But to them, even if their life histories never go out into the universe, they have a legacy to leave for their family, or for themselves. But what this process does, that I want to go through—and I realize that some of it is probably going to be painful—is to write this story because it's important."

Wayne finally interjected, stressing the urgent need for me to realize that such inner reflection can emerge as a difficult task on an emotional level.

"Yes, honey, I realize that," I told him. "There are some things—secrets that I have never told people—that I haven't even uttered a word to you about, Wayne. These are things that I haven't told my own kids, stories that I have kept hidden deep within my soul, locked deep in my memory. But, this is going to be a good, healthy thing for me to go through. Everything in my universe right now, this very second, is telling me that I have a story to tell.

We're only here a short time, and our lives are really vital.

All of our lives are as important to tell, as much as any celebrity's. This is about my adventures, my path, my spirituality. It's about who I am, and if nobody even reads this book, I'm going to write it for me alone—plus my children and grandkids."

"But do you think it's going to be hard to tell your message?"

"Definitely," I said, cutting to the chase. "In a book, how do you bring across these feelings that you have, deep within your soul? Yes, it's going to be hard. It's nice, Wayne, that you're a ghostwriter, and that you've been successful with a lot of other people. But this is part of it—I could never do this at any other time in my life except for right now. All the pieces are coming together, there are no accidents. You're in my life, because you're a ghostwriter for other people. I'm an 'okay-writer,' but I don't have the eloquent words that you have to bring this story across. It's the right time, the perfect time for us to tell my story."

"So, let's do it, Patty," Wayne said, smiling and summarily proposing another toast.

"That's right!"

Chapter 5

Shortly after darting unexpectedly from Twin Falls, we entered a little town where scores of people—perhaps hundreds of them—enjoyed a morning community pancake feed. Within several hours after abandoning our family dog, Laddie, my dad parked the car and I quickly joined my parents as we enjoyed the free meal.

To this day, I lack any specifics on the name or precise location of the town. The community must have been in Idaho since we had not driven more than a few hours.

God knows where we were heading, because my parents never bothered to tell me. All I can say for sure is that we just kept traveling. From there, we began staying in motels, one after another, as dad landed a never-ending succession of low-paying, short-term auto-body repair work.

Then, suddenly we entered Salt Lake City, Utah, exactly 220 miles from our starting point in Twin Falls. Through calculation many years later, I determined that during the initial days of that phase we must have wandered to a wide variety of towns. After all, a direct drive from our starting point to Utah's capitol, only would have taken just more than three and a half hours.

From the eyes of a six years old girl, Salt Lake immediately impressed me as by far the largest community that I had ever seen. To this point I had always visited towns rather than cities. At the time, Twin Falls was bigger than Reno, which dwarfed miniscule Las Vegas. Shortly after arriving in Salt Lake, my father dropped my mother and me off in a park before he went to look for work.

Forty-seven years later in 2000, Wayne took me on a romantic surprise four-day vacation to Salt Lake City. Without any effort whatsoever at age 53 one afternoon I took my husband directly to the same park that I had visited just one afternoon with my late mom. My memory and sense of direction had always been nothing less than stunning.

And, I remember that caterpillars were falling off the trees from directly above us as I sat on a park bench with my mother. To this day I vividly recall trees everywhere. The two of us stayed in the park for most of the day.

During subsequent weeks and months, mother and I ended up staying in the car a lot while my dad went inside a potential employer's shop to talk with the owners about employment. More often than not, we invariably ended up back on the road because father had failed again to land work. This initial pattern got riddled with consistent rejections; the trend and strategy changed markedly a year or so later when dad started landing temporary jobs on a much more consistent basis. Perhaps through trial and error he had honed his skills in the art of how to ask for things in such a way that you're more likely to hear "yes."

At the early stage, we usually stayed in any particular community for just one night at most. One time, either in Utah or Idaho, I had to go potty in the restroom of an auto-body shop. That's when I saw my first naked ladies. Remember, the people who worked in these places were men. The first images of nude women that I saw were all on a large poster affixed to the restroom wall, many gals each with different boobs. They had long ones, skinny ones, fat ones, and perfect ones.

I had never seen boobies before. I had never even seen my mother's boobies.

But there I stood alone in this bathroom at one of the places where my dad tried to get a job. I paid no attention to the faces on this particular poster. Intrigued, still at age 6, I was more interested in looking at the various sizes and shapes of those many super-interesting breasts. Not all of them were very attractive, especially the loopy ones. The enormous tits seemed to carry much more weight than the embarrassingly flat chests. Looking back, to this day I laugh when recalling that moment, my startled eyes simultaneously affixed to images of no less than about 50 women—a total of perhaps 100 individual boobs.

Certainly, little girls weren't supposed to go in there, but bathroom chores dictated otherwise. This led me at that very tender age to realize that gentlemen craved images of naked adult females.

Unexpected events such as this made these adventures interesting. Besides seeing the great outdoors, I got a peek into a part of the 1950s American culture that most little girls probably never saw. In those days, body shops were in the bad parts of towns, often behind nefarious businesses such as seedy bars or perhaps even strip joints. So, a lot of the time when my dad would visit potential employers I ended up sitting with mother in the car, looking around at less-than-ideal scenery for a child.

For the most part, these were towns where consumers owned older cars from the '30s and '40s rather than newer makes and models. These communities emerged as primary targets for my dad, since older automobiles for the most part needed the greatest attention. Every moment of this journey, I became a keen observer of that world, always closely watching everything that people wore, the architecture and how folks spoke.

My environment and my parents' journey left me with nothing else to do other than to look at life through the window of a car's back seat.

The Salt Lake excursion probably lasted one day at most. We never bothered to stay the night there. We must have briefly headed northwest back up to Idaho, before cruising down to the small, high-desert community of Jackpot in extreme northeast Nevada. My dad was probably thinking from that pivotal juncture: "Well, let's go to Reno, or let's go to Las Vegas."

Certainly at that point Reno must have been far from my dad's priority, since the inner need to avoid his highly critical in-laws must have remained pivotal. His numerous so-called failures several years earlier coupled with his recent inability to keep a job surely would have generated loads of criticism. Dad hated anyone telling him what to do or how to live, particularly people who disliked him and vice versa.

Whatever father's particular motivations on that day, he and mother decided that we would spend that night in the matchbox-sized community of Jackpot. Dirt poor, we apparently stayed in the car. All I remember in that town was seeing gypsies, in the era before everyday consumers began purchasing campers and trailers. These colorful people stayed in uniquely

85

designed trailers that they had either built for themselves from scratch or crafted from a hodgepodge of vehicle parts.

I walked with my mother near a camp set up by and for these transients. They wore bright clothes, and the children seemed happy while scurrying around their families' campfire and hollering in a happy-go-lucky tone. I yearned to play with them, magnetized by a sense that these people looked like they enjoyed having lots of fun. My eyes told me that their trailers were a blast to look at, everything jammed close together.

"Who are those people?" I asked mother, holding her hand.

"Gypsies."

Perplexed, I needed more detail: "What are gypsies."

"They travel all over, and they go from one town to the next to find jobs, good work for their families."

"Well then, mother, are we gypsies?"

"No! We are not gypsies!"

That conversation abruptly ended. Then, we blasted out of town. Avoiding Reno to the west, we instead headed straight south to Las Vegas. I remember keeping awake as he drove all night while mother slept.

We stopped on a hill overlooking Las Vegas, and I could see the lights of that tiny town during the final hour before the sun rose.

"I just need to rest for awhile," he said.

While my parents slept beside me, I gazed at the tiny town of Sin City's twinkling street lights; nearly nine years later entertainer Frank Sinatra's famous Rat Pack would hit town as the population boomed. After father's quick shut-eye, he drove us to town where we spent a couple days. Dad visited his friend and former partner, auto-body shop owner Ray Bandle. Perhaps my parents entertained the notion of living in Las Vegas.

After a short while, my dad must have failed to land solid, steady work because we summarily left to the northwest toward Reno. Maybe father found himself with no other choice, taking a so-called path of "last-resort." Goodness knows his various other attempts had fallen flat.

By this point, my mother was probably telling him: "No more of this, we're going to Reno. We know the town, my mother is there, and you've had work there before. The place is an obvious choice for us."

The mere notion of heading back to the Silver State's biggest city must have made his skin crawl, as if slowly and cruelly gnawed upon by persistent army aunts.

Little could father have known then that the difficulties would only worsen from that point forward. Getting shot out of a cannon like a circus freak probably would have been a much more pleasant experience for him than what was about to occur.

My excitement intensified during our final approach to Reno, delighted at the prospect of seeing my beloved Grandma Eve and Grandpa Oscar.

The sight of downtown Reno's nighttime lights up ahead made my body and spirit sparkle like a Christmas tree, primarily because I adored and cherished my Grandparents.

Luckily, they still lived at the Hill & Sons motel where they remained highly popular among tourists. Soon after our return, Grandpa Oscar resumed one of our favorite activities, as he made me yummy breakfasts of dunk-eggs and toast. Resuming their usual pattern, my Grandparents immediately started spoiling me.

While I felt delighted, my father soon became agitated at the mere notion of having to stay under the same roof with his nagging in-laws. As tensions approached the boiling point, my dad needed to make an urgent decision to get the hell out of there fast.

More than ever, I wanted the house to look as fantastic as possible. A primary goal became getting Wayne's room to look reminiscent of the F. Scott Fitzgerald era, spiffy, polished and high-class in every regard. At the same time, I found an old Kerak Shriners hat that my Grandpa Oscar once used, something important to me. In the 1950s, 1960s, and 1970s, Grandpa served on the drum corps and marched in downtown Reno parades before cheering crowds.

For some reason, without even thinking I fetched Grandpa's maroon Shriners hat from our basement storage area and summarily placed the garment atop the highest shelf above Wayne's desk. Compelling pictures of my husband's mother, Marilyn, his adult daughters, Annie and Bonnie attracted the eye near the U.S. flag and Nevada's state emblem. As he always has, Wayne kept a black-and-white, gold-framed photo of me next to his computer screen.

The hat added spicy, eclectic character to his workplace. Adding zest, 18 months earlier I had purchased a 90-year-old ribbon Underwood Standard Typewriter. Wayne always kept the machine atop a work storage station to his left, beside his upstairs office window overlooking the front yard.

"I don't want you to move my desk or purchase another one for me just for this event," Wayne had asked me shortly after our decision to open up the house to the tour. "Everything that I have is really important for my work, and I'm always comfortable knowing precisely where everything is kept."

I felt just a tinge of disappointment at this request, since I had wanted to purchase a classic old desk to replace his 7-year-old modern-era work station. Be that as it may, this home office also had plenty of interesting antique furniture, including a 50-year-old dark leather recliner that I had recently purchased via Craigslist online.

My challenge emerged in balancing the need to spruce the room up, while also careful to avoid disturbing his working implements. Even so, I could still bring artwork into the room to increase the aura of comfort coupled with a scholarly atmosphere.

Then, I got hit with a decision that came with ease. A round, solid table beside the recliner certainly could serve as the ideal place for the ancient Native American stone cutting tool that Pan had just found while building the path across the yard. Determined to display the stone in an honorable manner, I found an ideal stand.

"This is fantastic!" Wayne said, once I showed the stone to him. "Wow!"

Speaking freely and without reservation from the moment I showed

Wayne this display, he told me of his sincere belief that the stone fit the message of my upcoming book.

"To me, this stone signifies time, the commitment humans have to survive, and what people need to do to prosper," Wayne said.

My husband also made no attempt to cover his delight, upon my revelation that I kept buying old appropriate items for the house at low cost. These included a charming old desk snatched up for just $50 from one of my girlfriends who had just closed an antique shop that she owned. The item became a perfect addition to my home's front entry, fitting like a glove as if always supposed to be there. Everything started coming together. With just a little more than a month to go, I still had tons of work to complete, to give people a great feeling about this experience.

Amid the hubbub, too late to turn back, I started wondering: "Why am I opening the house for all these people to see? What am I going to get out of this experience?"

Would I finish on time?

Straight from Reno, I finally entered the first grade in Portola, California, a small timber harvesting community 49 miles to the northwest of my Grandparents' home.

Could this location have been a compromise between my parents, close enough to Reno so that mother and I could still enjoy lengthy visits with Grandma and Grandpa? Did dad like living nearly an hour from his in-laws, away from potential nagging and unnecessary criticism? I'll never know these answers.

Whatever the case, I felt overjoyed upon finally being able to enter school. We moved into a non-descript, ugly apartment. About the only nice feature soon emerged when we realized that lots of shade-giving pine trees surrounded the residence. I remember the crisp smells, playing among pine needles everywhere.

Nearby, I enjoyed a children's play area featuring a swing and monkey bars, a huge deal in my life as my energetic playground experiences opened me up to glorious, delightful possibilities. Sure, such a short while earlier I had yearned to attend a Twin Falls school with my friend Kathy. But I pressed such concerns out of my mind, excited to start learning.

Unaware of the rules and afraid to ask questions, I suffered a severe case of diarrhea one day during class. I pooped my pants, unaware that I could ask the teacher for permission to visit the restroom. This emerged as perhaps the most embarrassing thing that ever happened to me in almost my whole life.

I cried as my mother picked me up from school and took me home. Loving, kind and sympathetic she refrained from scolding me. My mom and the teacher said: "No matter what, if there's anything you need, Patty, all you have to do is raise your hand and ask, and then everything will be okay. This way such accidents will never happen to you again."

They obviously sensed that the incident traumatized me. This was a whole new world, because until that time I had spent every waking moment with my parents or Grandparents. I had never even stayed at anybody else's house.

Soon afterward, a delightful change erupted when I saw my first movie during class. The projector made rickety sounds prevalent in low-grade technology used in most U.S. public elementary schools at the time. The continuous "ch-ch-tick" sound intensified, and I asked myself: "What's that?" Consider this as a natural reaction, since I had never seen a movie. This marked the first time I saw visual images that appeared to move.

Right away little children appeared on the screen, all from different countries. This marked the first time that I realized that the world had many nations.

"This is Holland," an announcer said as the film showed a little girl wearing Dutch shoes. Right after this initial scene came a collage of youngsters shown in their communities everywhere from Japan to Germany, France, England and Spain.

Delighted, right after school that day I scurried home, telling my parents: "I saw places that were far away." My folks had never even told me about other nations. My dad had never even told me that he served in the Army in England during World War II. In fact, I didn't even know that there had been a huge war.

A stupendous world opened up for me, giving a clear glimpse of unique places other than Idaho, Nevada, Utah and California. I kept telling myself, "Wow, this is incredible." The burning passion to learn filled me more than ever. I eagerly soaked up as much information as possible. My favorite reading included the required textbook "Dick and Jane." More joyful sensations came when I started to draw with the other children. To that point, I had always drawn by myself or with my mother. Now, suddenly I sat in a room surrounded by many other youngsters who drew stick figures, and suns that looked far from realistic. By comparison, my images of horses and people had lifelike volume, texture and expressions.

I became puzzled when other children my age drew images that looked goofy. While I never felt somehow better than them, there could be no denying that I created vastly superior artwork. My parents and the teachers never commented on this, but instinctively I knew that my artistic talents excelled.

This became especially apparent to me upon walking past the fourth- and fifth-grade classrooms. I spotted their artwork, similar to mine and more sophisticated than classmates my own age. I vividly recall these revelations as becoming an important part of my thought process. I got struck with a realization that I did something different.

Halloween arrived fast. The last time I had gone trick-or-treating came a year earlier when my parents took me to gorgeous Twin Falls homes, where residents told us: "Come on in and have cookies," before asking all kinds of questions about my life and family.

The arrangement seemed far different in Portola, when I scurried to a next-door apartment, forced by a snowstorm to wear a huge coat over my outfit. My mom quickly took me to a few houses near our apartment, before we hustled home to escape the cold, miserable storm. I felt disappointed since this depressing experience seemed far less enjoyable than in Idaho.

Also for the first time I began enjoying school for the pageantry. Throughout the remainder of that autumn my class rehearsed traditional holiday songs. Those were stupendous days, before the current era of political correctness where stupid rules prevent public schools from mentioning the meaning of Christmas.

The holiday pageant became such a big deal that my Grandparents drove all the way from Reno for the performance. I felt proud that my beloved relatives would come all that way just for one show, so I concentrated on memorizing every word.

With all the other children I practiced and remembered the entire classic poem, "The Night Before Christmas." We sang all the wonderful classics like "Noel" and "Away in a Manger." Learning came easily back then. A huge part of my life became the glorious process of cramming in as much essential knowledge into my eager mind as possible.

During the holiday break, I went with my parents to stay with my Grandparents in Reno for Christmas. Until then, I had always learned that Santa Claus always comes through fireplaces. I told them: "But Grandma doesn't have a fireplace. Where is Santa going to come?"

"Oh, Santa finds places to bring presents when there are no fireplaces," the adults said. "Don't you worry at all; Santa will take care of you."

So, of course by the time I awakened on Christmas morning Santa had left me loads of presents at the Hill & Sons Motel in the tiny manager's apartment. For the first time, I saw Christmas cards that arrived from my Grandparents' many friends all over the country, mostly tourists who had stayed at the motel.

The Hill Family Christmas card impacted me most, depicting children lined up in front of a fireplace with stockings above them. For me, this marked the epitome of a perfect little family. I had never seen anything like that, and I'll never forget those now-deceased elder Hills shown in their finely appointed residence. This middle-class Reno family's delightful card spoke volumes to me, giving my heart a clear and distinct message of what I wanted from life.

For the first time ever I yearned for normalcy, to join the ranks of average Americans. But for me these vital questions came: Would such a lifestyle ever come, and how?

Chapter 6

Curb appeal, the essence of capturing and mesmerizing a person's eye, hails as among the most significant qualities that a home possesses.

For many years people had exclaimed "Ohhh," and "Ahhh," while walking past my house on formal, organized strolling historical tours of the classic old university neighborhood.

But at this point I urgently needed to get the fence fixed, because the wood front gate had begun to fall due to extensive age and excessive use. Focused on preventing the fence from falling before or during the tour, I became increasingly anxious upon realizing that Pan s had just left Reno for New York.

"What am I going to do?" I asked myself, while Wayne remained immersed in the urgent need to meet a pressing book deadline for one of his clients.

Keep in mind that Wayne would have been no significant help anyway, unable to differentiate between a hammer and a screw driver while concentrating on what he considers more pressing concerns. Like I say, I adore my husband with all my heart, although he fails miserably in matters of what he calls: "Home-fixin'-uppin' chores."

Shortly before leaving, Pan gave his truck and all of his customers to a handyman named Dave who desperately needed work. Before departing for New York, the Indian told my new handyman of the vital need to strengthen the fence as soon as possible.

Suffering from cancer, Dave showed his sweet side right away: "Patty, I'm going to take care of that fence for you."

Within a few hours Dave dug up and removed a primary section of the old fence, installed a vital concrete support and put the fence back up—all in one afternoon. Once again the fence stood firm and strong, which to me in a round-about way represented the same type of stability seen in Grandma's 1953 Christmas card from the Hill family.

In some regards, this is what having a good home is about, ensuring that your life, career or family never fall by the wayside.

At least I had the fence fixed, but lots of vital chores still needed urgent attention as the date for the home tour quickly approached.

Without any warning whatsoever, shortly after the 1953 holiday season, my dad landed a job in Sparks, Nevada, just outside Reno.

We left the logging and railroad community of Portola behind with little thought as my parents continued their endless pursuit of happiness. Still in the first grade, I started attending Robert Mitchell Elementary School by mid-February.

My parents got us into a dilapidated duplex right across the street from Sparks High School. The harsh northeast California winters had probably pushed my father back to these much more temperate climates, although doing so forced him to live closer to his in-laws. Mom still contributed as a full-time housewife. Each morning I made the four-block walk alone to my new class. More than ever, I enjoyed learning, unaware that this would be the first of countless school transitions through the coming decade.

Looking back, I would like to have stayed in one school, most likely in Idaho, to get a good, solid education and to develop lifelong friendships. Needless to say, attending five or more schools almost every year would gradually make keeping up with necessary schoolwork extremely difficult if not impossible.

By this point I knew how to raise my hand if I needed to visit the restroom. As a child, you just did what you were supposed to do, never saying things like: "Oh, dad, I want to stay here in this school forever." Your parents just did what they wanted; they moved you and never asked for your opinion. They didn't tell you anything, they just did it. And you better not say, "Oh, I don't want to do that." A child just never protested.

And, besides, if I had made my feelings known or asked them a pointed question on the issue I probably would never have gotten a complete, accurate answer anyway. From that point forward, most teachers lacked any faces in my mind, at least from the perspective of my memory today. They weren't in my life long enough to make them memorable.

So, I fail to recall specifics about the Robert Mitchell School teacher, and I lack any memory of most classmates from that period. I just remember learning things, and that's what I liked. Nothing really popped out at me, except for something that happened at recess. Now, nearly sixty years later the schoolyard looks exactly the same. I remember playing with a kind little boy. That day after getting home from school, I told my mother: "I met a new friend today! He's so nice, and I really like him. But, you know, it's really interesting. He has different color than me."

"What do you mean a different color, Patty?"

"Well, he's dark—he has kind of brownish, blackish-colored skin."

Yes, this had marked the first time I ever saw a black person.

Then, my mother said, "Well, that's nice, honey. I'm glad you're happy, and I'm glad you're having fun. But I don't' want you playing with him."

"But why, mom, I don't understand."

"Well, this is what I've got to talk to you about. White people do not associate with black people."

"But what's black—you mean his skin color?"

Taking her parenting responsibilities seriously, mother explained cultural differences to me in the best way that she knew how. She strived to pass along to me the value system that she had been taught to embrace. Hoping to put this societal system into perspective, she showed me one of my childhood books, "Little Black Sambo."

An innocent child, unaware of the wicked or selfish ways of the world, at the time I thought of this as a simple innocent story. The notion of racism had not yet been introduced to my curious little mind. At least from the start, I never associated the storybook Sambo character with the little boy that I had met.

"He's black," mother told me. "And, they're called Negroes."

Sparked with curiosity, I asked streams of questions about such people. All her answers essentially conveyed the message that: "You're going to run into them sometime in your life, and all I'm telling you is that whites stay with whites and Negroes stay with their own kind. And, you don't associate with them."

In keeping with the supposed morals of the time, my dad had to talk more about Negroes to me after he returned home from work that evening.

"Why can't I play with that little boy?" I asked.

My dad answered by starting to talk about his family experiences. His mother and father had told him about their association with Negroes when they had lived in Texas. The senior Edwards had worked in a Lone Star State casket factory alongside black people that my father described as "very stupid *niggers*."

Yes, whether I like to admit this or not, my dad used that horrible, repulsive and sometimes confusing "N-word," that still generates hate, confusion and animosity. My father never said "Negroes." Instead, as I sat on his lap, a highly inquisitive 7-year-old girl by this point, he called them: "A bunch of stupid *niggers* that don't know anything. You've got to realize, Patty, that my parents didn't like them because they were stupid. And we never saw many of them while I was growing up. But I've had a few people I've known who were black—I did know some guy who was a real nice *nigger*. Just do as we say, *niggers* stay with *niggers*, and whites stay with whites. Don't you ever associate with them."

This marked my first experience with prejudice. As commanded by my parents, from the following day forward I ignored the little black boy because my parents had told me not to go near him. A good little girl, I always did what my folks told me to do.

Of course, at the time I lacked any notion of how racism would impact my life, discovering much later that I definitely lacked such hateful attributes. In fact, racial equality has been among my favorite topics. During the summer immediately prior to my home tour, I had downloaded from Amazon.com a riveting book about early African-

American history, "Up From Slavery," an autobiography by the historical icon of that heritage, Booker T. Washington

Definitely far from racist as an adult, I enjoyed the riveting, compelling stories by the famed political leader, orator and author. I've never been prejudiced at all, careful to refrain from disliking people due to their skin color. The only prejudice I felt remained contempt for what I call "stupid people, whether they be white, black, brown, yellow or green, I don't care."

In fact, the first book that I downloaded upon purchasing my new Kindle e-reading device was Washington's autobiography, primarily because I remained intensely interested in the black culture. I've felt strongly about this since high school, watching the courageous and compelling work of the great, late American civil rights activist, the Rev. Dr. Martin Luther King Jr.

Whenever my father said that horrible word, "*nigger*," that really bothered me, especially during my teenage years. Only one black person attended my high school. One of the first books that I read was "Uncle Tom's Cabin, or Life Among the Lowly," the iconic, world-changing 1852 anti-slavery novel by Harriet Beecher Stowe. I remember crying my eyes out, and from then on I read so many things on the black culture. One of my other favorite books is "Five Smooth Stones," a novel by Ann Fairbairn, about 1950s African-American college students who made something of themselves.

A ferocious reader throughout my life, I couldn't put down "Roots: The Saga of an American Family," the classic 1976 book by Alex Haley, a novel based on his African-American family's challenging history—starting with the story of his ancestor, Kunte Kinte in 1767.

As a mature white woman, the movement for freedom among Americans of African heritage remained very deep in my heart. My instinctive passion on this topic went far beyond merely having close friends "of color." Maybe my burning internal yearning to learn as much as possible on this topic stemmed from my parents' insistence that I avoid my little elementary school classmate.

Without disliking my parents, in a sense perhaps I've stepped beyond them by taking a different path. This divergence emerged as a primary reason why I decided to chronicle my life here, however painful and emotionally difficult the task.

No, I do not hate the memory of my late parents, nor do I think of myself as far better than they due to these differences and numerous other diverging pathways that we chose. The more that I convey here, the more I discover that I have loads of bursting, pent-up passion to convey through this process.

My soul ignited with continually increasing energy, at the start of this book project upon Wayne's insistance that I should sit down and using a pen and paper—not a typewriter—write a one-page letter. Shown here, the message is addressed by "1-year-old Patty to me when I was 15 years old:"

"So, you are now 15. At this time being aged one and looking ahead at 14 years from now and even longer into the future ...I must say that I'm a very happy little girl who is much loved. I'm not thinking about anything, other than being taken care of....I would say to you this: Remain and become a loving person, learn as much as you can. Grasp everything from everyday experiences. Try to remember all the good things that have happened in your life until you turned 15. Cherish the love you received from mommy and daddy, and of course from Grandma and Grandpa. Remember all the wonderful places you have seen in the last 15 years. Yes, I know some of the memories were unpleasant.

You learn from them, so what should I try to become? A good person, kind, loving and spiritual!"

Increasingly fascinated by this assignment, and at the persistent urging of my husband, I also wrote a fantasy letter from myself at age 64 to the same 15-year-old Patty:

It's time to learn. Don't be lazy. Educate yourself. You really haven't applied yourself these last 15 years. Okay, I know you weren't supplied with more books, or you weren't told to study by your parents enough. ...So, you were lazy and didn't do your homework like you should have. This means for me today that if I had a true hunger for education, I would have been happier right now with myself. Yes, I know it was hard for you, Patty, going from school to school. And you did the best that you could. I really do acknowledge you, though, for really seeing and taking in the life challenges that you've had the last 15 years. You saw so much from traveling that you learned "street-smarts." You learned and appreciated nature and beauty. You learned to draw out of boredom, and manners. Because of those early years, you have made me a good person, a talented, gifted artist and an adventurer, and ...I love that little girl who never really looked 59 years ago into the future to think about what I would be like at age 64. I just thought at that time that 64 was really old. At 15, she just thought about having fun, school, family, my hair, clothes, and that one day I would live in a beautiful home and have a good life.

I soon found myself mystified to discover that these emotions and internal revelations started springing forth during this journey of self-discovery. I suddenly found myself motivated to delve even further along this vibrant pathway. The opportunity to write a "fantasy" letter from 15-year-old Patty to myself now in my mid-60s proved just as eternally graceful:

Hi, Patty (Grandma, Mother, Adult Woman) ...Wow! I would like to be healthy when I'm 64. I would like to have had many experiences in life. I would like to travel. I would like to have a marriage, had a couple of kids, grandkids, my friends. I want to be beautiful, I want to be loving, a good mother, wife and friend. I want a cottage with a beautiful garden. I want to read and enjoy a spiritual life, surrounded by others who think like-minded. I hope to be in a loving relationship. I want to work at my creativity. I want to paint and draw. I want to be active in my community, and to be a good citizen. I want to enjoy good meals with good friends. I want to see more of the world ...I think I will have some positive notoriety, as I am very confident with myself. I know that I will need to live until I am over 100 years old because there will be so much to learn and so much to accomplish. I will be a happy person who has somehow become accomplished in the arts, a good wife, mother, grandmother and friend.

Upon completing this phase, I broke into tears of joy. So many divergent emotions flowed freely and willfully into my heart. The realization that I now was at age 64 at the precise stage that my mother and paternal grandmother died made me tremble with gratitude toward our Creator. Thank you, for giving me good health, far past the point that so many others have enjoyed.

These delightful, easy-to-accomplish tasks soon inspired me to delve even more into that brief pivotal period when we lived across from Sparks High School, four miles east of Reno. Then, the vivid, undeniable realization struck that a little boy my age, Richard, lived in an adjoining unit from ours in the same duplex. The boy's parents had loved him dearly, with all their hearts as any mother and father would.

One day his mother, whose name I fail to recall, knocked on our front door and asked if I could come to visit him. At first my mother seemed perplexed, since the child wasn't on the porch as well. The child's mother explained that he was seriously ill, but didn't have any other kids to play with. Soon afterward, with my mother's blessing, I went next door one afternoon to visit Richard.

The child remained bedridden, afflicted by an irreversible bout of acute leukemia. Such a diagnosis for a youngster in those days became an almost-certain death sentence. Burning with fever, sweat covering every pore of his skin, the child kept rolling on his bed in obviously extreme discomfort.

"He needs another little friend to be close to him," the boy's mother told my mom and me one afternoon. "He is so very lonely and afraid."

Eager to give comfort and to help in any way that I could at the encouragement of my mother, one afternoon I held Richard's hand as he lay in bed. Like him, I didn't have any friends my own age. Like him, perhaps, I was dying, but in a much different way. His body was fading fast, while a little part of my soul was passing away amid the deep thought that I didn't actually have a permanent worldly home.

Increasingly empathetic, I crawled into the bed beside Richard and hugged him tight—in a sisterly way, almost as if I had always known him, almost as if I had always loved him, almost as if we were relatives. It was interesting. Loving. Graceful.

On the verge of fast-approaching physical death, Richard wept lightly.

As did I.

And, so Richard's journey continued into another phase, another realm while my pathway on this Earth steadily increased in difficulty and intensity.

The burglars struck at 1:30 in the morning while Wayne and I were asleep, tucked snuggly in our cozy upstairs bedroom overlooking the front gate and yard.

Our precious Diva awakened, startled by a noise that she must have heard from outside as one or more intruders slithered like snakes toward our front door.

Diva always slept at our feet each night curled up like a little Easter bunny. The dog looked so cute that upon seeing her people could swear that she would never hurt a fly. On this occasion, though, she proved her worth right away. Our little heroine bolted from the bed in a flash, scurried down the stairs with the tenacity of a wolf, and jumped up against the front door—barking her little head off.

"What's going on?" I thought, not bothering to awaken Wayne, who remained fast asleep. "Our little girl rarely gets so excited during the middle of the night."

Fully unaware that actual danger lurked just outside our front entrance, I lay motionless in bed on my back. I began thinking that the dog had probably been startled by college-age party-goers from down the street.

Much earlier throughout the evening the sounds of Friday night celebrations by university students rocked the neighborhood. Such hoe-downs kicked into gear on a fairly regular basis, primarily in the late summer and late spring when each school year was just starting up and eventually winding down.

Since we both had been young, vibrant and energetic college-age revelers ourselves several decades earlier, Wayne and I always understood the motivations of such youth. Thus, in all our years in this house, we had never called the police to complain about loud parties. "Let them be kids," the two of us would often tell each other. "Let them have fun, since life is invariably going to get tough soon enough for most of them when they finally enter the so-called 'real world, the dog-eat-dog universe.'"

This live-and-let-live philosophy had seemed to work well. After all, on several occasions those past few decades, Wayne and I had hosted a few loud parties of our own, some guests generating enough noise to awaken the dead. Well, almost anyway.

The tide had turned for us at the height of one of our bashes in 2005 when two cops showed up at our front gate close to midnight. Wayne greeted the officers and promised them: "Yes, we will turn the music down. My step-daughter, Zoë, is throwing a party to say goodbye to her friends, before she moves to Costa Rica."

The cops took Wayne at his word. The police left, vowing to return to arrest my husband for disturbing the peace and any obnoxious party-goers if neighbors issued more complaints that night about excessive noise. As he had promised, as soon as the police left Wayne told my daughter's revelers: "The cops were just here, and they asked us to turn the music down. Otherwise, there is going to be hell to pay."

"Yeah!" several of Zoë's guests cheered, while summarily turning the outside stereo up louder and cheering at the top of their lungs. Some of them told Wayne, "This is great. You know you don't have a great party until someone calls the cops."

Of course, at my insistence that night the music quieted and these party-goers calmed down as tranquility gradually returned. These were not the type of gatherings that I had become accustomed to hosting. By sharp contrast, the vast majority of my parties involved sedate, well-to-do people and common folks who enjoyed light cocktails and hors d'oeuvres. Easy-listening music, Hawaiian-style bamboo tiki torches, light salads and tropical drinks often emerged as major hits.

Our numerous wintertime get-togethers had often entailed quaint functions for maybe eight people at most. Yes, to me a house was not truly a home unless used as a unique place to share and experience joy. Thus at Thanksgiving the house became a virtual museum of how grateful that Wayne and I were to this community and to the freedoms that we enjoyed. The wreaths and decorations changed markedly, transitioning to deep, vibrant autumn colors.

The Christmas seasons, of course, always marked a much more obvious theme, and the character and uniqueness of this cottage-style house enabled me to transform the property into a virtual, vibrant and unforgettable Winter Kingdom. For the first seven or eight years or so that Wayne lived here that process became difficult.

The first week of each December he would start whining when I asked him to haul about 15 boxes filled with Christmas decorations from the basement to the ground-floor living room. At the time at least, getting my husband to perform any helpful work, these necessary chores, was about as easy as getting a stubborn mule to do its job.

Was Wayne lazy? Did all this challenge stem from the fact that he simply didn't care? Could it have been true that the guy lacked a single domestic bone in his body?

Certainly his wonderful mother, Marilyn Melton, could not have been to blame. From everything I had been told and seen first-hand this kind, intelligent and generous woman had done everything imaginable to raise him right. She and her late husband, Rollan Melton—Wayne's father—had each earned well-deserved reputations for their diligence and strong work ethics.

Despite Wayne's whiny, almost child-like protestations during those early years of our marriage we somehow managed to transform my house into a Winter Wonderland every holiday season. Although my guy always seemed to be living emotionally in an apparent fantasy world, his mind continually focused on other things, intellectual pursuits. We somehow always managed to cooperate enough to get these chores done.

Then, unexpectedly another transformation struck Wayne for an inexplicable reason that left me stunned, amazed and literally flabbergasted.

On his own, with no nagging necessary whatsoever, around 2005 he started throwing all his gusto, energy and creative spark into this annual holiday process. Sometimes when I would arrive home from early

December errands, he already would have the living room stuffed with the Christmas decoration boxes.

My guy started becoming so excited that he sometimes went overboard. "Wayne, you've got some of the Halloween boxes here as well; what were you thinking? You're scatter-brained and never pay attention," I would say, or words to that effect. Whatever happened to ignite his pizzazz I could never say with any certainty. From that point forward he became almost like a little kid, overly eager for the holidays to arrive and frequently asking for ways that he could help me prepare for these joyful seasons.

Wayne and I decorated our Christmas tree each season. I would crank up holiday tunes while we enjoyed hot-buttered rums. But through the 2005-to-2008 period our synthetic green tree had begun to crumble or at least disintegrate to the point that we literally had to fight with the thing to make it look right.

In December 2009 we forked out significant bucks for a silver-colored synthetic tree. Our blessings spilled forth in abundance when Cheryl Andrews, one of my most cherished long-time girlfriends, unexpectedly gave me dozens of genuine, unused 1950s Christmas tree ornaments that she had inherited from her mother.

Rather than over-decorate the tree with the many ornaments I collected over the years, Wayne and I began an annual tradition of employing a "less-is-more" strategy. The simple, round, colorful ornaments seemed to sparkle every year from then on. Nestled by the arched fireplace, the fire-resistant tree sparkled each season as if decorated by God's most cherished angels.

These various holiday seasons, the much-welcomed transitions from winter through spring and beyond marked what having such a wonderful, delightful home meant to me. Through my decisions, tenacity and perseverance I had indeed created the exact home that my late mother had once so desperately wanted for herself.

With each passing year, I have learned what having a home, a permanent physical place can mean: a stupendous place to share with long-time friends and new acquaintances; a place to cry and to laugh and to mediate; a place to learn and to share precious time and to learn about the deaths and births of loved ones; a place to cope with extreme financial difficulties and to thankfully cherish short-term money windfalls; a place to grow and strengthen a marriage, always spreading into new and wondrous possibilities; a place to escape from the ravages, wickedness and cruelties of the outside world, sometimes by reading books or watching television; a place to jump out from, racing to new jobs and new possibilities; a place to create artwork and graphic designs; a place to write books and a place to enjoy pets that have given my open heart stupendous joy.

And so there, on Saturday, Sept. 10, 2011, exactly two weeks prior to the scheduled tour cowardly, sneaky invaders had decided to hit my home.

As we slept upstairs.

As we lived our dreams, working hard and smart with as much diligence as possible.

Embracing my usual custom shortly after sunrise that morning I opened the front door, en route to depart for my daily exercise at Saint Mary's Health Center. Right away I noticed what had happened and thought: "Someone has left the front gate open! We've been robbed!"

A quick inspection revealed the loss of three solar-powered night lights that I had installed around a fountain near the front door a few days earlier. A bright lavender light, another solar device with an angel at the top also disappeared from the other end of the yard. At least for the time being the devilish, bold, brazen thief or thieves had either ignored or failed to see a unique feature that had been near the angel—the wood Indian statue that Pan had made.

These cowardly burglars hadn't stolen much, but still I felt invaded.

My mind began to swirl with amazing, positive possibilities amid this research and writing process—thanks to Wayne's persistence and dedication to me and to my heart.

More than ever before, I realized that each of us—especially in our maturing adult years—still has ample time to benefit by clearly analyzing our early lives. Yes, as I've clearly found, each of us at my age can take time to see how we tick.

Take great pleasure and care to travel back to that era when you're a little child. Acknowledge what you have learned, and from this perspective experience the joy or even the heartache of accepting your early environments. Smile or cry in the sensation of vividly recalling the emotions instilled by the people who surrounded you then.

Accept what you might have learned from them, or conversely how you might have failed to teach them vital lessons. Just as essential, embrace the process that enabled or made you into the person that you became. Up above the clouds, an omniscient Creator could easily see that this emerges as a fantastic assignment for each of us.

With each passing hour as I embraced this writing assignment and house tour date fast-approached, I kept learning more about myself. To my great joy, I continued discovering how I could become more effective when interacting with other people. That's precisely what our world is about, sharing and interacting with other individuals while learning and growing spiritually, emotionally and intellectually from those experiences.

Conversely, of course, you could live all by yourself as a hermit. But most of us dwell in environments with people all around. So, with those individuals that keep coming into our lives, we can and should become somewhat of an influence—especially those of us who have reached my stage in life.

At age 64, thanks largely to this book-writing process, I found myself blossoming out of my proverbial cocoon that I had been encased in as a child.

Maybe in this regard, now, I'm like a butterfly. My spiritual, emotional and intellectual wings have spread. Like I say, the greatest happiness has permeated my very being, a sharp, divergent contrast from my first 20 years of life. Thanks to my tenacity and stick-to-itiveness, I eventually enjoyed and came to appreciate many of life's greatest experiences—particularly having children.

Sharing and making friends, including with people of other cultures, has opened my spirit to the greatest possible outcomes that life can offer. Again, however, I still have a hard time with stupid people. That's my prejudice. Maybe this signals my need to visit some specific region of our world where I can interact with streams of ignorant individuals. Common sense tells me that I should avoid disliking any specific culture or segment of society. God only knows that I easily could have ended up evolving into a dirt-stupid person myself, taking another route in life into a world of drugs, alcohol or poverty—all pathways that I carefully avoided.

Largely as a result, perhaps more than ever before, with each passing day as the house tour date approached I felt a steadily increasing need to finish writing this book.

Within days after the death of my little neighbor, Richard, my father suddenly and unexpectedly decided that we needed to move 201 miles from Reno to Empire, California.

Rather than a burning need to hunt for more employment, this time dad's motivation stemmed from a desire to see and help his mother, who had become increasingly ill.

My parents acknowledged a desperate need to assist his family. Yet they never told me the specific reason. This Grandma lived with her brother, Jim, each managing a migrant workers camp near Modesto at the center of Central California's agricultural district in the lush San Joaquin Valley. Fruit trees spread out in seemingly every direction, in some instances for as far as the eye could see.

Some white and others Mexican, these migrant workers lived in a camp. Except for the very youngest children, the vast majority of these people worked the farmlands for extremely low, poverty-level wages. While living with my parents, great-uncle and Grandma Mamie, I began observing a completely new culture and environment. Really cool paintings covered the walls of Grandma Mamie's home. These were vibrant, compelling, professionally created paintings the likes of which I had never seen. While growing up, we never had paintings in our houses. In fact, our walls were bare. Then, all of a sudden, one painting filled me with fascination. The image of a warship sparked my imagination, capturing a smoky, bloody moment at the height of battle.

Flashes. Glorious colors. Emotional inspiration.

My little mind spiraled into another universe. It is the first time I noticed a painting on a wall. This grabbed my full attention, until shortly afterward when I started noticing much smaller paintings nearby.

Although Grandma Mamie lived in that tiny, dumpy apartment that her employers provided for managers, she had managed to install the most fabulous artistic images that I had seen until that point. Grandma had furnished the residence with 1930s furniture, generating a unique, distinctively comfortable setting. This environment immediately filled me with a lifelong appreciation for Depression-era furniture.

Remarkably, these mirrored the era, style, ambiance and authentic styles that fill my home today. People who tour my home will get the same warm, comforting sensations that I first felt upon visiting that grandmother's home nearly 60 years ago.

Although we stayed in Grandma's ugly little apartment, her furnishings made me feel cozy, warm and well-protected. Just as impressive, I instantly appreciated the many doilies, cups, saucers, and a wide variety of other keepsakes that Grandma had kept from her past.

To this day, I still own and cherish an eight-inch tall pitcher from this Grandma's home. An image on both sides of the container shows a little Dutch girl innocently kissing a boy of the same heritage, each standing near a little windmill. This priceless keepsake emerged into an essential, highly coveted part of my soul.

Amazingly, this Grandma's tiny house with a thimble-size living room, two dinky bedrooms pinched together and a tiny kitchen made me feel more comfortable than ever—thanks primarily to her cozy furniture.

Grandma Mamie never seemed sick to me, so I didn't understand why we had gone there. Apparently someone had mentioned that she was ill. Just as interesting, I failed to fully grasp that this was the woman who had instilled a sense of bigotry in my father.

This woman looked and acted in a much different way than my Grandma Eve, who always looked attractively dressed. By comparison, my father's mother at the time was younger than I am today, but she looked like about 100 years old, from a child's perspective. Embracing a style that would have made my Reno Grandma cringe, this woman wore what I can only call "old-lady shoes." Grandma Mamie's gray, severely short hair made her look quite ancient to me. She always wore long, funny skirts with aprons on them. Naturally, this impression made me think of what all old women must look like.

And, now here I am more than a decade into the 21st Century, proudly wearing stylish clothing. While preparing for the house tour, my hairdresser told me that my hair looked: "sexy." As a modern gal, an indirect product of the women's liberation movement of the late 1960s and early 1970s, plus a former "hippy," I prided myself in keeping my fingernails polished and my make-up applied so I would be ready at any time for any occasion. No, I would never allow myself to evolve into an "old lady," such as my Empire Grandma had become. No, I would never think of myself as worn out and useless. And, no, I would never discount the memory of that "Old Grandma," for just being who she was—the woman had unknowingly taught me who I could become and evolve into.

The mere thought that at the time in 1954 at age 61 she was three years younger than I am right now makes me appreciate our many sharp contrasts and distinctive similarities. I grew up as fashion-oriented, a lifestyle that Grandma Mamie never would have embraced. With just as much vibrancy, her keen taste for furniture became mine.

Another sharp difference came into play when I realized that this grandmother never talked to me in a chit-chatty, sharing way like my other grandmother.

Grandma Mamie's brother, Jim—my father's uncle—impressed me as kind of a "curmudgeon-dude." This man seemed like a complete opposite of my Grandpa Oscar, who lavished me with yummy breakfasts.

A few times I mustered up enough courage to ask Uncle Jim for a cookie, but all they had were Fig Newtons that I disliked.

"Don't you have any chocolate cookies?" I asked one time.

"I don't have any of those!" Uncle Jim grumbled.

"Well, I don't' like Fig Newtons."

Like the mean giant that the fairy tale character Jack encountered at the top of his beanstalk, Uncle Jim bellowed in a deep, monstrous voice: "Good, that means there's more for me." The man smiled wickedly as if he were a scary Halloween character when he said this. His mean-spirited tone filled me with either fright or contempt or fear—or maybe even all those reactions.

His slovenly appearance contrasted my father's movie-star features. While my muscular father wore crisp pants and finely-fit Pendleton shirts, Uncle Jim wore bib overalls and a huge farm hat.

My father and that guy could not have possibly looked and behaved more differently.

Although unfriendly, at least Uncle Jim never had much to say, which suited me fine. More than ever before, this made me appreciate my father's good, loving heart despite his own numerous flaws, not the least of which were bigotry and instability.

Unlike Uncle Jim, who never seemed to show any compassion whatsoever, my father had dropped everything in his own life because he wanted to make sure that his mother was okay. Keeping with his usual pattern, my father needed to find another auto-body shop job, this time in the Empire and Modesto area.

Luckily, as far as I know, dad landed just such a position in that community, right in the nick of time in order to help put food on the table.

I never spent any time with the children who lived at the migrant-worker camp, since my parents prohibited me from going near them. These people lived in barracks, crammed into units that looked somewhat like seedy, dilapidated motel rooms. These people lacked trees for shade or even a decent park. Dirt, dust and grime surrounded their accommodations, a God-forsaken place where I'm sure rats would not even want to live. As the years passed, these were the kinds of people that I would come to appreciate. These were the kinds of people that I would yearn to help. And these are the kinds of people that all of our society would continue to depend on, even as I grew much older and began to associate with highly successful individuals of many diverse professions.

My relatives always ordered me to play inside. They never said why, and I never bothered to ask. While in Empire, I moved with my parents, great-uncle and Grandma Mamie from the barracks into a house in the town of Empire.

About this time I finally started figuring out that there was something wrong with my grandmother. Until this point, I had thought the term "sick" only referred to feeling yucky in your belly or something. That changed one night when my Grandma dashed by the room that I slept in, and I saw her naked for just a brief few seconds. My mother promptly shut the door, and I knew something was wrong.

Someone had apparently mentioned the phrase "senile dementia" around that time, but I lacked any concept of what that meant. No one bothered to explain any of this to me, but the running-naked incident had warned of Grandma's behavior problems. Looking back now, I realize that my dad had taken a much-needed leadership position, ensuring that his uncle and my grandmother were all right.

As a result, I went through the rest of first grade in Empire, my third school at that grade level. My wardrobe at the time consisted primarily of dresses for school. Memory tells me that I probably had only a handful, because every time we packed up to move somewhere we took only about four suitcases. That's all we ever took.

We probably rented only places that had furniture. We always left things behind. I remember mother washing clothes in a ringer-style washing machine before hanging them up on a line.

At least one positive transition came. Once settled in Empire, we finally had a TV, owned by Grandma Mamie and Uncle Jim. Can you imagine the joy, curiosity and sense of wonderment I felt, when finally watching television for the first time at age seven? Of course, most American toddlers these days get bombarded with moving visual images before they even start to jabber.

I clearly remember that during the day mom would handle ironing chores while watching soap operas. She did everyone's laundry, and the ironing process emerged as her only available time to relax—at least somewhat. With just as much urgency, mother became obsessed with putting pin curls in my hair, handling this chore daily to make sure I looked immaculate when heading off for school. To her credit, mother always showed an appropriate level of concern about my hygiene. Without fail, she made sure that I brushed my hair and brushed my teeth before going to bed. These same mandatory tasks were performed like clockwork each morning before a small breakfast and departure for school. Just as impressive, mother always made me a lunch, because I hated the school's food. Most meals that mother packed included fairly nutritious selections such as peanut butter and jelly sandwiches.

Before I barely had time to get settled and become fully comfortable with our living environment, we started packing up again.

Following her usual pattern, one morning mom suddenly started stuffing our meager possessions into suitcases. This time no one discussed what was happening with Grandma Mamie or Uncle Jim. My father summarily started to load my immediate family's few possessions into our car.

We were now cruising along another highway. My parents kept me in the dark about exactly where we might have been heading. Perhaps they lacked any distinct concept of any specific destination.

Although this marked more of the same pattern of constant moves, the adventure soon evolved into a much greater challenge than I could have possibly realized.

My entire being yearned to look fantastic for my grandchildren during their upcoming visit, when they would arrive soon from the Czech Republic.

We last saw each other four years earlier in 2007 when I was 60. Filled with anticipation, I rummaged through my closet in anticipation of taking my 13-year-old granddaughter Eva to lunch, along with her mom, Hana. With any luck, my 19-year-old granddaughter living in Reno, Hannah Torvick, would be able to attend.

Determined to look spectacular for Eva, I started thinking of my late Grandma Eve, who always dressed first-class. Now blessed with a closet crammed with clothes that I took pride in, I started thinking: "What on earth should I wear?"

If everything went as planned, I would take my cherished female relatives to Harrah's Steak House, my favorite Reno dining establishment. I could have taken them to anyplace in town, but I yearned to give Eva a joyful experience that she could remember with fondness for a lifetime.

"I want her to remember me as a Grandma who was always beautiful," I thought. "I don't want her to remember me for being an 'old, curmudgeon Grandma, like I remember my grandmother from Empire. Clunky old shoes and frumpy garments are far from my preference. Not me, I'm a stylish grandmother."

So I looked carefully through my closet before finding a pair of white Saint John Knit pants. I chose a perfect white shirt to go with my favorite pants.

Filled with delight and anticipation for the "girl's afternoon," I put this outfit on in my upstairs dressing room. Momentarily, I inspected myself in a full-length mirror at the top of the stairs, delighted with my appearance and feeling quite fashionable. Satisfied at this point, I wanted my hair to look "just-so," determined to let my granddaughter Eva see me as one classy grandmother —thinking fondly of when she's age 64 in the year 2062, telling herself: "You know, my Grandma Patty was gorgeous. She was stylish. She lived in a lovely home with fabulous things"—not like I'm thinking back at my grandmother from Empire. Dead set on providing Eva with a memorable experience, I avoided entertaining the notion of taking her to a cookie-cutter chain restaurant. Cognizant on the need to create fine memories, I decided to give Eva, her mother and Hannah some spending money.

"I will give this cash to them at Harrah's," I thought. "And by God, that's where I'm going to take them to lunch."

As planned, upon picking Eva up, I told her: "I came to take you to my favorite restaurant, Harrah's Steakhouse."

Then, Hannah came over and she said: "Yeah, Grandma is taking us to the best restaurant in town; it's my favorite."

When we finally arrived, the delighted expression on Eva's face told me that the breathtaking ambiance had left her mesmerized. Imagine the surprise that Eva felt when waitresses placed butter before us, all fashioned into the form of roses.

The hostess Debbie told me: "Oh, Patty, it's so nice to see you," before ensuring that we were comfortably in our seats. A favorite waitress, Patty came over and gave me a huge hug, before I introduced this classy woman to my granddaughters.

Harrah's Steakhouse hailed as a five-star restaurant, undoubtedly "the place to go in Reno, bar-none." I had told this to Eva when I went to pick her up with Hannah.

"They're getting an experience, this is wonderful," I began thinking. "Yes, they could have gone to a boring big-chain restaurant and not had any classy atmosphere or first-class service. And to think, just by going here I probably spent only $35 more."

Family means everything to me. I've always had tremendous love for my daughter, Zoë, unable to attend the lunch due to work commitments. As the meal began, we still remained hopeful that Zoë could join us. Just like me, Zoë cherished fine wine. Thirty-nine years old at the time, my daughter worked in a wine shop where she had learned everything possible about such beverages, and she really would have appreciated this meal.

Zoë had turned out to be a smart, bright woman and a mega-talented writer. Hopefully, someday Zoë would be able to write about her life's many diverse and unique experiences, along with accomplishments still ahead. A bright, shining soul, she had her own daughter, Hannah, one of the loves of my life.

Somehow all the women in my family got prettier with each new generation. Of course, physical appearance is far from the most important attribute in life. Even so, the females in my family from each successive generation sparkled in their beauty, both inside and out. Eva shined as well, in my eyes a gorgeous 13-year-old girl already taller than me. "This has been a great girl day." I thought halfway through the meal.

Determined to step up the fun, I gave Hannah, Eva and Hana their spending money for a surprise shopping spree that I had planned for the four of us that afternoon. We darted straight from lunch to the shopping mall. This spiraled into tremendous fun for Eva, delighted by the fact that she was in America—able to shop with her cousin. Just as I had hoped, Eva's afternoon developed into something that I know she will always remember.

"You've got to give your kids memories."

This turned out to be a "girl day," but my love for my son Chris, a resident of the Czech Republic and Eva's father, still held a tremendous piece of my heart as well. My son, who had been over here to help his dad, my former husband, was excited to have his family coming here for the first time since they were little. During the afternoon of that "girl's-day-out," Chris and his 10-year-old-son, Mickey, my grandson stayed home in Reno and went off on a motorcycle ride together.

"I'm so proud of your dad," I told Eva, determined to show how wonderful her father is—so I told her: "You haven't seen Reno in a long time. Let's take Virginia Street. I want to show you what your father has accomplished."

As planned, I drove her to a park that my son had built in downtown Reno, the widely acclaimed Powning Park. During the late 1990s, my son, whom I consider a very talented sculptor, built the official statue of this city's namesake, Civil War Union Army hero Jesse Reno.

"Oh, I've always wanted to see that!" Eva said as we stopped at the park. "There it is, the statue that my dad made."

"Eva, look at that," I said, pointing. "Look at all the benches he made, and all the stone structures. Your father built that entire park with his own hands."

Until you see something tangible before your eyes, you need to tell your grandchildren how wonderful their parents are, and what they've achieved.

Until this point, Eva had never seen her father's downtown Reno artwork; she had only viewed flat photographic images on his Website. Just three minutes earlier, we had driven by the Thompson Federal Court Building at the southern edge of downtown Reno.

"Look!" I told Eva, as we passed by in my car. "Inside this huge stone building, in the beautiful rotunda you can see a bust of your father's late uncle Judge Bruce Thompson, the namesake of this famous building. Your father created and built that sculpture, dedicated in a huge public ceremony just a few days after you were born."

"Oh! I've seen that on my dad's Website, too," Eva said. "And, there it is."

This experience drove home to me the importance of being proud of your parents, and so I told Eva: "Yes, you've been over in the Czech Republic, and you've known that side of your family—but now you're over here for awhile, but you're also getting to know your dad's side of the family. Your Grandpa Fred Atcheson is a highly successful, respected and prestigious lawyer. You need to know more about your father's side of the family. There's even a building named after one of your ancestors at the University of Nevada, the Ruben Thompson Building; he was a wonderful and extremely intelligent person—and that's probably where you get all of your smarts. Your father and grandfather Fred hail from a long line of very brilliant people."

This had helped establish for Eva the fact that I had married very smart men.

"I don't want to go home, Grandma," Eva said. "Can I come and stay with you, because I really enjoy listening to all the things that you're telling me about my family. Can you tell me more?"

While moving her things into the bedroom, Eva spotted a photo of me at age 51 in 1998, beside my Grandma Eve—who was only 95 years old at the time, nine years before her death.

"This is a picture of your great-great-Grandma Eve," I told Eva.

"I remember Grandma Eve, Oh, yeah, she was so sweet."

That evening we sat outside eating dinner together while Wayne remained busy on his latest major book project. Eva kept telling me that she loved the stories, the house and the yard and how good it felt to be back in Reno.

Sparked by relentless curiosity, Eva asked: "Grandma, can you tell me a little bit more about Grandma Eve?"

Chapter 7

Straight from Empire, we ended up in the heart of the historic Gold Country community of Angel's Camp near by Grandma Eve's birthplace.

Unaware of exactly how we got there, I suspect my mother might have played a major role in this choice.

Nestled on the west side of the famed Sierra range, this community nestled on the edge of the central Golden State's San Joaquin Valley marked the start of the famed California Gold Rush of 1849, near where my great-great Grandparents discovered gold with James W. Marshall.

Again, my mother must have had something to say here, since Angel's Camp had emerged as a happy place for her, living near Stockton as a young girl in the 1930s. As a teenager mother had gone from Stockton to Angel's camp every summer to ride horses.

The community impressed me as stunningly beautiful. We lived near a creek, close to a huge playground as I began enjoying summer there.

I soon found happiness, delighted to discover lots of children to play with. Finally, my mother started telling me about the history of Angel's Camp. For once I got some honesty about a particular place where we stayed. Bitten by a keen sense of nostalgia and apparently eager to find joyful times again, mother told me about her own childhood when she had often enjoyed staying there.

Her words and memories spilling forth with the ferocity of a wide-open fire hydrant, mom told me everything she knew about the region's rich, vibrant history. As my much-awaited entrance into second grade approached, she started telling me about the magnetic, true-life past of that community's Mark Twain Elementary School.

Both my parents loved the author for which the building had been named. Dad had read all of the famed 1800s comic author's many classic novels several times, including "Tom Sawyer," and the "Adventures of

Huckleberry Finn." Father told me a lot about the famed writer, plus tales of the novels' key characters, Sawyer and Finn.

Dad took great delight in telling me how Mark Twain once lived in or at least visited Angel's Camp, plus tidbits from Twain's famed tale about that region, the "Jumping Bullfrogs of Calaveras County." Just as compelling, I took great delight in learning my own family's history within that region. The news that my beloved Grandma Eve had been born in 1903 in the nearby community of Sheep Ranch filled me with a boundless sense of awe and sincere appreciation for the many difficult struggles of my ancestors.

The notion that my ancestors were among California's first citizens increased my boundless thirst for knowledge about the region's pioneers.

Luckily, my father landed an auto-body shop job, this time in Angel's Camp, and my parents also hit pay-dirt by getting us into a tiny rented house instead of an apartment. The back of this quaint home rested on the bank of a peaceful little river adjacent to Main Street. Historic, irreplaceable old homes filled the community. Soon after we got settled, I liked entering the second grade at Mark Twain Elementary.

Once again, I began to enjoy the much-awaited experience of resuming my education. This time for Halloween I dressed up as a gypsy, similar in some ways to those wandering people we had seen just 15 months earlier in Jackpot, Nevada. Going door to door with my bag stuffed with candy, we got to go to the neatest historic homes that anyone ever could possibly imagine. The generous, homey smells to this day bring back pleasant memories. Within several weeks, I could already smell the distinct tinge of the coming Christmas in the air. In the evenings, chimneys filled the sky with just a perfect tinge of aromatic smoke, the odor of singed pine soothing to the senses.

The delicate, auburn smells of decaying autumn leaves on the wet ground, and the musky odor of the Gold Country foothills captured my imagination forever.

"It's nothing like you've ever smelled," I would later tell some of my girlfriends. "It's my favorite aroma."

Since then, I have been back to Angel's Camp one other time in the fall, and then those sizzling sensations came right back to me in an instant. And, I'm going to return there again soon, because you've got to experience smells and use your senses to make you feel alive. That remains one of my very favorite sensations of all time.

At Mark Twain Elementary School, all these children would have their mothers come in all the time to talk with the teachers. And, so, I thought: ""Oh, I want my mom to come in, because my mother is so beautiful. And, I want all my friends to see my mom, because my mother is prettier than all of theirs."

So, I went home and told my mom that the teacher wanted to see her at a certain time the next school day. My mother, said, "Oh, okay."

As I had hoped, my mother came at the appointed time, and yes—just as I had suspected—she was the prettiest mother in the entire community. Mom walked up to the front of my class, where the teacher said: "Hello, what are you here for?"

"My daughter said that I was supposed to come and see you."

"She did?" The teacher said, obviously confused.

Then, the women took me out into a hallway and the teacher said, "Patty, did you tell your mother that she had to come in here."

"Oh, I just wanted all the children to see my pretty mommy."

Hearing that, how could these women be mad at me? But they gave me a little lesson, which in this instance became: "Just don't ever tell your mom something that isn't true. I know it was nice, and you wanted to share your mommy, but that's not the way to do it."

Despite all the non-stop changes that had occurred in my life to this point, I still had absolutely no inclination that our nomad, gypsy-like lifestyle would soon resume at a relentless pace. I loved walking home, because the little town of Angel's Camp seemed to come straight out of a romantic, good-time movie reminiscent of early Americana. Every building was old, authentic, welcoming and warm, from tiny community stores to a quaint corner barber shop. The repair garage where my dad worked gleamed with just as much charisma, and for the first time in my life I was even able to visit his workplace.

"Hi, dad!"

There I was just in second grade, and my family felt safe and secure, knowing fully that I could safely walk by myself along that small community's main street. The four-block stroll straight through town led right to my family's rented house. I often walked home with a little girlfriend, Jennifer, who lived in a large Victorian-era house directly across Main Street from our tiny rented home.

On the few times when I would venture into Jennifer's house with her, streams of genuine antiques would fill my senses with unending glee. At first, I lacked any knowledge of what antiques were. Before then, I had visited numerous Idaho homes where people in large houses had owned fantastic furniture. But the furnishings in this girl's Victorian home impressed me as much different, much more refined, classier than I had ever laid eyes on before.

All the huge homes on Jennifer's side of the street had been there since the beginning of the 20th Century, built by ancestors such as mine, direct descendants of those who participated in the initial gold strike and the subsequent mining boom.

As a little child, all I could see when looking to the other side of the street were magnificent, powerful monuments to mankind's architectural achievements. So, I went to Jennifer's home to play quite a bit. All this history wrapped around that residence, while engulfing my entire aura as well.

Around this time my mother introduced me to various relatives who lived in Murphys, California, just up the historic California State Route 49 from Angel's Camp. Whenever the mood struck, mother would take me to visit an aunt and uncle who owned a butcher shop in Murphys, even more historic than Angel's Camp. Believe me when I say this was the cutest little town imaginable.

Right now, nearly 60 years later, Murphys is "the place to go." Just to stay in a Bed and Breakfast there visitors now have to fork out at least $200 per night. Now distinctive wineries lure streams of tourists to the region; these features never existed during my childhood, when Murphys remained a perfect place to go see my Aunt Ella. Then, I saw where my mother would stay all the time at Ella's house, back when she was a teenager.

One of the world's most kind, generous women, at least in my mind at the time, Aunt Ella showered mother and me with tons of yummy cookies and milk. Although not yet familiar with the works of highly acclaimed artist Norman Rockwell, I felt as if I was growing up inside one of his many famous illustrations depicting the true, family-oriented, placid Americana.

Upon my initial return for a pleasure visit with my good friend Jan Weiss and my grandmother, 30 years later at age 37, I felt great delight in an unexpected surprise. Aunt Ella's adorable old home had become a popular Bed and Breakfast, adjacent to a quaint hotel.

As a child I already had the feeling this would emerge into a popular place, luring people eager to go back in time. Mother would take me upstairs to see the bedroom that she had often felt safe and comfortable staying in as a child. The room's expansive windows overlooked a yard so fabulous and full of colorful flowers and delightful birds.

"This is where I would come in the summer, the happiest that I had ever been in my whole life," my mother told me as we gazed in silence out the window, holding hands.

Her voice vibrant and displaying unbridled excitement, mom told me about how much fun she had riding horses with her cousin, Bill Riedel to her heart's content as a teenager on those ranches and gently rolling neighborhoods.

"I love this house so very much, Patty," she said as we walked downstairs. "These houses are historic and they're one-of-a-kind."

My love for history, horses, classic old homes and warm family times grew thanks to these experiences with my mother. My little body burst with intense pride as she told me delightful tales about my many relatives throughout that historic region. She told me of her humorous uncles, mischievous cousins and long-lost boyfriends who had each made a unique, indelible mark on the Angel's Camp area.

Family. Friends. Deep, unbending connections. Roots.

Now I fully understood beyond a shadow of a doubt why mother apparently had played a vital role in my parents' decision to move us there. You've got to have something to hold on to in life, places and friends that give purpose and meaning.

"Oh, no!" I started thinking within a few months. "The suitcases are coming out!"

My mind raced as usual, struck with fear that we would soon leave another community that had captured my heart, especially such a perfect town. As usual, my parents never bothered to explain specific, in-depth reasons for their plans.

"We've got to go," mother finally said, as she stuffed our over-used, dilapidated suitcases in the trunk of our family car. "We're going to Idaho."

"Why? But I don't want to go!" Protesting for the first time, I had never before put up any semblance of a fight and now I decided to make my true feelings known. "But mom, I love it here so much! ...I love my school! I like everything about this place, just like you loved it when you were a little girl!"

"Sorry, but we're leaving."

"But I love my house," I said, getting choked up as my father summoned us to get in the vehicle. "I love my friends. I just love this town, it means so much to me."

I sat in the back seat, while mom sat up front beside father. Momentarily, we began to cruise away from that wonderful little community. "No!" I said in a loud voice, as the town disappeared from view out the back window. "This is where I want to be forever. I want to be close to my aunt and family, and ...Mother, I want to do what you did when you were a little girl and go ride horses."

As I wept alone in the back seat, my parents remained quiet in the front seat. My protestations went unanswered.

I began crying more forcefully and with the greatest intensity that I could ever remember to that point. Still without answering me, mom began softly weeping, not wailing forcefully such as I.

History, time and memories, all erased.

It wasn't until we arrived in Idaho two days later that I fully understood the compelling reason for this sudden move. An emergency had forced my father's hand. Just how he would manage to cope would end up impacting all of our lives for generations to come.

Every day I take a break from my fast-paced graphic design work duties to visit the internationally popular Facebook social networking Website.

If time permits I spend five minutes or so, or maybe up to a half hour, saying happy birthday to people or checking for updates on my friends. Shortly after Pan finished work on the garden trail, I logged in to the site and checked out a listing hailed as "You know you're a long-time Reno resident if you remember..."

Hundreds of maturing people who lived in Northwest Nevada in the '40s, '50s, '60s and '70s use this vital network to share memories and to reminisce. Always curious and interested in their comments, I checked the page and told myself "Oh, my God!" upon seeing a classic photograph of downtown Reno's former Mapes Hotel.

Vivid memories inspired me to write comments on the Facebook posting, although I usually avoid giving personal commentaries on social networks.

I caved in to a burning need to tell these bloggers about my deep feelings for the classic site and of the huge place that history fills within my heart. Imagine the frustration and anger that I feel to this day whenever I drive by the famed former hotel's downtown location, now the site for a shabby, run-down trailer owned by the City of Reno.

From the late 1940s into the 1990s the classic hotel reigned as the most significant landmark in the city's history. Many people fail to realize that for more than a decade through the bulk of the 1950s the building had reigned as perhaps the world's first and foremost hotel-casino.

Many of America's most popular entertainers from the era entertained at the top-floor Skyroom of the Art Deco-style structure. Top headliners ranged from Frank Sinatra to Jimmy Durante, Milton Berle and Mickey Rooney.

The Mapes attracted streams of tourists from around the world in the decade before the tremendous economic boom and growth of Las Vegas, eventually surpassing Reno.

Although I was only a girl during Reno's mid-20th Century heyday, unable to visit casinos alone due to my tender age, the Mapes played a major impact on my life.

You see, this is where at age 13 in 1960 I met the iconic, legendary sex symbol, movie star Marilyn Monroe. That year she spent several months living at the Mapes during filming of the classic movie "The Misfits," co-starring Clark Gable, Montgomery Clift and Eli Wallach. On the morning that I unexpectedly met Marilyn, I had taken a bus to downtown Reno from where I lived in a trailer park south of town.

On weekends I always took the bus alone to downtown, where I invariably would visit the Mapes coffee shop while careful to avoid the casino that prohibited minors. I often sat by myself at the coffee shop counter to enjoy a Coke. That particular morning as I started walking out the hotel's main doors a giant entourage of people working on or affiliated with "The Misfits" film started marching out of a parked bus.

Marilyn Monroe walked among these people as they all strolled inside the Mapes. The first several people quickly went past me. I recognized the starlet in a flash since I had seen her in many hit 1950s films. Some of my favorite Monroe movies included "Gentlemen Prefer Blondes," with Jane Russell in 1953, and "Some Like It Hot" with Tony Curtis and Jack Lemmon in 1959.

Marilyn suddenly stood right in front of me, and I said: "Hi!"

Marilyn stopped, knelt down to me, and then she used her world-famous, sultry, sexy, friendly, mysterious and magnetic voice to say: "Hiiiiii."

Her smile beamed, as if she somehow wanted to have her own little girl just like me, although at the time I failed to realize that she might have had such a motivation. I'll never forget her expression as we looked eye-to-eye, her cute face mere inches from mine. Marilyn was holding my hand, and all of the sudden members of the entourage jerked her hand and took this sex goddess away from me.

The Mapes had already become one of my favorite places during the previous decade, including when I had lived with my family in Carson City 30 miles south of Reno. When I was a little member of the Brownies organization for girls, our troop leader took us for an exciting visit to Reno for the day. With more than a dozen other girls, I went into the Mapes—my first time in a big hotel, as our leader took us to lunch in the coffee shop. For a little small-town girl to go into a huge hotel like that, the experience swelled into a major, eye-opening experience. My imagination cranked into high gear upon seeing an elevator for the first time, operated by a person whose only job was essentially to push certain buttons and to announce the arrival at specific floors. From the perimeter of the casino, we children stood in awe watching adults play slot machines, labeled by many gamblers as "one-armed bandits." With other Brownies, I watched grown-ups walking to and from the dining area, many wearing the type of crisp, classy, stylish, period-oriented garments that I had never seen before. This instilled within me a never-ending desire to evolve into a successful, attractive and well-to-do person—a far cry from my so-called "trailer-trash" background.

For me, this evolved into an amazing, wonderful experience for a little kid. The Mapes caressed my spirit, embodied with an irreplaceable impression of this as a stupendous hotel that the world should cherish.

From that point forward, through my pre-teen and early teens and beyond, whenever possible I spent many hours in the coffee shop. That simple, basic activity gave me a glorious feeling, no matter how many times I returned. With the Mapes considered the heart and soul of Reno, from the 1950s through the 1960s downtown held a well-deserved reputation as the only place in all of Northwest Nevada to shop—before the regional and national expansion of cookie-cutter malls began to infect the community. Prior to this change, wealthy women bought some of their most stunning clothing at Lester Conklin's and Joesph Magnin's. Lovers and successful families bought their jewelry and fine dinnerware at Herz. All primary U.S. department store chains maintained business downtown, including Sears and J.C. Penney. The Lloyd Gotchy shoe store offered the ritziest shoes available in town, while Lerner's outlets would later attract plenty of my attention as a young woman. Dress shops also helped make downtown an exciting, fun-filled place along with the action-packed 24-hour casino atmosphere. Harold's Club just down the street from the Mapes featured a lively sign that depicted a waterfall, a realistic campfire and pioneer American settlers. The club's promotional signs erected beside roads worldwide brought Reno worldwide fame, saying: "Harold's Club or Bust," also listing the specific number of miles to this community hailed as "The Biggest Little City in the World." Throughout my family's travels, we always got excited upon seeing Harold's Club signs across the West.

At the time Reno kept busting at the seams with excitement. Quaint, friendly corner drugstores helped give an irreplaceable small-town feel. Since this was the only major U.S. city at the time that offered legalized casino gambling, people eagerly trekked here from around the globe.

Clean. Sparkling. Gorgeous.

The Truckee River flowed through the heart of downtown at the Mapes' southern edge, streaming from Lake Tahoe in the Sierra to the high desert's Pyramid Lake.

Keep in mind that some of the world's wealthiest socialites at the time traveled here to spend the minimum-required six weeks in order to qualify for Nevada's famous "quickie divorces." Some of these gals, many loaded with cash and sometimes booze, married rugged cowboys or temporarily stayed at dude ranches to fulfill their mandatory residency requirements. Some wealthy divorcees ended up staying in Reno for good, leaving their rich lifestyles behind due to unstoppable attraction to the healthful fresh air, the stunningly scenic outdoors and a chance to grab a new, fresh start in life.

Stories of Reno's vibrant history yanked the attention of anyone lucky enough to get at least a quick glimpse into the community. The NBC-TV runaway hit western "Bonanza" show from 1959 to 1973 pulled more positive attention to the region, based on the fictional Cartwright family, living in the mid-1800s at the famed Ponderosa Ranch at nearby Lake Tahoe—hailed by Mark Twain as the "finest picture the whole earth affords." In the summer of 1959, children crammed the former Majestic movie theater in downtown Reno to watch the world premiere of the first "Bonanza" on the silver screen, shortly before the production's official TV launch in September. The theater presentation featured real-live, in-person presentations by the show's then-unknown stars; soon afterward, they became popular worldwide, Lorne Greene, Michael Landon, Parnell Roberts and Dan Blocker.

These were just some of the features that made Reno great.

As you might imagine, my love of Western history, the Mapes, classic architecture and this community swelled into my teenage years and beyond. For me, the Mapes served as the cornerstone for all this, a symbolic connection between our past and present.

Sadly, downtown Reno today hails as a somber place. As my husband sometimes says, "It's a city with a gorgeous smile. But there's one huge problem. Lots of the teeth are missing." Except for a few exceptions, the heart of the old casino core no longer reflects a vibrant, authentic, historical ambiance. City leaders will say they're striving to preserve the town's legacy, but the stone-cold truth reflects otherwise.

This hails as a primary reason why I care deeply about the mission of the Historic Reno Preservation Society, which organized and sponsored the tour of my home. This admirable organization, comprised of concerned citizens and history aficionados, truly cares about preserving authentic 1800s and early 1900s structures.

Throughout preparations for the tour, I remained dedicated and fully committed to doing whatever I could to help the organization generate vital funds. The society, commonly known as "Harps," uses donations to keep historical preservation a priority.

As these powerful sensations coursed through my veins more than a half century after the Mapes' heyday, the comment about the former hotel on Facebook drew all my attention.

Throughout the late 1990s, I had been instrumental in a failed community-wide effort to save the Mapes building from an official government plan to implode the structure to smithereens.

My house—the dining room—had been the place where a small group of committed, concerned people gathered to start the Truckee Meadows Heritage Trust. Our primary initial goal became to save the Mapes as the city's elected leaders, supported by significant campaign donations from casino corporations and construction companies, used all of their political energy in planning to obliterate the Mapes facility—

which had closed amid an economic downturn in the late 1970s and early 1980s.

At the trust's encouragement, in 1999 the National Register of Historic Places put the Mapes Hotel on its list of the USA's 14 most endangered historic sites. To that time, no structure ever placed on the list had ever ended up getting razed. Those of us who founded the Heritage Trust appreciated the fact that such a prestigious national organization had thrown its support behind us. And, with such significant help, we thought, "How could anyone let the Mapes building go down?"

And yet, every time we went in front of the City Council, they would give us our three minutes of presentation and look at us as if we had rocks in our heads. These elected officials conveyed the impression that we were crazy for wanting to save the building. Cronies for the city complained of rats in the closed-down structure, getting engineers to insist: "No, this has got to go down."

But we knew otherwise, bringing in historic preservationists who proclaimed that the Art Deco-style, high-rise building could and should be saved. I worked almost non-stop for three years, holding frequent meetings in my home to help keep our valiant fight alive.

Upon issuing press releases and public announcements about the city's selfish, misguided intentions we started getting letters from all over the world. People nationwide and from many nations begged Reno's city leaders to reconsider their goofy politics. Even so, heart-felt letters failed to grab the attention of Reno's misguided political leaders.

Every time I stood before the City Council for the maximum three minutes, one of my primary jobs was to serve as the unofficial representatives of countless cities that had mailed in objections to Reno's misguided plans. You would think that from these compelling letters that our elected leaders would say: "Yes, people from all over the world care that this building stays up; we've got to listen to them." But, no, the politicians sat there as if a trillion miles away from many of Reno's most concerned citizens. This time the Council members glared at members of the Truckee Meadows Heritage Trust as if our skulls were filled with horse manure.

Besides holding weekly meetings for three years in my home,

I personally designed and placed political advertisements focusing attention on the controversy. The Heritage Trust's financial needs became so desperate that I even met with the late Charlie Mapes, former owner of the hotel, to ask him for a sizable donation to put critical advertisements in the newspaper. The man seemed proud when he took me into his home office to discuss this vital issue.

"Mister Mapes, please give me some money," I said. "We need cash for this vital advertising."

"Well, uh, I..."

"No, look at all of us. We're all working hard to keep this building alive. You need to give me a couple of thousand dollars to put these ads in."

Then, Charlie Mapes, whom I had heard was a pretty frugal guy, ended up handing over a couple thousand dollars to the trust. So, we tried as hard as we could, but it went down. On January 30, 2000, several thousand people crowded downtown Reno to watch the evil-minded implosion concocted by Reno's politically disturbed city leaders.

Amazingly, some people with no sense of history whatsoever planned "imploding parties" that day, on the eve of Super Bowl Sunday.

I didn't want to watch, but my commitment left me with no other choice than to witness the God-awful destruction. So, I went with my son, Chris Atcheson, 32 years old at the time. We parked in a downtown parking structure, which would afford a clear, unobstructed view of the planned implosion from a safe distance.

The Mapes took a mere few seconds to fall, and then I cried for all this hard work that I had done along with hundreds of people committed to common sense. City leaders at the time blew hot air through their own mouths, their slimy, stinky politics encased with a virtual sewer of greasy, unforgivable scum.

Reno's mayor at the time, Jeff Griffin, shall go down in history for what I personally consider his slimy, selfish politics. At the time, Griffin and his cronies insisted that the land on which the Mapes stood at the heart of town would desperately be needed for some sort of other development—in order to pump up tax revenues. Yet the city never bothered to take decisive action to build, plan or support such a project.

The former Mapes site remained an eyesore, undeveloped and covered with concrete—the location of a single seedy trailer—nearly 12 years later as I made final plans for the public tour of my home. Nearly eight years earlier in 2004, four years after the Mapes' destruction, I had run for the City Council's Ward 5 seat. I faced incumbent Dave Aiazzi, whom I considered a ringleader in the Mapes downfall. My 2004 campaign focused on a wide range of issues; and by that point the Mapes never became a primary focus of my election effort.

Aiazzi amassed nearly 10 times more in political contributions than my campaign collected, thanks largely to his support from casino chains and developers.

As a definite underdog, outspent nearly 10-to-1, I campaigned hard and with tremendous efficiency. Many people throughout the community liked my strong stand in support of more sensible government.

Reliable sources later confirmed that Aiazzi looked sickly that election night, when I led in initial polling results. He emerged victorious by less than a few hundred votes out of tens of thousands of ballots cast.

Four years later in 2008, Wayne made his own unsuccessful bid against Aiazzi for the same Ward 5 City Council seat. This time, Aiazzi used his lessons well, throwing up a barrage of campaign advertisements designed to give himself a "mister green" environmentally friendly image. Overpowered by the political machine that had destroyed downtown Reno, although campaigning on a diverse platform, Wayne got slaughtered in a landslide.

In the process Aiazzi grabbed a final four years in office as dictated by state-mandated term limits. Frustrated and worried that political cronyism dominates our local, state and national landscape, Wayne and I have separately and individually decided to leave our political activism in the past.

Rather than showing bitterness and contempt, together we have moved on with our lives while careful to push our energies into a positive direction.

However we might have felt, to this date the Mapes still hails as the world's only building ever placed on the National Register of Historic Places endangered list—to ever eventually get destroyed by a slimy, selfish government. To this day, I admire the Historic Reno Preservation Society—the sponsor of my home tour—for avoiding any type of adversarial political confrontation. Instead, rather than endorsing political candidates, this valuable organization concentrates on appreciating and recognizing buildings of historical significance that remain standing.

After all these years, I posted my fond memories of the Mapes on the Facebook historical memories blog. Soon afterward, countless streams of people sent messages about their disappointment stemming from the Mapes' destruction, coupled with emotional testimonials of their many fond memories of the former hotel-casino.

These words of encouragement helped convince me that I had been taking the right path in deciding to open up my house for the upcoming tour.

Wayne's computer started running slow, and by that point I needed to step up efforts to help promote several of his ghost-written books.

Problems with my own Apple computer then left me with no other option than to drive to the Apple store 12 miles south of the downtown core. The drive would take a full 30 minutes, a long way by Reno standards, and I still refused to take the freeways—especially amid the ongoing summer road reconstruction projects.

Shortly before departing, I installed historic images of the Mapes on walls in my home's interior entryway.

"Perfect, a tribute to the Mapes," I thought, seeing the hotel's images while leaving out the front door. "Yeah, this helps put into perspective more than ever why I'm holding the tour, to help historic preservationists. They're at least trying to save what history we have."

Although I've never been obsessed with the Mapes, personally categorizing that failed battle as a lesson from the past, on that particular day while driving to the Apple store I began to recall the importance of that building.

"I'm just going to drive through the center of town while en route to the computer place," I thought. "Well, maybe when people are going out the door while they're on the tour, that's the last thing that they're going to see, too—images of the Mapes. Maybe they'll start thinking about history, thinking to themselves, 'Yeah, look at the Mapes. It's gone.' We've got to save our tangible reminders of history."

So, I drove through the center of downtown, past the site where the Mapes once stood. The tacky trailer made me angry as I drove past, just as it has every time that I have gone by the once vibrant location. Then, for the next few miles, the buildings along South Virginia Street looked pretty much like old Reno, but unlike the classic warm ambiance of my childhood.

Momentarily, however, my spirit sagged when everything to my left and to my right started looking like what Wayne and I call "Anywhere America." I passed countless malls and store chain facilities, all looking identical to those in other cities nationwide. The same street scene that I saw while on this errand looked precisely like the roads of Sacramento, Fresno, Los Angeles, Phoenix, Chicago, Dallas, Nashville and countless others. Without exaggeration, if you took a person who volunteered for an experiment, blindfolded her and left her beside a commercial area in Jackson, Mississippi, and took off her eye coverings—the gal might think she was in Atlanta, Tampa, Kansas City, Saint Louis or any one of hundreds of other cookie-cutter towns.

Yes, welcome to "Anywhere America," the era where most of our nation's small, once-quaint communities lack unique spunk or any semblance of a mom-and-pop aura. Thank God, limited numbers of unique communities such as Quincy, Angel's Camp and Murphys—all in California—still exist, and in other states as well.

While on my errand, I began to appreciate the fact that Wayne and I take great pleasure in enjoying back-road, out-of-the-way drives off the beaten paths. This way, we've found the occasional, infrequent community that has managed to retain at least some sense of Small Town America, refusing to bow to greedy, selfish, uncaring mega-corporations.

Amid my excursion, I realized that the mall-like atmosphere along

South Virginia Street stretched for nearly eight miles non-stop on both sides of the road.

Whether or not we like this, our nation's many cities are crammed with their own specific versions. From my perspective, their politics seem to say: "Damn the people; let's ram this development through to fruition. To hell with common sense politics. To hell with sensible planning. To hell with listening to the concerned citizenry. And to hell with quaint, unique and cozy-looking communities."

When I finally got within five miles of the Apple store, I realized that once-sprawling, lush, green farmlands, dude ranches and classic motels had been replaced by cookie-cutter "Anywhere America" shopping mall facades.

Just thirty years ago, this would have been a pleasant, leisurely, carefree country drive far outside Reno's city limits. Back then I would have passed a smattering of people-made structures, all of them unique, scattered here and there.

"The Reno that I remember from when I was a kid is gone," I thought, mindful of the need to accept this transition since people with my perspective have no other choice. "It's changed, and that's why it's so important to save whatever history we have."

This made me think of when I was a little girl, traveling non-stop, back during an innocent era when "Anywhere America" never existed.

Chapter 8

Stricken with deep sadness upon our sudden departure from Angel's Camp, at age 7 at least I could enjoy the great western scenery as we drove back to Twin Falls, Idaho.

My parents revealed that my father had needed to return to the Potato State to help Uncle Lehman care for my Grandma Mamie. She and Uncle Jim had moved from Empire back north shortly after my parents had taken me to the Gold Country.

By this point I started to enjoy the traveling, being on the road and looking at the Great American West's diverse outdoor setting from our vehicle's back window. My imagination clicked into full gear, delighted every time we visited a fuel station or entered an isolated country store. We went past or through countless little towns on winding two-lane highways, before the U.S. government built interstate freeways.

The food stops and hardware stores usually took us off the road for a few minutes at most. Long before "Anywhere America," I felt free and unencumbered. Most of the time we usually went about 15 minutes or so before seeing another car, usually on the opposite sides of these isolated roads from lanes where we traveled.

Many people might fail to realize this now, but at the time the American zest for cramming the highway and interstate system had yet to reach a fever pitch. We probably stopped briefly in Reno to see Grandma Eve and Grandpa Oscar on the way to help my dad's mother. In all likelihood, we took Highway 40—at the time the largest east-west route through the central United States, only a two-lane road.

Old motels beckoned, usually at least every hundred miles or so, eight years before the onset of a widespread boom of big-chain motels nationwide such as Holiday Inn. Until then, almost all motels were unique, none looking exactly like any others. The innumerable styles ranged from structures shaped like wigwams to donut-shaped units, log cabin facades, the appearance of Old West Union Army forts and many others. Most were mom-and-pop operations that depended on one-time visitors intermixed with frequent loyal customers. During those peaceful times when folks seemed friendlier and more trustworthy, many proprietors took the time to get to know their customers—unlike these days when many weary travelers only see motel clerks through bulletproof glass. Back then, the notion of a strong-arm robbery seemed far fetched. More often than not, motorists received everything from offers of hot coffee and donuts to opportunities for board games with other guests.

The fun sometimes accelerated for lead-footed drivers. As odd as this might sound today, it's true. Many rural desert or isolated areas of the West at the time had no speed limits whatsoever, particularly in some sections of Nevada, where the stretches between towns sometimes went for 100 miles or even much more. Long before Washington, D.C., bureaucrats forced individual states to impose speed limits, many western states embraced a proud attitude that inspired senses of personal independence and freedom. Nonetheless, as far as I could see, a vast majority of drivers such as my father adhered to a more leisurely lifestyle.

The slower-paced atmosphere and rustic settings enabled dad to drive at a more methodical pace than the hubbub that makes many of today's motorists go bonkers. From my perspective, we never seemed rushed, despite the pressing need to come to my Grandma Mamie's aid. Senile dementia's cruel, destructive symptoms emerge in a slow, methodical way unlike the sudden pain of a heart attack. Thus, if memory serves me well, we took our sweet time heading back to the community where we had abandoned our loyal little dog Laddie one year or so earlier.

Lacking a car radio while still en route, we sang Americana-style tunes and made up stories. Our games included: "Okay, what type of car is going to come next? What would you like to choose?...Patty, would you like a Chevrolet or a Pontiac?"

Thanks largely to these delightful activities, I knew all types of cars, every make, model and year of specific vehicle designs. With little effort my dad taught me how to instantly name every type of vehicle that went past. Eventually if a car zipped along that I failed to know, my dad promptly gave me the answer. Sometimes I'd say, "I'll take all Fords this time," a delight because I sneakily had figured out by then that far more Fords than Chevrolets traveled the West. Mom often took Cadillacs, perhaps because she knew only a small number of those vehicles traveled those routes. Dad would say, "Oh, I'll take Studebakers," and of course, none of those rare vehicles came into view. While always determined to make such games fun, mother and father seemed to set up their choices in order to ensure that I would always win.

We learned "car things" thanks to my dad's extensive automotive knowledge. Eventually, to make the driving time pass in a lively manner, we would start games where each person had to choose the color of the next car that we would see. Most of the time I chose white, since huge numbers of vehicles back then sported such a theme. Mom took red cars, or dad would take black or whatever.

Eventually when we got to the next town we always added up our scores to determine who won. I usually emerged victorious because white cars and Fords dominated the rural and desert highways.

In those days, travelers such as us always saw and appreciated everything around them. My dad often taught me, saying: "Patty, look around you. Don't look just in front of you. When you drive down the highway in life, you don't want to look just in front of you. You want to look all around you, because that's where you're going to discover things in life. And, if you're just looking straight ahead, you're going to miss things on the other side."

So, I embraced that strategy. More than ever, I started to appreciate or at least to analyze and fully recognize everything that my eyes beheld.

"Oh, look!" I would remark on occasion, delighted at pointing out to mother and father any unexpected and interesting point of interest. Rarely a nap-taker, thank God I never became a nauseous child who always got carsick. Such an illness might have been understandable, since I rode in cars a lot.

At this point instead of the Plymouth we rode in a used pickup truck that father had purchased. So, things were a little different. Unlike in our previous excursions when we had been limited in the amount of items we could take by suitcases and small car trunks, this time we hauled more things. The larger pickup space had enabled us to take lots of household items.

This isn't to imply by any stretch of the imagination that we were somehow like the fictional Jed Clampett from the 1960s and 1970s network TV sitcom. After striking oil thanks to an errant blast from his shotgun in the South, Clampett had struck it rich before loading most of his worldly possessions in a pickup truck before heading with his family straight for the luxurious Beverly Hills, California.

By contrast, if you ask me today, I would have to guess that for the most part during that 1954 excursion we in the Edwards clan were probably dirt poor—at least in a monetary sense. But like Jed's goofy relatives, mother, father and I had boundless, unending love for one another. Certainly we had endured many tough times, and I'm sure that on occasion dad reached low points where he was either at or very near penniless.

Maybe at least in a sense we were gypsies, except not the authentic kind that mother had pointed out for me a year earlier. Objective observers might have come to the conclusion that we were wandering aimlessly, never taking any one direction or staying on any particularly favorite route.

Adding spice to the mix, someone gave my mother a cat back in Angel's Camp shortly before our departure. She called her beloved pet Sam, which accompanied us on this trip. To put this into clear focus, picture this—three people living in the front seat of a pickup truck, right beside their beloved, smelly little feline every mile of the way. Oh, well, that's an exaggeration because Sam the Cat never stank, at least most of the time anyway.

But I will tell you this. The self-centered animal would just sit there on my mother's lap or on the floor of the passenger side, and whether anyone might have protested or not, my mom had insisted: "Sam is coming' with us."

Mother probably thought we were going to get to Twin Falls lickety-split like we had before, and promptly get a house. And then, right away, the cat would go into the home, and everybody would become hunky-dory, but things didn't turn out that way. When we got to Twin Falls, for some reason mother enrolled me into an elementary school right after we started living in a one room motel that had a kitchen.

Unbeknownst to all of us at the time, this marked the unofficial beginning of a phase where we would end up living in a seemingly non-stop series of motels for several years—with various spurts, stops, starts and resumptions.

If anyone were to choose an ideal location for a seedy, down-and-out classic 1950s-style motel for a TV sitcom based on our lives, this motel would have fit the bill. Think in terms of ratty, hole-filled curtains, a rug so old that the concrete floor below pushed its chilly attitude up into the room, and a shower that whined louder than a cranky steam locomotive.

On the plus side, at least I had lots of coloring books, diving into that creative process at a far more intense pace than ever. The room lacked any TVs, radio or other forms of family-oriented entertainment. Without fun reading material suitable for a 7-year-old girl, I promptly became—at least in my own mind—the World Champion Coloring Book Princess of 1954.

Chomping at the bit to resume my education, almost with the determination of the infamous world-champion race horse Seabiscuit within the starting gate, each morning I jumped at the chance to get to school as soon as possible. As soon as I enrolled, my heart became captivated with this authentic early 20th Century schoolhouse. Upon walking in the front door, the comforting lunchroom smells soothed the senses while permeating the hardwood floors. My huge classroom was loaded with enough desks that each student received an individual study station.

I had my own desk, mine all mine. I carefully lifted the desktop, storing everything neat and tidy inside. On my first day, I looked around the room; I loved seeing pictures on the walls. Images of George Washington and the cherry tree, the first such illustrations I had ever seen.

My delighted eyes danced around the room, catching my first view of our legendary 16th president, Abraham Lincoln. A colorful artistic rendering showed Honest Abe working beside a log cabin.

Near the top of each wall all around the room hung images of vibrant historical American events. The teacher started telling us about specific, compelling stories—each associated to an eye-catching illustration.

We had arrived around Thanksgiving. The teacher displayed fun, distinctive images of early American pilgrims. Until then I had never learned about them. This teaching system drove the essential basics deep into my willing psyche. The Pilgrim scene featuring autumn settings, and turkeys got emblazoned on my mind. For the first time, I fully grasped and appreciated what Thanksgiving really means.

More than ever, I found that my mind craved knowledge. Mrs. Robertson taught in an easy-to-understand manner that enabled me to appreciate the joy of learning. Looking back today, I have no idea how long I attended this school, perhaps two months at most.

Shortly before I was to turn eight years old on January 6, 1955, I began telling my parents of my deep desire for them to celebrate my birthday for the first time ever. To this point, I had always gone to other children's birthday parties, and I became increasingly excited because mother started talking about having such a celebration for me.

I wanted a birthday celebration like my friends, because they all enjoyed pin-the-tail-on-the-donkey and other fun games. At my friends' celebrations, everybody would bring gifts, and those parties were fun. But my parents had never bothered to organize such a celebration for me.

A few days before my birthday, while walking past a store with my mother, we spotted children's toys in the display window. Bowing to my wishes, my mother took me to a department store, buying me a doll, a puzzle and a play watch.

All of a sudden, on the day following my birthday—without having thrown a party for me—we suddenly started packing up again. As usual, my parents never bothered to tell me where we would go. In the rush to pack, they stuffed all my new toys underneath a tarp that covered our possessions at the back of the pickup truck.

That evening when we stopped at the next town somewhere in Idaho, I asked my parents: "Can I go get my doll, and my things to play with?"

Several minutes later my father returned to our room in yet another run-down motel, and gave me some crushing news.

"Your toys must have blown out, Patty," father said. "They're gone."

This essentially would become the story of my life for many years to come. Things vital to my heart always essentially blew away as soon as I began to grasp them.

While living in Reno nearly 25 years later in 1977, as a divorced 30-year-old woman something deep within my soul started telling me that I needed to have a sense of place.

Inexplicable emotions at that time started grating on my spirit. Perhaps my milestone age entering my fourth decade and challenges in my personal life at the time made me feel as if I had never really had a home, a sense of place. Eager for some sort of emotional closure, I started talking to my parents and asking: "Mom, how long were we in Twin Falls when we lived there when I was seven years old, going on eight? I really feel there's something that I have to go find out about that school. That school and that teacher, Mrs. Robertson, were very important in my life."

"I'm not sure, Patty," mother said. "I think we were only there about eight weeks."

"Yes, that's what I'm sensing," I told mother. "But I have to go back. Maybe it was because I was born in Idaho, or that we didn't really have a house in Idaho—only for a little while—but I have this sense that I have to go back there."

So, I decided to write my dad's brother, Uncle Lehman and his second wife, my Aunt Eloise, and see if I could come and stay with them. Meantime, my parents would look after my children, son Chris at age 10 and daughter Zoë at age five. Then, I took off on my own for a week-long getaway.

A misunderstood, confusing and mysterious deep inner need kept compelling me to make the 450-mile drive from Reno to Twin Falls, Idaho. "I need to find my roots, or whatever exactly this is—I'm unsure precisely what," I thought. Perhaps turning 30 had emerged as a pivotal time in my life.

Becoming extremely independent, I drove almost the entire way, spending the night in Jackpot, Nevada, about 30 miles south of Twin Falls. Exhaustion had prevented me from driving any further that night. During my brief stay in the small Northeast Nevada town, memories kept rushing back—particularly of seeing the gypsies there at age six.

Suddenly I started to remember many little details, able to clearly understand where things were. Always blessed with good visualization and superior memory, I realized that the gypsies had camped in an area that had now become a parking lot.

Rather than stop in Twin Falls first thing the next day, I drove past that community to Gooding, Idaho, a short drive past Filer. I went straight to a cozy home that Uncle Lehman had built for Aunt Eloise and himself.

I had always cherished my uncle, who reminded me a lot of my father—handsome, even taller than my dad. I felt great excitement to see them both. Then, after spending a few hours visiting these beloved relatives, I drove straight to Twin Falls. Now, keep in mind that I had not been to the schoolhouse since spending a few months there in the second grade.

But I drove right to the school, found the site immediately without even needing to study maps. I just drove straight to the building at 3 o'clock in the afternoon. Shortly after the end of the regular school day on a weekday, I walked into the building and immediately smelled those vibrant aromas that had remained deep in my soul for so many years. The same feelings that had made me feel happy for a brief few months as a child in this schoolhouse temporarily swept over me once again. In an instant, I found my second-grade classroom, and opened the door.

Right away I saw two teachers in there just talking to each other.

"Can we help you?" One of them said.

"I've just come back to see my old room, and I was here in second grade."

And, then I just started bawling. I darted from the classroom, shutting the door behind me. Without hesitation I ran through the hallway, scurried down the stairs, and hustled out of the building.

I jumped into the driver's seat of my car and just sobbed.

Why was I doing this? Why did I feel this way?

I could not at that time fathom why I had started going through this thing about trying to find my roots or something.

Maybe I felt overwhelmed or somehow unattached, although at the time I had significant parental responsibilities of my own. Or, perhaps a relationship problem with a man had added further wounds to my psyche.

I felt disjointed.

Suddenly after previously being married, I had become a single parent.

I keenly felt the lack of a place to return to for comfort. Some people can go home, especially many individuals who were my age at the time. Lots of young adults from my era had lived middle-class lives, growing up in one place.

This sudden attempt to seek answers had not stemmed from needing to talk with my parents, because they already lived in their own Reno-area trailer home separate from my residence. I still could have talked to them about such issues any time I wanted.

At this point, I yearned for a sense of place that my heart still yearned to find.

Getting no answers, I stayed in the parking lot in my car and cried for awhile before returning to my relatives' Gooding, Idaho, home.

Did this exercise tell me anything? Not really, it just made me still feel as if I had been a nomad or a gypsy, at least in a sense as a child.

I spent a week with my aunt and uncle, enjoying time with them before returning to Reno to move forward with life the best way that I could.

Nineteen months after Wayne and I married, in early January of 1998, he threw a surprise 51st birthday party for me.

The celebration has turned into an annual event. Each year, a few dozen of my best girlfriends gather in a Reno wine shop; we talk, laugh and share memories late into the night.

This tradition had started when Wayne concocted the initial surprise. On the sly, he had called Jan Horton, one of my girlfriends. With Jan's help, my husband arranged to have 20 of my friends gather into a back guest room at Harrah's Steakhouse, my favorite restaurant.

Wayne had purchased gifts for each guest, giving every woman a flower and adorning the dining table with giant flower arrangements.

That initial gathering left me breathless—the first time that someone had planned a surprise birthday celebration for me since my parents had promised but never came through with a party for my eighth birthday.

That initial gathering became such a hit that early each January through 2006 he helped organize these delightful gatherings of girlfriends for me at Harrah's. Every year, my friends showered me with streams of gifts. Then, in 2007 I moved the celebration from lunchtime to the evenings, changing the location to the wine shop where Zoë works.

Yes, life is about change and transition, plus our ability to grasp and appreciate the boundless love all around us. All this became possible thanks to my husband.

With just five weeks before the scheduled house tour, I awakened shortly before sunrise. Without taking time for breakfast, I drove straight to an abandoned, fenced-off hotel in downtown Reno. I snapped several pictures of the building, for a coloring book I'd been working on the previous few years.

By this point I already had completed ten hand-drawn images of separate motels, each a historic Reno-area location.

The site I visited this time was boarded up and fenced off as officials made final plans to raze the structure, The Heart of Reno Motel. My urgent deadline motivated me to stand in the middle of North Virginia Street to get a good photo before traffic increased.

This project had evolved into a coloring book, which I wanted to complete by December. By this point I doubted that deadline could be met due to my extensive backlog of necessary chores.

The motel life while growing up inspired the project.

Visitors to an Annual Nada Dada Motel arts event every mid-June had enjoyed using color crayons and water colors to add their own unique pizzazz to my pen and ink renderings of these old motels as I displayed them in the motel room.

During the week-long event, Nada Dada artists used rented motel rooms creatively. Attendees could have a unique experience seeing visual art as well as performance art set up in motel rooms. In recent years, prestigious publications such as the "New York Times" had mentioned the Nada Dada gathering, putting Reno on the map for coming through with a unique venue for art. This event became a way for me to bring my motel-related experiences to the public. At each year's event, I introduced more renderings of these old motels, and people told me they were anxious to see the publication.

As the home-tour date approached, my many ongoing projects still included plans to publish a full coloring book, featuring some of the West's—and Reno's—classic old motels, many of them closed or razed to make way for modern developments.

The lifestyle whirlwind kicked into full blast upon the departure from Twin Falls with my parents. From that point forward we lived in a steady succession of so many motels that I could hardly count them. Remember, we had left the day after my birthday.

That first night we stayed in a motel, probably somewhere in Idaho. This stay lasted a day or two at most.

"That car, I can fix it for you," dad would tell body shop owner. "I'm a really good auto-body repairman. I can fix that car for you for a rock-bottom price. My daughter and wife are in the car; we need a place to stay—and if you don't like what I do, you don't have to pay me. But I need fifty bucks right now, so we can have some food in our bellies and a roof over our heads."

"Okay," some prospects invariably said, ensuring our short-term survival.

"Like I say, my word is as good as gold," my father would say. "I'm going to fix that car, and if you don't like it, you don't have to pay me."

While noticeably grateful that his attempts had been successful, dad worked diligently while we stayed in another motel for a week. Mom kept just as busy, washing our clothes by hand. She hung the wet garments up to dry, stringing the clothes across our motel room. To this day, I still fail to grasp how she managed to accomplish these arduous chores. More than ever, mother kept me super-clean, while making sure my hair looked pleasing. Although essentially a homeless child, thanks to mother's persistent and crafty efforts I always looked like a typical, immaculate, and well-nourished American middle-class girl.

A horrific cold storm swept into the region at the same hour that we left for another town. A bitter chill took huge bites out of each of us. While riding in the pickup with my parents and Sam the Cat, I felt like a reindeer frozen solid at the North Pole.

With father driving as best he could, visibility plummeted to near zero amid blizzard conditions as winds approached perhaps 75 miles per hour. The extreme weather slowed us to almost a standstill. The vehicle slipped, stalled and made slithering motions to and fro as we went along the edge of a huge cliff—so high that the bottom of the canyon below was obscured from view during intermittent brakes in snowfall.

"I'm not going to make it," my mother said, cradling her arms around me as dad handled driving chores as best he could. "My hair is going to turn white, just with fright."

After a few minutes I looked down through the passenger window. Desperate to see at least something, I used my arm to wipe moisture from the glass. Then, the horrors struck me. Far below off the edge of the cliff I saw numerous crumpled, battered and obliterated remnants of cars. The vehicles had obviously careened off the same precipice upon which we were driving at that moment. Common sense told me that no one possibly could have survived those crashes.

"I fear that we're never going to make it off of here alive," my mother said.

Courageous, brave, stoic and keeping focused on his vital duties of staying on course in order to save his family and to keep us safe, my father remained quiet. From the passenger seat, I gazed up into his face, which somehow seemed either serene or at least showing the bold expression of someone who remained fully in command of himself. Had dad survived numerous death-defying situations before? Had he cheated death somehow in the past, giving him the necessary experience to get us safely through this trauma? Rather than tremble or jerk nervously at the steering wheel, father allowed his eyes, reflexes and arms to essentially become one with nature, to essentially make the snowy road and our rickety old pickup merge into a single unit.

His rock-solid confidence and determination somehow seemed to put my mother and me at least a bit more at ease. From father's sturdy demeanor, a person would think that he had driven this same road 1,000 times before in similar conditions. Yet my intuition told me otherwise. Yes, my father showed me that night of the great strength that becomes possible when reaching a Zen-like state, merging as one with the universe.

Call him "Lucky Larry."

Indeed, it would not be until quite some time later that I eventually learned the full truth about his past. Unbeknownst to me during that arduous trek, my father had previously cheated death many dozens of times before I was born.

For the moment I lacked full knowledge of the truth. By that point the Grim Reaper must have been angry with father for having the nerve, the guts and the good luck necessary to escape death many times.

Oh, thank the Lord that my father had been a hero during World War II, like so many millions of men and women that our great and enduring nation had spawned.

At present, as an innocent and fairly naïve little girl, I lacked any indication of the many harrowing, bloody and deadly battles that my father had endured along with his war buddies. Dozens or hundreds had fallen to their fiery deaths before his very eyes. Goodness knows, at that moment I didn't even know that a war had even occurred.

All I knew for certain in those moments high upon that mountain was that my father became my personal hero, rock-solid in my eyes for all time. He may have been making horrible decisions in life. He may have been hampered with an inability to communicate well with my mother and me. And, he may have been seriously flawed, unable to keep a steady job and to manage our finances the right way. But at least he was a true example of swirling, brave and confident masculinity. Maybe these were among the primary characteristics that motivated mother to stay with him. Perhaps she loved the adventure, however harrowing, or could settling for a much weaker guy have left her bored and wandering just as aimlessly?

Either thanks to dad's determination or because the proverbial playing cards simply fell in our favor, fate dealt us a "survival ticket" that bone-snapping night. Along with Sam the Cat, who had slept through all this, we finally got off the mountain in one piece.

Exhausted as the storm continued full-force, we checked into a motel in a small town at the bottom of the mountain.

We stayed there at least four days until the skies finally cleared.

As if things weren't already difficult enough for us all, this is where Sam the Cat decided to wander off and get lost amid the relentless snowfall. Mother had let the cat out to do his business. But the animal made the selfish decision to disappear.

"Where is Sam?" My mother kept saying.

Gripped with worry, mom kept looking out our motel room window. Failing to see any sign of the little guy, she even ventured outside a few feet in an unsuccessful attempt to look for him. Mother's worries intensified with each passing hour. To that point, I'm sure, at least in a sense Sam the Cat had become somewhat of a stable force to mom. Until that morning, father had always been the wandering, aimless soul in my mother's life. At least to some degree, Sam must have represented stability, a living being that you could always trust, that never snatched you away from any given place.

"There he is!" My mother finally exclaimed.

More delighted and excited than I had ever seen her in a long time, mother darted outside in the deep snow, fetched Sam, and returned to our motel room. Both shivered while I fetched them a blanket. Somehow this wily pet had managed to escape any serious injury or even a hint of frostbite.

To this day I can sense the distinctive aroma from that morning, not that of the animal but rather potatoes frying or something of a similar nature. Every once in awhile these days nearly sixty years later I still unexpectedly smell the same distinctive aromas from that exact place and time.

Survival. Basic human necessities. Food. Clothing. Shelter.

Instinctive sensations sometimes drive a person's motivation to remain alive. Every time I smelled that same unique order during my 60s amid winter settings—in parking lots while near restaurants or grocery stores—my mind immediately returned to that snowy Idaho motel.

Despite our tenuous financial condition during that stay, mother took me to a nearby store during a short break in the storm to buy children's books. Finally, I had something fun and educational to read.

Within several days we scurried to a nearby town where we landed in a much nicer, newer motel.

For the time being, we found ourselves in a high-end motel room far more respectable and cozier than any from the past. Maybe dad had essentially landed a good job at this town's body shop, snatching up enough green for us to prosper for awhile. My suspicions in this regard left me even more boisterous than usual as we walked into a nice restaurant— something we rarely did.

"Why don't you have something, like spaghetti or a steak, Patty?" My mother asked.

Paradoxically both delighted and stunned by this request, I insisted on my favorite evening meal.

Plain. Inexpensive. Hamburger.

"Oh, honey," mother said, persistent. "Don't just have a burger."

"No," I said, at this point old enough at age eight and bright enough to realize that my folks must have come into much more cash than usual. "I just want a hamburger."

"Come on, Patty, have something different."

"No, that's fine, mom."

I clearly remember the motel where we stayed that night had two big beds in the same room, a far more modern accommodation. This marked a significant transition, a definite improvement from all of our previous motel dives. This surprised me almost beyond belief, especially since the building's exterior had looked like a typical motel. Then, dad went down to the store bringing back Cracker Jacks. To typical families these days, such a treat might seem mundane. More than the tasty treat, I enjoyed the time with my parents, just having some fun, plain fun. The cheap, paper-made prizes from these containers made me feel rich enough to kiss my father's cheeks as if he were Daddy Warbucks. Of course, we probably only had enough funds on hand to survive another day or two at most. So, as I recall we stayed there for at least three weeks while he worked in that town, before we all re-entered the rat race of humanity elsewhere.

Chapter 9

More tenacious than monarch butterflies hunting for the best flowers at the height of spring, we fluttered aimlessly from town to town. Dad always picked up enough nectar to provide adequate energy and sustenance before continuing this unplanned journey.

After landing consistently in too many successive towns where similar butterflies had already been, we blew into the huge city of Idaho Falls. As soon as we settled down so that dad could scout out the community, he found the proverbial mother lode, an ideal place for him to join all the other worker bees.

We had arrived in this town at mid-day. I remember dad parking somewhere downtown. Left inside the pickup with mother, I sat there looking at all the people walking past us. Filled with awe and inspiration, I looked at all the women wearing finely-pressed suits and crisp dresses. Businessmen kept their paces lively and well-focused, their gentlemanly hats and finely polished shoes making them the epitome of social acceptability. In my little eyes, this hustle and bustle made everyone seem to fit in his or her own particular place in the grand social scale, everyone perfectly positioned within the pecking order of things.

Yes, for the first time in my life, I had suddenly landed within what I considered a huge metropolis. Even Twin Falls, Reno and Las Vegas had lacked anything close to shining with this big-city atmosphere.

"Wow!" I exclaimed while sitting with mom in the pickup. "This is a city!"

Stunned, mesmerized and fully appreciative of this opportunity to study the order of things on a first-hand basis, I kept my eyes glued to all the people.

My entire being yearned to suck up as much of this metropolitan information as quickly and as efficiently as possible. This filled my spirit with vital knowledge, helping to satisfy my insatiable, boundless need to learn.

During those few precious hours, my eyes, ears and other senses taught me lessons about life that would remain formidable and impacting for many decades to come. Viable, essential answers sprang forth in rivers without any adults needing to tell me so. Life has a distinct pecking order in big cities, just like the scenes that I had seen in nature while hunting and fishing with my family in the great outdoors the previous several years. The eagles were the ones who flew the highest and boasted the strongest claws, probably those guys in the snappiest, glitziest business suits. Power or at least the illusion of strength helped determine where these individuals went in life. A female could capture a suitable male of sufficient sturdiness, especially attractive, alluring young women who carried the snazziest purses that I had ever seen. The posture and demeanor of these gals told me they were definitely going places, particularly the swans. Gals from this particular breed sported short, natural, slightly curled hairdos, reminiscent of Elizabeth Taylor, Ava Gardner and Audrey Hepburn—mega-popular, top-bill female movie stars from that era.

Idaho Falls impressed me as a fantastic mating ground for the adults, although of course at that point I was still too young to spread my own wings or to fully understand—let alone to verbalize—such characteristics within nature.

Thankfully, at least for those few hours, I failed to catch a glimpse of any women who displayed even a small resemblance to storks. Sitting in the pickup beside me, my mother had a flat stomach and a firm, healthy, womanly chest. Although she wore rather bland clothes in comparison to those women on the streets of Idaho Falls, I knew from instinct that she had never come anywhere close to a stork—at least for the previous several months.

On many previous occasions, I had begged her: "Mommy, please have another baby—I want a little sister so badly. Can't I have a sister, please?"

Mommy told me, "No," that no such plans were in the works. And the firmness and determination in her answer let me know in no uncertain terms that she didn't want to have anything to do with storks.

For the time being, dad had once again failed to join up with an appropriate outfit within the Idaho Falls breeding area. Because at the time he was far down the rung of the pecking order on the grand scale of things, we only stayed in that big city for another few days—this time in a boggy, soggy, run-down motel.

A positive development finally came into play when we ended up staying in Jerome, Idaho, where my mother promptly enrolled me into school. God only knows how long I had been away from the educational system, perhaps several weeks or maybe even a period of months.

Although still in the second grade, these children all read much different books than what I had become accustomed to before. Able to plow through much harder publications than I could comprehend, these classmates unintentionally made me feel really stupid.

Catching up with them became impossible, at least in my mind. Unlike my earlier school experiences, by this point I found the notion of talking with kids my own age extremely difficult. Worsening matters, my abilities to make friends had declined to the point where I started shying away from other youngsters.

By the time I ever made any buddies, my parents would suddenly snatch me up and fly me into a completely new environment. More confused than a fish out of water, I felt as though I didn't really belong with anyone.

For the first time in my life, I wanted to avoid school—the very concept of which had fully magnetized my entire being just a year or so earlier.

My emotional, spiritual and physical transition had swept over the essence of my body and mind in a flash. The very notion of even attempting to catch up with the other students seemed far too hard for me to even contemplate.

This time when my parents left the town with me in tow I felt really glad. I had probably attended the Jerome elementary school for a couple of weeks, although at the time that stay seemed like an eternity.

From there, we went straight to Missoula, Montana, where my parents never attempted to enroll me in school. My biggest memory of the Treasure State involved milk containers that my mother never needed to refrigerate. Instead, she simply placed the drink on our motel front porch, where the beverage got cold enough for a Polar bear to enjoy. Each afternoon I would go outside, super excited to eventually see my father come home from work. His truck had a metal plate that a kid could hop onto outside the driver's side front door. So, every day I would run up to meet him. Dad let me stand on the plate, hugging the pickup as he drove the car down the street.

I loved my dad so much that excitement burst forth from my little body whenever he came home. Always ecstatic to see him, I would walk with dad when he strolled through our motel room front doorway to say hello to mom.

While in Missoula, a little girl, Julia, lived in a home across the street from the motel where we stayed. I loved going to play with her, largely because she lived in an actual, real-live house. Like my little friend Jennifer from back in Angel's Camp, Julia had her own room—something I never had.

One day after I scurried to Julia's house to play, her mommy told me: "Patty, you have to go home because of the storm." But I could have stayed there and played. Looking back after all these years, I still have a sense—judging by the mother's demeanor—that she just didn't want me there.

Motel trash?

Was that a term used even then? Before the era of so-called political correctness, had such people begun to shun me due to my family's apparent "low position in life?"

Whatever the case, she sent me home, and I never remembered having gone back there to play with Julia after that. This apparently marked my first experience of people trying to get rid of me due to my insignificant social stature in the pecking order of things. Yes, selfish, mindless, insensitive people like Julia's mother became the proverbial crows in my life.

All I knew for sure was that as a little girl playing with my friend Julia would have been fun. I felt bad because I knew in my heart of hearts that I could have stayed there and kept playing with her while rain continued falling outside.

Making what you might call a "round-robin," somehow father ended up taking mom and me straight back to Twin Falls to the motel where we had stayed before.

"Mommy, can I go to school here, please?" I asked, shortly after our arrival.

"No, we're not going to be here very long," she said. "After a little while, we're going to be heading off for Reno, so you cannot go to school here."

"Oh, but I liked the school in this town so much."

My mother's insistence left me perplexed since I knew the school year remained underway. Within several days after our arrival back in Twin Falls, I went with mother into a grocery store. From clear across the entire length of a shopping aisle, I spotted the second-grade teacher, Mrs. Robertson, who had taught me about Thanksgiving, George Washington, Abraham Lincoln, and other vibrant lessons from American history.

"There's my teacher!" I hollered to my mom, unable to hold back my exuberance. "There's my teacher!"

"Don't say 'Hi' to her," my mother told me in a commanding whisper, firmly grabbing my left arm. "Don't."

Without any additional explanation or discussion, mother promptly took me right out of the store's back door. We stopped our shopping in an instant, and left our groceries without paying for them.

Nearly 44 years later, I attended a Reno black-tie gala and fundraiser with my husband, Wayne. As the society columnist for the region's primary general-circulation newspaper, he received dozens of invitations each month to many of the region's glitziest parties and major fund-raising events.

Also the newspaper's entertainment columnist and a lifestyle journalist, at the time Wayne seemed to have dozens of friends, acquaintances and news contacts. A few years earlier, at a mansion owned by Wayne's parents in April 1996 we hosted 150 people at his invitation-only 40th birthday bash. At the time we were boyfriend and girlfriend, inseparable lovers.

At the time, I thought of him as a major catch, a guy filled with boundless, seemingly unlimited potential. Here was a guy who was going places, and by that point well before meeting him I had made my own significant mark on the Nevada economy.

A highly successful businesswoman, commuting weekly between my graphic design business operations in Reno and Las Vegas kept me constantly on the go well into the mid-1990s.

Although many guys competed for my time, a part of me still felt lonely. Those yearnings for sharing and giving were finally satisfied—at least for awhile—once Wayne and I finally found each other.

We had been married for two years when he finally accepted an unexpected promotion into the newly created society columnist position. I liked the fact that at the time he held a solid, steady, stable job. By then he had been employed by either the newspaper and its parent company for 20 years, his rock-solid stability—at least at the time—far surpassing any such soundness that my late father had ever hoped to achieve.

Shortly after Wayne's promotion, together we tore into new ground in the journalistic field. Using my own funds, I bought a digital camera long before the vast majority of other Americans had ever heard of such devices. Unlike today's high-quality, lightweight cameras that sell for as little as $100, my first unit seemed to weigh at least a pound or more and cost upwards of $900.

At least three or four times a week, I accompanied Wayne to various private parties and public functions. Working as his unofficial, unpaid assistant, I snapped photos of the so-called high-society people, the folks from the top of the proverbial pecking order.

A vast majority of these individuals had already become my close friends, thanks to my own business associations, successes and personal relationships through the years.

At the time, Wayne and I were each lean and well-built. Within seven years, his girth would balloon by more than 50 pounds.

My husband would later insist that much of the transition anyway—

had stemmed from the natural aging process. Such excuses failed to carry much weight with the likes of me, however. For a two-year period, I nagged him non-stop to get off his lazy butt and get some much-needed exercise. Otherwise, I was sure, he would end up getting diabetes or some other horrible disease, and perhaps die right on top of me—God forbid!—perhaps even in the middle of the night.

Thankfully, in keeping with his lifelong habit, using his own can-do attitude and focused energy starting in 2008 at age 52 he launched a dedicated exercise program that continued almost non-stop ever since. Every morning without fail, Wayne walked at lightening speed, always going a minimum of six to ten miles or preferably much more if he mustered up the time and energy.

As a result, his massive girth disappeared and has never returned. During the few years immediately prior to our scheduled home tour, his energy level had skyrocketed, far surpassing the doldrums experienced in the first five years of the 21st Century when he moved about with the vibrancy of a drunken tortoise.

Yes, like me, my father, and my mother and just about everyone else I've known in life, Wayne had seriously flawed characteristics. My own weight, for instance, had increased somewhat during my 50s. Worsening matters, I suffered a severe knee problem that made walking difficult if not almost impossible in around 2003. Like Wayne, I eventually embraced the chance to change for the better. Every morning almost without fail starting in 2006 I awakened early to enjoy exercise workouts, primary swimming pool activities, at the Saint Mary's Health Center near my home.

Largely as a result, my weight stabilized to a much more manageable level, although not quite as thin as I would have liked. My increases in physical activity coupled with highly effective acupuncture treatments given to me by Dr. Maureen Mckenney eliminated my knee problems. This combined with my dedicated efforts to eat healthy, non-fattening, nutritious foods enabled me to achieve and maintain good health.

I refused to have a handsome young husband while letting myself go to pot. Although far from insecure, I preferred to work hard to look and feel the best that I could, for myself and for my spouse.

Like I say, the guy was far from perfect, but I wanted to keep him. Any woman worth her weight in salt should get the most out of her man that she possibly can, and believe me I became increasingly determined to wring my husband dry for all his worth—even during times when we happened to be struggling financially or riding high atop the roller coaster of success. Ups and downs occur almost in a predictable pattern. Individually and together we preferred to concentrate on the high-goal spurts, because the other option could only cause economic and emotional pain.

Back when we rode high on that proverbial success train, Wayne worked as a society columnist while I ran my own company. Every step of the way, I enjoyed spending quality time with lots of friends. A majority of these individuals had already been my close pals. Before Wayne decided to leave the newspaper, he and I also started meeting streams of wonderful people who had just moved to Reno.

Thanks at least partly to my nightly forays on the town with him I got to meet many more friends, lots of them still close to us today.

Since we already knew so many long-time Nevada residents, from late 1997 through the middle of 2000 at most parties and public events we always went to tables where we didn't know someone. That way we generated new friendships, learning—and sometimes writing about—the lives of these many interesting individuals.

All along, the vast majority of people rarely asked about us. Maybe most folks felt a need to keep to themselves, worried they might come off as overly nosy or pushy by asking potentially unwanted questions. Just as essential, we were far more interested in what these people were doing, as a steady succession of them became "our new best friends."

At the time, I had numerous favorite dresses, and other garments that I would change and mix around. We went to so many functions that I could not possibly purchase or maintain a new outfit for every single night. So, I would cleverly inter-mix my wardrobe.

I needed to get creative and learn how to dress properly, especially because many of these events were black-tie functions. This period emerged as a very valuable time in our lives, especially due to the lifelong friendships that emerged—bonds that I still cherish.

More than 11 years after Wayne left the newspaper to pursue other interests, we occasionally hosted dinner parties in my home. Many of these guests were friends that we met during Wayne's newspaper career.

Anyway, thankfully during my lively times accompanying Wayne on Reno's party circuit, no one seemed to notice or care that I never owned many garments. For the most part I suppose people were far more interested in their own wardrobes, than any possible worries about what I wore on any given evening

I managed for a 30-month period to make people think that I was pretty well dressed, when in fact I was merely being creative.

At least for a time, Wayne had been a member of the Reno's prestigious Prospectors' Club social organization, before voluntarily leaving in 2009 to pursue other activities.

During the first decade of this century, Wayne had launched his full-time independent career as a ghostwriter of books. His association with the club had enabled him to meet various business leaders who sometimes gave him essential information critical to his research and writing. But after several years for the most part Wayne's only ventures into the club or its activities were to the annual gala Christmas party where spouses could attend. After awhile, we just decided to cut back on such activities, especially because Wayne never participated in the club's frequent social functions such as golfing, target shooting or getting tickets to boxing matches.

Been there, done that—we simply stopped.

Within a few days after mother dashed me out the back door of a supermarket to avoid my former first-grade teacher, more startling news came.

Mother informed me that we were about to leave for Reno, just like she had hinted about a few weeks earlier. This marked the first time that my parents told me of our intended destination well beforehand.

"We're going to leave right now," mother said, giving me little time to prepare emotionally. Even so, any thought of the upcoming reunion with Grandma Eve and Grandpa Oscar filled me with delight. Mom wanted to get there as fast as possible.

But for some inexplicable reason we broke our usual pattern, this time never stopping anywhere along the way. After driving through Jackpot, Nevada, we entered the Elko area, where we noticed a motorist stranded on the other side of the road. The guy kept his hood up as steam oozed from his engine.

Always a Good Samaritan, my dad pulled over to help the man. Father always would stop to assist people in distress simply because that's the kind of a guy he was—always helpful to anyone in need.

"Thank you so much for helping me," the man said, handing my dad his business card. "My name is Peter Harper-Collins, and I'm a lawyer from Reno. If you ever need an attorney, come to me and I'll take good care of you."

"I'll remember that," my dad said.

Little did we know at the time that we soon would need the lawyer's assistance following our involvement in a fatal car wreck.

We went straight to Grandma's at Hill & Sons Motel as soon as we got to Reno.

Joyful sensations made my heart blossom like a rose right away as my Grandparents continued their usual process of spoiling me. But a major problem erupted.

I finally learned why my mother yearned to get back to Northwest Nevada as soon as possible. She planned to divorce my father.

Dad just dropped my mother and me off, and all of a sudden we started living with Grandma and Grandpa.

My father left after saying a quick goodbye to me. This marked my first time ever away from him for any extended period, other than when my parents had separated in Las Vegas when I was an infant.

As soon as father dropped us off, my mom began the standard Nevada quickie-divorce process. The system began with a required six-week residency requirement.

No one told me where dad went. All of a sudden, my mother enrolled me into Anderson Elementary School, at the time on South Virginia Street south of town. Frightened to attend another school, I worried that students there would far surpass my basic knowledge, just as the others had several months earlier in Jerome, Idaho.

Unlike before when I had cherished the mere thought of going to school, this time the mere notion of attending sent chills down my spine. Faced with no other option as a mere child, I started going to classes as my mother got a waitress job in a small diner across South Virginia Street from what is now the widely popular Peppermill Hotel-Casino. In fact, the bulk of this major destination site boasting thousands of employees today sits on what once was the Hill & Sons Motel property.

For the first time in my life, my mother had to step up to the plate to support us, no longer willing or able to depend on father. Sink or swim, she was on her own. Determined to put my dad in her past forever, she strived to make her way in life while doing everything possible to support me. Mom probably still loved my father with all her heart, but his wandering ways had pushed her over the edge.

My psyche got a sudden wake-up call, upon seeing mother suddenly adopt a can-do, take-charge attitude concerning her own life. Her declarations failed to fool me though, because I sensed my mom missed me desperately during her work shifts. This seemed natural, since to that point she had been with me whenever I was away from school.

Anger filled her to the boiling point, yet she always managed to avoid expressing such feelings in front of me. To her credit, I recognized even as a little girl that she had started taking full control of her own life. Keep in mind that at the time fathers were perceived as the primary providers of any average American family. So, in a sense at least when viewed by societal values at the time she also had assumed the so-called masculine role along with her feminine duties.

Pretty soon, the two of us moved into a tin shack in a field on Lakeside Drive, a half block north of a people-made feature constructed in the early 1900s, Virginia Lake. Every day mother walked to work. As if pieces of a puzzle, each of our lives soon fit into an individual appropriate place, although I worried about what might have become of my father.

Attending school became difficult, partly due to fears that any attempts to make friends would only end up breaking my heart further following any sudden, subsequent move. The notion of continuing the pattern of making friends before getting pulled away from them left me feeling anxious. I just remember spending a lot of the time with my Grandparents and walking through fields. A crummy match box, the one-room tin shack seemed even less comfortable than a trailer.

"Patty, you're going to have some mush and some toast before you go to school," my mother commanded every morning. "You need this."

On a cranky old radio each morning during breakfast we listened to Bob Carroll out of Carson City, Nevada, mother's favorite announcer. On cool days, she bundled me up and sent me on my way.

"Where is my dad?" I kept asking, never getting a solid answer. He never came around. My relatives also refrained from using the word "divorce." Making such a statement would have done little good anyway since I didn't know what the word meant.

All they would say: "Your dad has gone off to work somewhere." Still, this wasn't so bad, because I still could spend quality time with my Grandparents and mom. Somehow I just remember walking to school every day through that field, straight down to Anderson School. Right after classes I always went to my Grandparents' motel.

My inner soul told me that these were hard, trying times. The situation left me with only one option, simply doing what society and relatives expected of me. From my perspective as a child, I thought that mother was doing just fine. I liked going to visit her at the restaurant, where she often fed me little dinners. This arrangement proved so delightful that she soon moved us from the seedy tin shack to a motel next to the diner.

Meantime, though, my schooling problems intensified. All other students still seemed light years ahead of me in the basic knowledge of reading, writing and arithmetic. This generated feelings that my classmates were far smarter than me, when in reality my problems stemmed from the fact that I had missed many months of school. My feelings of inadequacy intensified. This may have been a major reason that I never made a single friend. My life became a treadmill, seemingly endless, non-stop excursions to school, home, the restaurant where mom worked, and to the Hill & Sons.

Amid the whirlwind summer barbecue and party period, leaders of the Historic Reno Preservation Society asked me to create a hand-drawn promotional poster of my home.

My excitement intensified while waiting to visit my best girlfriend—almost sister—Kathleen Conaboy's for a huge summer bash. She had invited 50 people, many of them my friends as well. Visiting with these delightful people on a warm summer evening on her beautiful outdoor deck undoubtedly would energize my spirit as it did every year.

Throughout my adult life, I felt lucky and blessed to have wonderful friends like Kathleen and her husband John. To me, close personal bonds make life interesting, having things to do and places to go. I felt honored to have them in my life.

For the time being, though, I needed to focus on my vital chore of completing a pen and ink rendition of my home. Organizers of the house tour wanted to convert the image into a coloring-book style piece that they could hand out to visitors at the house. In addition, I needed to get a print made of the black and white, before coloring the image for use on promotional posters and post card-sized flyers promoting the tour.

Determined to get all this work done in time, I continued my usual lifelong pattern of remaining a busy lady. I felt honored to have received the request

Chapter 10

Dead-set to take a different professional path in life so that she could leave the restaurant profession, my mother embraced advice from our good longtime friends, Franny and Bill McCabe. Remember, my parents had become good friends with this couple at Victory Heights at the University of Nevada several years earlier.

My mom had relatively few friends. Mothering responsibilities coupled with my father's wanderlust had prevented her from establishing many significant bonds with anyone. In some ways mother had experienced the same sudden moves that prevented me from seizing any chance of developing long-term acquaintances.

By that point, the McCabes lived in Carson City 30 miles south of Reno, where Bill did well in his new position at International Business Machines, commonly called IBM. Bill told mother about new jobs being developed primarily for women, highly trained professionals, "keypunch operators." Bill explained to mom that she likely would land a solid, stable profession if she learned the necessary skills. Never one to waste time or dillydally, mother seized the opportunity right away.

This marked a major transition for mom, straight into what people at the time considered the high-tech new world of computer technology. She promptly took required courses, and soon landed a great job as a keypunch operator for the state of Nevada.

For many years to come, this gave mother the opportunity to land a job anywhere she went thanks to these unique, valuable skills. Never again would she have to depend on unreliable guys such as my father, or to slave her life away in greasy restaurants.

Thanks to mother's can-do attitude and focused determination within several months she moved the two of us to what looked like an old boarding house in Carson City a half hour drive south of Reno. Our place on the upper floor had a little bedroom, a 1920s-style furnished apartment with nice pictures on the walls.

But the elementary school drove me bonkers. This emerged as a far worse experience than my Reno classes. These kids' vastly superior reading skills made me seem like a moron although I was a super-bright child. I only needed to go there about a month before summer break started, and that made me feel great.

Little did I know that another major family conflict would soon erupt, actually making me dislike the very sight of my father.

One of my mom's dreams came true, but only for a short time.

Bill and Franny asked us to stay with them at a ranch where they also lived, perched on the eastern side of the Sierra overlooking Washoe Valley about eight miles north of Carson City. Right next to the iconic List Ranch, the McCabe's rented property captured our hearts the moment we arrived.

Finally, mom got to start living in a rural setting on a significant spread loaded with glorious horses, clearing the way for us to enjoy her dream lifestyle. Although someone else owned the property, we rented our own living quarters, and began enjoying the wonderful outdoor ranching life that dad had always promised for mother—but never provided.

While mom maintained her government job in Carson City, I took great delight spending fantastic summer days riding Oliver, my stick horse, all over the place. Mother and I had finally found joy, all thanks to her efforts and help from friends. After our many struggles, the dreary quest for happiness had finally started to click into gear.

Stupendous views from the ranch shot sensations of fun and delight into my heart. Looking at the Sierras just to the west made a person appreciate the majesty of the great outdoors. Each long warm day ended with a crescendo of crickets as the last streams of sunlight began to flicker away from the reflective Washoe Lake. Hawks overhead gave me a sense of comfort, even when holding their prey of typical rodents and desert snakes. Yes, the non-stop, rush-rush pattern of my earlier life seemed to have fallen by the wayside forever. Mother and I felt that with any luck we would end up living there for many years. This gift of a non-pressured, unhurried lifestyle proved just what my inner spirit had deeply yearned for, the chance to live a sturdy, stable life in nature's great playground.

Giant trees surrounded the dwelling, a respectable western-style house with a huge porch all around. The home had lots of rooms, enough that mom and I each had our own bedroom. The living room and kitchen provided a homey, cozy atmosphere. The McCabe children had their own rooms, while Bill and Franny had a giant bedroom for themselves. A picnic table smack-dab in the middle of the huge yard gave the place a friendly feeling. The ranch owners who rented this site to the McCabes even offered to sell the property to our friends at the rock-bottom price of $80,000. Unable to afford that, our friends preferred to rent.

The rustic barn and irreplaceable chicken coop sent out an all-American aura, telling everyone without saying in words that this was the place that a person should never want to leave. I played with the McCabe children as we let our healthy imaginations run wild. The expansive property provided countless opportunities for fun.

Every Saturday morning while living there I eagerly watched Western superstars Roy Rogers and Dale Evans on TV, plus "The Lone Ranger" and "Hop-Along Cassidy." The shows launched my passion for the ranching lifestyle into full orbit, amid realistic visions of gunfights and arrow-shooting attacks between cowboys and Indians.

When the programs ended, I skedaddled outside and ran up the adjacent hill on Oliver, my reliable, always-trusty stick-horse. The property gave me endless room to run, scenic views for many miles—as far as the eye could see ...I was so happy!

Gone forever, I hoped, were the motels and the endless traveling.

Then, suddenly, everything turned for the worse.

My father unexpectedly showed up on the property, leaving me in shock. Although I had missed him dearly, I knew in a flash that he would take us away.

"I don't want you here," I thought. "I like living in this wonderful place. And I don't want you to ever take us away to more motels than a person can possibly count. I don't like what you've done to me, moving me from school to school so that I feel dumb."

Even so, I refrained from voicing my deep inner feelings. I had never once spoken so harshly in all my life, and I wasn't about to begin such a pattern. After all, I had always been a good little girl, and I never would have contemplated disobeying my parents.

However I felt, dad could not possibly have reappeared at a worse time.

Mom did really well on her own, doing a great job taking care of me. I had finally settled in school, and the ranch gave me a delightful place to play with the two McCabe children, both about my age. The ranch had been the perfect spot to live, the exact type of place that mother and I had dreamed about for many years.

Yet, now, without dad having to speak a single word, I knew right away that he was about to take us away from all that. Whenever traveling in the past, he would always point to various properties and say things like: "Oh! There's a ranch that we're going to have someday!" He had continually put something like a carrot in front of us.

"Oh, we're going to have a ranch like that with horses," he would always say, all the time when we had been traveling. "One day, mom's going to have a horse, and you're going to have a horse, and that's what we're working toward. We're going to get that property."

So, then all of a sudden mother and I had ended up on just such a spread. But dad wasn't there when she had accomplished this for us. He never gave us the ranch; she accomplished that herself in a round-about way.

Bill helped, but she did this on her own and got us there. And like mother had been, I felt super-happy on that property. To be quite honest, I had started feeling delighted for awhile when dad wasn't around—although I still loved him with all my heart.

And, before his reappearance, I began to remember his drinking and some of the stuff he would do, like coming home late or pulling us away from wherever we happened to be living without any warning.

My mind refused to live that way again, and I wanted to see my mother continuing to experience happiness. Finally, we had just started to enjoy living without conflict, far away from the greasy motel lifestyle. For the first time, we lived in a great place. Mockingbirds awakened me with their delightful songs each morning.

Predictably, dad picked me up in his arms, holding me high, saying: "I missed you," and everything like that. But with steadily growing intensity I wished that he had not returned. Yes indeed, the moment my dad reappeared my skin must have suddenly turned red with revulsion. If I had been my mother, I would have put him out of my life forever. And, I clearly remember thinking, "I don't want him to come back."

"Your dad's here—aren't you excited?" My mother said shortly after his arrival.

"Yes," I said, lying through my little teeth, but deep inside I hurt as if an angel thrown into the depths of hell.

I hoped that our crappy on-the-road lifestyle would never resume, but my heart warned me to expect otherwise—and rightly so.

Five weeks before the home tour, I sat eating dinner with Wayne in the front yard, refusing to let him go back inside the house.

"Honey, we need to enjoy these summer evenings," I said, hugging him as he wiggled to move away—one of our usual games.

These warm late August and early September days often quickly faded into cool autumns, too blustery to enjoy outdoors. Our usual hectic pace dictated that we needed to strive to rest and recuperate in advance of the upcoming chores.

"Let's go inside and watch TV, and ..."

"Not so fast" I yanked Wayne's arm and made him sit back down. "We've got to take advantage of this great summer weather, because we're going to be inside all winter long."

Sometimes on such nights we would stay out long past dark and just talk, chatting about some of the things we were going to do. Our goals, dreams and tasks always became major topics. We had as many diverging interests as similarities, which often made our relationship just as steady as it was unpredictable—all at the same time.

We always worked so hard during the daytime hours that we enjoyed the serenity of evenings. So, we just sat there, calmly looking at the birds as we had for the past several nights, never getting tired of studying nature's pecking order.

Suddenly, moments after the sun disappeared, our solar-powered lights all around the yard started popping on, followed by the soothing songs of crickets.

This made me think back to when I was a little kid listening to these insects. Mindful that such creatures signified the most special sounds of summer, I always remained cognizant of the need to relax and enjoy the tranquil moments that life had to offer. These tunes starring Mother Nature reminded me of those sounds that I had heard at the Washoe Valley ranch in the evenings, back before my father returned—spoiling everything.

Although at present I felt rushed to get everything done before the tour, while releasing various books and paintings, I remained focused on the need to spend more time with my grandchildren as they visited from the Czech Republic. All along, I needed to enjoy plenty of time as well with my various friends to maintain those vital bonds.

My favorite thing of all to do remained sitting outside, enjoying a soothing glass of wine and talking with my husband. I loved that more than ever, plus resting in the evenings, slowing down, smelling the roses, and watching the birds—pulling a worm here and there, and watching the puppy's excitement as joggers and evening walkers eased past the home.

Any famed, highly acclaimed and talented artist from throughout history would have loved to study those compelling images, from a "True Magazine" on the coffee table of our tiny Carson City apartment.

Vincent Van Gogh, the iconic Dutch painter of post-impressionist tendencies would have scoured the publication, hunting for deep bold colors, riveting emotional honesty and any hint of rough beauty.

Taking a far more different approach, if the legendary Italian painter, sculptor and scientist Leonardo de Vinci had been alive in Carson City during the 1950s, he would have hunted for magazines depicting brave new techniques and creative designs.

Mother probably had little knowledge if any of such legends. At least in matters of those publications, her preferences focused on current ladies' fashions, vital tips for homemakers and anything to do with keen advice on buying goods at bargain rates.

"These magazines are nothing but pure nonsense," the notable and temperamental 17th Century Dutch artist Rembrandt would have proclaimed upon visiting our dwelling. "These images prove that Americans have very little class. Their morals stink."

Spanish surrealist painter Salvador Dali, popular during the 1900s, would have avoided any attempt to come to Rembrandt's aid. Instead, Dali would have either filmed the confrontation, or set his sights on wooing my mother while Rembrandt's antics distracted my father.

And, as for me, what should a highly imaginative, creative talent do with her free time, even during such domestic hubbub? Why, of course, oblivious to any artistic shenanigans all around me, I continually plowed through the magazines whenever possible. All those images, Wow!

Could Pablo Picasso, the mysterious cubist-style Spanish painter, have been looking over my little shoulder as I opened up the pages of those magazines? How would Picasso have painted the pictures of the Nazi concentration camps shown in that issue of "True Magazine?" Would Picasso have wept at the sight, or as I imagined would he have flat-out refused to paint such a horrible scene.

Upon seeing another "True" page that showed starved, emaciated bodies of Jewish people, would 15th Century Renaissance painter and sculptor Michelangelo have tried to erect statues in honor of those people?

Yes, what is a creative, artistic little girl—a budding talent—supposed to do, when she accidentally discovers the ravages of war for the first time? All within the pages of a magazine? Should the child have ignored these graphic images, instead running outside alone to play hopscotch? Ignore the issue. Remain innocent. Go into denial. Hide.

"Patty, you are so naïve—for God's sake, look at the big picture," early American landscape painter Charles Harold Davis would have told me right then. "Stop living in a fantasy world, kid. Sure, you've got it rough. But it's about time you've faced the truth. Millions of other little girls just like you have been slaughtered during wars."

The mind-blowing photographs of all those dead people—hundreds or thousands of them, piled on top of each other like so much garbage—made my heart stop.

"At least you are alive now, little girl!" Guatemalan and New Jersey abstract painter Alfred Julio Jensen whispered into my ear—trying to drag me outside, away from this magazine. "The other painters are dead wrong. Patty, you should run! Go!"

Flabbergasted, unable to even think of putting down the magazine, I continued flipping to more pages—each showing a specific war scene that made my skin crawl. Did Colombian painter, muralist and sculptor Alejandro Obregón create such images in his heyday during the mid-1900s? Had Maron Watchel, a plein air painter of oils and watercolors managed to capture such blood, guts and gore?

Oh, and yes, would I grow up to find myself living in such a deadly scene, far from my mother the keypunch operator and my father the auto-body repairman? Did my parents know about these terrible things—about war? Should I have rushed to tell them right away, so that they could somehow protect me?

To that point at age eight I still had not learned in school about World War II. I had not been told about Adolph Hitler, the Nazis, the

Holocaust, kamikazes and those atom bombs that pulverized hundreds of thousands of people 16 months before I was born.

Surely the American gothic painter Grant Wood would have known this was all some sort of trick. I know! The people who printed "True" must have put phony images into their magazine to fool me and my mommy and daddy. Scare us, before Halloween.

"What?" I kept asking myself, while trying to read a story that accompanied the black and white war photos. "What is this all about?"

Determined to get answers from a reliable source, I went to my father who knew absolutely nothing or probably very little about the intricacies of fine art. From what I could already tell, dad undoubtedly lacked any sense whatsoever of how "True Magazine" must have created such fraudulent images. Even more impressive, through the previous several years, father had shown me his own vibrant artistic skills. Remember, he could make a dented car look shining new, and he would flick his rod during fly-fishing in such a way that the master Colombian painter Santiago Martinez Delgado would have become enraged with jealousy.

Yes indeed, I knew that my father could tell me the truth, that the graphics art departments of the magazine were fraudsters. And, this I knew could generate my father's contempt. If there was anything he hated, it was phonies. Liars. Crooks. Con artists. Politicians. Surely dad knew a slime-ball when he saw one. So, I realized without question that he would help set the record straight for me.

"Dad, what is all this?" I asked, holding the "True" magazine, jumping onto his lap, while he relaxed on a brown leather chair in our apartment living room. I don't understand any of this. Are these really dead people? Why are all these bodies piled on top of each other? And it says here that people were gassed, entire families."

My dad then proceeded to tell me about World War II, where he described Germans who painted a swath of red terror across the landscape of Europe. Francisco Goya, the 19th Century Spanish romantic painter would have made a devil named Hitler's mustache look like mincemeat.

At my urging, dad told me why the Third Rich had gassed and burned millions of people, incinerating them to the point where old master painters would have wept for the remainder of their lifetimes—

unable to recreate gorgeous nudes such as Giorgione's irreplaceable circa 1510 classic Sleeping Venus. Father explained how billions upon billions of tears had flowed in streams, enough to fill the Hudson River art school, which generated such classics as Fredrick Edwin Church's 1859 "The Heart of the Andes." Bombs had sprayed across Europe, as if splattered against an unprotected canvas by American abstract expressionist painter Jackson Pollock.

Without giving specifics of his own creative involvement, for the first time in my life my father told me—as we gazed at the "True " photos—that he had gone to Europe four years before I was born. Imagine my pride and awe upon learning that my father had gone to England in 1943, determined to plaster the Nazi regime.

Going into full detail, at least as much as an innocent eight-year-old girl should hear, father described the urgent need to encase the enemy in a bombardment of destruction.

His job, dad fully admitted, was to sit in a tiny shell while working as a top turret gunner in American B-24 bombers. A tall man, he never should have been selected to squeeze into such a tiny space within the aircraft. Breaking their own rules, commanders ordered dad to serve such duties due to his vastly superior sharp-shooting scores during military training.

In order to fulfill his basic requirements and to qualify for an immediate return trip back home to the states, father needed to go on a minimum of 35 missions. He described soaring like one of those eagles that I had seen back in Idaho, zooming over allied France to paint the landscape below with colorful blood-red bomb blasts.

Firebombs called "flack" had filled the sky all around the aircraft of my father's crew many times, generating a red glare that I sensed would have made Francis Scott Key—writer of the "National Anthem"—extremely proud. Many times in those years shortly before my birth, enemy planes had zoomed toward the Belle of the Brawl aircraft on which my father served. It seemed that the enemy had fashioned themselves as crafty artists, determined to shoot giant holes into the aircraft, in hopes of sending my father and his buddies into oblivion.

In order to fight for the lives of his fellow crew members, time after time, my father had blasted his guns—always aiming to kill, with the craftiness of a fine sculptor, who wanted to make those adversaries stone-cold dead.

Carefully trying to censor the details to protect my innocent little ears, father gave just enough info that day as I sat dutifully on his lap, to make me understand in the best way that I could. I envisioned the many times that he had slain these adversaries. These scenes became vivid in my mind's eye: many of my dad's good buddies, burning to death before his very eyes as their aircrafts erupted in flames; my dad's reactions as his heart beat at thousands of miles per hour, seeing several or perhaps dozens of his friend's planes plummet to earth; sweat cascading from his forehead and neck, as he concentrated on making one kill after another in rapid succession—with the same poise and dexterity that he had used when hunting with his own father back in Idaho; men literally barfing their guts out, including others on his own plane after they had been shot while he continued to fight for his own life and for those of his surviving comrades; and those deaths—day after day, after endless days, in rapid, steady, never-ending succession.

They called him "Lucky Larry."

Yes, this was the man who had developed creative ways to escape from the line of fire during my childhood. This was the man who would move us from town to town, always searching for a safe place, a sanctuary.

Go now. Quick. Don't even think about wasting time. Let's get creative about this situation. If we stay in one place for too long, we might get shot or burned to a crisp, or is that an exaggeration?

Do all these artists, Goya and Van Gogh, Rembrandt and the like, realize that warriors and auto-body repairmen have their own artistic skills as well? Did my mother know? Was this a secret, that my father had shot his way across the skies of Europe, following orders—putting his life on the line, just because some captain, or colonel or general told him and his buddies to do it..."They were expendable," as the famed old movie title proclaimed, and so on this day I finally learned that my father was indeed a Master, deserving of as much acclaim as M.C. Escher, the 20th Century Dutch graphic artist who explored what critics proclaim as "impossible constructions." Like Escher, my father had managed to create a double image of himself.

Could my dad's various bosses at many dozens of auto-body shops have realized his creative strengths and heroism? Or, perhaps even more importantly, had my father cringed when they gave him orders in the workplace—his mind potentially thinking of them as those commanders who had ordered him and his buddies to go to their deaths?

There sitting upon my father's lap that afternoon, he felt strong to me. He felt as sturdy and everlasting as that statue created by artist Daniel Chester French of our 16th President, the Lincoln Memorial. In my eyes, as my father spoke to me, recounting stories of the war, he had the same wise, kind, ever-loving and courageous expression as seen by millions of people yearly when gazing upon French's statue—a perfect likeness of the man some simply called "Abraham."

Born 109 years before my dad, Lincoln surely could not have envisioned that like so many millions of other Americans nearly 80 years after the Civil War era, my father would play his own integral role in fighting for freedom.

Latched upon my father's every word, he told me about his nickname, "Lucky Larry." On numerous occasions, as far as I can recall, only a handful of B-24 aircraft would return to England after specific battles. Perhaps sometimes only three or four planes limped home, after dozens or possibly scores of others were all shot down during the same missions. Memory tells me that perhaps on a single occasion, or maybe more, just one smoking, shot-up, battered B-24 returned home.

And, my dad happened to be the tail gunner on those aircraft. So, he survived.

But was he truly lucky?

Well, his new comrades, the fellows who had been shipped in to replace the dead, certainly thought so. Perhaps these allied airmen played poker games at night, to pass the time away. Maybe they would place extravagant bets. Could it be true, that the victor of these wagers won the right to fly on the same plane with the man that they nicknamed "Lucky Larry."

"Yeah, I want Lucky Larry on my plane!" A rookie pilot might shout. "His regular commander got shipped stateside today, and so it's a good idea if he goes with my crew."

"No!" Some other flyboy must have shouted. "That guy goes with us!"

Or, maybe everyone got creative, flailing away, fighting for the right to go with dad, or maybe those apparent legends about his military reputation never rang true.

My Grandma Eve sure disliked him.

And my Grandpa Oscar certainly felt contempt for the man.

As for her part, at least by this point, my mother had lost every ounce of respect for her husband, until taking him back into her life. Indeed, for the first time, I finally had learned that my father was as creative, as talented, and as lucky as all those various artists combined, from Goya to Rembrandt and Van Gogh or even Michelangelo. If these legends had been eavesdropping on our father-daughter conversation, certainly they would have shied away by that point.

Until that time, I had seen duffel bags and other remnants of the war, things that father would carry around as if the necessary accessories of a watercolor painter.

"When I took off in that plane, I seriously assumed my duties both for myself, and for the rest of the crew," dad said matter-of-factly. "My job was to keep them safe, no matter what the odds."

"But dad, did you have to shoot people?"

"I just did whatever I had to do to keep my crew safe."

Without question during that two-hour conversation with my father, I felt protected within the confines of our pint-size Carson City apartment. The kitchen was as small as a phone booth from the perspective of a child, but probably actually large enough to use for a typical prison cell. During the winters, we needed to hustle outside in the extreme cold to plop quarters into machines that dispensed quart-size containers of oil—necessary to heat our rat hole of a dwelling. The run-down place lacked a single picture on the wall. One of my few opportunities for entertainment became a rickety wood chair, which I used when pretending to drive a car.

Blessed with boundless imagination, when playing alone in our living room, I often pretended that I was a school teacher speaking before a classroom crammed with wide-eyed students. Lacking a TV or many things to read, I did whatever reasonably possible to avoid getting bored. Transient children who came and went like blowflies from our barracks-style apartment building never grabbed any of my attention. Any chances to develop solid friendships with children my own age became a million-to-one shot.

Needless to say, this unexpected chat about the war with my father provided much-needed entertainment.

To dad's credit, instead of telling me horrible things or why the war had been bad or any of that gory stuff, he told me stories about going off with his friends and getting drunk. Rather than get into any detail about his many fiery fights tens of thousands of feet above earth, he told me about the time that he suffered from an abscess tooth. Physicians gave father morphine to battle the pain. Yet without anyone realizing that he suffered a severe allergy to the powerful painkiller, he started chasing cute nurses up and down the hospital hallways. The tooth pain and the narcotic made him crazy, to the point that hospital orderlies had to pull him down.

Rather than concentrate on death and destruction, he kept telling me funny stories. He made light of having to live in a place that he called what sounded like whip-snip or something like that. Creative guys such as my dad certainly had a way of coming up with goofy names. Artists such as he saw only the positives in life, the sunrises and the sunsets rather than the fires in between.

As father continued telling me these relentless yarns, making me smile and even laugh, he avoided bringing out his personal, hand-written journal of what he had endured during D-Day. He also refrained from going into more intricate detail of why or how he had volunteered to risk his life far more than necessary. For a reason that I'll never fully understand, he went for more than the minimum 35 battle missions, the point at which flyboys had earned a guaranteed, no-questions-asked return ticket home.

Amazingly, to this day in my mid-60s, I still have dad's many war medals and his D-Day diary. Somehow my parents had managed to hold on to these keepsakes, even after they had always left almost everything behind amid our countless moves. Someday, I will be giving these to my artistic, creative and highly inventive grandson, Mickey, who lives with my son, daughter-in-law and granddaughter in the Czech Republic. This boy admits to his pride in his Grandpa Larry, whom he never met, the man who battled to free the enslaved, captured or ravaged people of Europe.

Back during my own childhood, my curiosity went into full gear when father told me these riveting, side-busting war stories. Rather than craving bloody details, my penchant for asking father non-stop questions stemmed from my passion to learn more about life.

Even as a small child, I fully realized and appreciated the fact that I had been born. One well-aimed shot or even an errant bomb could have erased any possibility of my birth. I wondered what it would have been like if my father had been killed in battle and all of his buddies came back, and they all ended up having children my age.

Either our loving Creator, or the nebulous God of Fate, had commanded that I come onto this earth. Each and every one of us, strong and weak, wealthy and poor, smart and stupid, stands as a monument to our ancestors—whether they are artists, or lawyers, or even greedy politicians or whatever.

An 1806 portrait of Napoleon 1 of France, by the French painter Ingres, still reigns as among the most iconic artistic images depicting a warrior—just as gripping as the famed sculpture of U.S. Army Gen. George S. Patton Jr., now a monument at West Point.

Each of us is—to at least some degree—an artist. As I learned thanks to my father, each of us suffers emotional and sometimes physical pains. As the age-old saying goes, "Life is a bucket of tears." Our perceptions of this life, or our view of what we perceive as morals and personal values, gets reflected by our own actions, plus any tangible assets we might choose to leave behind in this world.

Blessed with my own God-given artistic talents, I reached with my heart and my spirit toward the heavens in the coming decades of my life. Like my father had during the war, in a sense I strived to take my drawing talents above the clouds. Art soars over all of humanity, lifting us up toward our own vibrant, unique and relentless dreams—even for little girls, as they become women, reach middle age, and enter their mature years. Herein rests those spirits who still speak to me and to all of humanity, the painters and sculptors and filmmakers and cartoonists and other artists, recognizing the undeniable pain of war but preferring tranquility, serenity, placid sensations and freedom from bloody deaths.

Dad's writing on the back of this photo, left to right
Barseth-Navigator, Baskins-Co. Pilot, Bartels-Bombardier, Paulnock-Pilot
Myself-Top Turret, Woolacott-Radio Operator, McCarthy-Ball
Riely-Tail , Fillman-Engineer

DFC AWARDED TO B-24 TOP GUNNER

First paragraph of a Los Angeles 1944 newspaper article ...
An Eighth Air Force Bomber Station, England Staff Sgt. J.L. Edwards, 25, formerly of Twin Fall, Ida., top turret gunner on the B-24 Liberator, "Belle of the Brawl." has won the distinguished flying cross for "extraordinary achievement... cool courgage and devotion to duty" during eight air force bombing attacks on targets in Nazi Germany and enemy occupied Europe.

Chapter 11

I became a certified, qualified and fully licensed dentist at the tender age of eight.

Well, this is of course a bit of an exaggeration. But the delightful truth sprang forth when I suddenly became an unofficial doctor of sorts.

All this clicked into gear when I finally started developing my first solid friendships in many years. All those children were orphans. They lived in the Nevada State Children's Home, a huge brick church-like structure right across the street from the barracks-like Carson City apartment where I lived with my parents in 1956. Called "Sunny Acres" at the time, the structure on Fifth Street just west of Stewart had served as the Silver State's official orphanage.

The original structure on the site, first opened in 1870, lasted more than 30 years until destroyed by fire in 1902. Using sandstone quarried from the State Prison, officials opened a replacement structure the following year.

Like I say, it wasn't until 53 years later that I became the facility's unofficial and unauthorized dentist at ages eight and nine.

Authorities prohibited outsiders such as me, "non-orphans," from associating with those scrawny little kids. Rules prevented "regular kids" from venturing onto the facility's state-owned grounds. Making matters even more challenging, my parents never even thought about inviting those children to visit our seedy residence.

Luckily, however, all of us children attended the same school, Fremont Elementary, named in honor of John Freemont, a military officer and explorer who had ventured into this region with the famed scout Kit Carson during the 1840s.

At recess one day, I suddenly and unexpectedly became the orphans' dentist.

Everything started after a little boy, Charlie, approached me during recess, complaining of an uncomfortable, wiggly front tooth.

"Oh, I know how to do that," I said without hesitation. "My dad showed me how to do this once when I pulled some of my teeth out. It doesn't hurt at all. Let me try it."

Whoever had oral problems would immediately come to me, requesting that I handle any necessary tooth-extraction chores.

Somehow I had learned a method to handle these duties without causing pain.

But the main thing that I remember from that period, I had friends for the first time. Although rules prohibited me from visiting their orphanage and prevented them from visiting my family's residence, at least we could play a lot together during recess.

So, for the first time in several years, I started to get excited about going to school every day. Also, this marked the year that school administrators had decided to hold me back in class, to take second grade over again. I felt happy to do so, because during the previous year I had fallen far behind in my studies. Finally, I had started to catch up while enjoying my new teacher, Mrs. Corbett. Although I hated my home environment, this school brought me great joy. Somehow this teacher managed to make me feel stable again, and I started enjoying walks downtown—a quaint, tiny, peaceful and interesting place at the time. Sometimes I met my mother for lunch at her work, as I fell in love with Carson City while hating our dingy apartment.

For the first time in many years I finally started feeling a "sense of place" again, as if I somehow "belonged" while my grades improved in school—shortly before the fatal wreck.

At age 53 during the summer of 2008, a sense of excitement swelled with each passing moment as we drove from Reno to Carson City.

Along the way, I kept telling Wayne about my dad, all the war stories about Lucky Larry that my husband had not heard in more than a decade.

A few days earlier, I had seen a newspaper advertisement promoting that weekend's appearance in Carson City. History buffs and aviation experts had arranged to put an authentic B-24 bomber on display, the same type of aircraft in which my dad served as a top turret gunner in World War II.

My toes began to shake just a tiny bit on that blustery day as I stood beside Wayne, looking at the historic aircraft at a hanger in the Carson City airport. Dozens of people lined up to see the plane. Everyone got in line for a tour inside the aircraft.

Every step closer to the entrance ladder increased my anticipation. My sense of excitement reached a fever pitch, as we got within 15 feet of the entrance. The stunned, respectful expressions on people ahead of us as they walked out of the plane let me know that the aircraft's interior definitely would be worth seeing.

Those final moments drove the point home that as a child and well into my teens I had always been a good girl. Young ladies should mind their mommies and daddies just as I had done. Those of us who behave want to please our parents so that they will be proud of us. Our lives hinge on family, on sharing, on doing what we feel is right, on striving to succeed.

More of these memories flew straight into my heart as we reached just ten feet away from the entrance stairs. I remembered those times back in Carson, when I had attended the Brownies. Mother and father will be pleased when they realize what a wonderful, well-behaved child I am.

Now, I'm walking to Fremont Elementary, careful to obey all laws every step of the way. Yes, I have been reared to be a good girl.

Good girls like me, we control our emotions. We avoid crying in front of other people. We strive never to make waves, to wander away from any path that might fail to please our mothers, and we want daddy to keep on loving us forever. My father adores me, as I sit on his lap and he tells me about the war, and I'll always be good. Finally, I place my hand on the ladder railing, taking that first step upward.

My daddy loves me. And I'm a good little girl.

Momentarily, I stand right inside the entrance, and I'm behaved because a little girl never protests and she has a solid place in the world, and I stand beside the cockpit. This is where my daddy is; he's in here somewhere. This crammed place, a crate of cold metal. These people inside here cannot possibly be adults touring an 80-year-old plane.

These are men in here, wearing Army uniforms, and it's in the middle of World War II, and the airplane is taking off. I hold onto my long blonde hair, so that it will not flap in the wind, and now we're suddenly flying over the English countryside.

My daddy is in here somewhere, and those other men in Army uniforms here are chattering into oxygen masks. Men wearing leather jackets.

Where is my daddy? I need to find him in here, to let him know that I'm okay, or is it true that I have not been born yet? Somewhere in here is the man who will someday be my daddy, the auto-body repairman, and I've got to find him to tell him that he must live through this—he surely has to live—because I'm a good little girl, and I want to be born, and I'm eager to live, and I'm willing to go through hell to be with him, because I love him so much, because I can't possibly say this enough—I'm a good little girl. Daddy has to know this, must realize that his tiny daughter adores him. I want to be born so badly, to learn what I already instinctively know—how to love.

As we fly over the English Channel, forget the fact that other people might be inside here taking a tour of an old aircraft from many decades ago. No, this is real, and now I see the coast of France.

"Dad, where are you!" My heart cries out. "I'm here."

I feel so cold, so terribly cold now, and I know how he feels at this very moment, if I can only find him, I'll tell him that right away.

Someone holds my hand, but I know this cannot be Wayne my husband. I know this because I'm still a little girl, and I haven't met my guy yet—or have I?

Then, I hear the gunshots, the rat-tat-tat, the continual non-stop blaze of constant gunfire. Smoke fills the air. They're firing at us.

I look to my feet to ensure my footing remains solid, and then I realize that I'm looking at the shoes of a grown woman. This cannot be the case. No, I'm a good little girl who wants to please her parents, and this cannot be—what, me, a woman? Nonsense.

All I want now is the man who protects his little child, and that's my father. Where is he, I'm so terribly worried. As the sound of gunfire continues, bullets rip through the fuselage all around me.

Now, finally, somehow, I'm standing beside a glass-shaped bubble at the back of the aircraft. There is my dad now!

"I'm standing right beside you, daddy! I'm here with you!" I yell as loud as I possibly can, but he must not hear me. I must not be yelling loud enough, because I'm a good little girl, and he's got other work to concentrate on for the moment. Dad keeps firing his weapon, non-stop. Through the glass, I see streams of Nazi war fighters streaming toward us from every direction. Dad fires straight into an attacker a quarter mile away, and the assailant bursts into flames.

Three more attackers approach us, as an American mustang fighter rips right behind one of the three pursuing bad guys. Just then, as the Nazi's blast continued gunfire in our direction, more holes rip through our fuselage.

"I'm hit!" Someone yells from inside the middle of our aircraft. This must be our bombardier. I look back there and see the guy, blood gushing from his neck as he maintains his position. The other tour-takers on this aircraft for the moment fail to realize any of this, and I can see that they're all in a fantasy world. These other people think that they're from the 21st Century, and that everything is A-okay.

But not me, I'm not that way, a good little girl. And, I see fully and without any denial whatsoever exactly what is going on. My dad is busy saving us all, a hero fighting for the freedoms of us Americans at home.

Then, dad takes a clean shot. Another enemy bursts into flames, as our pilot announces over the radio: "Charlie is dead," referring to the co-pilot at his side. Worried, I look straight up the fuselage and see the carnage. Charlie's head has been shot clean off.

"Kill them, daddy!" I keep hollering. "Kill all the bad guys, so that you can live! Please live, dad. Kill them, so that I can live!"

Dad keeps firing, all of his attention—his total body and soul—focused fully, and unabashedly on slaughtering our assailants.

Then, out the glassy tail-gunner position, I see five of our planes, all of the B-24 bombers from the Good Old USA, each going down in flames. These are my father's buddies, in the process of being fried, or struggling to jump from their burning aircrafts.

Suddenly, I realize that I have begun to cry. I'm as sane as ever, and Wayne is holding my hand, and my husband loves me—in a different way than my daddy had loved me. And now, why? Daddy isn't here. He must be heading back to England now.

They called him Lucky Larry.

And now we're standing on the tarmac near the still-parked plane, many decades after they took this gal out of service. I retrieve a tissue from my purse, and wipe my eyes. The tour had been a growing process for me. I enjoyed the experience every step of the way, teaching me what my dad must have gone through. Now, I fully began to understand what my father must have endured.

I understood why he had felt so much pain and heartache through the remaining 46 years that he lived after the war. His drinking, rowdy behavior, non-stop moves and occasional distant demeanor all came into clear view for me.

"That plane was so small—and I mean small," I told Wayne, as we walked through the airport parking lot. "I'm five-feet-nine, and I felt crammed in there. Imagine what it must have been like for my dad; he was six-foot-two!"

"Literally amazing," Wayne said, almost speechless.

"When I saw that turret, where my dad sat for hours on end, how in the world did he ever do that? Seeing that, I was actually even more intrigued than I had been the first time dad told me his story. Until you actually go into one of these planes, you have no idea what these men went through during the war."

"Boy, you're right, Patty. That hit home emotionally, even for those of us who have known little about these details."

"I just kept thinking how these men coped. When they got back from a mission, how they must have felt—when they were alive, after seeing their buddies killed. I can hardly begin to imagine how my dad must have coped."

This visit had been well worth the drive. As sound-minded and as sturdy as ever, I grasped tightly onto Wayne's hand. Dad had taught me to be tough, to do the right thing, to be a good girl, and to become a moral, trustworthy woman. Just like almost every maturing adult lady, a little part of me beamed forth every now and then as if a little girl. The childlike part of me, the imaginative Patty, knew this had been a healthy exercise—emotionally and spiritually.

"Are you okay?" Wayne asked me, as he started the engine of our Saturn SUV.

"I'm great," I said, briefly kissing my husband's cheek. "What a wonderful day, the wind is dying down. Let's go for a long afternoon drive. There is so much of the world for us to see, to explore."

I thought I could keep myself together, holding a brave face. As Wayne slowly pulled our car to the side of the road and shifted to park, I wept for my father, as my husband put his arm around my shoulders.

"I understand more than ever, why my dad drank. He drank because he didn't know how to cope with what he had seen. But he was a man's-man, so he couldn't tell people. They didn't have so many psychiatrists then, to help these men who were coming back from a war that was just horrendous. So, my dad coped the best he could, and he coped by not talking about it. But I never heard him talk about the experience, to his friends or anything. But now, today, being here at this place, I understood the pain and the suffering that my dad was going through. But I didn't understand it back then. And, now, he's gone. And I want so much at this moment to go to him and say, 'Dad, I understand now what you went through.' But I can't go tell him, because he's not here anymore."

During the years following that unforgettable tour, I searched for as much information as I could find about B-24 bombers and the lives of our heroes on those aircraft. I hunted for every piece of information that I could get my hands on about my father in the war. I became obsessed with knowing about the history

I watched everything that I could about World War II on TV, and I actually came across a book about the plane and his crew, the "Belle of the Brawl." A relative of a pilot who had served with my father wrote a book about their battles.

Inside, I found two pictures of my father, standing beside his fellow crew members. Today, that book holds a place of honor in my home.

The moment that I awakened on what soon would become the day of the fatal wreck, I felt so excited because we planned to see my cousins in Reno.

At age nine in 1956, I cleaned up and put on the best of my few dresses in order to look great. Following our usual custom, my mother spent quite a bit of time brushing my hair so that I would look perfect for everyone.

Mom always took great care to place just the right amount of pin-curls in my deep blonde hair.

"Aren't you excited to see your Grandma and Grandpa?" She asked me, as if somehow sensing that something lay ahead of us all.

To this day, I even remember my mother telling me during that final hour before the wreck that she loved me. Of course, my mom adored me. But she never said this too much, so I'll always hold those comments of hers dear to my heart.

At the time, we owned two cars. My mother drove a small 1954 Ford, and my dad had a large, roomy, sturdy Buick.

My father asked, "Which car should we take today?"

"Oh, let's just take the Buick," mother said.

On a normal day, the Carson City-to-Reno drive was a leisurely 35-minute jaunt, over a few hilly areas, and along Washoe Lake in the high desert, easing past the eastern edge of the great Sierra range. I always loved that drive, especially when we would always stop at the Jubilee for a meal at Dead Man's Curve just on the other side of Washoe Hill. Now, this might sound like a corny attempt to use a phrase from a popular tune made famous about eight years later from a popular Beach Boys hit. Yet, in fact, many people across the region had already hailed that section of highway as "Dead Man's Curve" due to the high number of fatal wrecks that occurred there.

On that beautiful clear day, we took off in the morning for a scheduled lunch with an aunt, uncle and cousins. After a having a great time with them in Reno, darkness had already fallen by the time we began our return trip toward Carson City. Mother wanted to get us home for a good night's sleep. I sat in front on her lap, falling asleep in her arms.

Gosh, I had loved her.

Suddenly I awakened, noticing flashes and lights while people were looking at me. Someone pointed a flashlight into my face and said: "Are you okay?"

Momentarily, I was somewhere out of the car. Dumbfounded and apparently dazed, I watched as medical crews drove my parents away in ambulances. Tons of cars, and flashing lights filled my senses. A short distance away, I could see the Club Jubilee, and then I realized that, yes, we were at Dead Man's Curve—although I had not yet heard of that phrase.

I had enjoyed numerous meals during the previous year at the Jubilee, where my mother had really liked having dinner. My parents knew the owners. The couple came out to the wreck scene, and the couple were the ones who had asked me, "Are you okay?" Shortly after my parents were driven away, they hugged me and whispered softly: "Patty, your Grandparents are on their way to come and get you."

"Where is my mom? Where is my dad?"

"They're okay. They're in the hospital, your Grandma and Grandpa will let you know what's going on, but don't you worry, because they're on their way."

Naturally, I worried about my mother.

Gosh, I had loved her.

My Grandparents soon arrived, taking me back to the Hill & Sons Motel in Reno. Due to the near-complete darkness at the wreck scene, they had not really gotten a good look at me there, and I guess my head was down the whole time.

"I'll make you a chocolate milkshake," Grandpa said soon after we arrived at my Grandparents' living quarters.

I thought, "Oh, good, that's wonderful. I love these shakes." Then, Grandma and Grandpa started looking at me for some reason, and they each started saying: "Patty, we have to take you to the hospital right away." Unable to understand why, I sat with them in their car as they drove me to the hospital, where nurses started looking at me, checking me out, and taking me to have X-rays.

I barely remember having fallen asleep, and the next day I started asking everyone who would listen: "Where are my mom and dad?"

"You can't see them right now," a nurse said.

I yearned to have my mother hold me as I lay in my hospital bed. I yearned to have her brush my hair, to help with my injuries, to make the hurt would go away. A doctor came into my patient room to check me over for a few minutes, casually mentioning that "they're in intensive care." As a child, I had no idea what that meant.

"Well, when can I see my mom and dad?"

"You can't," a different nurse said.

Then, my Grandma and Grandpa came.

"What's wrong with mom and dad?

"We don't know yet," Grandma Eve said. "We're just finding out, but they're okay. Everything is going to be all right."

I started to wonder if my parents were really all right. Just as pressing, I realized that my Grandparents were worried about me. Grandma eventually fetched a compact mirror from her purse and held it up to me, "Here, look in this mirror. Do you feel okay?"

Finally, I realized that I looked like a frog from a Disney cartoon. The sight made me feel odd emotionally, but my body felt fine. My chin had grown to the size of a giant water-filled balloon. To this day, I have never known what exactly happened to me, and I guess that the doctors never figured out the specific nature of that injury. All I can say for sure with extreme gratitude is that the lump or bruise eventually subsided. Thankfully, I felt fine.

I stayed in the hospital for about four days before the swelling started to disappear. I must have hit the dashboard, and I was okay. I kept begging to see my parents, to hug them both. Finally, on about the fourth day when my Grandparents came to pick me up from the hospital, they said that I could see mother. I still could not see my dad.

I went into my mother's room, stunned to see that she had suffered broken legs. Bruises riddled her face, making her look as if she had miraculously survived the world's most violent championship boxing match imaginable.

Everyone finally broke me the news that my father's legs had been crushed, plus various other problems—the details of which the adults kept from me.

Smack-dab in the middle of Dead Man's Curve, another driver—a drunken man—was killed instantly when he drove over the double-yellow center line and collided with our vehicle.

Upon my sudden decision to write this book, I had to become an expert flyer in the literary world seemingly overnight. Legendary American literary greats such as Ernest Hemingway, F. Scott Fitzgerald and John Grisham had earned their wings in the book-publishing industry through many years of difficult trial and error.

Naturally, I feared a crash landing in writing about my difficult early life and details of my life today. I knew that on my own I could never possibly write a compelling book.

The moment that Wayne and I had instantly and instinctively agreed that I should write this book, the reality hit me that my writing abilities and speeds were as slow and meandering as that of a turtle.

I feared that any effort done alone to chronicle my life would crash and burn. "I'm terrified, Wayne," I admitted.

"Nonsense," Wayne tried to hug me. "Soar above your fears."

"But you've seen my writing, far from the best."

"Leave the worrying to me," Wayne insisted. "All you need to do is relax."

Through the years, I have seen Wayne make similar assurances to his many clients. As a professional ghostwriter of dozens of successful books, Even prior to this point, his skills had left me stunned, admittedly in awe of the man that I happened to adore.

During the six-week period before my book project began, he wrote and published three books in vastly different genres—including one that quickly soared into a best-selling category at Amazon.com.

"Everyone needs to write a book about his or her own life experiences," I had been telling many people on my own initiative the previous several years, while serving as the graphic designer for all of Wayne's books. Throughout that period, I had written some 150 pages, mostly writing about my grandmother Eve. I always found excuses to do other things rather than venturing on such a formidable task as writing my autobiography.

Through the years I had often heard Wayne talk about the process. He always started every book by listening to his clients for an entire day or even for several days if necessary, all without taking a single note of what his clients had initially said. The whole time he fully heard every word, letting his mind, heart and soul envelope the details into a finely wrapped package. This phase takes every ounce of Wayne's spirit, or so he told me—and I would soon come to believe him fully, every word.

Following the initial day or two of absorbing all primary details, Wayne conducted an intensive interview of each client. Sometimes these lasted for up to 20 hours or more. For the client, as I soon discovered first-hand, the process became relatively easy except for the much-expected emotional trauma when recounting heart-wrenching personal details.

Determined to write this book we set September 1st as the initial launch phase of Wayne's research. Yes, I would essentially provide the vital information required to get this book off the ground.

Wayne spent the first few days of our book project probing the inner reaches of my mind. Herein I feel a necessary urge to ask any women readers: "When was the last time your husband spent two full days, 12 hours each day, fully and completely listening to every word that you had to say—all while keeping his mouth shut tight?" Well, as my ghostwriter, he truly had to listen and *actually hear* virtually everything that I said. This phase proved critical, his mind swirling with each new detail, mentally absorbing all the information possible while also envisioning how we would craft the book.

Following that intense two-day initial phase, I found myself falling in love with Wayne all over again. By listening and actually hearing, this was a man who proved that he cared about me—the guy who had agreed with me about the possibility of this project in the first place, and then actually carrying out what he had promised.

Wayne spent the next five days straight interviewing me. The guy took rapid-fire notes with much intensity, gleaning just the right amounts of appropriate information.

Starting promptly at 10 o'clock in the mornings, Wayne's upstairs home office became both our literary flight command center and the proverbial cockpit designed to soar straight into my heart, my soul, my mind, my spirit—delving into my passions, my hopes and my dreams. During these 12-hour daily sessions, each with intermittent breaks, Wayne flew straight, steady and true. These therapeutic mental flights required that I serve as our navigator, since my mind held the secrets, experiences and compelling details.

We took these flights together as we soared above the landscape of my entire life. Our proverbial, imaginary aircraft soared like a glider above every scene of my childhood. Wayne's inquisitive mind essentially served as a spy camera affixed to the outer wing of our plane, taking snapshots of my life. Our combined mutual energy came together in a glorious collage of emotions and visions, capturing images of my various apparent motivations, my own personal secrets, and at least some of the failures that make us all human.

Wayne made no judgments whatsoever as we zoomed into my family's psyche, delved into the inner canyons of my heart, and took dive-bomb runs toward the enemies of fear, confusion and insufficient knowledge that had riddled my childhood. For five straight days, I opened up my soul, telling my husband of my many lost loves; of my passions for life and for people; of my many hopes and dreams for happiness; of the many times that specific people have disappointed me, including him on at least a few occasions; of the countless joys from vibrant exploration; of my love for him, for great food, and for exploration; of the pride I have in generating certain knowledge; of my humble disappointments with myself for sometimes failing to learn enough; my discouragement from when people failed to keep their promises; of my yearning to travel more and to meet vibrant people, and of how I pulled myself—with no one's help but my own—straight from a "trailer-trash" world, pole vaulting into a new realm. Along this interview journey, I did plenty of:

Laughing. Crying. Smiling. Sharing.

Just as it should in a healthy marriage, I found myself able to fully open up every fiber of my entire being, of my spirit, my soul, my heart and my mind.

Skilled and keenly focused during every phase of this journey, Wayne always started the subsequent days always asking me if there was anything he could do to make me feel more comfortable or to voice any questions or concerns that I might have had.

On the rare occasions when I expressed any worries or potential problems, he always put my mind at ease by attending to necessary details.

I began to feel as if my heart had always known everything about Wayne, but also as if an elusive section of his spirit remained difficult to see—as if a bald eagle too far way and too high to clearly focus on, even with binoculars. Finally, as the interviews wound down to the last hour and minutes, I began to feel confidant about the writing of this book.

Chapter 12

Severe injuries prevented my father from working during his first few months after doctors released him from the hospital.

As he stumbled and struggled to walk while recovering from his crushed legs, mom still hopped around on crutches as her broken limbs healed. While my parents recuperated in our crappy Carson City apartment, the situation dictated that I stay with Grandma and Grandpa. Without "pushing" the point more than necessary, my life needed to take a different course until mom and dad "got back on their feet."

Once again family situations forced me to stay out of school for at least one month. Then, I finally got to return to class and resumed living with my folks, who finally gave me basic details of the drunken driver killed when he hit us. His passenger had suffered severe injuries.

"Thank God we took the Buick, or we would all be dead," mother said.

God knows how many people died at Dead Man's Curve until the government erected a concrete barrier at the site. This prevented cars from swerving into oncoming lanes.

Authorities even erected a plaque to commemorate the fatal accident victims. If my mother were alive she likely would have considered the memorial as too little, too late. The crutches and bruises left my parents with no choice other than to take many months for extensive recuperation.

My mother managed to resume work before father, due to his inability to walk and injury-related stomach area problems. Besides ravaging father's body, the wreck had severely wounded his already damaged spirit. From my view at the time, only a miracle would re-energize dad's once-vibrant zest for life.

Amazingly, just such an event would soon occur.

Since the late 1700s, rugged, vibrant explorers and independent scouts in the American wilderness have often been dubbed as "mountain men."

Trappers, guides and other frontiersmen grasped their own sense of personal pride and accomplishment, often living like hermits far away from other people. Carving out a new image for himself, one of the most interesting characters of this bent was John Jacob Astor, a German-American business magnate who explored the American West, the Pacific Coast, the Great Lakes and even huge sections of Canada.

Like Astor had, dozens of so-called Mountain Men that followed developed a feisty, rugged, independent spirit. To guys such as these, no man worth a dime followed the commands of big-business concerns—unless the fellow happened to own such ventures himself. A true mountain man depends on absolutely no one but himself.

As a bright young girl, I quickly learned that my dad was just such a guy, a mountain man—a courageous, independent spirit born long after what would have been his most ideal era. Like Charles Bent, a fur trader that explored the New Mexico Territory in the early 1800s, dad had been eager to leave the military in search of adventure. And like Hugh Glass, a frontiersman in the American West, dad was the type of guy who would have willingly fought a grizzly bear if necessary to save his family.

"Hey, Patty, do you want to go fishing with me today?" dad would ask every now and then, while continuing to recuperate from his auto accident injuries.

"Yes!" I would say, never requiring any serious thought on the matter. Like father, I always yearned to enjoy the great outdoors, far from the hectic city life.

Yet at the time I failed to fully grasp and appreciate the fact that by going fishing along the Walker River in Northwest Nevada, dad was essentially going where he belonged. Yes, he was a mountain man, a guy who never should have had to go up shooting guns in a plane or to move into a city. His spirit, his aura, his countenance and his motivations belonged with the bears, the deer, the mountain lions, the fish and with any birds that might have passed our way.

Always magnetized by father's masculine attributes, his boundless sense of adventure, mother strived to get in on the wilderness action with us as well. As her legs gradually healed, she seemed more vibrant, more energized, more filled with life's great possibilities whenever with him—especially outdoors.

Did mom have any inkling at that time that dad still possessed the wily, feisty attitude of the American Old West mountain man Ben Lily, a big game hunter who tracked cougars, black bear and grizzlies—from Arizona to Mexico, Idaho and Louisiana in the late 1800s and early 1900s? Or did she realize that dad still possessed the feisty, never-say-quit spunk of William Sublette, a fur trader and mountain man from Kentucky who engaged in the fierce 1832 Battle of Pierre's Hole—involving more than 100 trappers asserting their rights in a bloody, deadly confrontation with Indians north of Salt Lake?

As a little girl, at least until that particular point, I did not know of all these many historical tales of mountain men. If I had realized this then, would I have appreciated my father even more? Could I have spoken to him about his many similarities to those independent-minded spirits, none of them willing to kiss up to corporate America?

Upon our return under one roof in Carson City, we all tried to get our lives back into a state of so-called normalcy—although we had never fully achieved such a situation anyway. My parents focused primarily on their job-related transitions, while collectively we took a path of mending our bodies and souls.

"We're alive, and we love each other—that's all that matters," mother said. "We're a family. We're going to make it."

Deep down, though, as a mountain man, dad kept fighting his internal wars involving the bottle—coupled with the divergent chores of simultaneously heading in opposite directions, toward the wilderness and to a regular boring day job.

With our family ravaged in the aftermath of the fatal wreck, father called the Reno attorney that he had helped a year earlier when the lawyer's car broke down near Elko, Nevada. Dad explained our situation to Peter Harper-Collins, who gave dad the fantastic news: "Sure I'll file the lawsuit for you, Larry, and you should expect to receive a settlement of about two hundred thousand dollars within a year."

In the wake of our tragedy, father and mother finally had something positive to look forward to, and they hoped that Harper-Collins was a man of his word. That's the kind of guy my dad was, and he expected others to behave in an honest, righteous and forthright manner as well. Although a drunk, one thing father had was his integrity.

And they called him "Lucky Larry."

Close to 1 o'clock in the morning, I turned over alone in bed. Wayne's absence from our bedroom makes me lonely for him, but for the moment he kept busy working at a ferocious pace finishing a book for a client in his upstairs office on the other side of the house from our bedroom.

Unable to sleep without my husband, I sat up in bed and closed my eyes. Deep in meditation, I hugged our little dog Diva while thoughts of the book interviews from the previous several days made me keep thinking of my parents.

My many revelations given to Wayne in a non-stop conversation the previous five days had placed them at the center of my mind. Covered and soothed by the late-night silence, I start appreciating the fact that I still loved my mom and dad so much. I could feel the love each of them had for me.

And, I still felt that they remained with me somehow. They continued watching over me. That bond that is so important beyond anything—beyond food, beyond a roof over our head—that love still kept us together. Even through trials of those many difficult times, my eyes still see the tenderness of their smiles and my heart beats in tandem with the relentless dedication that they had for me.

This closeness, which transcends death, goes beyond understanding. Whenever certain foods such as round steak are cooking, distinctive aromas send me back to those times with mother. When fishing with a friend on the river, that's when I feel my father right next to me saying: "Go get that big one, Patty. Look right over there at that hole. That's where they are. Pay attention."

All these little things just keep coming back to me at just the most important times. A smell. A breeze. Sometimes while driving I just start crying, because I feel their presence. I feel like when we're driving in Idaho. At such times, I feel the air, those glorious clouds above, the sky or something unexpected reminds me of those wonderful times that I had spent with them.

All of a sudden I just pull over, alone behind the wheel, and I feel the presence of my parents. They're right beside me, here, as I break out in tears.

They're putting their arms around me, and they're saying: "We love you! We're still here." So I unexpectedly feel them at certain times, once every several months. These sensations could hit right before bed at night. Something happens, and I feel their presence, and I feel their love—which never leaves.

I was so loved as a child, and I knew that I was loved.

And, that's why I never questioned a lot of the things that they did when we were going from town to town, or where we were going—because I always sensed their love, and that they would never leave me—even though my dad left us at times—I knew that he was always there, and that he always loved me. There was no question.

Maybe I was just a more mature little kid, and I knew there were problems going on with my mother and father, and that was their thing. Maybe I didn't like where our life was going, but the one thing that I knew was that my dad loved me—and he told me so many times. My mother always was there, and told me that she adored me as well. Beyond a shadow of a doubt, they adored me with all their hearts and I cherished them.

Oh, God, I yearn for them to this day.

That's why I have pictures of them up all around my home, for the house tour visitors to see.

My treasures in my house reflect this. If I was to run out the door, and there was a fire, I'd go running to get my pictures of my parents. They're so important to me right now. And I miss them very much, desperately hoping that my mom was here.

My mother especially would cherish this house. She would become funny about the whole tour thing, thinking of that as kind of strange. But she would be delighted in this home, pleased that I have this wondrous, eternally castle-like cottage. That's how I feel about my parents.

I catch them with a song that comes on, I catch a glimpse of my mother, as I walk down the street and I see other children with their mothers—when I was little, and she would be holding my hand. Taking me to the dime store for treats. Whenever I see children, I think of my beautiful mom.

Today, when I'm fishing, I see a glimpse of my dad standing in the water. Doing this beautiful thing that he does with the fly when he casts.

I can see him in the rivers, as if he is there today. Memories are so poignant, and you've got to have them. That's what life is about.

They might be gone, but the memories are here as if you could go touch them, and hug them and tell them: "Hi, dad. I love you. What fly should I use to catch that fish?"

He's here. In my memory, he's living. My mother is here, still living.

They're not gone, as long as we have memories they live.

And when I tell these stories to my granddaughters Eva and Hannah, and to my grandson Mickey, and I tell them about these stories, saying: "My parents are not gone; they live. They're alive." And I cherish what was, and what is.

I catch them in the wind.

During the summer following the fatal accident, my dad would have to go rejuvenate his damaged body. Exercises such as fishing and camping re-energized his physical being while his zest for life seemed to reappear.

While fishing, he would walk through the water, and for some reason that helped strengthen his legs and midsection. Although much healthier than he, my mother experienced similar benefits. So, in 1956 we went every single weekend to Walker River in northwest Nevada's Lyon County past Douglas County going into Bridgeport.

We preferred the desert side of the river, rather than a tree-lined area within California south of the Topaz Lake region. Dad liked fishing in desert-like ground-level areas laced with lots of willows, thick brush and vibrant vegetation unique to the area—but no trees other than an occasional pinion pine.

The river emits a serene, soothing sensation. Either holding my hand or guiding the way, my dad would take me into the river to show me holes where hungry fish preferred to congregate. The smells of spring and summer contrasted sharply, while the autumn aromas emitted a generous, musky, slightly pungent aroma. Fond memories.

Clear through spring, summer and well into the fall of 1956, the vast majority of that year emerged as a fishing period for us. This activity slowly and steadily made each of us begin to feel whole again. Besides rejuvenating their bodies, the fishing brought my mom and dad back together. Even as a child I noticed them allow their motivations and preferences to wrap around each other, as if interdependent branches on a single tree.

A time to thrive and learn about nature, mother always made us wonderful picnics. The coolness, the outdoor setting, the changing seasons, everything about these adventurous excursions really gave me an abiding, lifetime appreciation for Nevada.

On one afternoon we got to meet a fun character.

"This is Mountain Man!" My father said after we came across the guy, and right away I sensed that these fellows—my father and that man—shared an unspoken bond. Could it be that mountain men of the true all-American bent sensed and appreciated one another

Throughout the first part of the year, almost every weekend we would bump into Mountain Man. Gradually, from what dad told me and from what I witnessed with my own eyes, I learned that this friendly guy went there solely for the purpose of trapping mountain lions.

Naturally, since deep within my father's heart he was a Mountain Man as well, my dad quickly became pals with the guy. They never needed to talk much about specific unimportant details the way big-city men did. Most weekends when we visited Mountain Man's camp, he greeted us as if we were long-lost family. Other times, he would be gone, probably off trapping mountain lions.

Back during those days when parents rarely minded whether their children talked with adults outside of the family, I would go up and chat with Mountain Man while my parents made initial preparations for fishing or as they set up our own campsite.

Mountain Man's stories about trapping, and his four gentle coon dogs, somehow reminded me of my dad except in a round-about way. Thin as a willow, he towered as high as my father at about 6 foot 2, considered extremely tall at the time. With absolutely no tell-tale signs of a city slicker, he wore blue jeans, crumpled old boots, and a nondescript, tattered shirt. Always sporting a cowboy hat, this rugged individual beamed, probably thanks to his nice-looking face.

Ceran St. Vrain, a New Mexico fur trader and Mountain Man who fought in the Mexican-American War, hailed from French aristocrats. Like St. Vrain, perhaps this Mountain Man at the Walker River also sprang from a wealthy, high-end past. As far as I know, my dad and this Mountain Man never discussed such matters, and I never broached the subject anyway—fully in awe of this guy's independent spirit.

Lacking any hint of an offensive odor, our buddy was fairly clean. In fact, the guy set up his camp in a very efficient order, everything in its own useful place, from tools and weapons to cooking utensils, beverages and food. I even remember my dad telling me: "This man lives out here, but I want you to look and observe, Patty, that this guy is a clean person. Gaze all around you. Everything is kept in order, including his dog's dishes. Mountain Man takes care of his animals."

Breaking his own pattern, my dad actually told me that he liked someone—this Mountain Man. Right away I had sensed my father's appreciation for the guy's unique characteristics—particularly his attributes as a gentle man, although rugged. A clean man, although living in the grimy, soil-caked desert. An articulate man, even though he had little if anything to say. A vigorous, hard-charging man, even though placid and calm when in our presence.

This is how my dad would describe Mountain Man: "Look at how a man can live in a camp, and still have it set up great. You can tell a man by how gentle he is. You can tell a man by how he talks to you. If you will listen to him, he speaks proper English. He doesn't say, 'Oh, I ain't got no...' He has been educated. He has chosen this way of life, because this is what he wants."

Hearing these keen observations, I fully appreciated and embraced everything my father told me. But at the time, actually, I failed to realize that in a sense my father was also describing himself as well—not just that "other" Mountain Man, the guy who trapped mountain lions. Yes, my dad was every bit as much a similar character himself, although none of us seemed to realize or acknowledge this at the time.

"This is not a stupid man," dad said. "This a person who is doing what he wants."

If not for my father's love for my mother and me, would he have adopted a similar lifestyle—lacking the responsibility of supporting a family?

Well, wouldn't you know, this clean, articulate man who lived in a camp alone made me a fishing pole one morning while my father and mother were nearby casting in the Walker River. I cherished the hand-made wooden gift. As I looked in awe, this man strung fishing line along the stick and told me: "You can catch a fish with this, just as well as you can catch a fish with your dad's fishing rod that he has over there. Go check it out and see!"

And, by God, I immediately headed for the river, leaving Mountain Man right then and there. I scurried across the isolated road void of traffic, got into the chilly water, marched up to a fishing hole that my dad had previously shown me, and stuck the line under the water.

Right away I got myself a fish. So, this evolved into a magical time, as we all became one with Mother Nature. We heard tales of the river, and yarns that my dad told me about fishing, giving me more stories about life as we drove back and forth on these much-awaited wilderness trips.

For me, lacking any fear despite the accident earlier that year, I still loved traveling in the car for regional wilderness excursions with my parents—just like I had felt a few years earlier in Idaho. But here, unlike in the Potato State, I knew that we were always going fishing, that we had a fairly solid, dependable home that we would never leave. The travels to and from fishing became some of the most wonderful times of my life, particularly because dad would tell stories about his childhood.

And we called him Mountain Man.

In many ways, as my second husband, Wayne hails as a complete opposite of my late father—at least in many regards.

Wayne's idea of hard labor is to pick up the TV remote and press a few buttons. My dad enjoyed intense, sweat-inducing physical activities like chopping wood, moving huge objects with his bare hands, and hauling away loads to the dump.

Wayne drank alcohol only in moderation and avoided seedy bars, especially establishments where the nightlife gets rowdy. Such a lifestyle would seem foreign to my dad, who enjoyed visiting neighborhood bars, getting drunk on a regular basis and joining in on the fun of drag-down, mirror-smashing fights.

For recreation, Wayne sneaked to movie theaters, preferring to take me along so that we could share snacks, possibly hold hands and argue light-heartedly about the film's quality afterward. Like the plague, my dad avoided such gushy activities. Rather than sitting for two hours getting bored in one place, father preferred to enjoy the great outdoors.

Desperate to go fly-fishing for the first time in many years, shortly after the 21st Century began I dragged Wayne along to go fishing with me. My heart, my emotions and my fond memories told me to enjoy that contemplative sport once again.

Trying to be a dutiful hubby, Wayne went through all the motions of pretending that he was excited about our upcoming fishing excursion. Yet deep down, I sensed that this was all an act since he loved me so much.

Sure enough, on a cool autumn afternoon, my anticipation began to heat up, my level of excitement pulsating as Wayne and I finally walked into the Truckee River near Interstate 80, about 30 miles west of Reno in the high Sierra. Once I started casting, memories of those pleasant family times from 45 years earlier began to make me feel at least a bit warm inside.

Then, splash!

Par for the course, right behind me, Wayne fell flat on his face in the middle of the river. By the time I turned around, he had already bolted to his feet, smiling and trying his best.

"I lost my pole!" Wayne said, frantically looking in an attempt to see the riverbed beside his feet.

"It's not a pole; it's a rod!" I hollered to this guy, who seemed hopeless in my eyes.

Careful to avoid hurting his pride any further than necessary, I summarily watched in seeming disbelief as Wayne flailed and scurried to and fro across the river.

Finally, after about two minutes or so, showing pity and striving to enable Wayne to save face, I promptly found Wayne's rod with no problem whatsoever and handed it to him. He offered a meek smile, his boyish face reminding me of a kindergartner.

"I'm just not wearing my glasses," Wayne said, trying to hold his rod in a way that would make him look like a seasoned pro—although to me he looked like a nervous, confused Cub Scout. "I would have found it right away and..."

Sitting on a rock at the riverbank, Wayne began pretending to go through the motions of putting his rod back into working order. Always intuitive about such matters, I knew full well that my guy had absolutely no idea of what he was doing...And then, his non-stop sneezing started.

Ahh-chooo!

From that point forward, Wayne sneezed so loud and so ferociously— every 15 seconds or so—that the fish must have been scared off for thirty miles in every direction.

Striving to keep my wits about me I went back to my original fishing spot and began casting. *Ahh-chooo!* This is the moment I have dreamed about, to return back to nature. I begin to think of how quiet my father had been, so sturdy and healthy during such getaways. *Ahh-chooo!* Oh, the solitude of nature, I want to think at that point. Appreciate the blessings that our creator has bestowed upon us, in creating such a placid, peaceful and awe-inspiring outdoor setting. *Ahh-chooo!* The dream of catching four or five fish now, and bringing them back home for tonight's dinner fills me with hope that Wayne's stupid sneezing will end.

Ahh-chooo! Ahh-chooo! Ahh-chooo!

"Wayne, are you okay?" I said, genuinely concerned.

"Don't you worry about me at all," Wayne said, still fiddling with his rod and shivering from the cold. "Must be pollen tickling my nose. *Ahh-chooo! Ahh-chooo! Ahh-chooo!*"

Ten minutes later, faced with no other choice, I drove us toward Reno, a 30-minute drive to home. Along the way, Wayne's sneezing subsided but he kept shivering. Wayne spoke non-stop about what a glorious day this had been. He spoke of what he considered his genuine desire to go fly fishing with me as much as possible from then on, because he had enjoyed the experience so very much and that he wanted me to finally begin to enjoy one of the few consistent activities that had helped stabilize my childhood—invigorating my soul.

From that day forward, about once every spring, summer and autumn, Wayne would bring up the fact that he desperately wanted to enjoy taking me on another fishing jaunt. But due to scheduling problems, or an apparent lack of genuine initiative, none of his declarations ever resulted in a single "Ok-let's-go" announcement.

Faced with no other option, as the next six or seven years passed, I could only rely on my memories. Lacking a knowledgeable and genuinely interested fishing buddy and fully aware of the need for fishing enthusiasts to travel in pairs, I at least took as much time as possible to fondly remember the distant past.

Then, a positive, unexpected change came to play, beginning at a charity barbecue on a Saturday afternoon in June 2008. There at the Swifterson Family Ranch for the first time we met businessman Bill McCready and his wife Teri. From among the celebration's 350 guests, the man impressed Wayne as gentlemanly, witty and highly intelligent. Blessed with a similar first inclination, I also viewed Teri as a beautiful, smart and delightful woman.

Naturally, from that moment forward, the McCready's became our new best friends. During the ensuing months and years, Wayne enjoyed getting business advice from Bill, as I cherished developing a delightful friendship with Teri. Then, a miracle.

One afternoon in the spring of 2010, Bill casually mentioned to me that he was an avid fly fisherman. Aged 66 at the time, Bill yearned to once again enjoy this contemplative activity, bringing back memories of his childhood in Oregon.

Finally, I would have a competent fishing buddy to help make my dreams come true, at least in the wilderness department.

Naturally, Bill and I promptly began planning as many weekend "fishing dates" as we possibly could schedule. Sometimes in the middle of the night as these planned excursions approached, I would awaken— filled with boundless anticipation. Over at his home about four miles away from my house, relentless anticipation also filled Bill. Crafty, conniving and sneaky, the businessman and futures trading expert landed a bargain deal, buying an entire set of fly fishing gear at a rock-bottom rate.

"I want to take you to the movies tomorrow afternoon," Wayne would tell me, usually on the day before one of these planned fishing getaways.

"I can't. I'm going fishing with Bill. I'm so excited."

"Are you going to use his rod again?" Wayne would ask, sheepishly.

"It sounds like you're jealous, Wayne," I smiled, kissing my husband's cheek. "You're not the jealous type at all, and I know that."

From that point forward, Wayne would always come up with some new line or other, as if to cast my friendship with Bill into a humorously suspicious light.

A few weeks later, Bill and Teri had us over to their house for a spectacular meal. For one hour straight, Wayne cast out so many of his naturally flowing lines that he hooked all the rest of us there at the McCready's dining table. Along with Bill and Teri, I laughed so hard that I nearly peed in my pants. At our friends' dining room table, tears sparked by our funny bones began to flow down some of our cheeks, trying to hold back the laughter. Wayne seemed to enjoy torturing us all with his non-stop, persistent and relentless lines about me preferring Bill's casting skills over his own.

Bill and I thought only of the fish, but Wayne took the situation from a whole different perspective. Making the most of the buffoonery, from that point forward Bill and I always started referring to each other as "my fishing husband" and "my fishing wife." For their part, Wayne and Teri separately failed to get bothered by such banter in the least. This transition suited each of them just fine, since both could spend Bill and my fishing time doing what they wanted—in special alone time, separately working, reading books, going to the movies, taking vigorous hikes, or snoozing alone in their separate beds in our different houses on leisurely afternoons.

Both Wayne and Teri expressed their joy at this arrangement, since from that point forward neither had to go fishing with us—an activity that they disliked.

"You're going fishing with a woman," some of Bill's friends would tell him.

"Yeah, she's my 'fish-wife.'"

"And your real wife doesn't mind?"

"No, Teri is delighted."

"Boy, Bill," some of these fellows, many of them fly fishermen, would tell him. "Where do we go to find gals like Patty?

Thanks to Bill's encouragement, I even managed to join a group of fly-fishing enthusiasts that enjoyed regularly scheduled one-day excursions to various streams, rivers, and lakes—all within a two-hour drive of Reno.

Most of the time, I was the only female, usually surrounded by dozens of guys. All of us focused on a single interest only, and that was to enjoy these getaways as much as possible while improving our fishing skills. On the few occasions when we managed to land a big one, we snapped photos of these throw-back trophies.

Sadly, soon afterward, Bill suffered from severe back pain from an unknown origin and almost died. Following an emergency surgery, physicians put him back on the road to recovery as I wrote this book and the house tour approached.

Luckily, word came that Bill was finally on the road to recovery, leaving me hopeful that he and I would soon be casting again.

"Patty, you're worried about your fish-husband, aren't you," Wayne asked, genuinely concerned during a brief rest break from his non-stop writing.

"I can't imagine how much pain he is suffering now. Bill's situation reminds me of what happened to my dad. Here, this time, is a man who was so strong—Bill would walk down along the river with me. He could walk on slippery river rocks and keep his balance. And, now he's bent over like a 90-year-old, incapable of doing just about anything."

Increasingly concerned, I brought a home-cooked meal to Bill and Teri's house before he entered the hospital. Visiting him in the hospital proved heart-wrenching. The pain-suffered by my "fish-husband" became so great that he could hardly even talk to me. So imagine my delight when his condition started to improve.

Finally, I seized an opportunity to visit Bill while Wayne stayed home working diligently on his book projects.

"Fishing was the one thing that helped my dad get back on his feet," I told Bill. "I think it's the activity that can help you, too. Try and hold off, Bill, until after the tour of my house. Once that happens, we need to go fishing as much as possible, That's what's going to bring you back to life—just like it did with my father. Bill, fishing together will make us one with nature, one with sounds, with smells—and with everything that's important in life."

Hearing this, Bill explained to me that he had similar experiences with his own late dad as well.

"Once I get back on my feet, Patty, we'll have many more fishing days together, for many years to come. We can sit out there all day long, and not even catch a fish, but it's okay—it's being in the wilderness, out on a river or on a lake. It's that whole serenity that fishing allows for you. That feeling of getting that big one on your line, there's nothing like it. It's the fight, the feel that's so incredible. Believe me, Patty. I'll get better."

Grateful for meeting Bill and Teri, for those many fishing excursions with him, and for his ongoing recovery, I thanked the Lord for giving me these new, vibrant opportunities to spread my wings at least for a short period of time, taking in all the joy possible from the awe-inspiring wilderness.

Chapter 13

Almost every little girl adores flowers, especially daisies, roses and lilies.

While in third-grade in Carson City following a full summer of fishing with my parents, I enjoyed having the most wonderful teacher in the world. In my eyes, Miss Craft was a pink rose in full bloom. She reflected sunbeams of knowledge into my eager mind.

Miss Craft's lessons in reading, writing and arithmetic grabbed all of my attention.

More delighted than ever at this chance to fully enjoy school again, I became a bumblebee—at least as far as our teacher-student relationship was concerned. At Miss Craft's beck and call, because she adored me as her favorite student, I would buzz beneath her pedals. There I eagerly sucked up as much nectar as possible, all coming to me in the form of boundless knowledge.

As a result, I began to blossom. My zest for life, my eagerness to learn and my excitement for going to school returned to my little heart.

Into that autumn, I had become the teacher's pet, the favorite of this sympathetic rose and I took the situation for all it was worth. Without exaggeration, the woman had somehow sensed my unhappiness, before injecting me with an unexpected new will to thrive.

All of my previous teachers in the many schools that I attended had either failed to notice me or to pay specific attention to improving my grades.

Finally finding myself in an ideal situation, I made my entire goal in life to convince Miss Craft that I was the smartest, craftiest and most delightful girl in the entire world.

I would rush home after school and finish all of my homework. This marked a first for me to this point in life, and my parents seemed to have no suspicions as to my true excitement. Naturally, Miss Craft became the center of my daytime weekday universe, and I strived to do everything possible to please her. So, I studied as much as possible in order to win my classroom's spelling bee. For the first time ever, I began to excel somewhat at math, and my passion for reading soared like a butterfly.

Striving to pretend as if she had no favorites, Miss Craft put one half of the children on one side of the room, and the others all went to the opposite side of the class. The child who ended up at the very beginning of the line was the youngster who got all the spelling words right. Due largely to compost and nurturing soils that Miss Craft provided, I always ended up at the very beginning of the line.

I became this teacher's pet, and I knew it.

This woman wanted me to transform into an educational success, and this change occurred seemingly overnight. Thanks to Miss Craft, I began to shine; she made me feel like I was the smartest kid in the class. Imagine my delight in realizing the fact that she fully understood and recognized my achievements.

With my newfound roots fully grounded within the soils of Carson City, I felt like I could grow and expand to my heart's desire. Indeed, the positive change that a great teacher makes in a child can impact the world for the better, for all eternity. Stupendous educators such as Miss Craft can change the course of history.

Thanks largely to her diligence and caring demeanor, my math skills and my passion for reading went into full bloom. Even as a little girl, I began to grasp the wondrous possibilities of my boundless potential. If all went well, in subsequent years a steady new round of teachers would help tend to my educational needs, providing enough eternal knowledge to eventually transform me into a potential success.

But sadly, familial situations suddenly ripped me out of the school.

Within an instant, my father resumed his previous pattern of moving our family to a new community without any warning.

My parents never gave me a specific explanation of why we had left Carson City.

Luckily, dad failed to land a job in the community north of San Francisco in a seedy part of Marin County filled with junky, trashy-looking auto-body shops.

From there, we made a 70-mile trek south to San Jose, California, where he landed work in his chosen profession within three hours.

My parents promptly rented first-floor rooms in an early-1900s Victorian-style home. For the first time in my life, I had my own place, a separate bedroom upstairs from my parents' living quarters. Mother soon landed a keypunch operator job thanks to her unique skills.

The essence of me blew through our San Jose neighborhood like a tumbleweed in an Old West cowboy movie. With my roots pulled out, my spirit lacked any firm ground to latch upon.

I ended up in a third-grade class taught by Mrs. Beck. To my great delight, this middle-aged woman emerged as a stupendous teacher, although much different from Miss Craft back in Carson City.

While I admired them both, my new San Jose teacher initially failed to recognize my potential. During the first few days, Mrs. Beck lacked any notion that I had been a teacher's pet a short time before. Could Mrs. Beck possibly muster up the power and grace necessary to re-energize my passion for learning?

Suddenly, I realized that in the San Jose classroom I could look out a window, gazing toward a bright new future. Sunlight streamed onto my desk, and within four days after enrolling in Mrs. Beck's class I started blooming once again.

Mrs. Beck made all this possible, thanks to her professionalism, coupled with her keen abilities to recognize my talents. Due to her careful daily nurturing, attending to my curious questions and assuring that my roots had once again found solid ground.

Thanks to my latest transition, I managed to develop new friends my age, just as I had done in Carson City. This time the experience took on a whole new dynamic, because I even had a phone in my upstairs bedroom at home. During the evenings and on occasional weekends I got numerous phone calls from my new friends.

I even received a handwritten letter from Miss Craft back in Carson City. The young woman who had made me her teacher's pet such a short while earlier wrote that she had married. Miss Craft also wrote, responding to a letter I had written to her, of her great delight upon learning that I had remained enthusiastic at another school.

While at home, my parents failed to recognize the fact that I had become excited by my latest transition. Because inquisitive children need loads of fresh air and freedom from everyday responsibilities, I watched a lot of TV including the "Mickey Mouse Club" as soon as I returned home every weekday from Grant Elementary.

At the time, Grant Elementary was just like the old schoolhouse that I had missed from Twin Falls with hardwood floors. At lunchtime in the San Jose school, distinctive smells gave me a sense that I had returned to a natural environment.

Mrs. Beck beamed, just a sweet lady. Every day after lunch, for all of us students she would tell a story. Thanks to a natural, God-given charisma, teachers such as she can grip you with tales that will instill in your heart, the passion and message of hope lasting a lifetime. Every day, we students sat quietly for a half hour as she read us the next chapter of a book—the first "Mary Poppins," nearly ten years before the tale became a hit movie starring Dick Van Dyke and Julie Andrews. By the time she read "101 Dalmations," I had started reading every book that I could possibly get my hands on, as the teacher noticed, fully recognized and appreciated my improvements. The illustrations accompanying these stories enabled my boundless imagination to bloom into every glorious shape imaginable.

Yes, my heart had found new hope in Mrs. Beck's classroom. Yes, my heart had begun beating with a never-ending passion for learning once again. And, yes, my heart transcended this universe, as these various compelling books brought me into other lands.

My burning need for knowledge and endless creativity magnified to the point where I realized that my drawing talents had somehow catapulted into a blessed, continual orbit around Mother Earth. I had drawn before all the time, but on one particular day Mrs. Beck gave us a lesson on Japanese culture. Then, she asked her students to draw something that we felt about that nation's society, so I created a geisha. I concentrated on specific features, especially flowers held by the woman.

"Patty!" Mrs. Beck exclaimed while standing dutifully over me, gazing down upon my picture. "Do you realize that you are an artist? That is the most beautiful picture that I have seen any of my students— ever—do...*Patty, you are an artist.*"

This teacher's brief, simple statement changed my life, influencing the positive pathway that I would eventually take both in my career and in my passions as well. From that day forward, Mrs. Beck instilled spunk, charisma and confidence. With her blessing and encouragement, I drew distinct images including illustrations of flowers on the classroom chalkboard for all my classmates to admire.

She gave me colored chalk, and I would get to go and draw on the board for her and for the entire class. Needless to say, I had been reborn on an educational level and even on a spiritual plane as well.

The courage of Miss Craft and Mrs. Beck, their passions for their professions and their genuine caring for students enabled me to grow emotionally, plus in mind and body. Collectively, they both launched me on the pathway to becoming a professional artist. Their passionate beaming colors and commitment to their professions turned my life around.

Floating like a swan, a former ugly duckling atop a tranquil pond, I felt soothed, at ease and peaceful. My latest experiences had taught me of the victories and great possibilities made possible by change.

Then, two months after we had arrived in San Jose, once again I got yanked out by the roots by my father. This time, he had decided to move me and mother to another place—destination unknown.

But at least at age 9 I had evolved into an artist, fully unaware of vastly different difficult times just ahead.

Chapter 14

At ages 52 and 53, from 1999 through 2000 I created a series of watercolor flowers.

I donated many of these paintings to auctions held by various charitable organizations. My efforts generated thousands of dollars for deserving organizations, especially charities designed to help needy children and educational organizations.

One of my favorite charities at the time was the Nevada Women's Fund, which helped girls and young ladies get their lives on track. For several years, I served on the fund's board as its leaders selected worthy women for college scholarships.

My favorite works from this flower series included roses and gladiolus, plus lilies, and geraniums. Each painting featured quotations and folklore about the specific type of flower depicted; these words helped bring zest and magnetism to the project.

Other charities that benefited from my flower project included the Sierra Arts Foundation, where I served as an executive board member for many years.

For the past ten years, I have purchased and enjoy arranging flowers. Each week, I place a new floral bouquet in a place of honor atop a beautiful desk given to us from Wayne's mother, Marilyn. This weekly present to myself gives me such joy to view the beauty that is displayed at the living room window.

When finances permit, I also regularly purchase a wide variety of other flowers, placing arrangements into every major room of my home.

Despite numerous offers, to this day I have refused to sell a couple of the most popular paintings from my flower series. Visitors at my upcoming home tour will see these images hung in the upstairs bathroom and in the master bedroom.

Yes, Miss Craft and Mrs. Beck, Thank you, I am an artist."

An unexpected magical event occurred in 1980 when I was 33 years old.

While rummaging through Reno-area garage sales with my 13-year-old son Chris on a Saturday morning, I discovered childhood school books that had changed my life forever. These were duplicates of the books during my blossoming years in the second, third and fourth grades.

Just by seeing the covers of these old school books I noticed in an instant that these featured the same images that had helped launch my artistic curiosity, sparked my imagination and ignited my lifetime of creativity.

Without hesitation I forked out a measly one dollar apiece for five books.

Yet an onslaught of personal duties at the time prevented me from sitting down for an hour or so to carefully read and to fully appreciate these publications.

Ten years later I purchased the house that I'm living in today. At the time the property lacked a yard, and there were absolutely no flowers. Only a handful of trees surrounded the outer perimeter.

About one month after completing the necessary initial first-step home improvements, one night I sat alone in the upstairs library. One by one, I emptied boxes of books and carefully arranged them on the shelves lining two complete walls, from floor to ceiling. Exhausted as midnight approached, from a small old cardboard box I pulled out the five books that I had read at various elementary schools.

Mesmerized, I leisurely looked through "Around the Corner," "More Friends and Neighbors," "Luck and Pluck," and "Sunshine and Rain." Child-hood stories and eye-popping images captured my imagination, igniting the same fireworks within my soul that I had experienced as a blossoming flower from ages seven through ten.

Feeling overjoyed but somehow confused as well, I then opened "The Friendly Village," published by Row, Peterson and Company out of New York City, Evanston, Illinois, and San Francisco. Illustrated by Florence and Margaret Hoopes, published in 1936 and 1941, the book grabbed my full attention.

Suddenly and unexpectedly, I felt almost as if a magnolia, my mind in full bloom. Now, once again, I was a little girl. My memories raced back to the time when I sat dutifully in Mrs. Beck's third-grade classroom at Grant Elementary in San Jose. I trembled slightly, filled with joy while reading through this delightful book's various sections entitled "Stay-At-Home Stories." Just as they had done during my childhood, these images inspired dreams of little neighborhood playmates, a peaceful town with a river running through it, enjoying a circus, riding horses and playing in an old barn. There, a little girl and her small male playmate find old artifacts such as ladders, bicycles and carts. Each subsequent page instantly enabled me to recall the joys of imagination, the blessings of having a quest for happiness—the hopes of making our dreams come true. Sure enough, the next section, "A feeling in your bones," inspired a child's joyful playtime with a goat, scurrying through a yard filled with delightful sunflowers. From there, a neighbor—Mrs. Hill—discovers the goat in her basement. Mountain stories, a yarn about blueberry pies, and fiddlers playing music at a family party made me feel the essence of what having a loving home truly means. Legends of cowboys and Indians, a train ride and a day on the range put me into a time and place where this book had enabled my imagination, education and artistic talents to grow straight and tall.

Surprise!

While looking at Page 210, my heart raced faster than a locomotive.

"That's a picture—a drawing—of my house today!" I thought, suddenly standing at attention in the middle of my home library. "That is an exact drawing of my home!"

The white picket fence, the cottage-style design, the precise window frames, and even the tree at the front entrance grabbed every fiber of my attention.

A miracle!

But this was just the beginning. A few pages later, I made a startling discovery. There, for the entire world to see was an exact duplicate of the wishing well in my yard.

Just as compelling, another page showed brilliant hollyhocks, each beaming skyward from a friendly garden. Well, remember, when I first moved into my home, the property lacked a single flower. Yet magically, within a few years after I moved in, hollyhocks had started to spring up all around my yard although I never planted them. As if to exclaim the power of our universe and the glories of Mother Nature, dozens of tall, healthy sunflowers suddenly stretched skyward along the side of my driveway.

At the time, not a single home throughout Northwest Nevada and in all of Reno looked anything close to my house. Flowers similar to those in the "Friendly Village" had arrived mysteriously and in abundance, but only after I purchased the property.

Stunned, with my spirit grabbed by this unexpected revelation, I sat down all alone in the center of my home library. A peaceful, soothing aura enveloped me. The undeniable, unbelievable, discovery made me realize that thirty-five years earlier as I child reading "Friendly Village," I had dreamed of the very home where I'm living today. Deep down, I realized that while attending Mrs. Beck's third-grade class I had begun to comprehend that having a cottage with a white picket fence and a wishing well was possible and maybe dreams do come true. More important, as an adult reading these old books I realized that hard work, determination, and visualization can enable each of us to reach across the stars, past the Milky Way and into the center of distant galaxies.

"Patty, this is your house!" Many people exclaimed as soon as I showed them this school book in subsequent years. "You have made your dreams come true!"

For me the trick had been finding a way to make positive transitions happen.

Hollywood movie stars from the 1920s through the 1950s lived in the lap of luxury.

To be a film starlet meant freedom from financial worries, far away from common struggles that nagged everyday folks from the Great Depression and beyond. The most popular movie actresses from child star Shirley Temple to steamy sensation Myrna Loy got buckets filled with mailed postcards and fan letters from around the world.

By contrast, while en route from San Jose to Los Angeles in my parents' run-down car, I was once again a mere weed, an insignificant nobody, a mere waif of an insignificant child.

With my little heart fading fast due to a lack of sunlight and ineffective nurturing, I saw nothing but grimy gray haze when LA finally came into view. This, of course, was the home of Hollywood, the place from which the stars shined bright, where pizzazz, big band music and all-night dancing gained additional fame on the Silver Screen. Bright lights, lavish galas, world premieres, Oscar ceremonies and red carpet extravaganzas caught the attention of the entire world—except for me.

Oblivious to such sparkly lifestyles, when that summer began I shuffled about as if my heart had been pulled out of my chest. I felt hallow, as if my soul had been carved away and somehow lost without anyone ever realizing what had happened.

If you have ever seen a sad child, a pathetic child, a little girl who had lost all hope, perhaps I was that person. Although with parents that loved me, in my mind I was truly alone.

Upon our initial arrival, my parents spent a brief visit with one of my dad's many war buddies.

Without any problem whatsoever, my parents both landed jobs. Rather than a house as I would have preferred, this time they got us a typically raunchy room at yet another motel on a busy primary route, Sepulveda Boulevard. Even on supposedly clear days, the Los Angeles haze made me feel as if stuck in inescapable quicksand. Shortly after our arrival, mother started hunting for a full-time child care service, which I considered an attempt to put me in storage like a piece of furniture.

"There's no need to pay a babysitter," I said, unusually defiant.

"I can take care of myself," I said. I don't need a baby sitter."

"But, Patty, there are chores to be done, and..."

Refusing to take "No" for an answer, I immediately volunteered to do the dishes every day, and keep everything tidy. At least to me, this seemed reasonable and easily done. Although a typically crappy unit, the place had a suitable kitchenette and even a fairly decent TV. The summer had just begun, with the prospect of school more than three months away.

I resumed my place in the world as a little girl—although invisible to just about everyone. Forgetting the fact that I still possessed an exuberant nature, as far as I could tell—excluding my parents and Grandparents—no one would ever care if I lived or died. No one cares about little girls who live in a different stinky motel room every week or so, or at least my senses told me. No one gives a hoot about stupid kids who spend most of their time riding in run-down cars and rickety old pickup trucks. And, the only place to go fishing was far-far from that wretched, stinking, scummy little place that my parents had chosen with little thought.

Left with no other option, I knew that we were supposedly living in the town filled with movie stars. Somehow my inner senses realized that those Hollywood icons lived in mansions somewhere nearby. Fame. Fortune. Fabulous fun. Financial freedom—what the hell do they know? Those popular film icons failed to give me any reason for thought. At that point, I had never even dreamed about enjoying such lifestyles. Dreams were for people with wealth and steady jobs. Dreams were for rugged, handsome men and sensational looking gals, anyone who had a potentially bright future.

Far from the imaginative, positive-minded child that I had been such a short while before, I realized that my only daily venture outside the motel room would be for a five-minute jaunt. Just run down to the corner store to buy a quick snack. Bored out of my mind, I flipped on the motel room TV.

Wow!

My whole life suddenly changed for the better, and my creative fantasy world clicked back into full gear. Non-stop movies from the 1920s, 1930s and 1940s played without letup, one after the other.

I suddenly found myself in a world crammed with wealthy people, attending parties—the men sporting tuxedos much of the time, while socially acceptable gals sang like sparrows and danced in a heavenly way, as if their feet were those of angels.

From that point forward, I became glued to the TV every day, from the moment my parents left for work until after they returned home. By the first several days, I yearned for these times by myself—actually preferring to live as a loner, at least then.

Yes, Hollywood movie stars live glamorous lives on and off screen. They drive fancy cars, and wear the best clothing. Depending on the situation, they're marvelously funny or appropriately serious. If the situation arises, film sensations will shoot each other, wear cowboy outfits, hop up high on to horses or blast down Japanese war planes.

I was now focussed on movie stars, like sex goddess Mae West, famous for her bawdy double entendres, salty language and aggressive demeanor. Olivia de Havilland always moved with the grace and charm necessary to become a popular mystical leading lady. Irene Dunn knocked your socks off in such films as "Love Affair" and "I Remember Mama."

Before long in my little mind I became a movie star, but more specifically the characters that these beautiful women portrayed. I became Franciska Gaal, the alluring Hungarian cabaret artist from real life, as she tantalized leading man Fredric March in "The Buccaneer." As Elisa Lancaster in "Bride of Frankenstein," I mesmerized audiences with my elusive character playing opposite that perennial monster Boris Karloff.

A mere two weeks into that summer, I leapt without any reservation whatsoever into my education about society. I became one with the movies, every Andy Hardy series film, all the screwball comedies, the dramas, the romances, the musicals and even bloody war films. Along the way, I learned and began to fully appreciate the distinctive clothing styles, furniture, automobiles, accents and societal behaviors of each specific decade.

I became the alluring, magnetizing and ravishingly beautiful Claudette Colbert in the 1934 Cecil B. DeMille production of "Cleopatra." Anyone who saw me as Eleanor Powell in the 1939 MGM musical Honolulu would have been sufficiently amazed with my undeniable star power and alluring movements. Anyone who saw me as the dedicated, brilliant and charmingly cute Jean Arthur opposite Jimmy Stewart in the 1939 Frank Capra classic "Mister Smith Goes to Washington" might have asked me for my autograph afterward, and I might have even taken the time to sign a movie ticket for them.

The culture, the music, the sights, and the sounds. Everything kept building up into a fabulous crescendo. That TV pulled me into all new worlds, vastly different cultures—exploring various lands, societies and periods that I had never heard about before.

And then, there were the ballroom dance movies, particularly the many films starring Fred Astaire and Ginger Rogers. That gentleman held me in his reliable arms, as I played the role of Ginger. He danced me all around the motel room as their movies played. He danced with me as I scurried from the kitchenette to the front of the TV, back in forth in continuous motions. Acting admirably as Ginger's reliable and talented stand-in, I held Fred's comforting hands as he waltzed with me in the 1933 classic "Flying Down to Rio," and during the next five years in "The Gay Divorcee," "Roberta," "Top Hat," "Follow the Feet," "Swing Time," and "Shall We Dance."

Thankfully, since the LA television station played these movies without any commercial interruption, I always had plenty of time to hug and kiss my many leading men exactly as any particular script dictated.

My star power wowed the entire world as Judy Garland in the 1941 musical sensation "Babes on Broadway." Re-energized, no longer lonely, and once again finding myself as a certified "happy girl" in so-called real life, I enjoyed playing my romantic role as the alluring, stunningly gorgeous Ingrid Bergman opposite Bing Crosby in a 1945 Classic, "The Bells of St. Mary's." Naturally, since by this point I was in high demand from Hollywood's top studios, I eventually buckled in and finally agreed to stun audiences with my ravishing, sizzling performance as June Allyson opposite Peter Lawford in the 1947 MGM musical "Good News"—a remake of a 1930 version, where I had played Bessie Love's character opposite Cliff Edwards.

By mid-summer of that year, my parents still lacked any idea whatsoever that I had become a certified, high-paid, glamorous Hollywood movie star. They failed to notice that I was no longer as depressed, that my creative talents had rebounded to the point of unabridged, boundless joy.

I kept another secret as well.

My folks also lacked any hint that I had become an interior designer and a ladies' fashion expert. I preferred the Art Deco style of architecture and clothing styles from many of my favorite 1920s and 1930s films. I knew exactly what kind of home a suitable woman of high society should live in, and how she should behave in social situations such as fancy high-end dinners. Just as important, a woman of any moral character and tantalizing charisma should know the perfect things to say to a man, if he tries to woo you, swirl you out on a dance floor, or whisk you away on a worldwide ocean cruise.

Stunningly attractive ladies such as I know how to pick a suitable husband. He must be handsome, super rich, courageous, adventurous, highly masculine, confident, brave and suitably unpredictable—plus a fantastic kisser.

"Are you sure that you're okay, Patty." Mother asked me one day.

"Sure, I'm fine. I'm doing all the dishes; keeping the place clean."

"That's not what I meant. You mean to tell me that all you do all day long is watch TV?"

"I'm reading some, too."

"Pat."

The mere mention of that word "Pat" signaled that unwanted fireworks were headed my way. The only time my parents called me that, a term I dislike, was whenever I happened to get into trouble.

"I'm not in trouble, am I?"

"Well, if I grounded you, you'd just have to stay here—and that's just what you're doing now anyway. All I'm trying to say is that there has been some sort of change in you, although I'm not sure exactly what."

"I'm just looking forward to the new school year," I said, telling the truth, since in all honestly my heart always yearned for education—if and when such a transition might occur. At the time, I lacked any inkling of course of the fact that I would someday look back at that as one of the best summers of my childhood by far—essentially locked into a motel room for three months straight. What other little "motel trash" girls from that era got an opportunity to spend virtually all of their hot summer days glued in front a TV, watching only classic old movies?

My new-found film star skills benefited me and my father as well as that summer ended. Blessed with poise, a far more mature attitude and a new-found wisdom, I went with dad to a party south of Los Angeles hosted by one of his war buddies.

"These people are..." Dad said over and over, amid the partying. He used a profane word to describe these party-goers, most of them wealthy individuals. "Just because all these people are rich, they think they're something special? Well they can..."

Father's offensive language intensified the drunker he became. With me by his side, he stayed away from most party-goers, watching them from across the back yard of a huge estate. From the way dad slurred his speech that night, his bothersome behavior and his intense anger, I could tell he would never make a suitable Hollywood movie star.

Blessed with poise that I had lacked just four months earlier, I managed to convince father to leave. He finally agreed to take me back to the motel, where mother waited for us. She had chosen not to attend the gathering, apparently sensing his bawdy behavior.

"Rich people stink," dad said, slurring as we cruised the final block to the motel. "Who do they think they are, anyway?"

Just like Myrna Loy would have done, or perhaps even movie sensation Bette Davis, I chose to keeping my mouth shut. This proved the correct move on my part. Sometimes when dealing with drop-dead drunks it's better to say as little as possible at the height of inebriation. After all, I had already learned that characters played by movie stars were experts at dealing with intense pain—both emotional and physical.

"I love you dad," I said, kissing him briefly on the cheek as he opened the motel room door. As the subsequent years passed, dad remained a celebrity, but only in my eyes and perhaps much of the time from the perspective of my mother as well.

With each new summer, and as the decades clicked past I never forgot my higher education thanks to TV that summer. I used those films as a model for my life, dictating everything from how to behave to fashions and home preferences.

Exactly forty-two years after that fateful summer, I became a certified "dead movie star." Literally hundreds of people can verify this transition, which they saw with their own eyes at a public park near the heart of downtown Reno.

That night in 1998 I was dressed up to look exactly like movie star Carole Lombard, while Wayne went as Clark Gable—the energetic hunk of a man whose most famous roles included Rhett Butler in the 1939 Civil War epic film "Gone With the Wind."

We pulled off this act in full view of everyone at the Reno Philharmonic's Second Annual Pops on the River Gala Fundraiser on the banks of the Truckee River.

Right after learning of the event, I rushed to purchase tickets as soon as possible. During the month prior, I contacted several of our friends and asked them to join us at my table—but only if they dressed as dead movie stars as well.

At the time, several hundred people attended the annual event from the early evening to a few hours after sundown. The second Saturday of each July, all participants decide their own individual theme for their 12-person dinner tables. Guests bring their own food and beverages, while most hosts and their friends install lavish decorations—almost everyone wearing interesting costumes to match their chosen theme.

The theme that I created, "Dead Movie Stars," along with our personal guests, Groucho and Harpo Marx, William Powell and Myrna Loy, plus other dead Hollywood icons was recognized by others for our creativity. Each of us wore authentic costumes and make-up, playing our roles fabulously, if I do say so myself.

The philharmonic proceeded to play numerous classical selections, followed by a variety of patriotic American standards from "God Bless America" to the "National Anthem" and early 20th Century marching songs by George M. Cohan.

With a bang, and a clash and a crescendo of applause the table that

I designed ran away with the evening's Best Theme Award. At least in a light-hearted sense, my hard work studying movies through the summer of 1955 paid off big time.

Unsatisfied with just one victory, the following year my table emerged as another sensation, although several other hosts had selected the exact same image at random.

The decision to host a "Beverly Hillbillies" theme came as a no-brainer to many people throughout the community, because at the time Max Baer Jr., a co-star of the 1960s and 1970s TV sitcom had proposed a casino in Reno themed on the show. I played "Granny," and Wayne did his best to look like the muscular "Jethro Bodine" character that Baer had played. Although at least three Pops on the River tables had a similar theme, my gang pulled off a coup. Thanks to Wayne's entertainment industry connections we were able to invite Baer, the actual celebrity, who immediately accepted our invitation.

Standing beside the real-live Jethro, my husband came off looking more like Bozo the Clown. But at least we all had a grand time that evening.

During the previous several years and even after that one occasion I met and associated with my share of celebrities including "red-blooded" Hollywood movie stars. For the most part—except for one major exception—I discovered that actual, certified, A-list film actors are just like the rest of us. Flawed. Flesh and blood. Normal. Real. Likeable and plenty of fun to be around, at least most of them anyway.

These revelations failed to shatter the mystique that my mind had created back during that long hot summer watching TV in a Los Angeles motel room.

By this time I learned perhaps just as well as anyone that creativity and the illusions of fun, comedy, drama and everything in between helps make life worth living.

Long before meeting Wayne, I even had a internationally famous celebrity try to wiggle me into bed—but that's quite a different matter, worth telling about later.

Sure enough, within a year of our initial arrival in Los Angeles. We finally stopped at what Dad hoped would be an ideal watering hole in Sunland 19 miles north of LA.

We needed acceptable accommodations. So, dad bought us our first trailer, actually a 23-foot-long, 7-foot wide fish bowl built in 1947 called a Spartan. Father then found a suitable park facility where other poor fish congregated, each living in its own miniscule trailer.

Mom helped choose this location because she wanted me be close to an acceptable school. Vastly different from motel living, this new type of accommodation presented other unique challenges.

My parents snuggled at night in a couch that they converted into a bed. Looking back today, I realize that our new home was probably no bigger than a very small living room of a home from one of the movies I saw during that summer.

Cramped together like sardines squeezed into a tiny can, we did our best with a kitchen no bigger than the front seat of our truck. My bed was tucked behind a miniscule space at the back, just beside a nook and cranny where I kept my own little things, like my drawing implements and coloring books.

Our Spartan lacked a bathroom. This proved a major setback hampered by biological functioning requirements. So, whenever struck by the need to "go," the sparse accommodations dictated that we use a communal restroom and shower—shared by many residents of the trailer park. As a result, like mother and father I strived to avoid guzzling more fluids than absolutely necessary during the final few hours before sleep time.

To this day, I remain amazed at how mother managed to get so much done in so little space.

I probably owned three dresses, just enough to appear as a cute little girl every time I gathered with other children at school. Each night and then again in the mornings mother worked diligently ensuring that I had the right amount of pin curls. Judging by mom's reactions, I must have looked cute as a button.

Each day mother went to work in order to congregate with other adult females at a suitable key-punching job. Dad would congregate somewhere in LA, working diligently to refashion man-made metal scraps—everything from crumpled bumpers and dinged hubcaps to scraped car doors.

I never griped about the situation. My attitude remained "this is what is," or "what kind of situation will my latest school become?"

Even so, at that juncture my parents and I had absolutely no inkling of a notion that a child molester and a potential killer—had suddenly approached near our trailer park. With the suddenness of a stalker, a man that appeared to me as if a serial murderer had me in his sights.

With mother and father away at their work one afternoon, the predator came straight in my direction. From my view his only objective was to obliterate me, perhaps after causing as much pain as possible.

Naturally, during those final moments of his approach, escape became my Number One priority. But how?

An orchestra played amid a picture-perfect sunset. Many of the world's wealthiest people, mostly billionaires had invited us to a Shakespeare Festival fundraiser on the northeast shore of Lake Tahoe.

I rested my hand atop Wayne's as an orchestra played Mozart classics. Food servers satisfied our every need as we proposed a toast to our many friends.

We had accepted the personal invitation to this $500-a-plate function from one of the 1999 event's organizers, back when I was oh so very young at a mere 52 years old.

Our personal host and good friend was Marilyn Strauss, a Tony Award-winning producer of a smash Broadway hit during the 1970s. Like other guests, we wore sneakers due to the beach's soft, all-encompassing sands. All men wore snappy tuxedos, while the women sported a vast array of high-end gowns.

At the time Wayne wrote a weekly society column for the region's mainstream newspaper. Everyone wanted to get to know him as much as he yearned to learn about their magnetic, interesting lives.

By this point at age 43, Wayne, a former Editor-on-Loan to "USA Today," had already worked at his society columnist position for two years. Attending about four parties or major social functions every week, year-round had become second nature to us.

This evolution had steadily evolved in my life because I took specific, positive and decisive action in the decade before marrying Wayne. During that period I met and became friends with best-selling author Leo F. Buscaglia, whose many books about the overwhelming and nurturing power of love gripped readers worldwide.

After initially meeting Buscagila at a Sierra Arts Foundation event, he taught me about how each of us can make his or her dreams come true. We need to fully envision and accept the positive reality of our desires, goals and aspirations in everything from family life, to professions, finances, friendships and lifestyle.

At the time, as a divorcee who had enjoyed my fair share of relationships with handsome, successful men, I lacked a solid bond with any guy whom I considered a potential mate. Deep down during those final few years before meeting Wayne, maybe I had been lonely. Perhaps my spirit yearned for the type of man who could provide, the specific skills and natural qualities necessary to satisfy a particular woman's unique needs.

So, in keeping with Buscaglia's many wise and timeless lessons, one day I sat alone in my living room and wrote down all the attributes that I yearned for in a man.

Kindness. Sharing. Empathy, Forgiveness. A positive-thinking, forward-moving force. In many ways, I yearned with every beat of my heart to find and become a lifetime mate with a good, stable, solid provider. I needed a man who would never leave me, someone that I could share with, travel with, laugh with, and tease, and have fun, and explore.

Fine relaxing dinners, nights at the movies, reading together, watching TV, and non-stop adventure were just a few things a wrote down.

So, yes, I met Wayne. But little did we know that just seven years after that black-tie banquet on Lake Tahoe's shore my husband would be living in a string of seedy motels..

I would be alone in my home, struggling to survive. Our lives would be shattered, tattered into tiny unrecognizable pieces in 2007.

His book ghost-writing business temporarily imploded, due to a lack of attention. In his absence, I lived alone in the home I cherished, my heart shattered into a million pieces.

Chapter 15

Within three months after moving with my parents into the Spartan trailer, alone one afternoon I scurried along an alleyway near a dentist's office.

Shortly after leaving school, little girls like me preferred to use such shortcuts to get to the corner store for tasty goodies. A dutiful and good child, I had taken this route many times. But on this particular day, a shark appeared in the form of a man who approached me on foot. This happened after I stopped to look at the guy. Curious, I had watched him park his white sedan.

Right away while walking toward me, I noticed that this fellow definitely had the teeth of a Great White Shark. He grinned as if the evil queen in Snow White, striving as best he could to act friendly.

"Hi," he said, sweet-like.

To me right away something seemed amiss. My parents had always taught me to avoid talking with strangers at all costs.

Stunned, I stood motionless—not yet struck with any thought of the urgent need to run. If she wants any chance at survival, a good little girl needs to scurry away as fast as she can. A crafty young child needs to trick her assailant. Or, better yet, quickly bite, scratch, and otherwise maim your potential assailant with lightning speed before darting away in a sudden escape.

"You don't know what you're missing," the strange man said to me, and at this point I finally noticed that he wore alligator shoes.

"What do you mean? I'm not supposed to..."

Obviously far away from his usual environment, this guy moved his hand toward me as if to indicate he wanted to give something.

"I'm going to the grocery store!" I said. "And, I'm not supposed to talk to strangers."

"Oh, you can take this quarter, can't you?"

"No!" I held firm to my position. "I can't take anything!"

Every day, many big fish gobble up smaller fish. This is part of nature. It happens so much that such deaths never make newspaper headlines. We're talking dog-eat-dog, buzzard-eat-buzzard and in my case big man steals away tiny girl. With my parents at the moment doing their regular day jobs, what was I to do? The hundreds of Hollywood movies that I had seen the previous summer at the LA motel room never featured scenes such as this. None of those films had anything to do with stories about monsters that snatched up little girls. Even the many picture books that I enjoyed refrained from such gory details, except perhaps for the likes of Hansel & Gretel of fairy tale fame, or Snow White, or Little Red Riding Hood, or Goldilocks. My mind raced for an answer, realizing that none of these fables featured sharks such as this guy.

"I have to go!" I proclaimed, as the man persisted, taking another step toward me.

If I screamed, would someone come to help? If I called out for my father, would he race to the rescue, turning into "Lucky Larry," the war hero who knew how to use guns with a vengeance? Kicking this man strategically with sudden force in his personal spot never became an option, since at the time I had not yet discovered such tactics. And, if I hollered for my mother, would she somehow ride up to lasso the guy as if she were Old West show superstar Dale Evans?

"Take this," the shark said, increasingly persistent.

"I have to go! My mommy is waiting for me right now, and I have to get home."

The man moved his hand toward my waist.

Too startled to run, all I could do was speak in the loudest, most authoritative voice that a little child can manage: "If I don't come home pretty soon, my mother is going to come and find me. So I have to go."

Before I had time to realize what was happening, the man tucked a single quarter into the cummerbund of my dress.

Overcome by an uncomfortable, eerie feeling, I immediately left him, scurrying to the little neighborhood store. After spending as much time as possible inside the establishment, I finally ventured outside—careful to look in every direction imaginable in those shark-infested waters.

I arrived home safely within a few minutes, fully aware from that day forward that danger lurked around every corner. Not even my father or my mother would be able to help when future hardships occurred.

"That's your house, Grandma!"

My granddaughter Eva said while filled with delight, as soon as she flipped through the "Friendly Village" school book.

"No, that's an illustration that women in New York created in the 1930s," I told Eva, standing beside her in my upstairs library—as our family enjoyed a picnic down below in the yard. "Those artists had never seen this house."

Naturally, I felt great delight on this occasion, the first time Eva and her 10-year-old brother Mickey had been to my home in seven years. Joy filled my heart throughout that evening, as Wayne handled barbecue chores, and Mickey enjoyed playing croquet with his father—my 44-year-old son, Chris.

On that day Wayne and I had been back together as a married couple for nearly four years. An internationally renowned sculptor, Chris lived in the Czech Republic with his children and wife, Hana. Seeing everyone enjoy such a great time on that warm summer evening in my yard soothed my soul and put my mind at ease.

With a yard nearly as big as a small city park, this emerged as a spectacular opportunity to enjoy outdoor activities that enabled everyone to bond and to create memories.

Still together upstairs with Eva, I explained to her my theory that the book's illustrators had fashioned their drawing of the home and wishing well after houses that they had either seen in New York State or in the South. Remember, the home identical to mine along with the same white picket fence is on Page 210 under the heading: "Away Down South."

"Grandma, I love this house," Eva said, reminding me of my own exuberant mannerisms as a child. "I love this yard; it's magical."

"I hope the people who tour my home next month feel the same," I said, hugging her. "Wayne and I are busier than you can imagine getting prepared.

Someone interrupted, yelling up from downstairs and urging us to come back outside and rejoin the fun.

More than ever before, my female intuition told me of the pressing need to leave a lasting legacy.

This book, in essence—or at least so I hoped—would emerge as my legacy to my children and grandchildren, for them to pass on to subsequent generations.

How would readers feel about me, about Wayne, about my family and about their own families and about themselves as well—as my entire story unfolded, fully and without any reservations whatsoever?

Everything changed for me the moment I laid eyes on Stephen Jefferson, a student in my fifth grade class at Sunland Elementary School on Hillrose Street.

His whispery brown hair and those eyes bluer than the vast Pacific Ocean made me blush. It wasn't so much Stephen's smooth voice that attracted me to him, but somehow his demeanor. The lad somehow seemed very near to me at all times, but also extremely far away as well. I felt as if stuck on him, although he remained a trillion miles away.

We never spoke a word to each other during those times when my stomach started to feel just a bit funny whenever I was near him.

The transition happened so slowly that at first I failed to recognize what was happening. I was having my first bonified crush.

Did this cute guy even know that I existed?

Hopefully Stephen had noticed me every afternoon when I watched him, pretending not to stare. My girly and wandering mind did somersaults, while watching him at recess, playing kickball with his buddies.

Crush!

Perhaps Stephen might have noticed as I checked my first-ever book out of a library, stories about Abraham Lincoln's life as a child. And maybe this guy even appreciated when our teacher, Mr. Houghton, had convinced the school's administrators to push me up a full grade in school so that I could study with children my age. This all worked out wonderful, since the transition had put me and Stephen in the same class.

My grades, reading, and math abilities all improved markedly. I now had a more solid, steady and stabilized course in life.

Could it have been true that innocent, delicate love made this all happen? Did love transform the lives of other little girls and women as well? Surely my favorite female stars from those Hollywood movies were right when they spoke of these emotions. But the famous actresses could not possibly have known the entire truth about love. Unlike I was at the time, movie starlets surely never had their stomachs feel this way when near the guys that they adored. Jane Russell and Marilyn Monroe never felt this light headed, this dizzy, this wonderful. No, those spectacularly gorgeous movie starlets could never possibly understand what I felt—even though I was not yet even a teenager.

How does it happen? Can this be just the beginning? Do all little girls know how glorious having a crush can feel?

If all this signals what romance is about, then I want as much of it as possible. Why in the world no one ever told me about love before, I'll probably never fully understand. Why does magnetism need to be such a big, huge secret?

Suddenly, our teacher, Mr. Houghton, arranged an annual school dance for our classroom. And, oh my God! The man posted a list of pairings, each girl matched with a certain boy. The virtual roulette wheel, the lucky ace card and the stupendous lottery windfall all came in at once for me that day. The teacher had paired me with Stephen.

Now, right away this decision seemed logical and sensible to me. No other choice would have made sense.

Finally, when the appropriate time finally arrived, Stephen held me gently—and somehow firmly as well—in his comforting arms as the first dance began.

I could tell that the boy, my handsome knight in shining armor, was excited beyond belief. I knew with all my heart that he cherished me, too, or at the very least he liked me a lot. This was only what they call a "crush," right? Stephen never looked me right in the eye, but I could tell that he adored me. He never made an awkward move, but I could tell that he was super-athletic just like me. And he never held me in the precise way that other boys and men would later in life, everyone with varying degrees of firmness, kindness, masculinity and charisma. But of course, for the moment, all those future excitements didn't matter a hoot. All my senses told me that Stephen really liked me and I liked him, although we never particularly knew how to tell each other.

Needless to say, I went home from the party with a hop, a skip and a jump.

More than ever before, I realized that boys will be boys, and that I finally had my feet on solid ground. My entire aura and body became grounded into the earth forevermore from that day forward, always to remain a girl, and then a teen, and a woman. From that period forward, being female made me strong even when I might have felt weak. Being female made me grow, even during subsequent times when I might have felt scared due to hardships. And, being female made me who I am today, an emotionally strong, loving and caring family matriarch.

A woman, tried and true, always moving forward and progressing through life.

Everything in the love department had started with that childhood crush on Stephen.

Angels beam with lights so bright that your eyes at first have difficulty seeing them. The essence of eternal love, kindness and sympathy permeates from such omniscient, spiritual beings. Anyone who has ever seen or heard an angel describes an overwhelming power that sparks both the essence of complete awe and a full acceptance of faith.

People who appreciate these eternal spirits find themselves thankful for God's healing force.

Throughout history, many people have sworn that angels appeared before them suddenly, showing grace, our Creator's everlasting love, and unlimited empathy.

Some cultures have taught that certain angels have wings while carrying swords, prepared to enter battles on behalf of those of us who suffer. Believers in God's boundless grace have described many heavenly angels, most notably Gabriel, Michael and Raphael. Many of today's believers swear that such beings generate miracles, often just at a critical point when all reason for hope seems lost.

To help put this into perspective, picture me as an 11-year-old fifth grade student at the end of the school year as spring edged into summer. At the time, I had absolutely no idea whatsoever that two heavenly, love-filled angels would suddenly appear to me that summer. The event would eventually change my life for the better.

Up to that point, I had no experience in the Christian faith whatsoever, other than attending Sunday school for a few weeks several years earlier when we lived in Idaho. Both self-described "agnostics," my parents never attempted to take me to church or to any type of worship services.

At the time, at least through that spring while living in our trailer in Sunland, I lacked any inkling whatsoever that angels truly existed. All I knew for sure was that I behaved like a good little girl, and that my parents still loved me with all their hearts.

Around this period my body was just beginning to transform out of what I would later call the "ugly-duckling" phase of my development. From ages ten through well into the following year, my gangly, awkward appearance made me feel out of place while pulling back just a bit at my self-confidence.

Before the angel appeared in my life, during April of that year my parents broke some delightful news that left me excited and overjoyed—

seemingly beyond belief. My parents had arranged for me to spend the entire summer with Grandma Eve and Grandpa Oscar, 505 miles north in Reno.

My excitement steadily intensified with each passing week until my parents took me to Reno, to drop me off for my summer stay with my Grandparents. Within a few days, we headed north for the journey back to the Biggest Little City in the World.

Exactly 50 years later during the same time of year I visited Grandma in her small room at Hearthstone of Northern Nevada in Sparks, just west of Reno. At 104 years old, she remained as bright, cheerful and sharp-minded as ever. As Mother Nature commands, her legs had given out, making any attempts at walking extremely difficult and her body slowed to a turtle's pace. But other than that she seemed as mentally spry, vibrant and talkative as ever before.

"I love you so much, Grandma," I said, trying to hold her hand.

"Why don't you take me to lunch, Patty? I want to play bingo, and you never take me to the casino as much as I want."

"I promise, Grandma, that I will, and..."

Unexpectedly, tears welled up in my eyes. I trembled ever so slightly, trying to keep my composure while using both my hands to hold gently onto her right arm. All these emotions kept swirling inside me. I wanted to tell Grandma in the right and perfect way imaginable how much I desperately loved her; how much she meant to me; how much she had changed my life for the better; how much I truly appreciated the fact that she had made a positive impact on me as a child—creating the pathway for a wondrous life.

Then and there, while gently leaning over to kiss Grandma on her cheek, I fully realized that—yes, indeed—she had been the angel that suddenly appeared to me that summer way back when I was just eleven years old. She had been the angel that opened up the spectacular world of possibilities to me. She had been the angel that had catapulted my soul into a universe filled with bright stars and endlessly fantastic possibilities. And, yes, she had been the angel that had spread her fluffy, light wings open wide to welcome me into a world of adult-oriented activities.

"I want you to understand what I'm saying, Grandma."

"I love you," I briefly kissed her cheek again, striving to emphasize my point.

"I love you, too, honey. Please take me to lunch and bingo."

I sat on a chair next to Grandma as she lay in her nursing home bed, the head portion cranked in a half-vertical position so that she could sit up. In recent months I had taken Grandma on occasional jaunts to casinos, where she often ended up getting away with plenty of loot after playing bingo and penny-slot machines. Surely this must have upset the casino management to no end, the very idea that a 104-year-old woman would legally walk out the doors with her winnings—sometimes only a few bucks, but hundreds of dollars at a pop on numerous other occasions.

On this particularly afternoon, though, I feared the end of Grandma's time here on earth would soon swoop upon us. After all, at her age a person had less than a 100-to-1 shot of surviving into any subsequent day. Thus, while holding this delicate woman's hand I wanted her to fully realize and appreciate the fact of how much I adored her.

Yes, without "sainting" the memory of this woman, refraining from putting her on any kind of undeserved pedestal, I knew beyond the shadow of a doubt that she had been my angel—along with my late Grandpa Oscar—during the entire summer of 1958.

Thanks to Grandma's fortitude, devotion and unstoppable caring during that three-month span she became the epitome of any angel that God could ever possibly create.

For me the span from June through August became a magical time, setting the pathway in life for me to decide what I wanted to become, my hopes for where I would live and my lifestyle—everything from dining preferences to fashion, nightlife and the type of home that I would eventually purchase.

Upon our arrival in Reno, Grandma and Grandpa had already landed co-manager jobs at the Town House Motor Lodge, at the time a notable high-end motel in Northwest Nevada. This marked a significant change from all those seedy, run-down motels where I had lived with my parents. Just as impressive, during this period Reno lacked any significant hotels other than the Mapes and El Cortez.

As the nationwide preference for lengthy road travel suddenly surged to all-new heights, Reno became the premiere place in all of Nevada for tourists to stay—many while traveling back and forth by car between the West Coast and East Coast. Meantime, keep in mind that Las Vegas was just on the verge of its Boomtown phase, several years before surpassing its Northern Nevada rival in size and fame.

At the time, I had been fully unaware that Grandma was an angel, although I already recognized her as a fantastic woman. As a Worthy Grand Matron of the Eastern Star, she wore gowns so glorious that just looking at her momentarily took your breath away. Grandpa drew plenty of well-deserved attention of his own, Grand Master of a prominent Reno Masonic Lodge.

Overjoyed upon my arrival, my Grandparents immediately began spoiling me rotten. Immediately putting the "trailer-trash" lifestyle behind me, I suddenly found myself being taken to lavish dinners at all of the Reno-area's most spectacular expensive restaurants at least two and sometimes even three times a week.

The most highly acclaimed, high-end dining establishments of the time eagerly greeted us. At my urging, we went to only the most extravagant restaurants, particularly Eugene's, Vario's, The Lancer and the famed Christmas Tree halfway up the Mount Rose Highway between Reno and Lake Tahoe.

"Come here, Patty," Grandpa asked me one afternoon in the office of my Grandparents' motel. "Let's go outside. I want you to see this."

My eyes started twirling like spin-tops the moment I saw a real live lion sitting in the back of a pickup truck. A man standing beside the vehicle, The owner of the Christmas Tree Restaurant encouraged me to pet the animal—which wasn't roaring, at least for the moment. By this point thanks to Tarzan movies that I had watched in a Los Angeles motel the previous summer, I realized that such creatures could easily eat an entire person in the blink of an eye.

With Grandpa's blessing, I petted this lion which was a favorite attraction at the Christmas Tree Restaurant.

"Come on up," the man said to Grandpa. "Bring your granddaughter and your wife tonight. It's our treat."

We jumped at the chance. As soon as I walked with Grandma and Grandpa into the Christmas Tree, two lovable Saint Bernard dogs came up to me, each begging for a pet. Relaxed and fully at ease, I walked outside to the back of the restaurant and petted the lion for a few minutes.

Then, in keeping with our usual custom, Grandma and Grandpa enjoyed a leisurely pre-dinner cocktail while I sipped a delightful non-alcoholic Shirley Temple, often called a "Pinky-Winky." A delicious steak dinner with all the trimmings soon followed, as I began a brand new custom of discussing my various favorite restaurants and menu selections. All of the sudden I started to develop into a mature girl—a budding young woman, actually—gradually steeped in fine culture, cuisine, the arts and entertainment.

Like I say, it wasn't until years later when I fully realized that my Grandma had been truly an angel whether she realized this or not. Her kindness, devotion and patience with me held no boundaries, imposed no unreasonable rules, and gave only encouragement.

Suddenly, she introduced me to the world of fashion, and I realized that although just 55 at the time, in my eyes she glistened as brightly as those famed movie starlets. Her smile rivaled that of movie star Lana Turner, and her overall complexion easily could have put sex symbol Rita Hayworth to shame.

Daytime activities transformed me into a virtual locomotive of efficient energy. From the lunch hour to late afternoon I played in the Town House swimming pool with a maze of children. These kids were on the road traveling with their parents or other relatives, who spent those daytime hours gambling in downtown casinos.

All this splashing and non-stop laughing began a few hours after I had slept in late. Treating me like a spoiled princess, Grandpa would lavish me with our favorite breakfasts of dunk-eggs and toast.

Yes, I had evolved into a real-live, All-American, boundless and increasingly sophisticated little girl. I knew this instinctively with every beat of my heart.

This inner knowledge increased full-force within a few weeks when Grandma and Grandpa took me on a stupendous, surprise six-day trip from Reno to San Francisco. This marked a significant difference from back when I traveling with my parents amid strange-looking skyscrapers in the City by the Bay.

This time, Grandma and Grandma made the experience much more vibrant and eye-opening than I possibly could have hoped for.

There, entire new experiences swept over me like a wind filled with nothing but glittery and charming sensations. Every night we dined at the fabulous restaurants, even more lavish and stylish than those in Reno. Watching the authentic rickety fishing boats come and go from Fisherman's Wharf, gazing with wondrous eyes at seagulls, chatting with a huge variety of street vendors, and leisurely strolling through Chinatown all captured every aspect of my senses.

More than ever before, my sensations of sound, smell, taste, touch and a blazing inner zest for life itself catapulted into a new universe. The crisp, vibrant and occasionally spicy aromas coupled with soothing, cool evening winds wrapped me up as if I were a tiny angel myself—warmed by the boundless love given by my Grandparents.

Angels do all these things to people, especially for little children that yearn for much-needed adventure. Angels can open up your world to new possibilities. Angels can pick you up from a mundane world, and then gently set you down into an exciting land loaded with fun possibilities. Angels can bring diverse, educational ventures straight into the heart of other interesting cultures. And, as I learned first-hand that summer, an angel doesn't necessarily realize that she is such a heavenly being, a spirit comprised of nothing but love.

Could my Grandma possibly have known that she was an angel, when taking me with Grandpa to the huge, spectacular Ice Follies skating show during that trip? Could she possibly have realized that she was an angel, when she took me into Macy's at Union Square—lavishing me with clothing so stylish and timely that my heart burst with pride? And, could Grandma possibly have known that she was an angel, in virtually everything that she did for me—from meals and playtime to good nutrition?

Perhaps even more important, an angel takes time to put faith into the positive possibilities of a maturing child. Sure enough, with Grandpa's blessing, she allowed me to walk through downtown Reno every so often—giving me enough money to eat at fun restaurants at the time, such as The Wigwam that sold the world's yummiest pies. At the El Cortez Hotel just across North Arlington Avenue from the Town House, I sometimes ate alone—proving to myself that I could enjoy adult food in style.

Occasionally I would skedaddle three blocks west to the former Crest Theater, where kids lined up using 7-Up soda bottle caps to pay for their tickets, all possible thanks to a beverage company promotion.

Almost as if they instinctively knew how to spread their own angel wings—without ever realizing they were such beings—on Friday nights Grandpa drove Grandma and me up and down West Fourth Street in Reno. His feathers glowing in a heavenly way, at least in my eyes, Grandpa eagerly looked for any vacancy signs at the various motels all along that route, sometimes called U.S. Highway 40. Our excitement always grew upon realizing that the Town House was—as usual—the only significant motel establishment throughout the entire region boasting a "no vacancy" sign.

This always proved to my Grandparents that the Town House essentially served as a beacon, beckoning tourists to enjoy the one-and-only true heavenly gates of Reno.

Our collective excitement intensified during the downtown Fourth of July celebration and parade, held along North Virginia Street at the heart of town in conjunction during that era with the annual Reno Rodeo. Eventually dubbed "The Wildest, Richest Rodeo in the West," the event emerged as a significant draw to the region's economy. At the parade, the horses, the cowboys, the World War II heroes, marching bands and the drop-dead gorgeous showgirls served as the icing on the cake for what had become my angelic, heavenly and unforgettable Reno summer. The time when I would develop my own future personality, the time when I would learn to appreciate and to communicate intellectually with adults, and the time to start blossoming into my teenage years—it all came together in one big package.

Then, just as any dutiful, dedicated and eternally loving angel would do, Grandma took me on a magical route when taking me back to my family's Southern California home as that stupendous summer ended. After briefly visiting my parents' trailer home, Grandma took me and my mother straight to Disneyland—which had opened in July 1955 just 26 miles southeast of downtown Los Angeles.

As just about anyone might imagine angels spoil little girls rotten. Angels will eagerly take you by the hand and then lead you into the Magic Kingdom. Angels are friends with Mickey Mouse and Donald Duck. Angels fully understand what rests deep within the hearts of their grandchildren. Angels see deeply into the souls of their granddaughters, kissing them not necessarily with lips but with dedication and commitment as well. Oh, and yes, by the way, never forget for a second that angels don't necessarily know that they're angels—until welcomed by God back into His Kingdom.

I felt the touch in Grandma's hand, the gentle and loving look in her eye, on a sunny June morning in 2008. The voice of a nurse on the other end of the line broke the news that I had come to expect but still dreaded.

"Patty, your Grandma died."

"Yes ... Okay ... Was it peaceful?"

"She went in her sleep. It was natural. Painless."

Without hanging up, I allowed my mind to give thanks to God, to give thanks to my family's newly deceased matriarch, to give thanks to Grandpa Oscar—who had passed away 20 years earlier—to give thanks to whichever Creator directs this worldly stage, to all caring and loving Grandparents from around the world in the past, in the present and in the future. Then, I asked the nurse:

"Did you know that my Grandma was an angel?"

Dad demanded answers right away from his Reno attorney, while we still lived in Sunland after my tenth birthday. By this time more than three years after the fatal-auto accident that seriously injured my parents we still had not received any positive news. Mom and dad's court suit remained pending against the deceased drunken driver's estate and his insurance company.

"What's going on?" my dad asked, after finally reaching that evasive Reno attorney Peter Harper-Collins by phone.

"Yeah, I'm working on it," the lawyer responded, giving his usual line while never giving any specific details or timeframes on when my parents should expect either a settlement or a court trial.

As the months and years passed, my parents vowed to put any future settlement funds or judgment monies to good use, perhaps to buy an auto-body shop for dad or even a home for mom.

After continually getting the runaround from Harper-Collins, my parents always shook their heads in bewilderment, essentially telling each other: "We just have to go on, and keep struggling to survive. But when will we get justice, and how?"

"We're getting out of here," father proclaimed to mother and me, three weeks after my return to Sunland from Reno. "We're leaving this place."

"Where are we going dad?" I asked, steady in my conviction to remain vibrant and confident—a far more mature girl than before that summer.

"We're going to Texas," dad said, and mother made no attempt to protest, at least openly in my presence. Prior to this my parents had never told me specifics on when or why we would be leaving someplace, let alone our intended destination—except for when we had left Montana for Reno six years earlier so that she could divorce him. So, this Texas excursion marked a major change at least in terms of communication.

Dad explained that his friends had been telling him that the Lone Star State would be a fantastic place to work, with plenty of good jobs. But before going there, dad said, we first needed to head up to Idaho to "get some things taken care of" with his brother, my Uncle Lehman.

Within a few days father hitched the trailer to his pickup truck, and we headed out of Sunland for our latest transition. My first thoughts focused on what school I would attend, and the possibility of making new friends.

Little did any of us know as we headed out later that day that a sudden twist of fate would change our lives forever.

The flat tire that changed all of our lives happened while en route to Idaho after we arrived in Hawthorne, Nevada, a small, desolate high-desert community.

"Oh, hell," dad said, as the demolished wheel on the trailer pestered us all with its Ka-ploop-ah, ka-ploop, ah, ka-ploop. Mom let out a mournful moan, as if this setback became far more than she could tolerate.

My heart sank upon hearing the sound. Father had always expertly fixed any mechanical problems through the years whenever our old, rickety vehicles had sustained mechanical failures. We had no reason to sense right away that this pesky problem would emerge as a major life-changing force.

The blow-out had occurred at around sundown, and the problem proved so pesky that we ended up having to spend the night.

"This is it," mother proclaimed the next morning. Complaining forcefully had been unusual for her. "Larry, I'm out of here."

"What do you mean?" father said, seeming perplexed, at least to me.

"This flat tire strikes me as an omen," mother said, while taking her luggage out of our trailer. "I'm going to Reno."

"Yeah! Reno!" I interjected, overjoyed at the prospect of seeing my Grandparents, and living near them. "Mom, I want to go to Reno, too."

"Reno?" dad finally piped in, as if stunned. He cringed, apparently at the thought of having to see or live near his in-laws. "I'm not going to Reno. We've got plans. Texas."

Mother piped in right away: "Larry, you can go to Idaho and Texas, or you can come to Reno. I don't care. I've had it with life on the road."

Dad grumbled that—yes, indeed—he would head out for Reno as well.

Unusually tricky and conniving, mother then promptly hopped onto a Greyhound bus headed to Reno, leaving me, and dad behind.

Thinking back, I know that mother wasn't even coming close to abandoning me. She knew full well that my father would chase her.

Intuitively realizing this, I decided to stay in Hawthorne with dad while he fixed the tire. Soon afterward, as father drove with me out of Hawthorne, heading straight for Reno, he made an assumption that hit the nail on the head: "Well, Patty, I think our traveling days are over."

And, they were.

Almost like baby magpies that get thrust from their nests for the first time, all of us eventually find ourselves either pushed or dropped into the dog-eat-dog world.

If a chick or hatchling falls to earth from high up in a tree, the tiny bird will either starve on its own, get gobbled up by predators, or instinctively discover how to fly and thrive, or get rescued by a parent.

For as long as I can remember, my heart has yearned to enjoy compelling and unpredictable stories where helpless underdogs overcome seemingly insurmountable odds to eventually achieve victory.

Fictional stories, such as the never-say-die attitude of the smash hit 1976 film "Rocky," where the primary character faces stiff competition have captured my soul since early childhood. The 1993 dramatic sports movie "Rudy" left me emotional, gripped by the real-life story of how University of Notre Dame student Daniel Reuttiger played on the school's football team despite significant obstacles.

Something about such sagas, especially true-life tales, grips every fiber of my being. Instinct tells me to appreciate anyone who at least tries to achieve his or her dreams, and especially those who have reached their goals. The quest for happiness and the valiant struggle to reach the highest mountaintop captures the imagination.

Just to live is to struggle. Just to live is to suffer extreme hardships, no matter who we are and whatever our lot in life. Just to live can become difficult, seemingly impossible for many people—challenging their abilities to cope. Just to live makes me wonder why some of us fail while others succeed in the continual quest for happiness.

My father's struggle to achieve his dreams had taken him off course, straight to the bottle and to a rambling personal journey. My mother's quest to achieve her dreams left her divorcing him two times, always re-marrying him—never achieving her deep desire to get a house of their own. They each eventually went to their natural deaths without ever fully grasping or holding onto what their inner souls truly desired.

As an avid movie-goer, my emotion leads to tears, laughter and smiles of joy, as characters up on the Silver Screen achieve victories in the face of insurmountable odds. Boy gets girl, poor family finds middle-class lifestyle, and weak athlete becomes super-strong in order to whip the snot out of bullies, these are the kind of transitions that help make the world fantastic—especially true-life tales.

"Cinderella Man," an award-winning 2005 movie starring Russell Crowe as heavyweight boxing champion James J. Braddock fit within the mold of the perfect true-life rags-to-riches drama that I admire. At the height of the Great Depression, as a struggling longshoreman hampered by extreme manual labor, Braddock barely earned enough to feed his family. After living in extreme poverty, their fortunes changed when Braddock confounded the odds-makers, eventually winning the heavyweight championship from Max Baer Sr.—father of the former actor whom Wayne and I had hosted in our "Beverly Hillbillies" theme party at Pops on the River.

Well, whether he knew this or not, at least in a sense my father had been a similar champion at least in some ways. Like Braddock, dad always managed to feed our tiny family during the worst of times, keeping food in our bellies and roofs over our heads.

The precise reason why I gravitate to such stories still remains difficult to pin down. Maybe the deepest reaches of my soul appreciate the winner in all of us, even characters such as my dad whom some people might wrongly think of as a "loser." Perhaps the creative part of my mind overrules any potential struggle to find logic or deep meaning in this—preferring to concentrate on "the struggle" rather than merely the goal.

Ultimately in this regard, Wayne sometimes insists that I fail to see or to fully acknowledge what he calls the irrefutable truth: "Patty, you're the winner—the same type of person that you get emotional about at the movies."

"I am? How can that be? Come off it, Wayne. You're trying to say I'm a winner, like Rocky or Rudy?"

"Exactly, Patty, think about what I'm saying."

"But I'm not famous, and I'm not wealthy in a financial sense. How can anybody call me a winner, like those characters we see in the movies? I think you're stretching this a bit too far."

For the next half hour, Wayne left me captivated. I latched onto his every word as he recounted my own personal story. He argued in no uncertain terms why I should start considering myself as the exact type of beat-the-odds character from the movies.

"Look at your own current situation, and your personal background, Patty. Wow, have you ever got a story to tell. Yeah, everyone has a story to tell. But your own actual personal tale is one about beating the odds."

I sat on our living room couch sipping my wine, as Wayne eased back in an adjoining chair. In that moment, my husband seemed so distant and yet so close to me at the same time. Deep down, although refusing to acknowledge his perceptions during that chat, I'll have to admit that he spoke the God's-honest truth, sometimes difficult to hear or to acknowledge, even if such statements happen to be complimentary.

Like most husbands, I suppose, Wayne was not usually this direct and focused at getting into a lengthy conversation about marital matters or verbally dissecting the other's personality and history. Still, his focus, his determination and his slow, methodical pace in driving this point home let me know that he truly cared.

"Look at yourself, Patty. Where you were in early childhood, and what you have made for yourself—building a solid life.

What a difference this is, compared to essentially living in the front seat of a pickup truck. And, don't you dare interrupt—let me do all the speaking for awhile—keep in clear focus your many professional achievements and personal hardships that you have overcome.

Patty. Like all of us do in life, you needed to make tough decisions when eventually going into the world on your own as a young adult. Surely like a lot of us have, many of your choices might have been considered 'wrong' or at least perhaps a less desirable pathway to take. Does this sound like I'm lecturing you?"

"No," I said. "But I still fail to accept this theory that I'm some kind of 'glorious winner' worthy of acclaim and celebrations."

"Okay, maybe not acclaim—not widespread fame, Patty. That's not what I'm trying to say at all. Each person, especially those of us over 40 or 50 years old has a story to tell, and yours just happens to be unique—all events during an era, a place and in situations that many people could very well consider as romantic.

If you don't want me to talk about this, then fine." Wayne said. "How many years have we talked about doing a book about your life? Come on now, you've got to admit that your story is worth telling."

For quite a number of years I had been urging people to have Wayne ghost-write their autobiographies. But to that point I had never gotten down to the nitty-gritty, other than to jot down a handful of pages while I spent a month in Costa Rica.

Now, this particular conversation about me being a so-called "winner" occurred in early 2008, more than three years before Wayne began helping me on the book that you're reading now. During the 43-month span in between, after reconciling and putting our lives back on course, we had talked off and on about tackling this project. But like I've already stated, it wasn't until we underwent plans for the September 2011 tour of my house that an unexplainable urge to conquer this task swept over us both.

During the initial one-week planning phase, amid the initial days when Wayne interviewed me for this book, he pretended to show little or no interest in specific details of my professional career. Baiting me on, without me realizing this at the time, he turned the tide. This time,

Wayne had me put into a position where I felt an urgent need to argue with him—to convince my husband of the vital process of how I had achieved numerous work goals in various phases in life.

Essentially, as I would discover much later, Wayne actually wanted me to drive this point home. In essence I had started to make a pitch similar to the proverbial hardball that he had lobbed in my direction during our living room chat more than three years earlier. At least in my mind, everything came down to this:

A woman or a man in our American society, still filled with many opportunities in the so-called quest for happiness, simply needs to make a plan, ask for what they want on a consistent basis and always remain eager to learn. These are all the decisions and lifestyle commitments that I had done in creating my own pathway in life.

Within several years after the tire on my dad's trailer blew in Hawthorne, Nevada, I landed my first job as a switchboard operator in my teens. Grandma and Grandpa gave me the position at the Town House Motor Lodge.

Any teenager or young adult has to start somewhere, and this seemed as good a place as any. Yet I'll have to admit that although people swore that I did an excellent job as a switchboard operator, the experience left me feeling far from fully satisfied. Please understand that I never felt like the type of person who would stay in a job that lacked huge opportunities. Everything that happened during my childhood taught me an important lesson.

During my elementary school years and beyond, father had stressed to me the importance of learning as much as possible and of asking lots of questions. During an era when females generally were viewed by society as less necessary to America's general workforce, dad would stress: "If you want to do something, do it right. Never do anything half-assed."

Heeding his advice, I looked for a profession that might interest me, upon my graduation from Reno's Wooster High School in 1965. Tests given by occupational experts indicated that I would be good in either the creative arts or social services.

I had heard of Oakland College of Art and Crafts and dreamed of attending this prestigious school in the Bay Area, but along with my family I lacked enough funds to pay for tuition. So, I enrolled in a downtown Reno beauty school, in hopes of getting a temporary job in that profession in order that I could work my way through art school.

My burning desire to get a good art industry job had remained since the third-grade, when Mrs. Beck had told me: "Patty, you're an artist," at Grant Elementary in San Jose. Deep down, throughout high school a part of me had said that, "Yes, Patty, you are really talented. That is who you are."

Going to an art school got temporarily pulled off track in 1967 at age 19 upon voluntarily leaving beauty school, partly because that profession failed to ignite my soul. Another motivation clicked into full gear when I had a baby that year, my son Chris. I needed to help support this adorable child and my husband at the time, Fred Atcheson, a university student.

The son of a prominent businessman, Fred had gained quite a reputation for himself while attending Reno High School—across town from Wooster High, which I had attended.

Looking back, the most important thing that I can remember about Fred at that time was the fact that I needed to be a supporting figure in his life. Fred had initially ignored my phone calls in hopes of giving the news that I was carrying his child. After some prodding, finally Fred gave a positive response after his father convinced him to marry me.

"Don't leave that girl hanging," Fred's father told him. "You need to make the situation legitimate."

For the initial seven years of my marriage with Fred Atcheson, I managed to help support our family.

At the start of this stretch while still living in Reno, I landed a low-pay accounting department job at a downtown department store, Gray Reid's. Math had been my least favorite subject in school. The miniscule pay was rough, however in those days you could get by easily on $1.50-per-hour. But little did I know at the time that this would serve as an indirect route to a lifetime career in the arts and graphic design industries.

While walking through office-area hallways in Gray Reid's, I often went past the illustration department that generated hand-drawn newspaper advertisements for the store. At the time, all major retailers of this kind featured print advertisements. Up to that point in 1967, big-name stores featured only hand-drawn ads depicting everything from people wearing garments to merchandise ranging from ovens to ironing boards.

Many people fail to realize this today. But most print ads up to that point did not yet feature photographs or even snapshots of fashion models.

Striving to generate a high-end image at all times, stores such as Gray Reid's maintained illustration departments that only employed highly trained artists. Commonly called "illustrators," these talented individuals were graduates of art schools such as the Bay area institution that I had hoped to attend.

Filled with envy, while working in the accounting department and doing a mundane job that required skills that a third-grader could handle, I watched the women artists who worked in the illustration department as they strolled through the halls.

Eventually as the weeks and months passed, I gradually began wondering every day about how someone like me could ever work in such a glamorous, creative environment.

Each time I walked past the illustration department's open door, I saw these women working diligently to make wonderful, creative print ads. Sometimes I would stand still in the hallway, staring in awe at these sophisticated women.

My yearnings to join that team intensified. "How can I make a positive change?" I asked myself. "How can I get the position that I desperately desire, within the illustration department?"

My heart gave me the only logical answer, telling me that I must generate the necessary courage to ask for such a position. So, finally one day I walked into the art department "How can I have a chance to work in your department? I asked Possie Edwards, its director, an imposing woman with bright blue eyes and a very fashionable, stunning figure.

Possie gave a no-holds-barred answer that struck me as challenging: "Patty, anyone who works here needs to have an art degree, such as the one I earned from the Art Center in Los Angeles." Although this might have seemed discouraging at least in the short-term, she also told me of an encouraging development. A short time earlier, Possie had hired a non-degreed young woman and had begun training her.

"Patty, we're in the process of hiring for another fashion illustrator position, so I would like you to bring in your portfolio," Possie said.

"Sounds great, thank you," I told her, never revealing that I lacked such documentation. I worked at home through the following weekend creating precise fashion-oriented artwork, using images from magazines as models while developing my own signature style.

The following Monday morning I entered Posie's office and gave her my instant portfolio. I assured her that the images were made by my own hand. Posie made no promises, saying only that she would review my portfolio and eventually let me know her decision after reviewing applications from qualified applicants.

Days and weeks passed. While no answer or comment had yet arrived, I strived to remain hopeful. Then, finally Posie invited me into her office.

"Patty, you've got the job. Congratulations."

"I do!"

Overjoyed, I latched on to the $1.72-per-hour job, a fair amount at the time—miniscule but at least more than some people earned. I used every penny to help support my husband and Chris. After more than a year or so, I got up the nerve to ask Posie for a raise. She gave me a flat-out "No," explaining that in order to earn larger paychecks an illustrator needed extensive experience in order to "pay her dues."

Unsatisfied with this answer, I soon landed an illustration job for a significant increase in pay, now $2.25, at Reno-based Tyson Curtis Wilson Advertising. Naturally, after seeing my artwork, that firm's management hired me on the spot.

The expert graphics team at Tyson, Curtis, Wilson started using me as their primary fashion model, because they said I happened to be convenient to use—"pretty." During this period print advertisements gradually started to feature photos. Since my employer already paid me for working there, the company saved big bucks by using me as their primary female model.

I learned a great deal from the creative team I worked with at the agency. They gave me a solid education in graphic design and production. I finally found a profession I knew I could grasp.

I had a huge thirst for success. In 1971, one year before the birth of my beautiful daughter, Zoë, Fred was accepted to attend McGeorge Law School in Sacramento, California's capital, a two-hour drive west of Reno.

"Patty, you have two days to go there, get yourself a job and find us a place to live," Fred said, and I did just that. After initially landing a low-pay position as an illustrator at a popular appliance store, I soon grabbed the prestigious position of Art Director for the California Chamber of Commerce—the first female ever to receive such an honor.

My career zoomed onto the fast track from that point forward. Following our three-year stint in Sacramento, we moved back to Nevada where I soon landed a Art Director position with the Nevada State Department of Tourism and Economic Development in Carson City—the same town 30 miles south of Reno where I had once pulled orphans' teeth. By this point, after building a positive reputation as an artist and for my unique, high-end graphic design and administrative skills, I continually pushed forward to new levels of increasingly greater success.

Along the way, I divorced and re-married Fred twice before finally setting myself free for good. Amid my continuous breakups and reconciliations with him, following two years in my state position, in 1977 I landed a three-year stint teaching students art in the Washoe County School District in Reno—employed by the Sierra Arts Foundation. This enabled me to reach deep into the heart of my community, showing children how to draw and paint, while giving them valuable information on how they could pursue full-time professions in my chosen career.

Always striving for greater success, in 1980 I began a four-year stint working in publications and graphics at the University of Nevada in Reno—also as a member of the faculty, an achievement that still makes me proud. After working with various publications and imaging projects there, I launched my own graphics design company, which gradually evolved into my current firm, WOW! Design Marketing.

Through the late 1980s and into the early 1990s, my business surged, employing five full-time employees. For for years, I commuted via commercial airliner on business at least once weekly between Reno and Las Vegas.

Certainly, the many lessons that my Grandparents and my folks had given put me on course for increasing success. My creativity and design skills put me on the cutting edge of the advertising industry. For many years I worked as the only graphic designer in all of Nevada and in perhaps much of the West to use computers to handle my craft. Along the way, I won more industry awards than I can possibly remember. Today, for the most part those honors mean very little to me. The important thing was that I served my clients, helping them to achieve the recognition that they greatly deserved.

But there still was so much that was missing in my life. Although I had close friendships at varying times with handsome, wealthy, and highly successful men, I felt a void. I yearned to find a man who could help fulfill my hopes and desires. A kind, loving, and generous man who would listen to my dreams, and share in my adventures.

Shortly after our arrival back in Reno, at age eleven the universe finally blessed me with my only private garden—the secret meadow where hundreds of magpies and I enjoyed a magical, peaceful afternoon together.

Other than spending time in my secret sanctuary or enjoying rides on horses at the nearby Bakers Stables, I hated my new environment.

Once again the requirement of sharing a communal bathroom and shower facility with lots of other poor people irritated me. A girl entering her teens needs quiet time in her family's private, clean rest room. That gangly period where we spout pimples demands at least some degree of solitude.

My escape to my secret hideout continued from September through October and into the first several days of November. With each passing day the skies became increasingly grayer, somehow as if the heavens knew of my unhappiness. More than ever before, I felt alone, isolated and without a solid place in this world.

Late one afternoon after I returned home from school I went directly to my serene place. Standing at the entrance looking at the pure stream, and giant healthy frogs, hundreds of Magpies sang joyfully for me perched on branches high above.

"Hi," I said to one of the smaller magpies, after it landed on my shoulder. The bird stayed perched silent, as if somehow sensing my loneliness, my heartache and my relentless deep inner yearning to find a stable place in this world.

Right on queue, as if following the signals from a great invisible conductor in the sky, the magpies began singing their unique song, as if playing Mozart "Piano Concerto Number 21." I smiled broadly, as their tune took me to a far-away peaceful place. I had become familiar with such great classics earlier that year, when I bought my first record, Dvorak's "New World Symphony." Classical music made me feel like a flower floating along that stream through the middle of my meadow, my own secret garden. As soon as I had brought my first-ever record purchase home, my parents looked at me as if I were some sort of an alien. My parents had thought I would buy current hit tunes from that era.

All I knew for sure was that this touched my soul, at a time when I desperately needed inspiration.

But to me, classical music generated the greatest sound the world could possibly imagine. The first time I heard classical music, I was ten years old in Carson City. My mother gave me a quarter to go to the movies to see the famed Walt Disney's "Fantasia."

And, now, imagine how my mind spun in wondrous anticipation, upon discovering that the magpies knew these same orchestrations as well. For only those few minutes at least, the birds proved to me that they knew Mozart's "Requiem," Beethoven's "Midnight Sonata," Joseph

Haydn's "Symphony Number 94," and Bach's "Brandburg Concerto Number 3."

Alone, I lay on my back in the grassy, slightly moist meadow. I looked straight above to those hundreds of magpies. Seeming to take great delight in giving this performance, the birds kindly and graciously played a full set for me. Although sad deep inside my soul, I found myself smiling. It was as if, for a full two hours those birds lifted me up— collectively flying me into the sky.

There, I became one with the harps, the violins—every kind of string, brass, woodwind and percussion instrument. The magpies' kindness coupled with their gentle singing lifted up my spirit, seemingly above the clouds. Perfect rhythm sections accented classical guitars, coronets, harpsichords, flugelhorns, organs, pianos and even occasional saxophones during limited selections.

A great composer skillfully inter-mixes perfect amounts of tingly sounds, everything from soft sensations to loud, thunderous climaxes. When done just right, everything comes together in a crescendo, a universal, soulful and spiritual overture such as that I experienced high above the earth that afternoon.

The hundreds of magpies held me protectively in their grasp, as if carrying me gracefully above the homelands of the greatest composers of all time. My many friends took me on a surprise tour over the French wine country, peering down at the graceful sweeping hills of Tuscany and up into the vibrant forests of Austria. They whisked me across the oceans and into the great outdoors on every continent. Gone were the dreary trailers, at least for the moment. Gone was the gloomy gypsy life, at least for as long as this orchestral journey might continue. Gone was the relentless maze of schools, where I had fallen far behind. And, gone were the continual yet unspoken conflicts between my parents, for at the moment thanks to my feathered friends I kept flying across the expanse of an all-new musical universe.

Oh, my God, I had thought, if only this music could continue. If only these birds could grasp me in their comforting expanse of grace forever, I would feel wholly free. If only the greatest conductors of all time knew how much I suddenly appreciated them, and for many years to come. And, if now I could only fly like a bird myself, I could feel whole and complete—the ultimate dreams that any little girl fantasizes about.

Blessed is this view, upon my sacred private meadow far below. Graceful is this vision, of the lush green trees, the frogs, and the horses grazing peacefully nearby. Charming is this land of ours, even in our times of distress.

Those who created these timeless orchestrations, thank you for touching my soul. Here these many magpies gently set me back into the heart of my secret meadow, amid compositions from the greatest composers of all time, all of them striving to win my attention. Great works from the Renaissance, Baroque, Classical and Romantic eras helped these caring, kind and eternally loving birds beam me back to earth.

Then, the music within my own private meadow had stopped—after the magpies disappeared from there. Fly away and leave me for the winter, as Mother Nature commands. Leave me with memories, as is the story of life's eternal changes and transitions. Make me remember you for all time with fondness and devotion, you birds who touched me—you winged creature, which never once feared landing on my shoulder.

As a 43-year-old divorcee in 1990, I suddenly went on a mission.

Every part of my heart told me that the ideal time had finally arrived for me to find a perfect home. One of my longtime friends had just purchased an ideal house in one of Reno's older neighborhoods, the Newlands Area, near downtown.

This emerged as among primary factors motivating me suddenly to move away from a cookie-cutter, boring house that I had owned for a couple of years.

With no success, a real estate agent started helping me to hunt for what I might consider a quaint and comfortable old-style house.

Frustrated after my initial failures at finding an ideal property, I got struck by the idea that I should drive around older neighborhoods to look for a suitable home. Right before going for that drive, I recalled a pleasant afternoon more than a decade earlier when I had taken my children, Chris and Zoë, for a walk when they were little.

After all those years, I still vividly recalled strolling past a quaint 1920s-style home in the Ralston neighborhood of what city planners call "old northwest Reno" four blocks west of the University of Nevada campus. I remembered that two-story house, which during that stroll I had thought of as a "real pretty" property.

This time, alone behind the wheel, I cruised up Ralston, turned onto a tiny street, Codel Way, and spotted the home right away. Then, right in front of the house I saw what I considered a message of fate, a signal to take immediate action.

A "for-sale" sign!

In those days before cell phones, email and social networking, I drove straight to my boring cookie-cutter home and phoned my real estate agent—telling him in no uncertain terms that "I want to see that house as soon as possible." My budget at the time was $120,000, respectable for that era in this market but not huge.

"You really don't want this place, Patty," Larry said, as we toured the home with my friend, Jim. They each pointed out the many drawbacks: a decrepit kitchen with '60s-style cupboards and '70s-style brown and gold linoleum; a drab sunroom with a glass container holding a huge, deadly-looking snake; a dungeon-like, dreary feeling throughout the entire residence; an upstairs library room without a single book; goofy furniture piled high in an upstairs bedroom; and a yard without any lawn, garden or flowers.

"This is my home!" I said, seeing nothing but potential.

"You can't be serious, Patty," Larry said. "This place is far more hassle than the offering price. "No, this place is mine. I want it," I said, still engrossed by a positive sensation that had struck me, an intuition. "Let's make an offer."

"You've got to be kidding. You don't want this. It's a lot of work."

"I have never been more serious in all my life. Let's offer $110,000," I said, thinking this as a reasonable amount, since the seller had posted an asking price of $120,000.

Within 36 hours, the seller promptly responded that she was firm on the asking price. The home had originally been put up for sale at $175,000, but potential buyers at that level had failed to qualify after a wait of several months. A similar scenario had played out when other potential buyers subsequently matched the seller's lowered asking price of $145,000. After that, the seller had pumped the asking price to what she considered a rock-bottom $120,000, refusing to budge downward another penny. So, her counter-offer to me remained firm at the current asking price.

"Let's take it!" I told Larry.

My mortgage application breezed through without any problem whatsoever. The lender's office was in the same small office building across town where my firm's headquarters was located. As professional neighbors, the lenders knew me well, fully aware of my competence and character. The loan breezed through without any problem. My income at the time was great, especially for a single woman, which my company's financial records proved in a flash.

Although blessed with the house of my dreams, my hard work had just begun. Many months of scrubbing and painting followed. Chris helped me with much of this work throughout that summer. The brother of Zoë's first husband installed a picket fence around the yard. I bought flowers and plants whenever possible, especially from gardening sales held every June at the nearby Rancho San Rafael Regional Park. Meantime, as you might recall, many types of flowers mysteriously starting appearing all around the property including hollyhocks.

After my father died, I sold his trailer, using the funds for my son Chris to give the kitchen a desperately needed remodeling. Meantime, old antique furniture that I had bought through the years fit perfectly in various rooms throughout the house. Rugs, carpets, couches, vases and many other items that had appeared out-of-place in my previous homes now seemed as if custom-made for this old home.

Everything fit in the "right and perfect place".

Like a female bald eagle comforting its confused hatchling, teacher Jackie Scarborough cradled me in her arms one afternoon at Reno's Vaughn Junior High School. Finally, a teacher had taken notice of me again and took time to pay attention, when I was 12 years old upon entering the seventh grade.

I felt stupid, while saddened that school administrators had stuck me into a bonehead math class. Getting my first monthly period was bad enough. I felt funny, strange to see all these new changes happening with myself. I sprouted like a beanstalk, already a gangly 5-foot-7 ostrich, feeling like a freak as I towered over all the boys and those cute girls. My gangly gate, those pesky pimples and those new little boobies of mine that I wanted desperately to hide made me feel like a freak in the circus that I had enjoyed way back as a 6-year-old, bright-eyed girl up in Twin Falls, Idaho. By this point when at home, I tried to hide from the world, tucking the covers over my head inside my family's tiny trailer.

My confusion increased one night. A strange, non-stop sound like a muffled drumbeat echoed from my parents' couch. Mother and father had recently gotten back together thanks to one of their numerous reconciliations.

"What are you two doing in there?" I asked, puzzled.

"Oh, nothing, nothing, nothing" mother briefly appeared to secure the door separating me from their sleeping space. It wasn't until several years later that I finally figured out the obvious answer. My parents had been trying to spend quality "alone time" together, "doing their thing."

Around this time, my dad went into a rage when his attorney, Peter Harper-Collins, finally called to say that the final settlement from the civil litigation involving the fatal wreck would be $20,000.

"Don't ever mention that man's name in my presence ever again," dad said, angry for the rest of his life that the total was less than a fifth of what the attorney had promised.

About three weeks after I heard my parents making odd noises in our tiny home, my father bought us a much larger trailer, perhaps using funds from the legal settlement involving the fatal car wreck. This was a much more expansive unit, 12 feet wide and 35 feet long and more important than anything—it had a bathroom.

Despite this insignificant improvement, I still felt downcast. The seedy, grimy and unsightly trailer park that we moved to on East Peckham Lane in Reno made me feel more disgusted than ever. These feelings remained during subsequent years as I transitioned into Wooster High School near the Airport.

As other girls grew closer to my height and my pimples subsided, one of my new friends became Margo Piscevich, whose father worked in administration at downtown Reno's Mapes Hotel—where I had once briefly met Hollywood sex goddess Marilyn Monroe. With her Mormon parents, Margo lived in the rented tenant side of a duplex owned by my future second husband Wayne's Grandparents, William and Dorothy Royle.

At the corner of Thoma Street and Kirman Avenue, the quaint residence served as the perfect place for this diligent girl to study, already well on her way to becoming one of the earliest, most successful female lawyers in Nevada history. Many of my other classmates from Anderson Elementary, Vaughn Junior High and Wooster High later went on as adults to earn themselves positive reputations in prestigious careers. Fooling everyone, I would later achieve success as well. Back then, though, I felt the stigma of being a mere "trailer person."

My family's meager income, motivated me to drop out of the Rainbow Girls, a Masonic youth organization that teaches leadership skills and sponsors social functions for young adults from ages 11 through 21. This had emerged into one of the few bright spots of my teens. I loved participating in functions, including two events that required me to wear different formal gowns in order to earn promotion to higher levels.

But lacking adequate funds to buy another formal, my mother gave me just enough cash to go to a Lerners store to purchase an ordinary dress. I felt too ashamed or embarrassed to wear such an inexpensive garment at the latest upcoming function. So, I told my mother that I wanted to stop attending Rainbow Girls.

One of the worst weeks of my life happened through the Thanksgiving holiday, right after the assassination of President John F. Kennedy in Dallas, Texas. During my sophomore year in high school. I felt dreary that weekend as Reno's weather became more overcast, miserably cold and more somber than ever. The entire atmosphere seemed to weep, as if Mother Nature herself had gone into deep mourning. My mother and Grandma Eve worked diligently to make homemade raviolis, our family's tradition for more than a century at that point.

Shortly before the scheduled meal, dad stumbled into the trailer while dead-drunk, far more inebriated than I had ever seen him. My heart fell onto the floor of our living room after the phone rang. I watched father pull a knob off the TV and hold the device to his ear as if to answer: "Hell-er-ooo? Hell-er-ooo?"

I disliked my father, I disliked our home, the trailer park, who I was and almost everything about my life. Mom and dad divorced a month later and mom and I were on our own.

Mom had the trailer moved to another trailer park, this time with an address on Kietzke Lane. Our trailer, though was situated at the end of a long row of mobile homes. Our home butted up to Yori Ave. I disliked this trailer park as well, but for some reason this space didn't seem as dreary.

The sinking feeling in my stomach always hit when men visited our tiny trailer to pick mother up for dates. By that point mom had become the primary, solid and steady breadwinner of our family. The mere idea of her spending time with men other than my father made me confused and bewildered.

Thankfully, mom never left for overnight excursions, and she initially avoided any temptation to invite these male companions to our residence for dinner.

This pattern suddenly changed when mother took me out to dinner with Stephen Cartwright, the old West illustrator whom she had been briefly engaged to in Las Vegas before meeting my father. Prior to this unexpected meal during my sophomore year in high school, mother had told me about Cartwright a few times.

"This is really neat," I thought during dinner. "Mom gets to see her old friend."

Right away Cartwright impressed me as average-looking, a sharp contrast from my father's tall, dark and handsome frame. I realized that if mother had married him she would have lived a comfortable life rather than struggling to make ends meet. Highly successful and widely acclaimed in his profession, at the time of our meal Cartwright owned a Grass Valley, California, ranch loaded with horses—one of mother's strident lifelong dreams. At the time, Cartwright was married with an adopted child.

I had never seen Cartwright before that meeting, and have never seen him since. Many decades later I remained unsure why or how mother and the artist had contacted each other and the reason why they had invited me to the dinner.

Mother told her former boyfriend at one point during the meal: "Oh, Patty likes to draw." Cartwright apparently took this comment as a positive signal, before briefly telling me the basics of his profession. Needless to say, this revelation instilled motivation within my heart, because until that time I had lacked a full understanding that a talented artist could potentially make a solid living as a professional illustrator.

Three months after my 16th birthday, my parents reconciled and got back together for the rest of their lives.

"Honey, there has been a murder," my mother urged him by phone, terrified. "Patty and I want you to come home to us now, to protect us."

Terror and unbelievable fright had filled mother and me in the initial days after the Reno murder of international Olympics snow skiing athlete Sonja McCaskie. Startled police found McCaskie slain just two homes down from where we lived on Yori Avenue.

At the time of the slaying, dad worked at an auto-body shop in Quincy, California, 79 miles northwest of Reno.

News of the McCaskie slaying shocked the entire community, the body reportedly slashed and decapitated, the head rolled across the floor of her tiny residence. The killing mortified us all, especially young women such as me who previously had little notion that murder could occur—an extremely rare event at the time in Northern Nevada and particularly in the close-knit, small-town Reno community.

With the killer unidentified and apparently on the loose, dad rushed back to Reno as soon as mother had phoned him at my request: "Please call him, mom. I cannot sleep. I'm a nervous wreck."

Gripped with intense fright, mother and I wrapped our arms tightly around father throughout the entire night immediately after his arrival. This marked the first time that I had slept in the same bed with my parents since infancy.

Within a day or so police arrested a Wooster High student, Thomas Lee Bean, just two years older than me. News reports or rumors indicated that Bean had been driving through our neighborhood looking for women's undergarments hanging from clotheslines. Thank God mother and I never used such techniques; we cleaned and dried all of our laundry at a local Laundromat. Otherwise, as I've feared to this day, Bean could easily have targeted us instead of McCaskie—who had hung her panties outside her residence to dry.

On several occasions during the preceding months, while walking past McCaskie's residence, I had waved and smiled at her. The beautiful 24-year-old Alpine skier had represented Britain in the 1960 Winter Olympics at Squaw Valley California, 44 miles southwest of Reno. Police announced that her slaying occurred in the early morning hours of April 5, 1963.

Just six years old at the time, my future husband Wayne also lived on Yori Avenue that year. The second oldest child of Marilyn and Rollan

Melton, at the time editor of the community's Reno Evening Gazette newspaper, Wayne lived with his immediate family a mile to the north of us in a middle-class neighborhood in a tiny matchbox-size home.

Police detectives identified Bean and tracked him down after identifying at least one of McCaskie's personal possessions that he had hocked at a Reno pawn shop. Washoe County District Attorney Bill Raggio successfully prosecuted Bean on a murder charge, before the court sentenced the killer to die in Nevada's gas chamber. Officials commuted the sentence to life in prison in 1970, and Bean has remained incarcerated ever since.

Nearly ten months after my 48th birthday I met Wayne for the first time—at least as far as I could recall at that point.

I promptly won him—indirectly—as a sort-of booby prize in a contest, before eventually making him my second husband.

The fun started shortly after 2 o'clock in the afternoon on September 13, 1995, when the phone rang in my home office.

"I want you to be a contestant," said the manly voice on the other end of the line, identifying himself as a features writer for the local newspaper. Intrigued, I listened as Wayne Rollan Melton explained that the hit "Les Misérables" musical would perform in a three-day stint in downtown Reno in just ten more days.

Wayne said that the newspaper was asking five top graphic designers to draw distinctive images of the show's promotional illustration. In every major city where "Les Misérables" appeared, a drawing featured varying unique illustrations of a primary character, Cosette. In the Windy City of Chicago, promotions featured her wind-swept hair, and in New York City she proudly held a torch posed like the Statue of Liberty. Wayne asked if, like the Reno newspaper's other contestants, I would create a Cosette image distinctive to our community. The paper, he promised, would then publish the five contestants' individual drawings and let readers vote for their favorite.

"Sure," I said right away, giving this promise little thought but also careful to refrain from revealing that at the time clients kept me extremely busy.

Wayne expressed his gratitude, before explaining that the absolute final deadline for me to bring the image to the newspaper was exactly one week away on September 20th.

A few days after making this commitment, I went on a whirlwind weekend pleasure trip with a my friend, Jan Weiss to the San Francisco Bay Area. Shortly after returning home to Reno as scheduled on Sunday evening, a mysterious illness sent excruciating pains through my abdomen around 4:00 that morning. The discomfort became so debilitating that I asked my good friend and employee, Margie Sibley, to drive me to the Emergency Room at Saint Mary's Regional Hospital just a quarter mile from my home. To this day, I still lack any idea what prompted this severe illness. All I know is that drugs that medical professionals pumped into my veins quickly made me feel somewhat better.

Around 10:00 that same morning—a Monday, my girlfriend Kathleen Conaboy's husband—also my good friend—John Bardwell picked me up at Saint Mary's to take me home.

"You look like death warmed over," Bardwell said right away. "What on earth is wrong with you?"

"To heck if I know. At least I feel a little better."

Well, right after returning home I went straight to bed to get much-needed rest. Finally, I awakened about 5 o'clock in the afternoon, feeling somewhat better. But suddenly I remembered my commitment to deliver the Cosette image to that newspaper guy named Wayne the following day. Throughout my career, I had never failed to meet a promised deadline. Partly because I felt at least a little better, that burning need to show professionalism motivated me to work late that Monday night to get the job done in time.

Shortly after the lunch hour the following afternoon, I arrived at the newspaper's front-entrance area with the promised Cosette image. A receptionist called for Wayne. Unbeknownst to me, he rarely went to greet delivery people, preferring to let them drop off their promised materials or press releases. This time, however, he decided to walk into the reception area after receiving the receptionist's call. The moment I laid eyes on him for the first time, my first thoughts were: "I bet he's the nicest husband to somebody."

Wayne promptly sat across from me, listening to my story of the sudden illness and how I almost hadn't finished this project on time. Wayne expressed his gratitude, especially since only two other graphic designers out of the five who promised such deliveries had come through with their commitment.

"Are you going to the show?" I asked him.

"Well, yes, if I can find a date."

This prompted an immediate thought to strike me: "He's not married!"

Wayne then told me he felt impressed since my version of Cosette was different from the two other submissions—each featuring that character either holding or beside a playing card, distinctive of Reno's casino image. Like Wayne, I considered those cards as predictable and off-the-mark, partly because at the time lots of other cities nationwide permitted casino gambling including Las Vegas and Atlantic City, New Jersey. Taking a much less predictable route, my design featured Cosette at the world famous Reno Arch—which proclaims the town as "The Biggest Little City in the World."

Saying thanks, Wayne wished me luck in the contest which offered no prize, other than the supposed prestige of victory. To my disappointment, later that week and a few days before the "Les Misérables" Reno premiere, the newspaper's readers voted to select one of the predictable poker-card images as the winner.

An unexpected call came to me about a week later from Wayne, who asked: "Patty, I would like to take you to lunch."

In a few days we met at the PJ & Company restaurant on South Wells Avenue. At first I thought of this as an informal get-to-know-you meal, especially since Wayne showed interest in my life and career. This guy explained that, yes, indeed he had ended up going to "Les Misérables," arm-in-arm with a brunette—one of numerous attractive women he had been dating at the time.

It wasn't until a few months later that he admitted fully and openly in no uncertain terms that during the week after meeting me in the newspaper reception area that: "All I could think about were your eyes—that certain sparkle that I had never before seen in any woman."

A few days after our initial lunch, I unexpectedly bumped into Wayne at a Nevada Women's Fund banquet. He recounted a vivid memory of first meeting me at a similar event about seven years earlier, when I had accompanied my former live-in boyfriend, Graham McKenney. As Wayne and I began dating in the mid-1990s, I still failed to recall this apparent first introduction—after which my current husband remembered having told Graham: "Where have you been hiding that woman!" Wayne had known Graham as an acquaintance for several years, interviewing my then-boyfriend for numerous business-related newspaper articles.

Wayne also claimed to have remembered conducting a phone interview with me in the early 1980s, when he researched and wrote a story about advertising trends of the time while I worked doing graphics and teaching at the University of Nevada. Conversely, as Wayne and I began dating in the fall of 1995 I had absolutely no recollection of such a conversation from nearly 15 years earlier.

Anyway, about two weeks after I formally met Wayne at the newspaper, he bumped into me and my good friend Margie and John Bardwell at a popular West Fifth Street lounge. From a respectable distance, Wayne watched in amusement as a tall, handsome, and well-dressed gentleman struggled and failed to pick up on me.

Shortly after I managed to avert that guy's attention, Wayne sat down for a little while beside us. By this point, Margie was nearly three months pregnant with her first child, Joshua John, nicknamed "JJ." My future husband stuck around for a few minutes that night, just long enough for me to realize that this was a guy that I might enjoy spending time with.

Midway through the following month in October, Wayne took me on a four-day road trip up the Northern California coast. This marked his first time staying at a bed-and-breakfast, a lifestyle that had stuck on him ever since. Like many couples falling in love, we would sometimes stay up until a few hours before sunrise, chatting non-stop, sharing our hopes and dreams.

Except for a four-month separation amid marital problems and extensive financial hassles in late 2007, we have been together ever since. In recent years we have occasionally found ourselves chatting about our hopes and dreams into the wee hours of the morning, seemingly with as much or even more excitement as during the first few months of our courtship.

Without realizing this at the time, as a high school sophomore I became a paid unprofessional hairdresser for the madam of a notorious legal Nevada brothel.

Also a good girl, I was fully unaware of Maureen Gunderson's involvement in the world's oldest profession.

Maureen's daughter Sandy Gunderson, a Wooster High classmate, became one of my very good friends. Guys everywhere went wild at the very sight of Sandy, whose big boobs, and Venus body made heads turn.

At the time, I was a fairly decent-looking blonde with the best flip in school in my junior and senior years at Wooster High. Yet upon launching my friendship with Sandy, I still remained as innocent as Bambi. Most other teens my age at the time were darling and cute, but by comparison Sandy beamed as nothing short of unbelievable.

During my sophomore year, Sandy and Maureen lived in a trailer just a few doors down from ours. Since Sandy and I were good friends, she had invited me to drive up to what at the time everyone considered the city's most prestigious neighborhood, Skyline Boulevard in a hilly area southwest of downtown. My parents had never driven me to that neighborhood, proverbially the "other side of the tracks" where Reno's wealthiest families lived. From sixth grade clear through high school this is where the vast majority of my schoolmates grew up.

While en route to our first excursion there, Sandy's mother Maureen—pregnant at the time—explained to me that: "Patty, I need to get out of this trailer, and I'm going to marry my boyfriend." Right off the bat the concept of moving from my seedy neighborhood into a comfortable community seemed somewhat foreign to me.

"This is where they're going to move?" I started thinking, as Maureen drove us around the Skyline neighborhood, looking for the type of home where she might want to live. Needless to say, the mother and daughter made their dreams come true. A short while later on one occasion I started helping Maureen do her hair at their new Skyline neighborhood residence.

"Patty, you are good with hair!" Maureen proclaimed. "You should go into hairdressing."

Fully unaware that Maureen worked as the full-time Madam of the notorious Cat's Meow Bordello in adjoining Storey County, Nevada, I visited their home three afternoons per week after school—for the express purpose of creating Maureen's hairstyles.

"Patty, you do a better French twist than beauty professionals," she said, always paying me a few dollars—a lot of money for a girl my age at the time.

This planted the seed in my head that perhaps I should consider attending beauty school, at least to get the required education necessary to enter that profession. That way, by working as a hairdresser I hoped to save enough money for tuition to a San Francisco-area art school.

All these years later, somehow I remain grateful that Maureen never mentioned her brothel-related profession. I gradually stopped doing her hair. While in my early 20s, I finally learned from mutual friends that Maureen had worked as a madam in South America before moving to Reno. Every now and then during the years after high school I would bump into Sandy, who always remained a sensational physical specimen of American womanhood and also a delightful person in my eyes.

Sadly, as I would later learn with great shock and sadness, my former schoolmate Sandy died of a heroine overdose at age 25, apparently without knowing that she had influenced my life, indirectly putting me on a pathway toward beauty school.

Steadily increasing amounts of new, and startling discoveries clicked into gear during the first several months after moving into my classic old home.

Following a long day's work, one evening I rested while leisurely sitting alone in my living room. Slowly sipping wine, I read the book "One Creature," a collection of poems and collages by my late personal art mentor, Joanne de Longchamps.

After flipping through the first few pages among the credits section I saw startling information about that original priceless limited-edition book—the listed publisher operated out of the same home that I had purchased!

Stunned and speechless, I carefully read that rare book. The publisher, West Coast Poetry Review, had printed just 500 copies in 1977. Her other book, "Warm-Bloods, Cold-Bloods," also featuring poems and collages by Joanne and published in a run of just 750 units, grabbed my attention as well—printed in 1981 from a different Reno address.

Mesmerized by this latest revelation of my home's history, pleasant memories of Joanne enveloped me like a protective halo. Joanne had lived in a classic house adjacent to my first husband's family home on North Center Street just four houses down from the entrance to the University of Nevada.

Through those years some faculty members at the university scoffed at my attempts to plan an art show featuring watercolor portraits that I had created. Some of these individuals thumbed their noses at my efforts, insisting that I should concentrate on more contemporary or avant-garde—experimental or innovative—art endeavors. During the early 1980s, a selection committee rejected my proposal to participate in an upcoming art show at the university's Getchell Library. Instead, they chose an artist who affixed the handle of a suitcase onto a wall, embossed with supposed explanations of what such luggage represented to society.

This struck me straight through the heart, a real disappointment. Through the previous several years, as a hard-working mother of two young children, I spent all my available time in the evenings creating watercolor portraits.

This process of developing images of my parents, various family members and interesting-looking people throughout the community essentially evolved into my "self-taught master's degree." Naturally, following the rejection by the university's art faculty, I grew somewhat discouraged.

"Don't worry at all—do your own thing, Patty," Joanne told me. "Follow your own course, follow your own heart—create the art that you know is right for you."

Always wise, extremely kind, patient and willing to give advice whenever I asked for her opinion, Joanne instilled within me the necessary gumption to stay the course.

Her late mother, Ruth Avery Cutten, had gained a solid reputation in the arts community when dancing with the famed, iconic Isadora Duncan—hailed as the creator of modern dance. As a child in the 1930s, Joanne had traveled with Ruth throughout Europe, particularly France, for studies in music and art. According to at least one published report after returning to the United States around that period Joanne turned down a movie contract offer from 20th Century Fox. Despite her apparent reluctance to become a film star, Joanne agreed to numerous professional modeling contracts, before appearing on the cover of numerous magazines that were popular in the 1930s and 1940s. One of these images caught the immediate attention of a young mining engineer, Galen de Longchamps.

"I would like to meet that girl," Galen reportedly said, and mutual friends arranged an introduction. The couple married in January 1941 in Pasadena, California. Her new husband was the adopted son of Frederic de Longchamps, a prominent Nevada architect credited with designing distinctive buildings—many that would remain some of the state's most classic, irreplaceable structures, still standing much later in the 21st Century. The father's notable projects included country courthouses across Nevada and the still-admired Art Deco-style U.S. Post Office on the south bank of the Truckee River in downtown Reno across from the former Mapes Hotel site.

For a 20-year-span starting in the 1950s Joanne continually enrolled in virtually every art class offered by the university, from ceramics to painting and sculpting.

By the time our close friendship developed while in my 20s and 30s, in the late 1970s and early 1980s she had served as a primary guiding force. She helped me to stay the course in fulfilling my dreams of creating the type of art that sparked my interest, no matter what others thought. Thanks largely to Joanne's encouragement I eventually became a much-sought-after watercolor portrait artist. People from many walks of life began awarding me lucrative commissions to create portraits and images of their pets or homes. A service that I continue to this day, this process served as a cornerstone of my thriving graphic design business.

Largely due to Joanne's encouragement, this transition began clicking into gear when the Reno Little Theater sponsored an art show featuring many of my watercolor portraits in the early 1980s. During this period, Reno's respected Deluxe Art Gallery gave me a highly-coveted invitation to display my watercolor portraits there in an exclusive two-women artist show, also featuring works by Deborah Cofer.

Sure enough, as if to exemplify my artistic style and subject preferences, during this same period some of the world's most prestigious art museums began featuring collections of classic and timeless oil and watercolor portraits.

The mere thought that Joanne had introduced some of her greatest works via a publishing company that operated in my future home—long before I bought the property—filled me with pride. Along the way, before Joanne's death in November 1983, she had become close friends with many legends in Nevada history. These luminaries included Walter Van Tilburg Clark, author of the landmark novel based on Reno, "The City of Trembling Leaves," and world-renowned artist Robert Cole Caples.

Adding even more unexpected, glorious vibrancy to my home, in my living room to this day I have two extremely rare paintings, perhaps the world's only remaining contemporary mid-1900s works by Caples—a cubist piece and a stupendous depiction of the Milky Way. Born in 1908 and reared in New York City, Caples had studied at the National Academy of Design and the Art Students League before joining his physician father in Reno in 1924. Continually growing and evolving as an artist, the younger Caples then attended Community Arts School in Santa Barbara, California, before opening a studio in downtown Reno's Clay-Peters Building. Caples' artistic heart took him on a pathway similar to the route that my own spirit would follow a few generations later; Caples started doing portraits before adding landscapes to his repertoire.

Some of Caples' most famous works included portraits of Native Americans, generated while serving in the First Federal Arts Project during the Great Depression. Unattainable in today's consumer markets, these works are considered among the greatest American classics of their kind. To this day, Caples' paintings remain some of the most coveted artwork in the American West. Sales of his pieces are extremely rare; some of his most widely acclaimed paintings still hang in a limited number of distinctive, classic Northwest Nevada residences.

As my friendship with Joanne solidified, she showed me dozens of handwritten letters between her and Caples, who had eventually moved back to the East Coast with his wife, Rosemary. These heart-felt letters expressed the intense interest that Joanne and Caples shared in art, culture and the American wilderness.

Blessed with the new-found revelation of Joanne's historical association with my home, I began displaying her two books in a place of honor under the portrait I did of Joanne—for everyone to see during the upcoming tour of my home. I owned two depictions of flowers by Joanne. I kept both of her most widely acclaimed collages on display in my kitchen; Just looking at these images soothes my soul. To think that she played such a significant role in my art career continued to fill my heart with gratitude. To think that she most likely stepped through the front door of my home long before I came here makes me humble. To think that her poetry and artwork will continue to live on in her blessed books bathes me in waterfalls of eternal grace. Oh, what I wouldn't give just to be able to say "thank you" to Joanne once again.

Would Joanne have been proud of my achievements? Could she possibly have envisioned what was to become of me, that I would eventually manage a book publishing company from the same residence—with my future husband?

Par for the course, Wayne insisted on engaging in his usual jovial banter with me, this time amid our slow 15-minute drive to the west Reno home of Sharon Honig-Bear.

"I hope there's plenty of good food," Wayne said. "What will there be to eat?"

"I don't know," I told him, as we drove slowly along Idlewild Drive, lined by a maze of trees that provided ample shade at sunset beside the Truckee River.

"Why go to an evening party, unless there is going to be great food?"

"You're just being silly," I answered, well aware that Wayne knew our host had gained a solid reputation for her tastes in great meals and fine wines. A New York native, Sharon had worked as a restaurant reviewer for the Reno Gazette-Journal, including during the 1990s when Wayne worked there. She had already gained a solid, positive reputation throughout the community before becoming president for the 2011-2012 season of the increasingly popular non-profit Historic Reno Preservation Society.

Just as Wayne had hoped, we soon discovered that Sharon had prepared a lavish backyard meal for us and owners of the five other historic local houses selected to participate in the Second Annual Reno Harvest of Homes Tour.

Sharon and other event volunteers gave us an enticing glimpse into the history of all the homes. Built from 1906 to 1964 in a variety of unique architectural styles, they included: three residents in the historic Newlands neighborhood of the southwest, just outside downtown; one residence in the Idlewild Drive neighborhood immediately west of the city's casino-area core; a classic house in old southeast Reno's South Wells Avenue district; and my house in the "old northwest Reno" neighborhood—immediately west of the University of Nevada campus, and bordering casino core's northwest edge.

Thanks to compelling and riveting research that society volunteers provided during the gathering at Sharon's home, and during the weeks immediately before that event, I learned jaw-dropping details that left me stunned, and in awe. Preservation Society volunteer Debbie Hinman, working in conjunction with other members, dug up hard-to-find historical information on homes selected for the tour.

Their intensive, dogged research revealed that the wife of the man for whom my junior high was named, E. Otis Vaughn, had attended a huge party in my future home in September 1929. That celebration drew plenty of attention within a few weeks before the Wall Street Crash of 1929, the onset of the Great Depression. Details from that party's guest list uncovered by Hinman from an 82-year-old "Reno Evening Gazette" society report left me speechless and humbled. Many early pioneers of Reno's educational system and business community were on the guest list. They included Professor and Mrs. B.D. Billinghurst; a future Reno junior high would later be named in his honor as well.

One of the most widely acclaimed invitees was Reno Mayor E.E. Roberts, a former congressman who had represented all of Nevada in Washington, D.C., from 1911 to 1919. According to a "Backyard Traveler" article by Rich Moreno, former publisher of "Nevada Magazine," Roberts had "scandalized the nation" while also amusing Renoites when he enthusiastically endorsed 1931 legislation that legalized casino gambling in the Silver State. Along with Nevada's liberal divorce laws, this innovative measure helped make the Silver State one of the world's pivotal, most coveted tourism destinations for many generations.

Roberts died while still serving as Reno's mayor in 1933, ten years after his initial election to that position. During the height of prohibition Roberts reportedly had proclaimed, much to the chagrin of many Reno residents at the time, that in spite of Prohibition during the height of the Roaring '20s, he would like to have allowed alcohol to flow freely from every street corner.

"I'm stunned by all this," I told Wayne, as we drove home from Sharon's party a few hours later. "All these important things happened in our house, and I never would have known any of this without the dedication and commitment of people like Debbie and Sharon."

As soon as we arrived home, I spent many hours well into the night reviewing the compelling information amassed by Debbie and other Preservation Society members, details that I had never known. The newspaper society item described the 1929 gathering at my home as a celebration of the 25th wedding anniversary of the house's residents at the time, Maj., and Mrs. Keith S. Gregory, who served as an instructor of Reserve Officers' Training Corps (ROTC) military courses at the university. This system would later play a pivotal role on Wayne's side of the family. His first cousin, U.S. Army Col. Ronald Rose, a 1980s graduate of the university's ROTC program, would later serve in the Rangers in the wars in Iraq and Afghanistan.

Others on the party's guest list included numerous university professors who would go on to play integral roles in the development of the educational system at the heart of the American West. Along with their spouses, these party-goers included professors Peter Frandsen, F. Armbruster, John W. Hall, A.E. Hill, Fred W. Wilson, Sanford Dinsmore, and Col. J.P. Ryan. A subsequent search of the "Congressional Record" showed that in 1899 Ryan had served as a lieutenant in the Sixth Calvary at Fort Riley, Kansas—where my husband Wayne was born 57 years later in 1956. As a lieutenant in the U.S. Army's Big Red 1, Wayne's father Rollan Melton had been stationed there about a year after graduating with the journalism degree from the University of Nevada.

Other documentation subsequently found by Wayne showed that in 1895 during the development of U.S. Army tactics, Ryan had written an article entitled, "Some Cavalry lessons from the Civil War." Other guests at the 1929 celebration included Lieut. and Mrs. Herbert B. Wilcox, whom records showed had applied to become a military surgeon in 1915. Also invited with his wife, Col. W.B. Standiford, who subsequently served in the late 1930s at the University of Indiana's ROTC program. Another report by the U.S. Secretary of War indicated that Standiford had served in the Philippines in 1900 in the wake of the Spanish-American War. In 1899, the "West Virginia School Journal" reported that Standiford would be shipping out to the Philippines that year as part of the 41st Infantry based in Camp Meade, Pennsylvania. In 1908, reporting out of Fort McKinley in the Philippines, Standiford commented on the "ignorance of militia as to the sanitary arrangements in camp."

Labeling the gathering in my home as a "unique and enjoyable" party, the society item said that the affair was also a fifth birthday celebration for the Gregorys' son, Bill.

"With quantities of sagebrush, Juniper trees and rocks in the living room, the home was converted into a realistic setting for a picnic supper served in true picnic style," the article said. "Cards and indoor horseshoes were the diversions following the supper."

From my perspective during the 2010s, the notion of dragging vegetation into the living room and playing outdoor-style games inside would have sent shivers down my spine. In any case, as the Preservation organization's superior, extensive research proved, ladies in Reno society during the late 1920s must have perceived the home as distinctive for its unique characters.

On Codel Way, "The Bonnie Briar Model Home at University Terrace ~ Now Under Construction," said the headline of a quarter-page display advertisement in the May 26, 1928 edition of the "Reno Evening Gazette."

The advertisement went on to proclaim that the property in the University Terrace neighborhood "offers an opportunity to every woman interested in better homes to watch building construction from the basement to the roof. This model home represents the last word in modern home design, construction and equipment and will interest every member of your family. The Bonnie Briar Model Home is being built in keeping with this growing, thriving, prosperous city where the latest in modern transportation is bringing a new era of growth and development.

"O.H. Paulsen and Company is building the Bonnie Briar Model Home especially for you and people like you who want the best in home design and construction within reasonable cost. This model home is designed and is being built as an inspiration for the many more new homes that will be built in University Terrace in the near future. Already, construction on other homes has started and these will multiply rapidly as people realize the certainties of increasing values of the limited amount of high land available for home sites in this city, where the population will reach 50,000 people in less than ten years."

Like the vast majority of American homes approaching 100 years old, my house has had numerous owners. Each added extensions or amenities that helped give the property increasingly unique characteristics—many that I would later remove or refurbish.

According to the Preservation Society's research, a wedding apparently occurred near my home's future site way back in 1915. The betrothed were a Reno High student, Ida M. Games, and Elroy E. Meckley who worked at a cigar store. Before the outbreak of World War I, the couple announced their intention to make their home at a residence at 527 Nevada Street, several blocks south of my current property.

In keeping with societal norms and practices of the time, married women during that period were often referred to in newspaper articles merely as "Mrs.," while the first names of these females were rarely printed. Records show that in 1932, three years after they lived in my future home, while still living there, Mrs. Gregory was listed as a member of the Trinity Guild Auxiliary.

A 1929 newspaper notice stated that E.E. Meckley, an excavating contractor, announced all excavating work for Sears, Roebuck and Co., at a property adjacent to and immediately south of my home. As of 1932, Meckley and his wife owned four adjoining properties on the street. A truck owned by E.E. Meckley overturned and a passenger was injured in 1933. Other auto accidents involving Chester Meckley, the homeowner's son, occurred in 1937, 1939 and 1941. Meantime, apparent financial problems had hampered the family during the height of the Great Depression in 1934, when government records show that the Home Owners Loan Corporation sued the Meckleys for $10,078 in delinquent payments. Two years later amid foreclosure the family was ordered to sell three of the adjoining lots.

At least a tiny bit of good fortune came in 1940 when Mrs. Meckley won a bottle of Clorox at an event marking the closure of a cooking school. After World War II erupted, in 1942 E.E. Meckley needed to apply for yearly permits to get the tires recapped for his trucking business. Nonetheless, the family's good fortune apparently picked up in 1943 when the Yancey Insulation Company applied for a remodeling permit on the home. Meantime, that same year, serving on the Victory Garden Committee, E.E. Meckley assisted homeowners in handling issues with soil on their properties.

Another development came in 1944 when the couple's son, Chester completed basic flight training with the U.S. Army Air Corps. After attending Reno High and the University of Nevada, Chester and his wife, Jean, made their home in the house where I live today. He served in Japan in 1945 as a member of the Occupational Fifth Air Force fighter command.

More tragedies ensued during the following decade, when family member Ida Meckley slipped on ice at Codel Way and West Eleventh Street. A resulting leg injury forced her to visit the hospital. Records show that a woman, Virginia Williams, also lived in the Meckley home in 1952. The following year, she was in an auto accident in which E.E. Meckley was cited for speeding at age 57.

The family's seemingly endless list of auto accidents and vehicle citations continued. In 1955, Ida Meckley was cited for failing to use proper precautionary measures when she pulled from a curb, resulting in an accident. As if he refused to be outdone, by this time in his early 60s, in 1955 Elroy Meckley was involved in a fender bender, this time cited for failing to drive with his eyeglasses.

The man's frustrations continued in 1955 when reporting the theft of from 15 to 20 cords of wood from his Mill Street lot, more than three miles away from the Codel Way residence. Ironically, 45 years later, in 2000 Wayne and I each worked for an online arts sales company, commuting to a Mill Street office near the former Meckley job site.

Mysteriously, more records surfaced in the Historic Reno Preservation Society research, listing 1127 Codel Way as the last known address of Florence P. Simon, who apparently had left the property in 1963 without claiming insurance funds.

Finally, Elroy Meckley's obituary in February 1966 gave additional insight into this man and his family. Born in October 1886 in Harrisburg, Pennsylvania, he died of a heart attack at age 79 in my future home. At age 21, in 1907 he ventured to Goldfield, Nevada, the same year that Wayne's grandmother was born in that mining community 265 miles southwest of Reno—and 187 miles north of Las Vegas. At the time, Goldfield bustled as Nevada's biggest city, when precious ore mining lured people from around the world. Apparently this same lust for adventure and potential riches had separately magnetized Wayne's late great-Grandparents and Elroy Meckley to the isolated, high-desert community.

The unincorporated town in Esmeralda County on U.S. Highway 95 had a population of only 440 people as the 21st Century began, a sharp decrease from the estimated 20,000 around the time that Meckley first stepped foot in that community. Like the vast majority of those pioneers, Meckley had left Goldfield as that town's mining boom gradually waned. Business analysts estimated that those mines generated the equivalent of nearly $83 million before taking a sharp dive around 1940.

Like other feisty pioneers and early Nevada residents, Meckley pursued a better life even during tough economic times. His obituary recounted that he moved to Reno, operating a trucking-contractor business from 1925 through 1945. Meckley was survived by: his widow, Ida May; sons Elroy of Sparks and Chester of Reno; eight grandchildren; and a sister in Pennsylvania. Internet records of the University of Nevada System Board of Regents show that three weeks after Meckley died Mr. and Mrs. Walter M Cummings donated $5 in his memory to the university.

Another news item uncovered by the society's research showed that a tiger skin rug with the animal's head was stolen from my future property in 1971, the night before an antique estate sale there featuring a whopping 10,000 items.

Adding even more luster to the property's history, widely known and highly acclaimed writer and editor William "Bill" Fox, had lived in my Codel Way home in the 1970s and 1980s. Excelling in a profession that Wayne would later bring back to the property, Fox had worked with Joanne de Longchamps in the 1977 publication of her book "One Creature," when the publisher West Coast Poetry Review listed its address as my future house. Fox's operations later moved to a home in a secluded, private neighborhood between Mount Rose Street and West Plumb Lane near the southern boundaries of the historic Newlands neighborhood.

"History—most people fail to think about it enough," Wayne told me, on the day after our delightful evening visit with other homeowners in Sharon's back yard.

My gut reactions told me that Wayne was right on target. People who live in historic homes such as ours are likely to discover a treasure trove of interesting information, just by checking through old newspapers, and government records.

Chapter 16

The future president of the United States briefly locked his gaze straight at me.

How would Ronald Reagan react the moment we finally came face-to-face? What would I say to him, and how should I behave?

The occasion in February 1974 came near the end of his second and final four-year term as California's governor. At the time Reagan, already world-famous as a former movie star, was strikingly handsome and still with a manly physique at age 62. By contrast, I was just 27—dressed in an inappropriately sexy outfit, lacking the experience and world-class sophistication at the time to know any better.

This particular day marked a significant change for Reagan and for almost everyone else in attendance. The occasion emerged as the first time in California's history that women were allowed inside a formerly all-male club.

As the relatively new art director for the California Chamber of Commerce, I became one of the first woman in Golden State history to be invited to this annual event. I attended with the first female editor of the business organization's magazine.

The only other time that I had personally interacted with a future U.S. president had been back in 1960 when I was just 13 years old. At the time a United States Senator from Texas, Lyndon Banes Johnson briefly visited Reno during a West coast campaign swing as a vice-presidential candidate on the Democratic ticket headed by then-Massachusetts Sen. John F. Kennedy. During Johnson's brief stop in Reno, he stayed at the Town House Motor Lodge managed by my Grandparents. That morning the Lone Star State politician and I ended up swimming together—just the two of us—in the motel pool under the close watch of U.S. Secret Service agents. Kind, gentlemanly and fatherly in demeanor, Johnson peppered me with casual and polite questions as we swam in the warm, soothing waters. After perhaps just 15 minutes or so, this man got out of the pool, dried himself off and signed his autograph for me on a photo of himself: "To Patricia, from Lyndon Banes Johnson."

Of course, at the time as a little girl I lacked any notion that I had been swimming with a future president. And, eventually as a young woman about to meet Ronald Reagan for the first time, I lacked any inkling that the famed actor and politician held presidential aspirations as well.

The two occasions involving Johnson and Reagan could not have possibly been more different. Johnson had handled our brief Reno chat with grace and natural kindness. Although also holding a reputation for having a friendly demeanor, perhaps Reagan lacked any inkling of precisely how to interact with me. This would have seemed natural, because the event marked the first time a California governor had to interact with women in a formerly all-men's playing field.

Along with the editor, I got the distinction of being invited because I served as a director within the highly respected and integral California Chamber of Commerce. We were the only two women professionals in attendance. Prior to then, throughout the organization's history of more than seven decades by that point all other directors within this system had been men.

Although never labeling myself as a "women's libber," or as a champion for the betterment of female rights within the workplace, I had soared in my career to never-before-heard-of heights—just as such efforts picked up steam by countless other women nationwide. To say that I was a trend-setter or the breaker of a proverbial glass ceiling might have seemed like an exaggeration to me at the time. Yet looking back after all these many years, I'll have to admit that yes, indeed, I had essentially helped to tear new ground for other women who would eventually follow into a pathway that I had helped create.

As the gathering began in a huge meeting room near the California Capitol Building, I realized that all those men seemed somehow unsure of exactly how to "handle" or interact with women within their formerly all-male bastion. For my part, I lacked any notion of how to look and behave during such a formal function. Needless to say, my cute green dress emitted a steamy, hot, sexy allure—sharply inappropriate and out of place for such an occasion. If I had known any better at the time, a finely pressed and dark-toned business suit would have given me a much more suitable appearance.

Our nation's future president already played the role of "The Great Communicator" to a perfect-T. Reagan worked the room with the grace and depth of a tropical parrot naturally interacting with other high-flyers and super-achievers within the male species. If he had asked anyone before we came face-to-face about my personal role or why I was there—a woman, of all things—someone might have told him "that's Patty Atcheson, our new art director." To this Illinois native, I suppose, that word "art" might have somehow enabled all those men to somehow set me apart from all the others. The Chamber's male directors held positions of high distinction, everything from top posts in energy, finance, business development and transportation. Perhaps those positions could easily be classified as far more important than someone like me, in their minds a "mere art-related professional."

When Reagan finally got into a position to meet me, I felt as if he was unsure of what precisely to say. And, God only knows, I lacked any clue of what to tell him. Momentarily, this tall, muscular hunk of a man shook my hand, his grip on my fingers and palm undoubtedly as tight as Hulk Hogan, the future wrestler, actor and TV personality. Regan's super-tight grip caused me physical discomfort, at least temporarily preventing me from saying anything of any import. All along, this crafty politician smiled like a delighted, joyful munchkin meeting Dorothy in the Land of Oz over the rainbow.

Within seconds Reagan was elsewhere in the room without having said a word to me, focusing his attention on the event's other guests. Looking back, I realize that his firm, manly grip might have been a clever way to put off or eliminate the possibility of any conversation between us. As a woman breaking new ground, entering the formerly all-male kingdom, perhaps I had upset the proverbial apple cart far too much. Maybe these men were still having difficulty figuring out how they should interact with director-level women at important business functions.

Lord knows my pathway to that juncture in life had been formidable. The mere fact that I landed the job had amazed me and many others as well. Everything had come down to the fact during the previous several years that I had developed the gumption to ask for and to often receive the things I wanted from life. Much of my perennially positive, can-do attitude had sparked into overdrive after my former Gray Reid's Department Store illustration department boss, Posie, had rejected my request for a 50-cent per hour pay raise back in 1968 when I was just 21 years old. Keep in mind that by refusing to take "no" for an answer, and finding my own pathway, I had asked for and received an illustrator position at Tyson Curtis and Wilson advertising firm in Reno.

"Now that you're hired, how much do you want us to pay you?" the firm's personnel director had asked me.

"Oh, two dollars and twenty-five cents an hour, that would be fine," I responded without hesitation, the precise amount that I had asked Posie for and this time getting my new request granted on the spot. Later that day, I submitted my resignation to Gray Reid's.

From that point forward, I credit much of my success on my continual, relentless and always unsatisfied thirst for new knowledge—while always striving to improve my art, graphic design and illustration skills. While at Tyson, Curtis and Wilson for several years, I eagerly learned as much about the advertising and marketing business a possible, everything from directing photo shoots to all basics of the publication process.

Amazingly, while working at the firm, one of my former arts classmates from Wooster High more than three years earlier entered the business to apply for a job. At this juncture, Bob Boisson had just graduated from Oakland College of Arts and Crafts. Bob had enrolled there on the recommendation of our high school arts teacher. During my senior year about an hour after school, I had entered the Wooster arts classroom to get some of my supplies. Startled, I had found the room filled with students—all of them boys, and each filling out applications for admission to the Oakland school.

"But what about me?" I had complained at the time. This male teacher didn't tell any of us girls about this opportunity. Of course, none of the boys could give me any answers, because they lacked specific details on why our teacher had failed to tell his female students of this opportunity. All my classmates knew was that he had told only the boys about this process.

"What are you doing here?" Bob asked me, right after he entered Tyson Curtis and Wilson to apply for a job. "This is a pleasant surprise."

"I work here," I said, matter-of-factly. "I'm an illustrator."

"Great, Patty. Wow!" Bob made no attempt to censor his obvious amazement at my accomplishment. "Did you go to an arts school?"

"No," I said, not wanting to make Bob feel bad. "I have been an illustrator for several years, and I'm still learning."

"That's great," Bob said, as he began to complete a job application form. "Guess I'll see you around sometime."

Bob went on to generate his own successful career as a talented and respected illustrator, while I concentrated on improving my own skills. Super-talented and highly knowledgeable at the illustration and marketing craft, Bob subsequently had a highly successful career as an advertising, marketing, promotion and community programs executive for numerous Gannett newspapers, primarily in the West Coast. His many duties later included promotion director for "USA Today" based in Washington, D.C.

Ironically, my second husband's late father, Rollan Doyle Melton, served as a board member for many years at Gannett, including when the company launched "USA Today" in the early 1980s. Wayne's own career began to blossom later that decade when he became a temporary Editor-on-Loan to that publication, the nation's largest general-circulation newspaper.

Every step of the way through my own career, I embraced a take-charge and perennially positive attitude, always telling anyone who inquired that "I can do that" whenever an appropriate task or skill was required of me. Packed with energy, I managed to help support the family as my first husband attended college. I still carried all these attributes with me after Fred eventually entered McGeorge School of Law in Sacramento, part of the University of Pacific.

Based on everything I had been told by Fred's fellow students, he quickly emerged as one of the brightest pupils during that period. Usually a good judge of character—but not always—Fred excelled in mock trials held at the law school, attributes that later would help him climb to the top of the legal profession. Several decades later, long after our second and final divorce, well into the 21st Century Fred held a well-deserved reputation as a sharp-minded businessman—the owner of numerous rental properties—and as a much-sought-after lawyer. Back in the mid-1970s, he had depended on the financial support that I provided for him and for our two children.

Initially upon our move from Reno to Sacramento in 1973, I landed what I considered temporary, a low-pay grunt job laying out ads for an appliance company. Yet eager for more success and to give Fred the financial support that he desperately needed at the time, I set my sights as high as possible.

The California Chamber of Commerce put me through a maze of job interviews. Each time I used my usual, casual and take-charge response of "Oh, I can do that," particularly whenever questions arose regarding whether I had designed and published magazines before. Although I never flat-out lied during these inquiries, I stretched the truth at least somewhat in several regards. After these interviews, I telephoned some of my friends and former associates in Reno, telling them: "You've got to help me."

Like champions or even coaches helping from my corner of a proverbial boxing ring, these Silver State professionals said all the right and perfect things during phone interviews with my future Golden State employers. To that point, for instance, I had worked some on helping to generate magazines but never fully held complete responsibility in getting all that work done. At least one publication industry professional back in Nevada still carried a deep crush on me, although nothing sexual or inappropriate had ever occurred between us. After my departure with Fred for Sacramento, I knew that the man still living in Nevada would do "anything reasonably possible to help me advance in my career." Sure enough, following my request this man must have given a performance via telephone deserving of an Academy Award for best supporting actor.

At the time, the Chamber's officials faced a great degree of pressure to hire women for director positions. For nearly a century to that point all executive-level positions within the organization had been held by men. The public outcry and the urgent need to hire a qualified woman for such positions must have been tremendous. As far as I knew, many qualified candidates had applied for the job that I deeply coveted—and all those who had traversed the initial gauntlet into the final-interview phase other than me apparently had been men. Partly as a result of these factors, I quickly found myself positioned on the precipice of potential success. But then a major setback occurred; a Chamber personnel department official summoned me to his office.

"I'm sorry, but you flunked, Patty," the man said, his facial expressions displaying genuine sadness, at least from my perspective.

"What do you mean, 'flunked?'" I asked, startled because things had seemed to have gone well to that point. My positive attitude had refused to even think of failure.

"The math portion of the test—you didn't get a passing grade," he said. "I'm so sorry." Empathetic, the man then explained that as a result, he would not be able to schedule me for any of the necessary employment interviews for the job.

Damn.

I had always hated taking tests of any kind, particularly anything whatsoever to do with math. The endless maze of public schools that I had attended as a child had never enabled me to catch up fully with my classmates, to get a complete grasp of numbers. And, now, there I sat, my dreams apparently crushed although throughout life my entire spirit and physical being had craved as much knowledge as possible.

"I guess you might want to hear this," I said, interrupting this man as this meeting seemed to be breaking up. "I was having a problem that day—a personal problem."

"A problem? What could..."

"I was on my period."

Silence filled the room for what seemed to be the next hour or so, but in actuality the delay in speaking probably lasted about five seconds at most. From my perspective, you could have heard a pin drop from 388 miles away in Los Angeles. Faced with tremendous pressure to hire a woman for a director spot, Chamber officials suddenly found themselves having to deal with a so-called "girl problem," although unbeknownst to them I was a pure, unadulterated dunce involving anything to do with mathematics.

"Your woman time..." the man started stuttering, clearly unable to think clearly as his face suddenly turned dark red. "I mean, Patty, you ah ... What I'm trying to say is that..."

"You mean, I can take the math portion of the test again?" I said, excitedly.

Apparently before any clear, rational thought could possibly enter his mind, the guy summarily found himself saying: "Yes."

During the days that immediately followed, determined to fine-tune my math-test skills in a rapid-fire fashion, I started to inquire with as many knowledgeable people as possible on how I could tackle such a task. Someone finally said: "Go to the library; they have samples of the exact kind of test that the chamber is required to give."

Eager to heed such advice, I soon went to the public library, got photocopies of a sample math test and studied the document non-stop throughout the weekend. Soon afterward, Lady Luck paid me a fantastic visit that put the remainder of my professional life on a positive course.

The sample test that I had copied and memorized was the exact same exam that was on the make-up test that I subsequently took. Needless to say, I aced this quiz before taking the required round of necessary in-person interviews with batteries of Chamber industry panelists.

Several weeks later during the winter holidays, Fred and I took our children Chris and Zoë on the two-hour drive to spend his brief time away from school during winter brake with our relatives back in Reno. Late one afternoon, I got an unexpected phone call while staying in the home of my mother-in-law at the time, Mary A. Atcheson—affectionately known as "Mary A."

"Patty?" the male caller inquired, as if needing to verify my identity. "Yes?"

"This is Harold Pinkerton," he said, the Chamber's top administrator. "I have a Christmas present for you."

"A present?"

"Congratulations, Patty—you're officially the new art director of the California Chamber of Commerce."

Overwhelmed with joy, and beaming with boundless happiness, I then proceeded to enjoy the most fantastic Christmas holiday ever with my immediate family—my parents, and with my husband's family as well. My father-in-law at the time, Merle Atcheson, had gained a solid reputation throughout Northern Nevada as the highly respected Executive Vice President of Sierra Pacific Power Company. My first husband's other relatives also had achieved—or were in the process of gaining—significant successes in the legal and medical professionals. Their jobs and activities ranged from a superior court judge to medical students. Suddenly I had emerged as the first adult female within their ranks to enter the cusp of future professional success.

Thanks to my stick-to-itiveness, my good fortune continued despite temporary potential stumbling blocks encountered during my first few months in the art director post. With help from my secretary and several staff-level personnel, my many duties included the development, design and production of promotional brochures, display advertisements, annual reports to weekly and monthly newsletters and the "Pacific Business" magazine.

None of my new associates at the time realized that I lacked direct first-hand experience managing every major aspect of magazine production. Right off the bat I hit home runs with no problem, developing a brochure and display ads. Yet I lacked the full mental concept of everything necessary to implement page layouts and typography for an entire magazine. Determined to get on top of the situation and to learn these skills rapid-fire, on the weekend immediately before my first scheduled California Chamber magazine production, I took home sample prototypes from a previous edition of our magazine; I studied the documents during the entire weekend. This effort paid off right away, upon completion of the first overall layout of "Pacific Business" under my leadership. However, at that point I also still lacked hands-on experience tackling the necessary chore of what industry professionals called "specs," or type specifications—the process of determining specific fonts and type sizes. Remember, back then printing industry professionals lacked the digital technology that helps simplify or at least streamlines the overall pre-production publishing process in the 21st Century.

Once I finally gained enough confidence to tackle this necessary "spec" process, Vonnie, our new editor, offered to handle the chore herself, saying: "I've always done this. You don't mind if I handle this, Patty?" From that point forward, my regular work process at the Chamber became a snap, everything handled without any problem.

The only disappointment while there came entirely as the result of a decision that I had made. A top-level executive had mentioned that management asked if I could personally paint an official painting of the California State Capitol Building. Officials planned to give the piece to Governor Reagan. Either stupidly or at least short-sighted at the time, I turned down the offer, insisting that another artist that I respected at the time handle the work. Looking back more than four decades later, I kicked myself at the realization that by doing the requested painting myself I could have essentially put a major "feather in my professional cap."

Certainly, I had ample talent to tackle such an assignment with distinction, as proved by another job that I would tackle several years later when employed at the Nevada Department of Tourism. While there, I generated limited-edition, pen and ink renditions of all 17 of the Silver State's county courthouses—many of them designed by highly acclaimed architect Frederic de Longchamps. Well past my 60th birthday, my series of Nevada's county courthouses remain highly coveted, displayed prominently in prestigious law firms statewide.

One of the most important lessons I learned emerged as the continual, pressing need for all of us to seize opportunity when such chances arrive.

As the years passed, and I steadily achieved ever-growing levels of professional success, my parents never once said to me directly: "Patty, we are so very proud of what you have done, what you have achieved in your career." And yet, all along, somehow I never needed to hear them say such things, instinctively realizing that any accomplishments that I might make should speak for themselves.

This pattern continued into the late 1980s and early 1990s, my father fully aware that at the time I owned and operated my own stable, fully operational statewide graphics design firm—while commuting by jet weekly between Reno and Las Vegas. Instead of mentioning my specific achievements or my overall career advancements, dad would say things like: "That's good, you'll need an office for your people."

The notion that his daughter had zoomed sky-high in a profession once hailed as a "man's-world" seemed far from my father's mind. And besides, such a direct statement, giving praise had simply never been his way of communicating. The most important thing in my mind remained the fact that my parents truly loved and adored me.

Whatever might happen in our future, I would always know that I could retain my pride in him. That's partly why I placed dad's many war medals, secure in their display box, in a place of honor in my home's upstairs library—in advance of the upcoming tour.

Chapter 17

Shortly after I graduated from Wooster High and got married to Fred, my parents bought a small property in Sun Valley seven miles north of Reno. Mom and dad moved the trailer there, living at the site for the remainder of their lives.

For several years, dad maintained his nagging alcohol abuse, working at several auto-body repair shops and at one point even briefly owning such a business himself.

During a stretch of nearly two years, he traveled the state selling the Bondo brand product to similar shops. Made by the 3M Company, the fast-drying, hardening paste was used to repair dents, rusty holes and leaks on virtually all types of vehicles.

Father contributed to my parents' income until he stopped working for good at age 56 in 1974. Perhaps his stamina had waned, possibly aggravated by the nagging injuries he had suffered in the fatal wreck nearly 20 years earlier. Maybe he had begun collecting Social Security disability payments; my parents never told me of his apparent income sources, if any. Meantime, mother maintained her job at Sierra Pacific Power Company, work she liked; she enjoyed helping people in the utility's customer service department, devising creative ways or payment plans so that they could make necessary payments. Thanks to mom's seniority with the firm, she had been able to land this position when the business phased out key-punch operations as those technologies became obsolete.

Father still occasionally enjoyed chucker hunting. Now as proud Grandparents, dad and mom occasionally took my son Chris fishing with them from early childhood through his teenage years. They also cherished time with Zoë as she grew into a delightful, intelligent young lady.

Because dad loved my mother so much, his alcohol abuse gradually and steadily began to decrease. For the first decade after dad's retirement this transition had not seemed highly apparent, taking shape at a snail's pace. While mother continued to work at the power company, my parents started spending more quality time together.

By the early 1980s, they started taking their camping trailer for weekend or vacation excursions to Pyramid Lake. This high desert body of water known as a "geographic sink" with no outlet 30 miles north of Reno served as the ideal place for mom and dad to enjoy fishing, their favorite leisure activity.

Mother also spent lots of her free time with my Grandma Eve. As a bonded, loving and caring mother-daughter team, they remained best friends. Mom and Grandma frequently enjoyed playing bingo at John Ascuaga's Nugget in Sparks just east of Reno.

At age 62 in 1986, mom finally was able to retire. Through the years she had been the best of my parents at saving and managing money. Unbeknownst to any of us at the time, however, mother's nagging habit of smoking cigarettes soon would take her life.

During the first two winters after mom retired, she and dad took their travel trailer to spend the holidays in the warmer Arizona climate. They quickly decided to end that short-lived tradition, because mother desperately missed spending the holidays with our family in Reno.

By the time doctors told us of mother's lung cancer, I suppose any hope of saving her life had already passed. In their small trailer home, when dad was 70 he did an excellent job caring for his ailing 64-year-old wife. She had been hospitalized several times, including for a brain operation after the cancer spread.

"Mother, I have a question for you," I told her at one point. "Why did you stay with dad after all your problems through the years?"

"Because we liked fishing," she said, matter-of-factly, blunt and to the point.

"Okay," I said, accepting her statement at face value.

Without speaking directly of the matter, all of us seemed to know that mother would soon perish. At one point I went to see mom in her hospital room, promising to bring her books on spirituality if she wanted, some detailing the positive power of healing.

"No, I just want to enjoy what I have right now," mom said.

I spent the next hour just hugging mother, to let her know how much I deeply loved her. After she was released from the hospital, I went to see my parents at their home.

"Mom, do you know what I want more than anything?"

"What do you want, honey?"

"I want you to cook me one of your favorite meals, round steak and gravy and potatoes. I want to watch everything that you do while you're making it."

In my eyes, mother seemed super-pleased that I would want to spend quality time with her. I watched her pound the steak, an essential phase of the process in those days before 21st Century technology made such work unnecessary.

The smells, the aromas, and the simple yet comforting taste gave me a protective, warm sensation. Several decades later I would continue to cook similar meals for Wayne or other relatives, especially Zoë and Hannah whenever I would have a "mom attack"—a healthy yearning to somehow bond with my mother in a spiritual way.

Following the loss of her hair due to chemotherapy, amid three hospital stays mother never appeared to me as if feeling badly and she never complained. So, the last time she went into the hospital, I thought, "Well, she's going to be coming home again."

Chris had just returned to Reno from his travels in Europe; I took him to see his ailing grandmother in her hospital room. Right away I realized the sight of my son's sick Grandma was hard on him, and Grandma Eve was there also.

"Can I have a banana?" mother asked. "I want a banana so much."

"Sure, Grandma," Chris said, before going alone downstairs to the ground-level hospital store and restaurant to get her the fruit.

While alone with my mother and Grandma Eve, I noticed that at age 85 she looked much younger and more wrinkle-free than her ailing 64-year-old daughter. Watching my mom as she lay on the bed, I kept thinking: "I just love her so much."

Finally, after Chris returned with the banana and the time came to go, I said: "Well, mom, I'll come back to see you in the morning. It'll be around 8 o'clock, while on my way to a business function."

"Okay, honey."

I arrived as scheduled first thing the next morning. Right away I noticed that mother wasn't in her patient room. I figured that they must have moved her, because similar impromptu transfers had occurred several times earlier. To find out her new location, I promptly went to the nurse's station.

"What room did you move my mother to?" I asked.

"She passed away in the middle of the night," a nurse said, as if commenting on the delivery of milk or a newspaper or a daily shipment of mail.

"And you didn't call me?" I said, stunned. "No."

This upset me, since the hospital had my contact information and my father's phone number as well. The nurses also never bothered to call him. This left me with the responsibility to tell my father that mother had died. The notion of seeing his beloved wife in a hospital had been far too difficult for him to tolerate, so he never had visited mother during her various hospital stays. Still, he had been a champion during mother's illness, tending to her every need while at home. To father's credit, he had been stone-cold sober during the final year of mother's life, fully dedicated to doing whatever he possibly could to help ensure that she was as comfortable as possible.

"Mother is gone," I told dad right after arriving at his trailer home. I spoke briefly and to the point, since this is the way we always communicated. "I'm so pissed at that hospital for not calling us."

Dad never cried upon hearing this. We all had expected the news for quite some time. Still, the motionless expression on his face told me that a huge hunk of his heart had been removed forever that day, leaving a sad, gaping hole in his chest that never could be filled.

"Patty, you handle the arrangements," he said. "Everything that needs to be done."

A short while later, I spread mother's ashes at Pyramid Lake, perhaps her favorite place in the world—where she had enjoyed fishing more than anywhere else with dad.

"Why in the hell won't you ever answer your phone?" I told father on the front porch of his trailer, about a year after mother died. "You should know how worried that I am about you."

"I've just been busy," he said. "I never heard the phone."

Those were the days before non-stop communications such as email, instant messaging and online social networks.

"Dad, I've been calling you for days with no answer," I said, far more concerned than angry. "I don't want to come in here and see that something has happened to you, and I haven't seen you for days, and you're stinking in the bed or something."

I still spoke with him in this pointed, direct fashion because that's how we talked to each other.

At my insistence that day, dad promised to do a better job of keeping in more frequent contact. I insisted that he call me every three days or so. During the three years after mother's death, I rarely missed seeing him at least once each week. Except on occasions when pressing business matters prevented me from seeing him, usually on weekends, I always grabbed a fast-food hamburger, a drink and French fries. I then shared these meals with dad at his trailer, often visiting him for however long that he wanted.

Through this stage in life he remained sober. Father kept pretty much to himself, always close to the trailer except for occasional brief excursions to local bars, where he drank only coffee while playing poker machines.

Lacking his favorite fishing partner—mother—dad stopped enjoying his favorite outdoor activity.

Following mom's death, dad seemed to at least go through the motions of taking care of himself. His favorite foods included lots of tomato soup with plenty of crackers. Although father might have tried to put on a bright face, he failed to fool me at all; I knew of his deep unhappiness.

"You could come live with me," I told him, after buying my home in 1990—two years after mother's death. I explained that a tiny cottage behind the main house could easily serve as an ideal residence for him. That way, I explained, dad could come and go as he pleased—enjoying meals at my main house whenever he wanted, while also having his own personal space and privacy in the back cottage. "Dad, I'm getting tired of not hearing from you enough. This way I'll always know that you're okay."

I made this same proposal several times, and his response was always: "Oh, Pat, I've got so many things to do."

My gentle, persistent nagging always failed in this regard, each time assuring that he could enjoy plenty of privacy. When I first bought the old home and took him through the property to show him around, he commented: "It sure needs a lot of work."

"I can do it; it'll take some time."

"Well, okay."

As I might have expected, dad never said anything like "congratulations" for buying such a unique home with great potential. More than ever, I never expected to receive any accolades from him. Any praise would have been unnecessary, since such bold, gushy talk was not our way of expressing emotion as father and daughter. His basic messages throughout my various career and financial advancements still remained simple and short acknowledgments such as "stay honest," "that's a good place to work," or "you can't cheat an honest man."

The last time I spoke with him was on the afternoon of March 30, 1991. The following evening at my house I planned an Easter dinner with my best girlfriend, Kathleen Conaboy. By that point like sisters, our friendship had been growing since the early 1980s when we had first met while both working at the University of Nevada.

"Dad, I want you to come over and meet my friend," I said.

"No."

"You're coming to dinner."

"I'm busy."

"Listen, please, dad. I'm insisting on it. I want you to meet my close friend, and I want her to meet you. I want her to know you."

"Okay," he finally said. "I'll think about it."

The fateful phone call came to my home in the wee hours of the following morning, probably around 2 o'clock. I answered, groggy and awakened from a deep sleep. It was Steve Mortensen, owner of Fisherman's Bar in Sparks—my dad's favorite place to visit on Saturday nights, on his infrequent forays away from his trailer.

"Patty, I'm calling to let you know that your dad died of a heart attack."

"What happened?" I asked, wiping sleep from my eyes.

"He was over here playing the poker machines, just visiting with us," Steve said. "He wasn't drinking. He was just having coffee and telling us stories. And then, without warning, he just fell off the bar stool."

"It happened that fast?"

"The paramedics said he was probably dead before he hit the floor."

"Well, if he had to go any way that he wanted—except for fishing—that's the best way he possibly could have gone."

Later that morning, at Easter sunrise I realized that my father—a lifetime agnostic—had just enjoyed a spiritual reawakening. Had mother welcomed him into her arms, full of forgiveness and showing him the way into heaven? Well, at least one thing seemed certain, his deep unspoken sadness finally had ended, and I felt more certain than ever that there really is a caring and eternally loving God.

Chapter 18

Envision a delightful "snow globe."

Many of us vividly recall or admire such miniaturized scenes, filled with water encased in circular glass. Such amenities increase in popularity each holiday season.

Anyone who has ever shaken such an object can never forget the eye-popping sensation of shaking these spheres. White flakes seemingly appear everywhere inside until the person holds the device motionless, causing the appearance of snowfall.

These particles gently cascade to the inside base or foundation, usually the site of cozy cottages, or Santa Claus and his elves, or a wide variety of other wintry scenes.

Nine months before the tour of my home, a few days after Christmas I felt as if in a placid, tranquil "real-life" snow globe with my girlfriend, Kathleen Conaboy.

With her husband John Bardwell out of town on an art assignment, I visited their home to tell my true sister that she really matters. I even phoned Wayne to tell him of my plans to spend the night there, without causing any clatter.

After having a fine dinner, we drank wine in front of the fireplace as the snow fell outside. Kathleen wanted to cozy up to the warm fireplace and watch television. In no uncertain terms, I told her "We are going for a walk. There have been very few times in my life that the moon gives a luster of midday to objects below. Ha Ha, it is as bright as day outside, come on, lets go for a walk." Like bunnies we snuggled inside our toasty garments, and slithered arm-in-arm in our warm fuzzy coats as snow fell all around. Anyone who has ever known such quiet, such eternally placid silence can never forget these heavenly sensations. The crunch of a person's boots in the snow below makes the ears tingle with delight.

Snowflakes meander everywhere as we parade super-slow down the middle of a quaint, out-of-the-way neighborhood road. To follow each other step-for-step is to form unity. To wrap around each other's arms in a sisterly, playful way marks the delight that only adult siblings can share, bonded friends for life. To dance in methodical silence here amid this brightness, the super-shine of these friendly white sparkles can only make us look like angles in each other's eyes. Oh, what a woman would give to have such a delicate feeling. Oh, what a woman would give to know that she is truly cared for by someone so dear, forever, always. Oh, this night becomes a gift, an unexpected frosting on the cake that comprises both of our lives.

Girlfriends!

Each sensing the eternal magic in this moment, each never feeling an unnecessary need to grasp all of these heavenly dustings that fall upon us, we both keep our eyes wide open—like children afraid to miss even a moment of this spectacular scene.

Yes, here we know more than ever that any little girl who grows up without a biological sister of her own can find such sharing later in life. Here, we never need to look back to keep track of where our footprints have taken us—at least initially. Here, on the snowy ground below, in the shimmering sky all around us, and within the delightful looks on each other's faces, we know this sensation will last throughout this lifetime—and perhaps far beyond.

We, girlfriends talk and share our dreams. We measure this moment with our hearts, we measure this moment in our words of love, we measure this moment with dreams about this exact second—and focused on our ever-evolving futures as well. Perhaps most important of all, we measure the moment with smiles.

As for me, I have changed as a person since childhood, no longer confused in a hectic world of non-stop traveling. Change has come to me, in the form of physical maturity as I edge deeper into my senior years. Change has come to me, in the form of learning and appreciating the blessings of forgiveness—for myself, due to the many mistakes I have made in life and also forgiveness for others who might have wronged me. Change has come to me, for now I find myself much-loved by others whom I had never yet even known as a child—by Kathleen, by her Husband John Bardwell, whom I cherish as an artist and as a friend, and by Wayne, and by countless new friends amassed during these past few decades.

Up, way-way up above us, perhaps from a distance of a mile or so, these snowflakes form. Up, as far as my gloved hands can reach, I can pull these delightful designs into my palms—each unique, each blessed and distinctive just like the souls of individual humans, at least to a point. Mother Nature dictates this. She commands silence at this moment, other than the hidden noise of our lively heartbeats—each still packed full of boundless curiosity. She requires nothing of me, although I decide to show my uncensored joy.

Momentarily, we girlfriends find ourselves on the front porch of one of our best pals, Kris Coppa and her husband Don.

"Come outside and play with us!" We tell Kris, and she soon helps make our sharing whole and complete. Good, soothing wine that requires the tongue to relax and the sensations to smooth out any unnecessary thoughts or worries eases us into a gentle breeze. Picture an object going ever so slow atop a sheet of ice, as if a person never worried about the outcome. Feel the cold, crisp air, just smart and tangy enough to gently bite the senses into a wide-awake tone. More than ever before, appreciate those who have gone before us—my mom, oh how I miss her so—my dad, oh how I smile knowing that his pain is gone—and my Grandma Eve, the angel, here I yearn to smile for her, to laugh for her, to cry for her, to jump for joy in gratitude for having had her, and to step once again in harmony with Kathleen and with our girlfriend Kris.

Somehow within this snow globe, the moon manages to shine—full, complete and bright as ever, as if unaware or perhaps ignoring the fact that the snowfall has become heavier than ever. A crack in the clouds? A crevasse from the heavens above? Who knows for sure, other than the cozy toes—our feet encased in furry boots.

At this moment, perhaps Kathleen and Kris realize as I do that the snow globe in which we frolic at this late hour plays holiday tunes. Maybe they fail to hear these blessed songs the way I do at this moment, these ladies' words as cheery as little schoolgirls at recess—like the clamoring of children sharing apples and other yummy snacks during playtime.

Careful to avoid mentioning this, so as not to disturb their delightful thoughts, I allow my mind to play the song that it knows and cherishes—"Silent Night." Oh, holy night, you are here for me, making me feel more alive than ever. Oh, silent night, the stars must shine way up there somewhere, far above this relentless shimmer.

Each feeling safe and warm, we soon re-enter Kathleen's home, basked by wise, giving and abundant heat from the quaint, old-style brick fireplace. Always a champion of the holiday season, my best girlfriend has decorated her home with many ornaments and Santa dolls, so lovely that the actual Saint Nick would become green with envy. More slow sips of wine pamper the soul ever so slightly, as cherished holiday tunes reverberate delicately from a multi-speaker stereo.

Surely my true sister here knows that this bond is similar at least in some ways to back when I enjoyed a shopping excursion with my mother and Grandma Eve as a 5-year-old girl back in Twin Falls, Idaho. Surely my true sister knows of the genuine familial love that I embrace for her always, and for her own lovable parents as well, and for the countless times we have already spent together, and for the hoped-for future gift of many good times still yet to come. Always there for each other, always there to listen, to cry together, to hug, to share and to talk about our men—we, us maturing ladies, we bring our legacies to this earth as best we can, for we are always and forever:

Girlfriends!

Three weeks after Wayne and I began dating back in 1995, I had a disclosure to make to him. This declaration emerged more as a matter of fact than any sort of confession. Healthy relations require truth. " I like younger men."

By this point in my late 40s, I explained fully and honestly to Wayne that during my late 30s and particularly my early 40s a feeling of great confidence fulfilled me more than ever in life—as a bold, brazen lady. Through those years, I had felt and behaved sexier than I ever had. Throughout that period, all of my adult male companions were at least 10 years and in some cases nearly 20 years younger than me. I had loved these guys and enjoyed them for their passions, for their energy, for their good looks and in some cases for their pizzazz, charisma and their great potential. I had held them and touched them as much as they touched me, as much as I would permit anyway. Far from a dominatrix or a mere sex goddess, I almost always had set the rules.

Once I selected a suitable guy, and he chose me, the fellow served my particular purposes, my individual needs and desires. But I didn't want any of them close to me emotionally and spiritually, and that's a big reason why I chose them so young. Maybe this was my way of protecting myself from getting my soul hurt, and yet—deep down—no matter how fantastic the physical and emotional sensations had been during that period, deep down I had felt a void.

An empty space.

For a period of several years, life had blossomed to a point where my heart felt nothing that really mattered, as if nothing had touched the very essence of me at all—either physically, emotionally or spiritually.

During the few years immediately before meeting Wayne, the vast majority of the time I had started telling them all "No," that I did not care to go out on a date. No, I'm busy with my business or with my family, or with my various obligations. I would convey without saying so in words—I don't want you to hold me, because I feel nothing for you. No, there is something missing in my life, and I cannot say precisely what it is, how to express the way that I feel to you or even to myself. Yes, some of you might have ignited at least some degree of passion. And then there was Ron, the guy with the rock-hard body, maybe even young enough to be my son. Off and on with ever-decreasing frequency for the final 15 months before meeting Wayne, this certain someone, a mere plaything, had been there for me—but that guy had never truly been close to my needy heart at all.

Finally, things got to a point where on the rare occasions that I did go out on dates, I would refuse the offers by these men to walk me to my front door when the evening ended or their occasional urgings for me to allow them into the living room for a nice visit.

Never once had I told any of them, at least toward the end of this phase, of my true reasons for this increasing physical and emotional distance between us. Deep down, I wanted a certain kind of guy with a loving, giving heart. Deep down, I wanted a man with a youthful energy, but also with potential. Perhaps more than anything, rather than just current financial wealth, I yearned for a guy who had a longtime stable, rock-solid career. Someone with the resources, vitality and ambition to care for me, someone to listen to me, to really see me, to have me, to hold me, to touch me, to share with me—in every positive way that a bonded man-woman couple can enjoy.

Every fiber of my mind told me that this fellow was out there, somewhere.

More than merely just the opposite of my father in terms of professional stability, this guy would need to listen to me—to actually hear what I had to say, like no man had ever done before in my life.

Call this what you will, but please for heaven's sake realize that I was far from one of those difficult-to-please women. Anyone who truly knew me at the time and fully understood my motivations would never have even ventured to label me as "high maintenance." To the contrary, I was a loving, giving and kind woman—eager to give my heart someday to someone who showed the ability to share his many positive attributes with me as well.

Indeed, as I told Wayne that night, even before our first kiss, I had banned all new men from even coming close to entering my front door— except perhaps for Ron, that temporary "play-thing." By that point, still only three weeks after meeting my future husband, I had discarded Ron as if he was an unwanted sack of potatoes. That young stud—nearly seven years younger than Wayne, who was nearly 10 years my junior himself— had never been close emotionally to me, nor was I to him. Certainly, this rush, this transition, this magical transformation within my soul occurred almost overnight.

Wayne had almost instantly and effortlessly changed everything.

Sure enough, he unknowingly unlocked the floodgates of my soul, and so with hardly any reservation whatsoever, I invited him to my home for dinner. I invited him afterward into my living room, a week or so before we had traveled together up the Northern California Coast. Also, on that night, I invited him to share a glass of wine with me after our meal in the living room. "No, thank you," Wayne said, "I don't drink alcohol; I have just never liked booze of any kind." My subsequent offer of ice water was met with his smile, the only imperfection his slightly crooked front teeth.

Without either of us ever having to say so in mere words, from the start the two of us had felt comfortable and far from nervous in each other's presence. Rather than positioning himself on my couch. Wayne sat casually on the floor of the living room. Momentarily, he started speaking of a bright, light-filled and glowing sensation that he felt in that moment—not *from* me, not *for* me—but rather as he said honestly in those moments, and I remember his words very well even to this day: "It's your house, Patty. Your home, I've never felt any such positive energy ever, from anyone's home before." Occasionally sipping his ice water, Wayne relaxed, his head propped on his right hand—his elbow planted casually on the living room carpet as if the roots of a healthy sunflower.

I already felt a rush, hard for my body and my physical being to stop. Finally, here, now, in this moment, is a man that I want—someone whom I can share with. Something about Wayne told me that he had all the right and perfect characteristics that I had yearned for, or at least I hoped.

Was I already falling in love with this man, fully and completely for the first time in several decades? How could this be, just three weeks after meeting him? By this stage in life I had prided myself in feeling and behaving wise and strong, and level-headed. And yet here, suddenly as if an autumn leaf that got blown into the middle of a raging high-mountain river, I felt myself getting swept away downstream both physically and emotionally.

God, please don't let me fall in love so fast. Let this bonding go slow. Allow the two of us to get acquainted slowly, enabling this new relationship to grow at a methodical pace. No matter how much I prayed in this regard, the feelings were too much for me to hold back. No matter how much I prayed, the floodgates within the very essence of my being had already started to open—whether I liked it or not. Ah, indeed, no matter how much I prayed, whatever I might have hoped for at that point, I already felt my heart beat faster whenever I was near Wayne.

For a full minute or so, I cannot truly say exactly how long after all these years, Wayne talked in a heart-felt, uncensored way about his sensations concerning my house—the light, the positive pulsations, and the boundless energy he had felt just being here. It wasn't until much later that I would learn first-hand on many occasions that Wayne was a "sensitive" person who actually picks up on the vibes of people, places and things.

Very early on, even during his first visit to my home, I had already sensed an inkling that he had a powerful sensory perception—his sensitivity, his kindness, his inner pulsations—his connectivity with the universe all around us. Ah, this had been exactly what I wanted in a man, a masculine tenderness.

Starting on that evening, and in the many nights that would follow, I opened up my heart to him, revealing: my purchase of a 1958 Austin-Healey British sports car for just $800 in the summer after graduating from Wooster High—selling the vehicle after a few months in order to help amass my $1,000 tuition for beauty school, only to later discover decades later that such classic vehicles were later worth as classics a whopping $175,000; of how I had cruised the main street in downtown Reno on warm summer evenings in the mid-1960s with my girlfriends—a community tradition at the time, one night meeting up with a young man named "Toby"—discovering that we were born in the same hospital on the same day in Twin Falls, Idaho; of when I had served as the president of Girls Athletics during my senior year at Wooster, an activity I truly enjoyed, only to get booed by several boys as I received an award at a school assembly—breaking part of my heart; of how while attending Wooster as a senior I became the only girl to date a college boy, Joel— becoming a sensation when he wore sunglasses while visiting our cafeteria at lunchtime, unwittingly prompting one of my female classmates to ask for his autograph; of my landing a deal that enabled my first husband Fred and me to buy a tiny home for only $7,500 in the early 1970s, smack-dab in the center of an African-American Sacramento neighborhood; of how my son Chris' black schoolmates often picked on him, unknowingly at the time helping him to grow up tough as nails; of my passionate love affair with a married man, a wealthy business executive, while working at a Reno advertising firm in my early 20s—during one of my numerous separations from Fred; of how my first husband and I had reconciled several months before we conceived Zoë, the love of our lives; of how my mother had given me a quarter when I was just eight years old living in Carson City, telling me go to the special showing of a movie "The Wizard of Oz," promising that I would enjoy the film and making me a lifelong lover of cinemas; of the time a model in a university arts class that I took failed to show up one day, before I volunteered to pose nude at age 28 for the entire class to draw paintings of me—only to discover, to my dismay, that people who were being taken on a tour of the building would walk through the classroom—some gazing admiringly at my fully exposed body; of the first time my father taught me to drive, a Jeep with a stick-shift—before sending me on my merry way to drive alone in the vehicle across the high desert east of Sparks, while dad enjoyed a beer with a buddy; of spending my 35th birthday traveling in Europe in early 1982—at one point standing alone for at least ten minutes in front of the Mona Lisa at the Louvre Museum in Paris; of living a hippie lifestyle much of the time in the late 1960s during the first several years of marriage to my first husband; of leaving the beautician business after visitors to the beauty shop where I worked in Sparks proclaimed to me, "Wow! What an artist you are, Patty—this is truly your calling," noticing that I drew sketches from magazine photos to kill time at the back of facility, where management had stuck me as "low girl on the totem pole;" and, of course, many of the most vibrant tales from my near-gypsy-like lifestyle during childhood.

I startled myself by revealing to Wayne detailed revelations about my early years on the road, essentially living in the front seat of a pickup truck and various other vehicles. The mere fact I uttered these phrases stunned me.

This marked a significant milestone in making such a disclosure. Many of my closest longtime friends still lacked any notion about my curious past. Showing nary a hint of discomfort, Wayne described his own compelling history, plus an off-the-mark public perception of him as a rich, spoiled and untalented "daddy's boy"—a member of the "lucky sperm club," the son of a multi-millionaire.

Such assumptions proved far from the case, as Wayne fully revealed. At the time he was a divorced father of two teenage girls that he deeply adored with all his heart.

Sadly, at least from Wayne's perspective, the divorce attorney for the first of his two ex-wives—his children's mother—had been my ex-husband Fred Atcheson. The divorce decree had left Wayne near destitute for many years, always making his child support payments without fail for nearly a decade up until the time we met. Yes, my ex-husband, hailed as one of the best lawyers in all of Northern Nevada, had taken Wayne to the financial cleaners in the divorce settlement in the mid-1980s.

So, although Wayne had a fairly good job, he was far from rich. Nonetheless, from that point forward many people throughout the community incorrectly assumed that as a couple he and I were super wealthy, perhaps in the top 1 percent of income earners.

Striving to make the best of things, on occasion Wayne got a fairly good laugh or at least a brief chuckle by stretching the truth—sometimes telling people in a light-hearted manner that "because that lawyer screwed me in my divorce, I went out and took his wife." This, of course, was not true but Wayne occasionally made this observation anyway, as if the mere act of saying so might somehow make him feel better.

As a child, in his teens and as a young adult, music experts and conductors recognized Wayne for what they called his superior, heart-rending operatic and Broadway-style singing abilities. These were among attributes that forced me to fall more in love with him during subsequent months and years. Through the late 1990s and several years beyond, I often heard him sing in the shower and a few times accompanied by piano at social parties held at the home of some of our good friends.

Throughout that period, Wayne's vibrant, magnetic character, his numerous talents and entertainment skills led me to believe he had boundless potential. Like almost every woman striving to concentrate on the best qualities in her boyfriend, I somehow overlooked or at least paid little attention to—either intentionally or inadvertently—some of his eccentricities.

Perhaps the worst of these forced me to at least momentarily face at least one truth. One evening a few months after we met, I convinced him to stop the nonsense of staying occasionally at his one-room furnished apartment.

Although Wayne never took me inside, through the open door as he moved out some of his possessions, I noticed that he had been sleeping on a bed without any sheets, or even a blanket.

Speaking honestly, Wayne explained to me that he paid little attention to so-called worldly things of that nature. While far from bizarre, his unique characteristics included dreams at night that almost never featured people, but rather of other-worldly objects, forms, shapes and dimensions of many kinds.

Still, Wayne boasted a well-deserved reputation as exceedingly kind and a genuine good guy—at least in most circles. While attending one weekend evening social function with him at a home design business, one of my girlfriends pulled me aside and tried to warn me to avoid Wayne because—as she said—he's "just different." My gut feelings told me to brush off this comment, which at the time I considered a mere nuisance.

Other events proved quite the opposite. Nearly 150 people attended Wayne's invitation-only 40th birthday party in the backyard of his parents' Reno mansion residence in April 1996. Scores of people enjoyed interacting with Wayne, at the time an entertainment columnist and features reporter.

The following month on the spur of the moment after living together in my home for just more than half of a year, we eloped to historic Virginia City, a 40-minute drive southeast of Reno in the Comstock. Neither of us wanted any fanfare or hullabaloo from this wedding, preferring to avoid drawing attention from our families.

During the next 20 months I continued working at graphic design from my home office, while Wayne maintained his co-called "regular day" job.

Our lifestyle took a dramatic change in early 1998 when the newspaper's management promoted him to the additional, newly created position of society columnist.

Although this transition opened up the boundless positive

possibilities for many new friendships and contacts, the newspaper insisted on paying him a very small salary.

Sure enough, as we wined, partied and dined at least three or four times weekly with some of northwest Nevada's wealthiest, most highly acclaimed and successful residents—including some billionaires. Wayne barely earned enough to put gasoline in our tank in order to attend these functions. He only owned a few good, decent suits that I had bought him. Luckily, nearly 100 percent of the time our hosts picked up the tab, everywhere from invitation-only parties in homes of the very wealthy, to major fundraiser events for huge charities.

My duties as his unofficial, non-paid assistant taking photos of guests at these gatherings played a key role in cutting back on my abilities to work full time at my own business. Partly as a result, we found ourselves falling further behind in paying our bills. Things got so bad at one point that I was forced to sell some of my precious jewels including an extremely rare diamond necklace featuring multiple-karat diamonds, inherited from my late Grandma.

Driven to the brink of desperation, finally Wayne asked his employer for a much-needed and much-deserved raise. Management had the audacity to scoff at my husband's observations that he earned barely enough income to perform his job. One executive even had the audacity to scold him, saying they were offended that he had asked for higher pay. Meantime, our accountant literally laughed when he first saw Wayne's annual financial records.

Meantime, his widely acclaimed and much-revered father, Rollan Melton, enjoyed a highly successful lifestyle. At the time, my father-in-law and his wife, Wayne's mother Marilyn, lived in a spacious mansion deemed by many people as perhaps Reno's most highly coveted residence by far. To their credit, and I will always be grateful and appreciate them for this, in 1999 Wayne's parents gifted to him funds that we desperately needed to pay for a new roof and exterior paint on our home.

Desperately in need of repair, sections of the roof were filled with broad, gaping holes—giving rainfall and snow runoff the potential to cause near irreversible damage.

The situation got so bad that Wayne literally feared our roof would cave in and disintegrate—falling into the attic, perhaps while we attend one of those Champaign and hors d'oeuvre parties hosted by one of the Reno and Lake Tahoe area's most coveted millionaires or billionaires. All along, my husband's popularity with the public seemed to increase at this point in his 20-year career, after working his way up the ranks as a crime reporter, general assignment writer, city government reporter, business writer and entertainment columnist. On numerous occasions in the early 1980s, he had literally filled the local section of the newspaper, chuck full with fast-breaking news stories all written by him. While he gained a reputation as the "backbone of the newsroom," at least in the eyes of some top editors, others seemed to show indifference. Meantime, some people in the community complained to Wayne openly, to his face that he was a crappy, non-talented Daddy's boy who never deserved his various jobs—although he happened to be well-liked by many within the newsroom and throughout the community.

The perception of Wayne as a non-talented adult son of a super-rich, nationally acclaimed Republican newspaper executive and columnist might have reached a fever pitch in the autumn of 1986. A handsome 30-year-old divorced father of two at the time, Wayne attended an evening party that his parents hosted at their mansion for then-Vice President George H. W. Bush.

That night Wayne arrived decked out in a snappy suit, well after the Secret Service had given the "all-clear" signal and as military helicopters flew above his parents' mansion to provide necessary security surveillance. While en route to the event, Wayne had parked his old beat-up, run-down car several blocks away, before walking through a gauntlet of community protestors—primarily staunch anti-Republicans. These folks enjoyed what they called a "cheap weenie roast, while the super rich—including our vice president—are over at Rollan Melton's house dining on caviar."

For several minutes that evening, Wayne sat beside Vice President Bush who spent an hour or so going to pre-designated open seats at the this quaint backyard gathering for less than 120 guests. Some visitors viewed this as a precursor for what would become Bush's successful bid for the presidency two years later. Wayne's father never proclaimed this at the time, but "H.W." was far from his own personal favorite as far as presidential-level politicians.

Straight from this invitation-only party, Wayne went to his unfurnished rented button-sized duplex apartment, where he slept alone on the floor—without blankets or even a pillow. That night, without even enough money to buy pajamas for himself due to crushing child support payments, he tossed and turned, finding sleep difficult, knowing that somehow, someday he might achieve at least some sort of success in his own right.

"I guess you damn Republicans are super-happy tonight," another journalist angrily told Wayne several weeks later, on an election night when the GOP retained its majority in the U.S. House of Representatives. Rather than respond, and cognizant of the need to refrain from arguing unnecessarily with others in his craft, Wayne never bothered to respond to this small-minded person. Keep in mind that reporters, for the most part, are trained to remain open minded and to avoid rushing to conclusions, lest their assumptions be dead wrong. Sure enough, Wayne was a registered non-partisan, not preferring either political party.

Two years later, during the second half of 1988, he served as an Editor-on-Loan to "USA Today" in Washington, D.C., before returning to Reno. Several of his Northern Nevada co-workers served similar stints to differing positions before and after. By that point an 11-year newspaper veteran within two months after returning to Reno, he got an unexpected job offer to return to Washington as an editor for the newspaper parent company's Gannett News Service. At age 33, Wayne carefully weighed this proposal, which he considered as a possible pathway to upper management positions—perhaps even as a managing editor or an executive editor.

Yet Wayne's top priority at the time remained his daughters, Annie and Bonnie. Without a steady girlfriend, still living alone and sleeping on the floor of his apartment, my future husband spent quality time almost every weekend with his children—who still lived the bulk of the time with their mother, his ex-wife at her Reno-area home.

Letting his heart rule rather than his mind, Wayne chose to reject the job offer and stay in Reno so that he could be near his daughters. Sadly, though, just a few years later Wayne's ex-wife was able to use provisions from their divorce decree arranged by my crafty ex-husband, Fred. Despite Wayne's protestations, the woman moved with their children to the Silicon Valley—where she landed a high-paying job after earning an electrical engineering degree from the University of Nevada.

Faced with no other option, for the next six years almost without fail Wayne made the eight-hour round-trip over the high Sierra range in his run-down old Suzuki compact car—sometimes in blizzard conditions—to spend every other weekend with his daughters.

As a married couple, Wayne's and my financial condition took a sharp turn for the worse in 1999 when a Nevada court granted the girls' mother a whopping 25 percent increase in child support payments. This order came even though Wayne's financial records proved that he had consistently paid the woman twice the amount that was agreed to in their 1986 divorce. Adding insult to injury, the court ordered that this electrical engineer—at the height of Silicon Valley's growth spurt—garnish those payments straight out of his paycheck.

Meantime, Wayne's duties and his strong work ethic mandated that we go to high-end social functions. Naturally, we did our best to try to fool the many party-goers into thinking that we were doing at least okay financially. Worsening matters, for the first time ever my home-based graphics design business dried up, at least for the most part. Although I developed steadily increasing friendships at the evening functions, my professional work load tapered off. Steadily increasing numbers of competitors dove into the Reno market; just about everyone with a mouse and design platform started fashioning himself as a graphics expert. Some businesses fell for this tactic, those with inexperienced eyes wrongly believing they were getting good-quality work—when in fact the vast majority of those cheap images stunk. The stress forced me to start gaining weight for the first time in my life, by this point in my early 50s.

Still boasting loads of energy, I spent much of my time during this period organizing those numerous Truckee Meadows Heritage Trust gatherings with my trusted friend Toni Harsh in hopes of saving the doomed former Mapes Hotel facility. I also earned enough to buy groceries and to pay bills.

At one point Sierra Pacific Power Company where my mother had once worked turned off the electric power to my historic home—taking me totally by surprise. Panicked, I got some immediate help from Wayne, who had either forgotten or failed to pay numerous utility bills for several months in a row.

"Wayne, my dad always told me the most important bill to pay is the utility bill," I told my husband that evening, as he put on his tuxedo and I pulled one of my best gowns out of the closet—in preparation for attending our latest high-brow society event.

Pushed to the limit of my ability to mentally cope, I broke into tears as Wayne explained that we barely had enough gasoline in the car to get to that night's event. On that particular evening, as I recall, we went to a lavish gala attended by many multi-millionaires on the shores of Lake Tahoe a one-hour drive from home.

When Wayne went to a Tahoe gas station so that we could fill up for the return trip, he suddenly realized that he only had $5.28 in his checking account. Desperate and hoping to save face, as I had left my purse at home, he put five bucks into the tank.

This left my man, the guy that I adored, the guy who had attracted me into his life, into marrying him, into loving him—famous locally for his close associations with the "rich and famous," with only 28 cents to his name, and absolutely no savings whatsoever.

This was high society? This was the epitome of success?

The executives at the newspaper and the stockholders of its parent company, Gannett, lived in posh homes, flew in private jets, garnished stock options worth millions, took multi-week golfing vacations, and high-level stockholders such as his parents earned God-only-knew how much every year. To his mother Marilyn's great credit, though, she paid to get a new set of teeth for Wayne's daughter Bonnie—each tooth rotten to the core, some to the level of the gums as his ex-wife supplied the children with mountains of candy paid for with funds from the child support payments. Thanks only to my mother-in-law's efforts and kindness, Wayne's daughter eventually could boast a smile suitable enough to land herself in a toothpaste commercial.

By this point, as Wayne's readership totals and the fan base grew for his extremely popular society column, he started telling me of his increasing unhappiness working at the newspaper and his sense the entire print news industry was on the verge of going straight downhill—faster and with more horrific results than a barrel of monkeys shooting off the edge of Niagara Falls.

"I'm losing respect for myself," Wayne told me at the time. "How can anyone have any respect for himself, when giving his heart and soul and talents to such a greedy, selfish and heartless corporation as Gannett?"

Amazingly, just at the breaking point, Wayne unexpectedly announced to the news media in March 2000 that he was considering a possible bid for the Ward 5 Reno City Council seat held at the time by Dave Aiazzi. My husband eventually decided to avoid entering the race.

This revelation stunned many people throughout the community, the vast majority of whom never thought Wayne would ever possibly entertain a departure from the newspaper. Seizing the opportunity, an executive for a local firm, a Dot-Com company that sold artwork online, gave Wayne an unsolicited job offer.

Eager for a change in life and for a well-deserved increase in pay, and with my blessing, Wayne accepted the proposal in May 2000. By this time, I had already started working as a part-time, mid-level internet administrator at the same Reno-based Internet company. At age 44, Wayne had served 22 years for Gannett, which gave him a grand total of only $22,000 in retirement. Needless to say, this angered Wayne, since he had been told by management while working at Gannett in the late 1970s and early 1990s that employees with at least 20 years seniority were guaranteed a lifetime of monthly retirement payments.

The company also neglected to give him a goodbye party. Instead, top editors—some of them earning well over $100,000 yearly—mentioned his departure at the end of a mandatory two-hour staff meeting, where reporters were taught necessary updates on legal skills they needed for their jobs.

Wayne spoke briefly, telling everyone how much he had appreciated them and saying a sincere goodbye. Then, right away just about everyone left the conference room about as fast as possible rather than take time to enjoy Wayne's goodbye cake—because they needed to get back to work as soon as possible after the extensive, mandatory work session.

"Thanks, dad," Wayne shook his father Rollan's hand, and my husband also hugged his mother—who had taken the time to attend. By this point my father-in-law was terminally ill, suffering from congestive heart failure. Five months earlier Wayne's father had suffered a near-fatal condition while traveling with Marilyn several hours before midnight on New Year's Eve in London, England, as revelers greeted the year 2000. Two of Wayne's siblings flew to the United Kingdom to be at their family patriarch's bedside, while my husband stayed home—near penniless—working on his extremely popular weekly column about Reno's high society, the rich and famous.

"This is one of the happiest days of my life," Wayne told me after returning home from his last day at the newspaper. "I finally have a much better job, glad to be away from that rat hole—the idea of sitting at that desk for another twenty years made me lose respect for myself."

Little did each of us know that this transition would eventually lead to financial ruin, with the IRS set to slap a lien on my home just six years later.

"Wayne, I have a secret place that I want to show you?" I whispered in his ear, as we drove back home toward Reno from our romantic trip up the Northern California coast, that first month after we met.

"A secret?" he said, weary following several hours driving.

"It'll be worth your while—I promise," I oozed, as we headed east on State Route 70 along the lazy Feather River.

"What is this secret all about?" Wayne said, obviously curious. "A surprise?"

Unable to hold back all the details at this early point, I explained that for the past five years I had owned nearly six acres of undeveloped land. The site was nestled near the heart of Dixie Valley, tucked in the high Sierra seven miles west of Frenchman Lake inside the Plumas National Forest.

"I've never taken anyone there before—any man, ever," I said, fully honest and open about revealing this secret.

After passing through the out-of-the-way town of Quincy and eventually past Portola where I had attended my initial first grade classes, I asked Wayne to turn left on an isolated country road leading north from the ideal little community of Chilcoot-Vinton. We drove another eight miles, the road surrounded on both sides by tired, flowering sagebrush—all vegetation weary after the brief summer, already prepared for the fast-approaching winter. A natural hazy sensation emanating from whispery, dark, breezy clouds high above cast the distinctive wisp of autumn on everything—from the varnished, reddish roofs of century-old barns, to the blushing clump of late-blooming blue wildflowers near the side of the roadway. Even the cattle, dozens of them, stood motionless across the field, all posing like cardboard posters, all far off in the distance—as if actually clever spots on an oil painting by my late mother's former boyfriend, Stephen Cartwright. A clever landscape artist would have had a field day with everything around us, as I could see from the respectful and amazed expressions in Wayne's eyes as he drove.

I asked him to pull to the side of the road at the entrance to Frenchman Canyon—a windy, steep two-lane road leading up to the lake. Eager to see my property, he parked and inquired: "We there yet?" I urged my new boyfriend to avoid getting too eager, too fast. Slow down, taste the positive sensations of life, enjoy the vibrant autumn colors flashing all around us, and breathe in as much of this cool country air as possible. Momentarily, we ambled hand-in-hand along Frenchman Creek, our eyes transfixed on a canopy of yellow and slightly orange leaves—all perched directly above on a maze of branches. Moments such as these come only to a few lucky people.

Finally, we paused for air as a sudden whispery breeze served as a much-needed reminder that the afternoon would only last for so long before nightfall—a definite deadline, since I yearned for Wayne to see my property well before dark.

"We need to go now," I said, gently tugging at Wayne's hand, urging him to return with me to his car. But he wanted to stay with me in that one place. No words were necessary for him to convey this desire, judging by the fact that he pulled me toward him for a long, and much-wanted kiss.

Still lacking any reason to rush faster than necessary, we soon drove up the three-mile canyon, before edging along Frenchman Lake's south side.

Wayne had been to this lake before, perhaps with other girlfriends. But with them, he had never ventured this far along the lake, he had never ventured to this realm of understanding within this natural environment, he had never ventured any deeper into this forest. All this suited me just fine, as I directed him to turn left onto a dirt road—the final seven-mile phase to my hidden property.

My secret, until that day.

During the final approach, we winded atop the dirt road. Up ahead, at a distance of about 80 yards, a clump of mischievous deer zipped across the road, leaving smoky-looking air behind them. A few errant raindrops had the audacity to plop on the windshield, which still afforded a fine view of indefinable, fairly average round hills to the left and right of us. The various valleys, ridges, peaks and crests within the 400-mile-long, 70-mile-wide Sierra always offer such surprises, nothing ever looking exactly the same from one day to the next. Sure enough, the threat of rain had suddenly ceased, at least for the time being—a typical day in the Plumas National Forest, where weather conditions haphazardly change.

"Wayne, there's Dixie Peak!" I said, delighted, as boisterous as ever, "We're almost there."

My new guy slowed momentarily, as if sensing the need for his brain to suck in every sensation of this sight. The late afternoon sun insisted on sending tendrils of ravishing, spell-binding light here and there upon this pyramid-shaped peak. Far up here in this generous, mountainous wilderness, a respectable distance from the faintest possible smattering of city smog, even for a person of mere-average vision a pine cone could be seen resting on a tree branch from many miles away. Time loses all of its regular meaning way up here, playing by rules that only Mother Nature can dictate, rather than the mindless structures of the continual deadlines and rush-rush attitudes of metropolitan society just 63 miles away, to the southeast of us in Reno. Far from such worries and concerns, I reached out to grasp Wayne's hand as he drove us over the final ridge leading into Dixie Valley.

"My property is down there," I said, pointing. "Up around the curve."

On my command, Wayne stopped on the dirt road and shifted to park; he sat still behind the wheel as I opened up the entrance gate. After he eased the car onto the entrance road, I hopped back into the front passenger seat. Fifteen seconds later we pulled to the travel trailer, formerly owned by my parents, which I had hauled to the property nearly five years earlier. On the west side of the dwelling, Wayne and I stood on a massive 4-year-old wood deck which my son had built over a period of several days. Under a wood-frame canopy, this perfectly positioned patio overlooked Dixie Meadow, through which a creek flowed lazily, spreading here and there in the form of high-elevation wetlands—a cherished, seldom-seen jewel. Rarely seen within the continental United States, such spectacular and irreplaceable amenities serve as a playground for wildlife and vegetation of many kinds, the games and the rules continually changing with each passing season.

"Wow" Wayne said, standing beside me on the deck. "You mean I'm the first guy you've ever taken up here? Unbelievable."

I reiterated this truth, sitting beside him on a wood seat and explaining the feast of landscape set out in every direction before our eyes. In recent years, and during the seasons that would follow, some of the world's most popular movie stars and TV personalities had made this valley their secret, untold getaway. The most popular among these household names had included Tom Hanks and Tom Cruise at varying times renting an adjoining property, and Sandra Bullock whose family had purchased nearby land. At the time, movie star Mare Winningham owned a property just on the other side of a nearby road, enjoying summers with her family. Just up the valley a bit, Anthony Edwards, then a co-star of the popular "ER" television series, owned a small A-frame structure on a wide expanse of land.

Amazingly, on a whim, five years earlier in 1990 I had driven through this remote back country and spotted a "for-sale" sign on the barbed wire fence. I latched onto the property as soon as possible, forking out a down payment of several thousand dollars and paying just less than a few hundred dollars monthly under a 10-year contract—the selling price a grand total of only $28,000. Longtime Dixie residents and my few girlfriends lucky enough to know the truth about this purchase swore that I owned "the choicest, the finest, and the most spectacular property in the entire valley, bar none."

They say that a person "makes his or her own luck." Well, if this is indeed true then fate certainly had helped out quite a bit. With no one's help but mine, my hard work, determination and stick-to-itiveness had begun to pay off big time. Without any man to help me, without any close advice from anyone except my deep intuition, and without any reservation whatsoever, I had seemingly pulled all this clay right out of the sky—figuratively speaking—with the help and guidance of my boundless faith in God.

My mother would have loved this place. She would have loved the idea of bringing horses here, she would have loved the idea of building an authentic log cabin with a smoky, authentic fireplace on this very spot, and she would have loved spending cool, refreshing evenings on this porch, sharing good times with family and friends.

Direct and to the point, taking a far more masculine stance, my late dad would have always brought his fishing gear—always eager at the crack of dawn from late spring into mid-autumn, to visit this vibrant forest's countless lakes, rivers and streams. Surely dad would have enjoyed roaring campfires late into the night, using a circle of well-placed rocks that surrounded a fire hole that Chris had dug just twenty feet out from the porch—close to the sagebrush line.

I told all this to Wayne as we sat there together on the patio, holding hands. Our gaze focused on the nearby meadow, on the mountains, the ever-changing skies above, and the overall crisp ambiance that already hinted of the winter season's first snows that would arrive within several weeks.

While looking out into the vast meadow, I explained that everything for the moment might look dry, lacking any hint of color, and actually quite dull or even lifeless at least to some degree. Yet this always loomed as one of nature's most mischievous, predictable tricks, part of the ebb and flow of the quickly changing seasons—each with its own life, its own aura, its own mysteries, and—God willing—its own sudden and vital discoveries. Gone for the time being were those many extremely rare high-mountain hummingbirds, which crisscrossed these meadows, particularly in the cooler mornings and fresh evenings—rather during the heat of mid-day from late June through August and sometimes well into September if Mother Nature felt in the mood. Gone for the time being were the many thousands of wildflowers that cover this meadow like a blanketed rainbow every summer, and the late-night riveting of frogs, and bald eagles and spectacular hawks that soared on occasion overhead—those regal reminders of our freedom. And, for the moment at least, gone were the deer, which timidly creep across the meadow onto my property, usually on summer evenings after venturing below to this level, coming down from the nearby mountaintops that surround us. This is where my spirit looms, where my heart soars higher than I ever imagined, as the very essence of everything that I am becomes one with heaven.

Well after sundown year-round on cloudless nights, especially when the moon is absent, a person's eyes fixate on every star imaginable in the Milky Way. Particularly on moonless nights, or before or after that caring, gentle orb makes its crawl across the sky, the stars beam so brightly en mass that the outline of the skyline—the top edges of the hills and mountains all around, become fully visible, even at 3 o'clock in the morning. During the next 11 years, Wayne would see these scenes many times, both of us as well as our various occasional guests becoming fully in awe of Nature's trickery, her kind attention to the minutest details, and of her seemingly endless ability to escape accurate description.

Some nights, especially during July and August, wild black bears would often roam through my meadow, occasionally overturning our giant ice cooler. With noses so sensitive that they could smell a jar of yummy peanut butter from many miles away, the cuddly looking but deceptively dangerous creatures did everything imaginable to fill their demanding stomachs. Like the most stupid human burglars imaginable, they invariably left behind evidence in the form of paw prints large enough to cover three footprints of an adult human male.

For protection and as a warning call, we always brought our best friend at any given time, first my chow-chow Sasha. Always protective and exceedingly loyal to me, as commanded by her breed this caring dog would have fought to the death if necessary in order to save me from any potential attacker. Her wails at night only came at the most ideal and important moments, especially during Wayne and my first summer together as man and wife—when we brought our new little 6-month-old chow-chow along as well. During that warm season more than 18 months before Wayne's promotion to the newly created social columnist job, the big dog Sasha's job became to teach her little friend Cosette on the important intricacies of protecting humans. Only bark at the right times, always remain positioned for sudden danger, and take a ferocious stance directly in the face of an evil adversary only at the most judicious moment—the ultimate point of danger. Like any infant, little Cosette got off to a rocky start, often barking at the wrong times, scurrying into the brush for scouting duties at inopportune moments and even wandering off too far and too long for us all to get relaxed, worrying about her. Two years later, after Sasha had passed on at age 13 to the Great Kennel in the Sky, we learned to our great pleasure and delight that Cosette had been taught well. Like Sasha had done before, by this point as a young adult Cosette got into the protective mode only at the most ideal moments. Yet the new dog had a much more mischievous, curious and wandering spirit than her immediate predecessor. Occasionally she would disappear for many hours on end, causing Wayne to sweat with worry. "Don't fret, she'll come back," I would say, and sure enough our much-loved little friend always returned, sometimes carrying a branch or stick that somehow had sparked her interest.

Marking a sharp change from my early childhood, for the previous few decades I had enjoyed a steady, unending succession of caring for and loving many cherished pets. The memory of losing Laddie after he had unsuccessfully chased after our car in Twin Falls when I was just six years old remained latched onto the inner recesses of my mind. Ever since, at least beginning in my adult years, I came to appreciate, understand and respect the endless joys and responsibilities of protecting and respecting domesticated animals and those in the wild as well. Up here in Dixie Valley, some 6,500 feet above sea level, the roar of a bear or the wailing of a coyote carries seemingly everywhere—the sound ricocheting from valley to valley, across numerous meadows, over rivers and even to the mountaintops.

Straight across to the west, a majestic cavalcade of looping hills always insisted on grabbing a person's attention. A person could sit on our porch for days on end, always seeing new visions, new images in these exact same ridges and crests, numerous inconsistently placed dark outcroppings, leftovers from apparent volcanic overflows many million of years earlier.

Without the sun and the moon there to mark the passage of time, one would think of how this same scene had looked earlier, perhaps as recently as just a few hundred years ago before white men first stepped foot in this region. Certainly this would have been an ideal place to hunt for game of many kinds, particularly in the evenings. By that point in the mid-1990s, a few hundred land plots through this valley had been privately sold.

Smack-dab in the middle of the Plumas National Forest, in its infinite wisdom the federal government had decided for some strange reason to allow private land ownership. I might have been wrong, but memory told me that all this started to click into gear in the late 1960s or early 1970s.

The summer before I met Wayne, Dixie Valley had emerged as a literal fantasy come true for my immediate family's guests from the Czech Republic—acquaintances of my son. A person would think these guys had died and gone to heaven, their dreams of landing at the center of the great American west fulfilled. To this point, the only visions that these mid-European gentlemen had of this region came from old Western movies and TV shows, the classic cowboy-and-Indian fanfare. Dixie immediately signified all of this to them and much more.

By mid-October most years, steadily growing white, massive and generous clouds would arrive with the tingly, crisp coolness signaling the unstoppable onset of winter. Then, by Thanksgiving Day or shortly thereafter, snow would pile upon snow in consistent multiple layers, sometimes in amounts exceeding cumulative annual totals of 150 inches. Sierra winter storms often come in rapid, relentless and tireless succession, never-ending spurts of cool, wet, frosty energy. Only the heartiest of human souls dared venture in these parts during the dead of winter, particularly from December and often well into the months of April or even May.

No matter how ferocious the storms, the sun-energy pokes predictable holes in winter's chilly plans, making for a near-continuous and almost constant snow melt. Thus, each successive snow layer weighs down heavily upon the previous, compacting the snow pack total downward. Nonetheless, all roads leading here remain closed and virtually inaccessible throughout winter, except perhaps to snowmobiles.

This cold season, this resting period, this endless collage of change, they all play an essential role in generating the magical summers that capture my heart. By the time Wayne ventured into my life, my soul had already melded into this place. Every summer weekend left me captivated, pulling me toward this mountain hideaway. Fridays, Saturdays and Sundays became the time that I would catapult into this heaven, with Wayne at my side or without him if necessary due to his heavy work load.

Steaks sizzled on the deck barbecue every evening, usually accented by coal-roasted potatoes or corn on the cob. My appreciation and love for Dixie Valley held no boundaries, held no grudges, and held the continual promise of either family fun or much needed getaways with my husband. Most mornings I would arise to the coolness, that invigorating fresh air, clearing all the senses and opening the mind to every positive possibility.

Some mornings I would cook bacon and eggs, the aromas undoubtedly wafting far and wide—fresh news to noses of any fox, domestic dog, coyote, squirrel or all other mammals including humans lucky enough to enjoy a nearby vantage point. Other mornings, I would enjoy a long sunrise stroll, taking in the sight of lengthy shadows streaming across the entire valley floor—sometimes no more than a half mile wide in many places. Especially during this period, the nose picks up the perfumes of these thousands upon thousands of wildflowers. Other more predictable, daisy-like plants show their colors every August and September, unembarrassed to blush during the most intense heat of day—willing to attract those necessary bumblebees.

In my wetlands, just 65 yards or so down a gently sloping grade from the trailer, occasional teams of hiding fish trickle about, always happy to show their joy at experiencing life. Only one tree, a 50-foot-tall pine tickles forth in the meadow below, everything else except for the wetland vegetation and millions of seasonal wildflowers covered in high-mountain sagebrush—which emits its own vibrant, yellowish flowers every September through early October.

When summer reaches its zenith, the stillness of almost every morning gives way to cooling, persistent breezes—usually making their intentions known by the noon hour. These whispery sensations often pick up to a non-bothersome degree by mid-afternoon, when thin mountain air invariably forces many an unsuspecting person to fall into what I call a "deep Dixie Sleep," whether he or she wants to or not. When this happens, the person invariably finds his limbs feeling as if virtually glued to the bed, to the chair or the hammock immediately below. Unlike at lower elevations, where the mental senses return almost immediately upon awakening, up here everything comes into focus slowly and deliberately.

A simple, non-fancy wood hut just 15 feet from the back of the trailer serves as the only commode. With no piped-in running water, and lacking a well pump, we always bring our own beverages or bottled H2O, just enough for the dogs and for spit baths.

Stress always kills, debilitates and ruins the body, particularly unhealthful tensions caused by life within the big city. The mind-numbing hassles of paying bills, meeting constant work deadlines and the mere struggles necessary to survive can result in cancer, irreversible illness, painful joints, premature aging or overall declines in health. Instinct tells me, actually requires me and commands me, to return here to Dixie whenever possible. On infrequent occasions while sleeping in my cozy old Reno home, during the dead of winter I sometimes dream about this place—this mountain meadow, these wildflowers, these hummingbirds.

Sometimes I dream of the moments up there with my granddaughter Hannah, when as a young girl she occasionally brought some of her best friends for overnight stays. The sweet smell of roasting marshmallows and chocolate to create yummy S'Mores remains vibrant in the mind year-round. Then, on one occasion little Hannah demanded—that after sundown Wayne stand in the middle of the meadow, the perfect place from which he sang the unforgettable, song "Maria" first made popular by the hit early 1950s Broadway show "Paint Your Wagon." Upon hearing my husband's heaven-sent voice echo through the entire valley, my heart virtually stopped for a full minute or so—the very essence of my being fully captured and open to all possibilities of his charisma. This, for the first time, told me in no uncertain terms that, indeed, it had been true—Wayne likely would have enjoyed a much more successful career as a professional singer. There, standing alone in the meadow, his gentle but manly face glowing in the reflection of this roaring late-night campfire under starry skies, I felt the heart within him, the creativity, the promise of hope, and the boundless legs of our Creator's unlimited possibilities.

"I will remember this moment for the rest of my life," I told Wayne, hugging him fully, appreciating him, wanting him to fulfill his dreams—to succeed somehow, somewhere at whatever sparked and ignited his positive energies.

Little did any of us know, of course, at the time that just 11 years later in 2007, I would lose my ownership of Dixie forevermore.

Without placing blame, Wayne's decisions would later take us down a path of financial destruction. Without placing blame, the facts rang true, speaking for themselves, six years after Wayne left the newspaper the IRS would slap a lien on my old Reno home. Without placing blame, my husband led me unknowingly down a pathway toward all-encompassing financial ruin.

How and why did this happen? How would I ever possibly learn to love him again? More important, when losing all respect for someone that we love, that we once adored, how can we reignite passions, rekindle dreams, and get on track for a better life?

Chapter 19

For the first time in years, I opened up my heart to Wayne just two days before the scheduled tour of my old home.

"Don't you die on me," I told him, tears streaming down my face. "I love you too much to lose you. You are my life, my best friend."

Four years earlier, together and individually we had been through pure hell during the ultimate personal and financial crisis of our lives. During that period, we had been apart for four months, each struggling to survive, to make ends meet.

But now, this time in September of 2011, life was much different. We had gotten our lives back on track, our incomes increasingly steady, and by this point we shared our souls more than ever before. The sharp difficulties of the past had honed us each until we transitioned into stainless steel. We had reinvented ourselves.

As we made final preparations for the house tour, Wayne had revealed to me that a week or so earlier he had exhibited physical symptoms of what we had greatly feared. Although in good, vibrant health for the most part, a continual physical condition threatened to end his life at any time—the "end" for him possibly within any 24-hour span. Physicians and medical histories of people with similar conditions taught us that sudden death could come seemingly without any advance warning.

"Don't you dare let anything happen to you," tears overcoming my every emotion—unable to even begin to entertain the mere thought of losing him.

Throughout the most severe part of our personal hardships four years earlier, I had never once failed to love Wayne with all my heart—although during that time I had lost virtually all respect for him as a man, and as a provider. In my mind, a vibrant and healthy man such as he should never have allowed himself to fail to earn at least some income.

The shock, the mere thought of the IRS lien on my home during the summer of 2007 ripped me with fear, anger, confusion and perhaps even contempt at least to some degree.

Only through patience, hard work, time, commitment and sharing did I eventually see the world from a much different perspective.

And finally, as the final 48-hour countdown had begun for the home tour, those particular worries had long since been buried into our past. Yes, Wayne had changed. No longer was he a slob with a messy office, but rather a much cleaner, more meticulous guy. Methodical and consistent planning replaced exuberance. Reasonable income goals replaced dreams of a huge windfall from a major success. No longer did he take ill-intended, unnecessary business risks, having fallen previously into a morass of money problems too deep to possibly dig away from. And, perhaps from my perspective, no longer did he strive to achieve in entrepreneurial endeavors that—at least to me—seemed pointless, and perhaps even recklessly stupid. In one sense, through this transition Wayne had found a boundless new energy, a vibrancy for one of his undeniable skills—writing a maze of never-ending compelling books, almost all of which I admired. But from his perspective, another candle within his soul had burned out perhaps for good—the realization that he either would or could never again strive for success in new creative realms he had once pursued. The result was a changed man, a new man, a guy who had essentially reinvented himself on the fly.

The new Wayne, had become a bright, inventive, super-energetic, and intuitive thinker, a visionary into people's very souls—a chronicler of their thoughts, dreams, hopes and aspirations, conveyed in the forms of successful ghost-written books, at least in my mind. Through the previous decade, he had written many dozens of books, some quite successful. An avid reader myself and also his harshest literary critic, I truly admired and appreciated almost all his books. Those were never the problem. His numerous other endeavors had caused our hardships, or at least served as the root of the underlying difficulty.

"This has been the best summer of my entire life," I told Wayne two days before the scheduled tour, still opening up my heart, soul and mind to him—fully, holding nothing back. "The past is the past, we both made mistakes, and I'm ready and eager to move forward with you."

"I know, honey. I'll be good."

"Then, Wayne, you're going to take good care of yourself. You won't let anything happen to you. Promise me."

"No one can ever predict his own health—but I promise."

Despite our hardships, although wishing those extreme hassles had never occurred, Wayne still viewed the first decade of this century as the best 10-year period by far of his entire life—come hell or high water. Conversely, I viewed the same period as a nightmare. Struggling to survive, to pay the bills and to save my home from potential foreclosure had jabbed a proverbial dagger into my lifelong personality trait of being perennially positive in almost every way.

This is not to say or to imply, however, that my husband liked or enjoyed the hardships that each of us had endured. For him, the great joy—even amid the most difficult of times—rested in the fact that he had escaped corporate America for good, the newspaper chain that his father had championed, the newspaper chain that from Wayne's personal view treated some of its most talented staff-level employees no better than rats. Free at last, for the first time in his life starting with his resignation from Gannett employment in the spring of 2000, Wayne was for the first time able to dedicate much of his boundless creative energies on entrepreneurial endeavors. While Wayne had admired, respected, and truly loved, his late dad, he disliked the path of the American newspaper industry. Rather than take an "if you can't beat them, join them" philosophy, Wayne had embraced a sharply different tactic: "If you don't like them, quit. If you don't like their shallow newspaper stories, quit. This is Gannett's business, and if that company wants to screw its workers and cheat the public out of any chance for powerful in-depth news, that's the company's choice. So, quit."

Always eager to be a good, loyal and empathetic wife, when Wayne resigned from his stable job in 2000 I supported his decision and told him at the time, fully and honestly, that I would eagerly back any decision that he ever wanted. Perhaps unconsciously at least at the time, Wayne had seized the opportunity to bolt from his employer at the exact time that his child support obligations ended.

Upon leaving the newspaper he was aged 44; six years later in 2006 the company announced the mandatory retirement of all employees of at least age 50 who had at least 20 years experience. So, the snotty corporate fat-cats would have jettisoned him from that sweat-shop anyway; the decision to leave early had merely put him into an earlier position to learn how to survive as an independent.

Vowing to put the negative, short-sighted Gannett Company into his past, Wayne threw all of his professional energies into his new career. The Dot-com company that we each worked at mirrored a trend of that era, drying up and fizzling apart by the end of 2000. Lucky for us, though, an investment banking firm that saw spark and intelligence in Wayne promptly hired him as their executive-level director of corporation communications. Working with Crimsonica, Wayne suddenly started earning a salary including bonuses that nearly doubled what he had been earning at the newspaper.

This transition enabled me to cut back at least some on my work duties as an independent contractor helping clients with their graphic design needs. Largely at Wayne's insistence, during the first several years of this century I cut back on my work efforts at least somewhat—devoting more time to my granddaughter Hannah, and my daughter Zoë; the pair lived off and on separately in the cottage behind my home and in a small upstairs bedroom of the main house that I would later use as a changing room.

At face value, my life seemed to have leveled off somewhat on work-related matters at least, while Wayne seized the reins in striving to serve as our chief breadwinner. All along, however, looking back now I should have paid more attention because unbeknownst to me at the time Wayne had started falling further and further behind in paying all of our bills. During this period, he had insisted on handling all of our personal financial management chores, wanting to be the "man" of the family. Worsening matters, although for those first several years when filing our annual returns Wayne would pay our tax obligations in a lump sum—gradually, he fell further and further behind in paying the IRS the required payments. Throughout this all, he had thought—incorrectly— that he could always earn enough to catch up with what Uncle Sam wanted, but instead he kept falling further behind.

Fully unaware of this increasingly serious situation, I began delving more into my art interests, spending time with girlfriends and helping to care for Hannah as she approached and eventually surpassed age 10.

Neither Wayne nor I knew this at the time, but his various decisions in making payments and juggling bills were just then beginning to position us to eventually fall head-first off the edge of a financial cliff.

All along, my husband dove full-bore into his new job, loving the challenges and the ongoing opportunities to learn and to achieve. Throughout the spring and summer of 2001, the investment bank sent him on numerous business trips to Las Vegas and eventually to New York City's financial district. Although Wayne's income had increased, he now held the responsibility of paying his own federal taxes. Gone were the days when all those chores were handled automatically, taken out of his paychecks as a relatively low-paid grunt worker as he had been before.

Compounding these unseen problems, the Attack on America of September 11, 2001, slapped a solid dent in the industry in which he had only recently begun to work. I thanked God that Wayne was not needed in New York on that particular day, because otherwise I might have lost him just like thousands of other spouses who had suffered the deaths of their mates. Yet like so many thousands of other executives and finance industry professionals, the proverbial writing on the wall soon surfaced. Wayne would need to find new work due to the sudden industry downturn sparked by the 9-11 tragedy.

Although Wayne received a $10,000 parting bonus, and regular $5,000 monthly salaries through the remainder of that year—he kept juggling our bill payments, never telling me of our growing problems and also failing to fully grasp these difficulties himself. His father, Rollan Melton, died the following January. Many people wrongly thought that Wayne had inherited many millions of dollars, when in fact the estate remained fully intact under the control of his wise, penny-conscious mother.

In the meantime, from mid-December of 2001 until early 2002, unbeknownst to me, Wayne had used credit cards to finance our three-week jet and road trip to visit my girlfriend Kathleen and John who at the time lived in Tampa, Florida. At the time, I had been under the incorrect assumption that my husband had used his $10,000 parting corporate bonus to pay for the vacation. Fully in the dark about our gradually growing financial problems, I told Wayne of my sincere support of his efforts to become a professional, full-time book ghost-writer. Right off the bat within several weeks after his father's funeral attended by nearly 3,500 people, Wayne landed contracts to write two motion picture screenplays plus a ghost-written book by the end of that summer.

Literally, within the course of two years Wayne had totally and fully reinvented himself. His income steadily increased to well above his old newspaper salary. Then, in the early fall, he landed yet another book ghost-writing contract. Packed with energy, eager to succeed professionally for the first time in his life, my husband seemed on a roll. All along, however, I lacked the notion of the increasingly desperate need to worry and to take decisive action on my own part; the financial situation had already started to reach a critical stage.

Although Wayne's income had increased substantially, he kept "robbing Peter to pay Paul," juggling bills and eventually going into credit card debt in order to cover regular bill payments—a definite "no-no" from the view of almost every financial planner.

Always motivated to achieve, to reach for even greater successes in life, in late October of 2002, he decided to move to the Los Angeles area to pursue a part-time career as a movie actor or even a TV star. Yes, finally set free from the supposed chains of big-corporate America, Wayne took decisive action in an effort to make his dreams come true. For the bulk of that time, he stayed in a run-down, seedy motel on Sepulveda Boulevard near Culver City, California, not far from Hollywood. Bolstered by his can-do, positive, take-charge attitude those of us at home started nicknaming him at least for awhile as "Hollywood Boy." Every so often, he would email me a humorous diary, so funny that I would laugh out loud when reading them. Meantime, while hustling to cattle calls in hopes of working as a movie extra, Wayne worked round-the-clock on a laptop computer in his motel room, sometimes toiling throughout the night, to write yet another movie screenplay—once again under contract to a private, anonymous client.

While steadily increasing numbers of clients were beginning to recognize Wayne's writing talents, none of us seemed to sense his difficulties at managing our money. At the time, on my own still doing intermittent art-oriented, graphics jobs and portrait commissions, I earned just enough to pay for my food, gas and incidentals while back at home.

Wayne and I had desperately missed each other during his absence. Finally, he paid for a plane ticket to fly me to Burbank, California. There, he picked me up before we spent several days in the Los Angeles area. While en route home in his car, I even took him to the Sunland trailer park where I had lived in a proverbial fish bowl of a trailer with my parents, during that time when I had been approached by a pervert who stuck a quarter in my cummerbund. To Wayne's credit, he had at least some degree of success during his two-month stay; he was initially selected to play a critical, prominent movie extra role in the much-awaited film of the time, "Seabiscuit." Sadly, though, Wayne got cut from those plans because he had suddenly gained too much weight, no longer the relatively skinny guy that he had been just a few months before. This marked the beginning of the era when Wayne had ballooned in size, a weight-gain phase that lasted off and on for the most part until launching his daily power-walking exercise regimen beginning in 2008. Another short-term success came in late December of 2002, when he got an unexpected casting call while in Reno to appear in the trailer of the movie "Ghost Ship"—which had premiered in theaters a year earlier, but was only now on the verge of a video release.

Following this unexpected call in the evening, Wayne drove all night from Reno to reach the Los Angeles filming site in time for the sunrise shoot. Filled with boundless energy, he worked non-stop on the set until late that night, before departing for Reno by car again in hopes of reaching home in time for a pre-scheduled 9 o'clock meeting with a book client the next morning.

While all of us have talents, each person also possesses his or her own unique flaws. Wayne shined in his personal sales efforts, gathering new ghost-writing clients—almost all of them contracted to pay him thousands of dollars. But the serious flaw remained, his juggling of bills, using credit card debt for some expenses as another new problem steadily began to emerge.

Although his overall client base steadily increased, he strived to come off within our household as a good provider—wanting to save face, unwilling to let me know that I should re-enter the workforce full-time. Because Wayne loved me so much, he wanted to protect me, to care for me and so he always told me throughout 2003 that "everything is okay." Either he was fooling himself, just plain ignorant or in good-old-fashioned denial, he failed to tell me of the credit card problems. Perhaps his widely fluctuating income from month-to-month had led him to believe that he would eventually catch up for good. Or maybe he hoped for a super-huge score, a movie screenplay grand slam or a runaway bestseller that would solve our financial worries forever.

Sure enough, throughout 2004 Wayne's personal income shot skyward, into full orbit through the upper stratosphere. Throughout that calendar year his income reached previously unheard of, much-dreamed-for levels for him personally, but he failed to pay any IRS taxes during that period—always thinking, wrongly so, that the "next paycheck will enable me to catch up with that debt once and for all."

Through that period, Wayne pumped tens of thousands of dollars of his hard-earned income into entrepreneurial endeavors that fell flat. The greatest of these, at least during that time frame, involved amassing highly experienced movie industry professionals in Las Vegas—in order for them all to jointly consider transforming a book that he had ghost-written into a major motion picture. Although Wayne did not personally pay for all these expenses, he forked out big bucks to rent himself a limo and other amenities—necessary to convey that high-end image. My husband even played a pivotal role in successfully finding an associate producer who successfully recruited numerous seasoned Hollywood producers and film-writers to attend those sessions.

At the time, however, I remained at least somewhat oblivious as to the specifics of all these endeavors. Locked in my heated, non-stop and eventually unsuccessful campaign for the Reno City Council, at age 56, I remained on a non-stop treadmill—designing signs, creating ad images, giving public speeches and attending events.

Throughout that period, Wayne and I lived and put our separate energies into totally different worlds. Each of us wanted to achieve success, while wishing the other the greatest possible achievements. I loved my campaign, putting virtually all of my physical and mental powers into the effort, unexpectedly losing perhaps 20 pounds in the process. The campaign became a whirlwind of non-stop activity, usually each day from well before sunrise to the wee hours of the next morning.

My life and Wayne's diverged into vastly different courses throughout 2004, our passions for our lives still ablaze. We each lacked any hint that the winds of change would soon erupt into a mighty conflagration within the marriage.

Chapter 20

From 2000 into 2006, I steadily visited Dixie Valley for three-day late-summer weekends alone most of the time. Wayne usually stayed home in order to handle his steadily increasing work load, amid his every-growing responsibilities writing books and other endeavors.

One of the few bright spots emerged in November 2004, when Wayne paid cash—rather than using credit—to upgrade and refurbish what had been the run-down, lifeless upstairs bathroom of our home. In late 2003 and earlier in 2004 before my campaign I had already selected and purchased the ideal old-style replacement tile. Wayne left all essential planning responsibilities up to me, except for a few requests: "I need a mirror that opens up to reveal a cabinet holding toiletries such as shaving supplies, right in front of a classic, antique sink affixed to an old table—with reliable running water."

Rather than follow his request, I found a vintage mirror that I preferred, plus a sink affixed to a stone countertop—held upright by modern-looking metal rods. From day-one, at least from Wayne's perspective, the sink failed to empty free-flowing water, but instead took about an hour or so to run down. Also, to Wayne's great displeasure, the mirror refused to open, backed only by a wall rather than a hidden cabinet such as he had requested.

"What I want, and what I ask for doesn't matter around here," Wayne complained privately to me.

"The bathroom looks great. What do you have to complain about?"

"I cannot even shave in there. What's the use of spending thousands of dollars for an upgrade, if the bathroom isn't even close to being functional?"

From that point forward and ever since, Wayne had to handle his shaving and tooth-brushing chores in the tiny ground-level bathroom adjacent to the kitchen. This closet-like space was just big enough to sit in when necessary or for standing in front of a mirror.

Every six months or so from that point forward, Wayne would complain to me that my ambivalence about the sink and mirror situation signified a crack in the marriage. From his perspective, he deserved at least a few basic amenities, while working as hard as he could as our primary breadwinner—at least in those early stages before everything drastically changed.

Taking a sharply different view, I saw him as whiny, small-minded at times and complaining too much about all the wrong things. Sometimes he screamed at me, yelling and expressing his pent-up anger. With increasing frequency, he expressed his frustrations—upset at my refusal to show him the basic respect he thought that he deserved. He never once hit me or moved in my direction in a violent way, but gradually I became leery of being near him. This was not the man I had married, once so kind and always listening to whatever my whims might be, catering to my every need. This was not the man whom I had married, always calm and level-headed. This was not the man whom I had married, always respectful and always on an even keel with me.

Drugs were not the problem, I knew that for sure since Wayne always avoided narcotics or even a sip of alcohol. Infidelity was not the problem, I knew that for sure because a woman knows and senses such things— never a hint of passion toward other women or strange unaccounted-for disappearances. And a lack of trying had not been the problem, since to me at least from 2000 through 2005 he seemed to keep working as methodically and efficiently as ever—at least from his perspective.

He kept demanding respect, but he was acting like a baby at least in some regards. He kept promising our financial picture would improve, but from my view we kept struggling to make ends meet more than ever before. From my perspective, getting him to sit down quietly and rationally to talk calmly about these issues was about as easy as lassoing a blue whale in the middle of the Pacific Ocean.

Taking a sharply different position, from Wayne's perspective I had begun to do whatever I wanted—without asking for his opinion or his input beforehand. He realized that I still pulled in my fair share of income, usually by graphic design work or doing commissions. Whenever possible, I went off on out-of-town getaways with girlfriends, my children or granddaughter Hannah. Wayne always acquiesced, wanting the best for me, eager for me to relax and to enjoy life. Still, from late 2004 into the middle of 2007 the friction between us seemed to intensify.

The first nine years or so of our marriage had blossomed and strengthened at least in many regards, primarily because we gave each other tons of space—while also sharing in activities and fun that really mattered to us. But suddenly a great divide had increased between us, as if Wayne lived at the South Pole and I lived up north with Santa. Our relationship grew cold and frigid at times, while also occasionally intense and filled with boundless, insatiable passion for one another.

On the positive side at least, we gradually began to understand each other perhaps even more than each of us knew ourselves. When alone together on infrequent out-of-town getaways, we often spoke aloud the exact same thoughts that the other person was thinking at that very moment. No matter what his flaws, and there were many, I still loved him deeply down to the core of my soul.

All along, Wayne began to understand, to appreciate and to accept my many imperfections as well. Except for the bathroom situation and complaints about never bothering to tell or ask him in advance when accepting invitations on behalf of us both, he began to take note of my numerous imperfections—which never actually bothered him or at least which he never complained about: my propensity to watch far too many reality TV shows, which he considered mindless; my preference for us to dine out in restaurants that he complained served too much "cheapy-Chinese food;" of my increasing tendency to run off to Dixie Valley on weekends alone, without first giving him ample notice—at least from his perspective; and of my refusal to create more artwork on my own, just so that I could enjoy the pleasure of such activities.

To say or to even try to imply that I was perfect would have been a boldfaced lie. Such an attempt would have been unnecessary anyway. All I wanted more than anything remained to continue being a good, kind and loving person.

For his part, Wayne became increasingly reclusive. Here was a man who had once seemed to have dozens or maybe even hundreds of friends or at least many solid acquaintances. And, now, all of a sudden I got faced with the reality that at this point around 2005 and 2006 he lacked a single, steady and reliable friend other than me. This man once so popular had evolved into a virtual hermit, a recluse—making no attempt whatsoever to share long-term personal bonds other than with clients that he happened to serve, mostly as a ghostwriter, at any particular time. During this juncture, he started spending up to 18 hours a day—everyday, non-stop, without letup—in his upstairs office, rarely venturing out of the house as his weight ballooned. Unlike before, when he had been so handsome, strong, well-built and vibrant, he moved like a giant sloth.

After a few years of this, my frustrations grew. I found myself telling him with increasing frequency and growing intensity: "I did not marry you to become your mother. I want you to be my husband and my lover instead." Wayne never whined or groaned when I said this, always promising to improve—while also complaining, at least in humble tones, that he deserved and wanted respect. But from my perspective, how can a woman respect a man who shows no respect for himself? What had changed him, and was he depressed? Maybe he felt that life had started passing him by, that perhaps it was true what some people had said about him—that he was a spoiled, stupid, dumb "daddy's boy" and a numbskull who never would succeed at anything at all.

Still packed full of pent-up eagerness to succeed, in 2006 and 2007 Wayne started revealing to me that while still generating countless ghost-written books he had started dabbling at Internet marketing. He worked at this round-the-clock, while also promoting a unique, password-protected credit repair program that he had created all on his own. The credit repair system actually took off somewhat, initially generating at least two sales per day via the eBay online auctions system.

Meantime, with a partner from Sacramento, my husband played an integral role in financing and securing the patent copyrights for a unique women's beauty product that Wayne assured us "will be a huge hit around the world. Every woman will want this." By mid-summer of 2007 as I prepared to visit my son and grandchildren in the Czech Republic,

Wayne declared that: "By the time you get home in September, we're going to be rich—guaranteed."

As his weight continued to swell, throughout that same period, he also started to dabble in the latest Web-based get-rich-quick schemes. Desperate for a winner, sometimes he even begged me to use one of my credit cards to buy into overnight riches; several times I bowed to his wishes, only to see these schemes fall flat. Wayne's propensity to make that "one big score" became so intense that he eventually even created his own online multi-level marketing system. To make this legal, he created a sound, reliable digital product as the integral sales ingredient, before essentially putting himself in the top management position as that company's owner and founder. Initially but only temporarily, this paid off for him as people from around the world sent cash necessary to purchase his product. However, his business model soon fizzled out, perhaps due to the glut of other Web-based money-making systems.

Then, the proverbial mud hit the fan when the IRS sent a certified letter, telling us that the government had slapped a lien on my home. God only knew how I would survive? How would I keep the house?

Abandoned and alone. I sat inside Wayne's former upstairs office, which I had transformed into a virtual war room. He had left me without notice in the middle of the night four weeks earlier.

Streams of paperwork, and debt collection notices stood in separate, appropriate piles—stretched atop a huge table at the center of the room.

Collection companies kept hounding me day and night, with no one to ask for help but myself. The emergency had forced me to sell my beloved property in Dixie Valley, in order to pay off the IRS and remove the lien on my home.

Unbeknownst to me at the time, from 2000 through 2007, Wayne had racked up tens of thousands of dollars in credit card debt in my name. This left me stunned and mortified, especially because I had not used a credit card in more than a decade. Lacking a regular full-time job, I had virtually no regular income other than the opportunity to continue hustling for as much graphic design work as possible. With barely enough money for basic necessities such as paying utility bills, I lacked any idea whatsoever of where Wayne had disappeared to—perhaps he had killed himself or been hit by a car or moved to South America. I had no idea.

All I knew for sure was that this sudden onslaught had put me into emotional shock. Until all this happened, I lacked any idea whatsoever of the extent of our money woes.

Survival!

While creditors kept hounding me, I lacked even a fraction of the funds that would have been necessary to pay for any lawyers to help me through this mess.

At the time I remained unaware that for several days, Wayne had lived in the front seat of his car. There, without food, electricity or normal shelter such as bathing amenities, he worked on his laptop to start ghost-writing a book at a much-hoped-for rock-bottom fee for a new client that I had recently referred to him through a friend. Desperate for income, Wayne had started that project for a Seattle woman without first getting a signed contract.

As if proverbially slapping me in the face, Wayne pulled thousands of dollars from one of my business bank accounts that he had access to—using the funds for basic living expenses. From that point forward, for a period of several months he lived in a steady succession of cheap, run-down, stinky motel rooms—just as I had done as a child. This former society columnist had turned into a virtual pauper, working feverishly at his writing chores in hopes that his new prospective client might see fit to pay him someday. If the general public had learned the truth, they initially would have considered Wayne's transition as a riches-to-rags story. Abandoned and alone, each morning I sat in my ground-level home office. My body rocked back and forth, as I burst into what some spiritualists call "tongues." Words of mysterious origin spilled forth in non-stop streams from my damaged soul. The love that I still had for Wayne and for my late parents remained stronger than ever. Each time this "tongues" thing happened without warning, those streaming phrases engulfed me non-stop for periods of maybe five or ten minutes.

Afterward I always felt at least somewhat better in an emotional sense. More than ever before in my life, at age 60 now I needed to be strong, tough, as hard as granite both emotionally and physically. Gone were the days when I had depended on my wandering parents for mere survival. Gone were the days when I had any kind of man beside me who might help to make things right. Gone were the days when I had hoped for a steady restful life at the onset of my senior years. This isn't supposed to happen, this isn't supposed to occur to good people with stupendous hearts. This kind of thing isn't supposed to happen to a kind woman who has been caring and loving.

But it does.

Determined to get back om my feet and dead-set on generating a positive outcome I started taking positive action on a consistent basis. Right away the biggest lesson came in the form of the need for self-reliance. Never depend fully on another person for your survival and for your ultimate happiness. Always take charge of your own life, even if you think that you're in a joyful, solid relationship. Use the wisdom within your own heart to help guide you into positive directions. All along, care for, manage and closely monitor your own finances. Never for a moment let anyone rule and dictate your own financial future.

Suddenly, five weeks after Wayne's departure, he gave me an unexpected phone call: "Patty, I want to help you in any way that I can. Let's meet where we can talk."

"Yes?"

"Then, you can meet me on Wednesday evening in the lobby of Washoe Grill ."

"I'll be there. I agree we need to have a serious discussion."

During the final few days before that scheduled rendezvous, I tossed and turned alone in my upstairs bedroom. What could I possibly even begin to say to him, if anything? Still slapped in the heart by a love that kept me gripped in fear and anger, I shook and cried all alone—with no one to hold, no one to talk with, no one to share my heart with, no one to share my dreams with, no one here that could possibly help me, no one here who could possibly understand what I had been through in life, and

God only knows how in the world I might be able to cope. No one but I could do all these things.

In the final few hours, I kept shaking with anticipation. The giant ball of anger within me and the giant ball of love all wrapped up together into one gigantic, confusing hodgepodge of indefinable emotion.

Then, Wayne stepped into the entrance area of the Restaurant at the appointed time. We sat together at a round table near the cocktail bar, within the main entrance room to the dining room. Right away I realized that within the past five weeks Wayne had shed at least 15 pounds or maybe even more. Being near penniless, all alone and living in crappy motels while writing a book in desperation to survive will do that to a person. Without hesitation Wayne started telling me his well-rehearsed speech, promising that he would do whatever he could to possibly help me with finances. Within a flash, my pre-set, well-choreographed plan went right into action.

Caught!

Faster than a lightning bolt, a process server handed him with the divorce papers that my lawyer had prepared. This dissolution of marriage was the only option as the attorney had explained. God only knew how much exactly my husband had pulled. Maybe there were additional mountains of debt that I had not yet heard about. My advisors had made this strategy crystal clear. Put this guy out of your life forever. Sue Wayne for the money that he took from your bank account without authorization. Get rid of this guy, cut clean and start your life fresh and anew, Patty.

A stunned expression crossed Wayne's face as he held the paperwork. He continued vowing to help me in whatever way that he could, whatever my decision. The precise words of what we had said during that ten-minute conversation remain fuzzy to me, as if somehow seen through a heavy fog on San Francisco Bay. This I knew would be the end of the two of us as a couple.

Within a few minutes we were outside sitting in my car, and saying: "Wayne, how did this happen to us? We're living inside a nightmare."

"Neither of us would have dreamed that something like this could ever happen in our lives, could we?"

A short while later, we departed, going in separate directions after promising to call each other within a week. A few days later I attended an afternoon Thanksgiving season banquet attended by a few dozen of my friends. Lots of them started asking me why I looked so terribly sad, so I answered—fully meaning what I said: "Wayne and I are getting a divorce. We're never going to see each other again."

Dictated and choreographed by Mother Nature, during mid-autumn white, ominous and reliable clouds make their predictable march into Northwest Nevada.

Signaling the onset of the coming winter, these fluffy pillows tease their way through the sky as if pretending not to signify precisely when Old Man Winter will arrive. Usually within a few weeks or so before Thanksgiving or shortly after, these white crystal showers blanket the entire region with the promise of peaceful times immediately ahead. Biting cold forces many people to stay inside, while many hearty souls prefer to play outside, or to shovel walks, or trek to the Sierra for wintry sports.

Many cultures view this season as a time of death, or even perhaps a much-needed period for rest and renewal. Thankfully, I had my family— my children—and many friends to offer emotional support. A few days before Thanksgiving, a generous snow fell, probably only an inch or two but enough to give us all that warm-hearted early-holiday sensation. I managed to feel fuzzy and warm inside at least a bit while making my late Grandma Eve's secret ravioli recipe—the family tradition of, at this point, more than 120 years. Perhaps largely for my benefit everyone remained positive, laughing and joking about our many good times through the years. With Wayne absent, everyone remained careful to avoid mentioning his name, kindly in order to prevent any unnecessary emotional upset. By that point I had already made my intentions clear to everyone—that I had no plans whatsoever of ever seeing the guy again.

With any luck, the divorce would slide through the courts with no problem by the first of the year, finally setting me free from the anchor that had pulled me deep into a financial quagmire. The wine flowed freely around the dining room table of my old home; much of the discussion focused on the bright future for me.

Everyone kept saying how great I looked, that I had not appeared more beautiful in many years. Although I might have looked good, although I smiled a lot, and although my words and actions focused on "fun" things, deep down my soul, spirit and heart remained seriously wounded. Numb. Nothing. Bland sensations. Dizzy, being so hopelessly alone inside.

And, worrying about Wayne.

"Are you okay?" I asked, reaching him by phone a half hour after my Thanksgiving guests departed.

"I'm more worried about you, Patty, than you are about me."

"But are you all right, Wayne? Did you have a Thanksgiving dinner?"

Rather than give a direct answer, he stressed his concern for my well-being. By phone, Wayne kept peppering me with non-stop questions, all while continuing to reiterate his vow to give me as much financial help as he possibly could. We showed our genuine concern for one another, neither mentioning the possibility of reconciliation. As midnight approached, following more than one hour on the phone, I suddenly and unexpectedly found myself blurting: "Do you have a girlfriend?"

"No woman in her right mind would want me now."

"Things change. Once you get back on your feet, Wayne, you will..."

Striving to take the focus off of himself, he promptly asked if any guys had asked me out on a date. Rather than tell a bold-faced lie, I admitted that at least one fellow—a businessman—had asked me out to dinner. But I had told the guy, "No," since I had other pressing matters, primarily survival.

"You're a fine catch, Patty," Wayne said. "That's great; when the time comes I want you to get yourself a highly successful guy who can take much better care of you than I have."

I countered that such a strategy remained the furthest thing from my mind, since the overwhelming and pressing need to get out from under the mountain of bills would undoubtedly consume all my energies for some time to come. Rather than argue, Wayne reiterated how sorry he felt that all this had happened, asking me to forgive him for his many horrible mistakes and the pain he had caused me. "I have already forgiven you; it's not a question of forgiveness. I still love you Wayne, but I have no respect—any, whatsoever—for what you have done."

"There's no way that I could blame you for feeling that way," he said, before we promptly agreed that each of us was extremely tired and needed to go to sleep in our separate accommodations. Before hanging up, he told me of his ferocious work pace alone in his motel room—ghost-writing a book "on spec," in hopes that a perspective client would want to pay him.

From that point forward, Wayne and I took turns calling each other every so often to check on each other if only briefly—yet some of these conversations stretched for more than a half hour.

By arrangement, on the Tuesday evening immediately after Thanksgiving, he came to the house for dinner so that we could discuss details of the divorce. Each of us hoped to get the details ironed out with little hassle so that we could move on with our lives. With any luck the paperwork would breeze through the courts, making me a free and single woman during the first week of January, just five weeks away. This marked Wayne's first venture back into the house since his departure. Upstairs in his former office, he saw the huge table that I had erected, piled high with bills and a court summons.

The guilty, ashamed expression on his face spoke volumes without him having to utter a single word. Before his very eyes, the horrendous tasks that still faced me became fully evident. Any possible attempt for denial got obliterated in its tracks. Following dinner, we talked until well past 3:00 that morning "I still love you, Patty," he said, his voice showing signs of obvious sleepiness. "You know that?"

"I love you, too." We promptly went our separate ways.

Little did I know while reading my third grade text book, Friendly Village, illustrated by two women, Florence and Margaret Hoppes(copywrited 1941) that I would one day have a home that looked exactly like the one in this book. I would get the house of my dreams with a picket fence in a village with a beautiful river that runs through it.

Away Down South

Once upon a time away down south where the sun shines most of the time there was a pretty green house with a rosebush growing over the door.

There was a white fence, too, which flowers of all colors looked through the cracks to see what was going on in the

In front of the house was a chinaberry tree that looked like a big umbrella.

Other trees grew all around the house and looked over the high back fence into the woods.

It was a lovely place to live in, this pretty green house with the rosebush growing over the door.

210

211

1. My mother, Audrey Chisholm Edwards at the Falmingo Hotel in Las Vegas 1946. 2. & 3. My dad J. Lawrence Edwards in his uniforms. 4. Mom and Dad, New Years Eve 1946 in Las Vegas, Nevada.

1. Me at 11-years-old at the Town House Motor Lodge, Reno, Nevada.
2. Me at 11 years-old in Sunland Calif. 3. Christmas in the Sparton in
Sunland. 4. Aunt Iva, Uncle Jim and Grandma Edwards in Empire,
California 1954. 5. Grandpa Oscar, Grandma Eve and me in 1953 in
Reno, Nevada.

1. Me, Senior year at Wooster High School, Reno, Nevada. 2. Graduation day, 1965 with mom next to my Pontiac.
3 & 4. Modeling for magazine photos in 1969. 5. Sitting with Fred Atcheson(with umbrella) and friend after modleing clothes for a Gray Reids Fashion show in 1969.

1. Chris and Zoë, 1974 in Sacramento California during the time that I was art Director for the California Chamber of Commerce.
2. Photograph I took of Chris when he was 16-years-old for a painting. I did the drawing and never finished it. I still need to paint it, even though he is now 44-years-old.
3. This photo by Photographer Harley Brown is one of my favorites of Zoë. 4. Chris, Zoë and our cat Pukey in 1985.

1. *My grandaughter, and Zoë's daughter Hannah Torvick ,19-years-old.
Photo taken in 2011 by photographer, Andrew Hatch. 2. Grandaughter
Eva Atcheson, 13-years-old, photgraph taken in 2011. 3. Chris Atcheson
at 43-years-old. 4. Grandson, Nicholas at 10-years-old and daughter in-
law Hana Atcheson, photos taken in 2010.*

1. *Unveiling of painting of Wayne at Addi Gallery with Hannah at 8-years-old. 2 & 4. Photos of Wayne and me at social outings we attended while Wayne was the social writer for the Reno Gazzett Journal. 3. Cheryl Andrews and me campaigning for City Council. 5. Wayne, his mother Marilyn Melton and Doug Smith, supporting me as I filed for office in May 2004.*

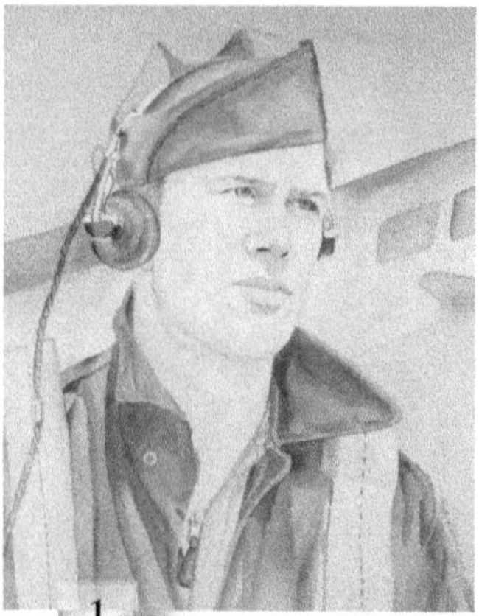

1

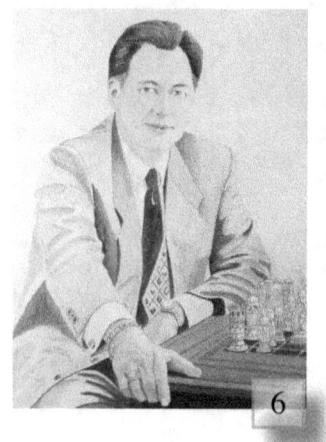

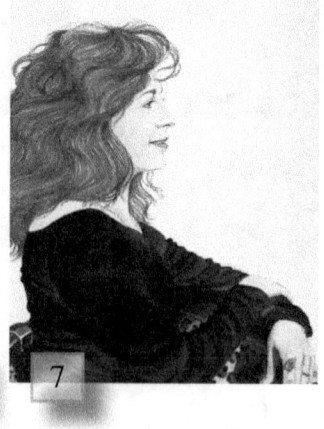

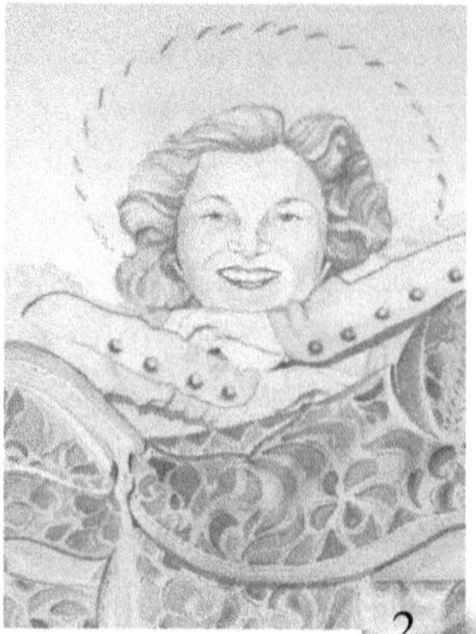

2

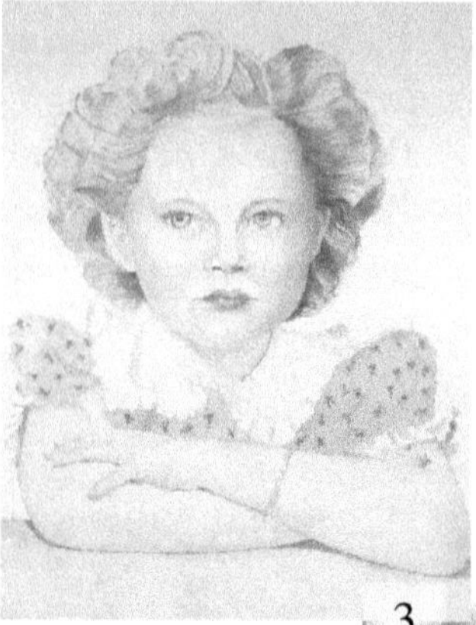

3

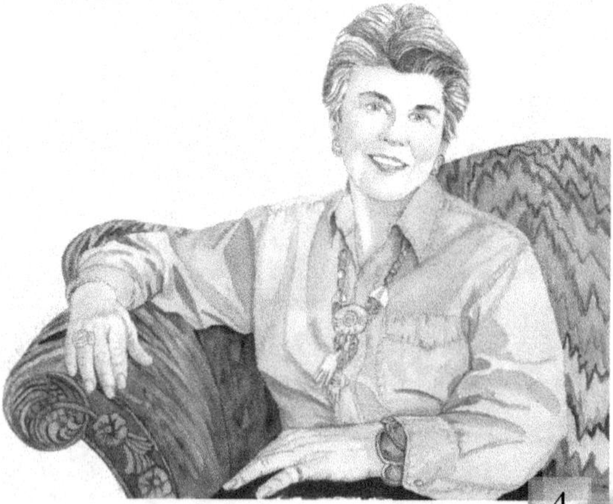

4

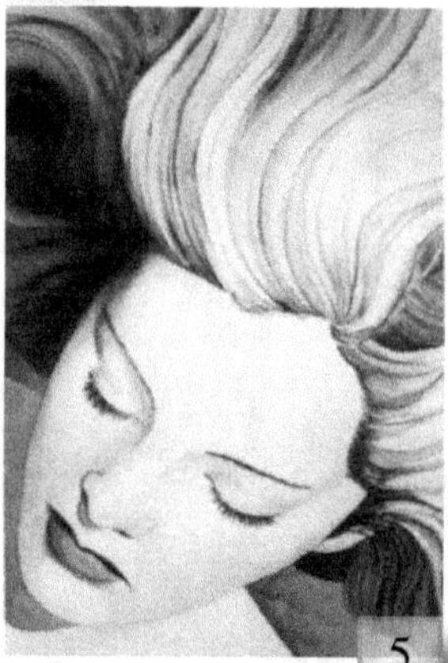

5

6

7

God gave me a gift and I look forward to painting many more portraits in the future. 1, 2, 3 & 5 Nostalgia portraits for a one woman show. 1. Dad in war. 2. Mom as Heldorado Rodeo princess in Las Vegas. 3. Me at 5-years-old. 5. Joanne deLongchamps 4. Commissions, Marilyn Melton 6. Sam Bornholdt 7. Susanne Pennington.

1 & 2. Drawings for a coloring book that I am working on of old motels in Reno, Nevada. 3, 4 & 5. Landscape paintings for a book project with photographer, Stephen Wheatcraft of photographs and paintings from each of the 17 counties in the State of Nevada.

Chapter 21

To pray is to give ourselves to God, to open our hearts to his wondrous possibilities. To pray is to hush our selfishness, giving our lives to nothing but endless love. Down to the bottom of our feet, and up above our heads we appear in quiet repose amid our internal conversations with the Creator.

Uniting in spirit and emerging into spectacular spirals of internal sunshine, we each can devote ourselves to betterment. For me, prayers exist as powerful rivers that enable the unseen love flowing through the universe to blossom and to open beams of ever-widening expanses of pure, positive light.

Each morning without fail from the Thanksgiving holiday celebration into mid-January, I went alone into my downstairs office. In silent repose, I always sat as each new sunrise sent streams of good energy through the revealing windows all around.

"Dear God, please bring a job to Wayne—a good-paying job," I prayed. "Bring peace and tranquility, plus hope to everyone around me. Give me strength to survive and prosper through this new day. Bless me, and all those that I love. Work your mysterious miracles for us, even at the worst of times when we feel reason to lose all hope."

On a consistent, humble and repentant basis, through the holidays and into the second week of January, Wayne had consistently asked me to let him back into my life. His former acceptance of the pending divorce had fallen by the wayside. He refrained from begging, but made his feelings known—promising to change for the better.

My heart and my intuition told me to take him back, but only under certain conditions. He still lived in a seedy motel, while I remained in my historic home still eking out just enough earnings to survive. By New Year's Day, we each had begun expressing our unstoppable love for one another. Yet lessons learned from the recent past commanded that we each make drastic changes. From my perspective, the most important factor remained for Wayne to get a steady, good-paying job. Only then, I had told him, would he be able to live under the roof of my home. Yet time was running out. By my birthday on January 6, he had just enough money to pay for one more week in his crappy motel room. I had no money whatsoever to give him. All his other options had run out. He had just finished his ghost-written book, but still had not been paid. All my senses told me to remain strong. The last thing I needed under my roof was a man there merely as a "charity case." By phone, Wayne told me that he had accepted his fate. The weather that year seemed particularly harsh. Snow fell almost every other day. His only shoes were a ratty old pair of boots, sneakers and a well-polished pair of formals.

Lord knows, I had enough problems of my own. Meantime, I worked feverishly to complete various graphic design jobs, and billing clients as rapidly as possible. Just surviving remained my top priority.

For his part, Wayne did plenty of praying as well. Taking a full, honest and complete assessment of his actions, he realized that he would have made many of these same mistakes during his 20s if starting out as an entrepreneur as a young man. Through his young adult years, he never had to juggle the ups and downs of business finances—since through that phase of life he always had a steady paycheck.

While wanting me back, he never became fully and completely repentant for what he had done, realizing that no success in business is ever possible without taking at least some chances. His only primary regret stemmed from the fact that I had suffered greatly as a result of his misdirected decisions. Never in his life would he ever have entertained the possibility of hurting someone, especially me—the person that he cherished the most.

So, as the deadline approached for Wayne's expected transition to yet another seedy motel, all we could do was pray and hope that he would find meaningful work right away. We maintained daily communication by phone, telling of our love and expressing nothing but the best for one another.

Each morning I opened up my soul to God, expressing my

thoughts and emotions while signifying my gratitude that Wayne had acknowledged his mistakes. Asking for forgiveness evolved into merely a first and necessary step from my point of view. Each of us needed to find within ourselves more strength and gumption than ever. Two days before Wayne's job hunt deadline, a harsh, unforgiving and biting-cold wind swept through northwest Nevada. Snow piled unusually high as the atmosphere yielded itself to deadly dips in the thermometer. Whenever Wayne and I spoke, he remained positive, showing far more concern for me than about himself. The extended storm opened up the heavens to a rush of additional snow. Most streets became impassable except for periodic melting in early afternoons.

The next day, my prayers reached a zenith, as I gave up all of my soul to the Lord our God: "Do with us as you will, forgive us for our sins, and allow both Wayne and me and our families to survive and to prosper." I asked the Holy Father to look at the good things about Wayne. See the many kind things he has done for people through the years, the way he loves all individuals as if part of himself. Take pity on him, the man who has made mistakes but who adores you, oh Lord, as much as I. Accept him into a better position. Put my husband in a place where he can do great and positive things. Allow him to prove to himself and to others what he should never have to prove, showing everyone he knows that true, boundless love is the one and only answer.

After finishing my morning prayers, I went to my daily exercise, ate a healthy breakfast and promptly went to work generating graphic designs in my home office. The middle of a super-hectic workday provides little or no opportunity for self-reflection.

At precisely 10:44 that morning, Wayne answered his cell phone in his motel room while packing up his few belongings preparing to become homeless.

"Wayne, would you be willing to take a job," said Margie, my business partner calling from her home-based office two miles west of my house.

"Yes! I need work."

"An editor's job."

Margie explained that she had just received a call from a Reno printing company. One of that firm's most reliable clients suddenly needed an editor, a graphics designer, and a seasoned professional experienced at magazine production.

Without hesitation Wayne agreed to meet Margie and the magazine's publisher at the man's Sacramento office the next morning. Margie explained that I should also be there as well, since she had just called to recruit me as the experienced professional.

First thing the next morning, Wayne checked out of the motel on the very day that he ran out of money. On the spot at the appointed time he met Margie and me in the front reception room at "Northern California Families Magazine." Just three minutes later, a receptionist ushered us into the office of Publisher Marcus Appleton. The four of us sat at the desk of a large, well-appointed executive conference room.

Marcus started off by spending a few minutes explaining that he needed seasoned, highly respected and experienced professionals to operate the magazine. Seizing an opportune moment, Wayne started to tell Marcus about our experience in the industry.

"There is no need to give those details—you are all hired," Marcus said. "Your positive reputations are well known. You don't even have to show your resumes. I need all three of you as soon as possible. When can you start?"

"Tomorrow," Wayne said.

"Deal."

Chapter 22

While life is never just a bed full of roses, Wayne started giving me his entire paychecks. He moved back into my house faster than a Saturn Rocket lifting a space shuttle into orbit from Cape Kennedy.

Wayne vowed to change, putting his misguided efforts into the past. He promised to lose weight, regain his youthful vigor and avoid stupid entrepreneurial efforts, while also putting me in full command and control of our family finances.

From the start on his own initiative, seizing this new chance at a good, respectable life, my husband also made his feelings clear to me. He insisted on never being mothered, determined to become the man of the house and my committed spouse and lover.

They say that "Rome was not built in a day." This age-old adage rang true with regard to Wayne's overall self-improvement efforts. So many changes were necessary that he found a complete and instant transition difficult. With each passing month and year, I steadily learned that his most marked improvements never came when I nagged about any particular issue. Instead, his most significant transitions came on his own initiative. Within three years, he gradually evolved into at least his version of Felix Unger, the spotless, cleanliness-obsessed character from Neil Simon's "Odd Couple" buddies of Broadway and TV fame. Of course, Wayne never came close to becoming a male version of Martha Stewart in regard to household chores. Each new success in Wayne's professional life and in his personal life as well seemed to motivate him to improve even more.

Yes, God had answered my prayers and Wayne's as well.

Margie started proclaiming that Wayne was one of the best writers and editors that she had ever worked with.

For each month's issue of the "Families Magazine," with input from me and others, he generated creative assignments for the entire magazine. Within a week of landing his new job, he also recruited a staff of independent writers from throughout the Sacramento and Northern California areas. Despite our admirable efforts, as that spring waned, the magazine's revenues plummeted amid advertising sales problems that were no fault of ours. Just then another miracle happened. One of Wayne's former clients form Portland, Oregon, suddenly paid him $15,000 in past-due payments from an old book contract.

As those funds began to dwindle, by late summer Wayne landed another book contract—this time a medical publication, after initially working on spec in hopes of impressing his client and a publisher. The only significant setback came, from my view, when my husband suddenly filed as a candidate for the Reno City Council. Wayne should have discussed this with me in detail beforehand, without jumping into the race without more definitive plans. Outgunned, outnumbered and slugging it out against a highly-financed incumbent, he got blown out of the water in the November 2008 general election.

To Wayne's credit, though, he walked to just more than 24,000 different doorsteps during the campaign. This door-to-door strategy failed to put a dent in his well-funded opponent's strategy. Nonetheless, I designed and produced Wayne's campaign image and materials and organized fundraisers in our yard. On the positive side, the effort helped instill Wayne's love and passion for brisk-walking. From that period forward, he maintained his active daily exercise regimen, and he started eating healthier foods thanks to my efforts.

All these various transitions challenged me throughout 2008, testing my abilities to cope. The pressures of lacking a steady, regular jobholder in the family tested my heart. The income of a book ghost-writer shoots up and down in vastly diverging and unpredictable directions. A boardwalk rollercoaster comes to mind.

Yet eventually, I started realizing that through consistency, dedication and perseverance—working as a team—Wayne and I had begun to develop a significant backlog of successful book projects for increasingly satisfied clients.

Through 2009 and 2010, the soft spots seemed to become less

frequent. Along the way, miracles still occurred for us—such as in mid-2011 when Wayne and I devised creative ways to generate significant cash through sales efforts. I also held down a variety of jobs as an independent contractor specializing in graphic design, marketing and public relations.

In fact, the happiest summer of my entire life started clicking into gear. This started one month before I learned of the one-day public tour of historic Reno homes. Everything started to gel. The most important things in life involve more than just professional careers, income levels or where a person lives. At least for me, the most important gifts of life involve caring, sharing and bonding relationships, plus family, personal growth, creative endeavors and good friends.

My creative and artistic tendencies swelled to all-new heights, always blessed with new ideas and steadily evolving artistic concepts. My relationship with Wayne grew more passionate, positive in every sense more than ever before. Our capacity to share and to openly express ourselves reached new heights. We developed and appreciated our separate and shared dreams, which always responded to us in kind. My once-broken heart healed, springing forth into a higher universe where hoped-for wisdom dwells amid the far-away stars. This personal growth, both spiritually and physically occurred in the secure environment of my home. Growing and evolving into my mature years left me with nothing but increased gratitude for all that I had in early childhood, those little things—primarily the love from my parents, plus gratitude for the many gifts that I knew were still to come from age 65 and beyond. I had learned so many important lessons, one of which taught me that a woman should never let her primary happiness hinge solely and primarily on any one thing—even her relationship with her husband, however much she might love him.

The hurling, falling and relentless storms during the first six months of 2011 had given way to clear skies and pleasant weather from July through most of September. Even more important, the atmospheric conditions within my soul began to shine eternally with just as much brightness.

Thank you, God, for the never-ending miracles.

Chapter 23

Three hours after hundreds of people began touring my home, Wayne and I sat together in a cozy booth at a restaurant in southeast Reno.

Relaxed, enlightened and tranquil sensations engulfed each of us as we ordered a late-morning breakfast. While people continued entering my home non-stop on the other side of town, unexpected warm and delightful sensations filled our hearts.

Wayne and I spoke of how lucky we were to have each other, still with many dreams to fulfill. Each of us expressed our sincere belief that we had never been happier, especially in the wake of so many hardships and struggles. The former times of mental pain, fear and trepidation had been replaced by peace of mind, confidence and Zen-like success thanks to our dedication and commitment.

Wayne opened up his heart to me more than he ever had in years, telling of his burning passion to write hundreds more books before he dies—hopefully at a ripe, old age. With my encouragement, more than ever he enjoyed helping make dreams come true for many people, enabling them to leave legacies for coming generations.

Certainly I had not been the only person to overcome hardship, to successfully reach and conquer an all-new pinnacle in life. Perhaps even more important, every house, dwelling and building worldwide has at least some unique features. My home was far from the world's only interesting property. Although no other house in all of northwest Nevada looked or felt anything like mine, our world remained loaded with innumerable one-of-a-kind, irreplaceable structures. Perhaps even more important, I believed that most people lucky enough to own homes understandably had great pride in their houses.

Indeed, just having a steady, standing and durable house made a person humble and grateful, especially in the wake of millions of home foreclosures during the previous several years. With people in virtually every state and major community affected, many of us with a reliable roof over our heads felt grateful and empathetic. The images of streams of houses swept away by the March 2011 earthquake and tsunami in Japan brought tears to a person's core. Through such hardships, our hearts overflowed with the knowledge that life remained precious, fragile and a blessing. My appreciation for what I had earned widened, pushed into an overflowing sense of empathy when seeing TV images of floods ravaging homes nationwide—everywhere from once-delightful houses in tiny Vermont communities to homes inundated with irreparable water damage across Oregon. Early that same year, spring tornadoes wiped entire neighborhoods off the map in Joplin, Missouri, and Tuscaloosa, Alabama, killing hundreds of people.

Increasingly appreciative of all that I had, I opened up to Wayne fully and honestly during that late-morning breakfast. I told him of my sincere, relentless excitement—an eternally burning flame—that I had in helping to create and design books for people. I told him, how I felt the greatest pleasure in my entire life thanks to our current and committed professions.

"The books that we help write, create and publish for people will play at least some role—however significant—in enabling humanity to improve for the better," I told him. "Can you imagine the power that we have together, working as a team, the tremendous things that we can do to help people get the recognition that they greatly deserve.

For me, I told him, every fiber of my body commanded that I live to at least 104 years old, as long as my Grandma. I wanted with my entire mind and every molecule that comprised my body, to continually and unabashedly bloom forward.

Any reason for tears disappeared, since each of us had already endured enough pain and heartache—paying our dues. Earlier that morning, after leaving our home just as the tour began, Wayne and I enjoyed visiting the five other historic Reno houses on that year's tour. Like us, each of those other homeowners surely must have had their own dreams—perhaps to some degree struggles and hardships—before acquiring their classic residences. These ranged from: a little Queen

Anne cottage; a Moorish or Spanish style eclectic; a stucco structure hailed by neighbors as "The Castle;" and a Colonial Revival structure, plus a sharply accented 47-year-old residence inspired by acclaimed 20th Century architect Frank Lloyd Wright. Thanks to the diverse and vibrant preference of their owners, each home boasted unique and unforgettable furnishings, artwork and special touches such as impossible-to-duplicate gardens and kitchens still featuring original tiles, sinks and in some cases appliances installed when the homes were built.

Adding to our amazement, perhaps like many of the hundreds of other tour-goers, Wayne and I had separately driven, walked or bicycled past many or all of these dwellings during the previous several decades. Imagine the sensation of legally being invited into classic houses in an old neighborhood—the things that you would see, the way that people live, signs of their unique tastes, preferences and quirky habits. Such visits offer a peek into the world of homeowners, essentially enabling tour-goers to delightfully step into the private universes of their neighbors—if only temporarily.

Sharing the same beliefs and perceptions, Wayne and I talked about all these things while driving back home from the restaurant. Yes, as corny as this might sound, we believed fully and without any doubt whatsoever that it's true what some people say: "We're all in just one big human family." When everything is said and done, the cold hard facts come down to the simple statement: "Almost every person universally wants and craves a home, a safe place to call his or her own—a haven from the many potential ravages of the outside world. As literally thousands of homeless children starve to death every day in Africa and in many nations around the world, the basic, primal and understandable need for people to have a home remains universal."

We all share this earth, we all share life within Mother Nature's realm, and we all share a quest for happiness—wanting the best for our families, our loved ones, our communities and for ourselves.

We all live in this one world.

Sharing our mutual delight, Wayne and I both spoke of our recent joyful discovery that my "fishing husband" Bill had steadily started regaining good health. With Wayne's blessing and Teri's as well, in recent weeks my outdoor companion and I resumed our usual practice of escaping deep into the wilderness together to cast our rods to our heart's content.

Adding to the steadily increasing intensity, Wayne and I realized that this book could not possibly come close to describing the wholesome and complete lives of my children Chris and Zöe. More than ever, giving birth to my children, rearing them and seeing them evolve into stupendous adults had evolved into the greatest treasure in my life. Each will have a sensational story to tell, giving their own perspectives—hopefully someday in books of their own.

Within several blocks of our return home, I told Wayne of my sense of fulfillment. A maze of inspirational activities the previous three years had helped make my life complete. My numerous projects and personal growth experiences reached a vast array of fun and delightful plateaus. Each step brought me closer to full bloom as one of God's many appreciative flowers. While continuing to awaken in spiritual faith, a steadily increasing intensity of encounters with creativity and learning subjected me to: generating a statewide Nevada personal art project, envisioning and eventually putting me onto the path of developing paintings depicting each of the 17 counties; a steadily increasing number of artwork commissions, including images of clients' homes or their getaway residences; a much-improved marriage, where Wayne and I began listening to each other, expressing our needs and working to fulfill each other's desires; a greater commitment to my physical health, improving my diet selections and continuing my exercise; and perhaps best of all, a naturally flowing and generous commitment to God. Through genuine forgiveness, understanding and empathy, a pathway opens toward the greatest wealth possible in the entire universe—the complete, strong, unbending and steady love for ourselves and for others on this our shared journey through life.

Herein rests a joyous and substantial revelation.

I have a sibling.

My little brother was born in December 1948, just 23 months—nearly two years—after my birth in January 1947.

Each of us has his or her unique, personal story to tell. Only my brother would be able to describe what he went through, an integral and much-loved part of our family every step of the way. Yes, he endured many of the same trials, tribulations and opportunities on our mutual journey through early childhood, adolescence and the evolving stages of adulthood.

From our many seemingly non-stop road trips, everywhere from Sunland to Empire, Twin Falls, Reno, Las Vegas, San Jose and many other cities and towns, I'm sure that my brother had unique experiences just as challenging and formidable as mine.

We are blood in what we have shared, although like all siblings seeing this world through different perspectives.

Herein rests the integral reason why I have waited until this juncture to disclose my brother's existence. It is not for me to say how or why our numerous transitions occurred. It is not for me to say what he may have felt, or how these challenges impacted his life. And, it is not for me to say why life provides so many diverse pathways for people from the same immediate families.

Still, I can declare with certainty, without any reservation whatsoever, that the beams of light from the sun above shone down upon us all. As we sauntered aimlessly from town to town, each new experience moved our shared world along every dip and curve. For you, dear brother, I owe my gratitude—for deep, deep down within my heart—I love you wherever you might be on this particular day, at this precise moment. We all sprang forth from the same family tree. We went fly-fishing in the same rivers and lakes. For better or for worse—mother and father, and you and I—we all flourished in whatever way that each of us knew how.

The throbbing, brooding and crowded sensations when all crammed together in the front seat of our pickup—along with Sam the Cat—collectively we became a single teardrop, a single raindrop, a single dream—all of us together on what we perceived as a hoped-for road to happiness.

Oh, brother, as the years click past, whether we see each other or not, we'll always have that shared mutual past. Let us dash much further into our senior years, manifesting ourselves every step of the way for the better. Like gardeners tending to our Creator's most precious flowers, we can snip away any thorny branches, tend to each of our souls as best we can, and exist in the best, most flourishing ways that nature might provide.

Little brother, I love you

Hope. Forgiveness. Understanding.

These were the things that Wayne and I talked about as we arrived back at the house, with 45 minutes remaining in the schedule time for the tour. While parking on our own street, we realized that at least 15 or 20 vehicles owned by tour-goers remained on the same road.

As we got out of our car, Wayne and I looked over the white picket fence in the front of the house—gazing admiringly at the delightful garden and trail that Pan and I had built earlier that summer.

"This is my new Dixie Valley in a sense," I had told Wayne, and he responded, telling of his appreciation and complete understanding of this commitment.

Preservation Society members greeted Wayne and me with opened arms upon our arrival at the front gate. Homeowners who provide their houses for the tour are welcome to stay on their properties during the event.

Wayne and I had chosen to give the Preservation Society ample space. The last thing any homeowner should hear is a visitor innocently blurting out commentary such as: "What a great house, but their drapes stink," or "This is the crappiest wallpaper I've ever seen—yuck!" or "Why in the world would anyone want to use a sink like that?"

Be that as it may, from that point forward Wayne and I separately enjoyed strolling through our own home as if tourists ourselves. The distinctive pitch of the roof and the Tudor-style dormer at the front drew just as many positive comments as the living room's curved, star-shaped, brick-lined fireplace. The two massive doors at the side of the living room, each with twelve windows affording views to my main-level sunroom and office, drew lots of attention, as my birds sang delightful tunes from their antique cages.

Wayne's upstairs office seemed to draw plenty of attention, particularly the stand upon which I had placed the ancient Indian cutting stone. The antique desk upon which sat a leather case holding my dad's World War II medals drew lots of "ooohs" and "ahhs." Vintage black and white photos of my smiling parents in the 1940s and 1950s drew plenty of attention, virtually none of the visitors aware of whom those attractive images were of—or about the significance each had played in my life.

The photo of me as a cute 4-year-old—taken at a studio in Twin Falls, Idaho was placed in a special area in the dining room, most visitors unaware that my late father had spent every penny he had to buy the image after seeing the photograph in a display window. Streams of gladiolas flowing from a wide crystal vase in the living room made people comment on how delightful the entire inside of the home looked—everyone in the dark as to the major significance such flowers had played in my life.

To our great pleasure, we felt honored and delighted when Preservation Society President Sharon Honig-Bear stopped by with just 10 minutes left in the tour. Like the organization's volunteers, she had worked non-stop throughout the day at numerous homes, ensuring that the event went off without a hitch. We told Sharon of our boundless joy in sharing the home with our community, glad to have played at least some small role in helping to support historic preservation efforts.

Thankfully, throughout the day Reno had been blessed with sunny, windless and warm weather. Yet storm clouds suddenly appeared overhead, just as the volunteers and final visitors started to leave. Among those departing were members of the widely esteemed and greatly appreciated Great Basin Costume Society. These attractive adults, men and women, wear authentic old-style clothing at numerous public events, including popular fundraisers such as that day's home tour. To our great delight, we had seen several of these delightful people that morning in the other homes.

"Have any of you seen magpies around town?" Wayne asked a couple of the costumed volunteers as they left. "Those birds are important to our story about this house."

Lauren Reeser, an attractive woman in her 20s wearing a flowing 1930s-style dress promptly answered: "Yes."

"Where!" Wayne said as I stood at his side, our ears at full attention.

"There are lots of them up near the base of Peavine Mountain,"

Lauren said. "They're up above the Somersett community west of town."

"Wow!" I said. "I wonder why the birds are way out there."

Lauren explained her theory that perhaps magpies prefer to avoid highly populated urban areas. Thus they had migrated to the latest outer reaches of Reno, which had sprawled in every direction in recent decades.

As if to celebrate this new-found, significant discovery, just when the final visitors and volunteers left the clouds burst overhead. Soothing, refreshing rain reinvigorated my garden.

Blessed with this new-found revelation, Wayne and I began to realize that figuratively speaking magpies had spread much farther than merely the outskirts of urban areas. Indeed, magpies—those loving, caring and vibrant creatures, doing everything possible to survive in today's increasingly hectic world—are at least in some sense just like us humans. All of us have magpies in our hearts. We want to do whatever we can to survive, to make our homes livable and attractive and comfortable nests—whether they are historic dwellings such as my home or cookie-cutter houses in sprawling pre-fabricated communities. At least in a small way, my parents were magpies, always wandering soles eager to return to nature for fishing—because they hated big-city life.

You and I, all of us, we're just like those birds. Long after I'm dead and gone, the many books that I have written or marketed or designed shall enable me to leave an enduring legacy. I shall emotionally fly like just such a bird—spreading my wings open and wide, to enable people to create their own enduring legacies, bolstered by their unique stories.

This way, I shall thrive, survive and help others throughout my life and then forevermore, for I am now and always will be one of them—those magpies.

I saw my first magpies in more than 53 years on Oct. 14, 2011. That afternoon two magpies took me by surprise, flying nearby as I fished with Bill in Smith Valley, Nevada, about 80 miles south of Reno. Bill and I had chosen to spend that morning fishing along the Walker River in the valley, the same spot where my late father befriended a Mountain Man more than a half century earlier.

Exactly one week later, while on a photo shoot, art-oriented trip for a Nevada Book project with Stephen Wheatcraft, I unexpectedly spotted one magpie while entering Jacks Valley—about 45 miles south of Reno.

These unexpected sightings filled me with appreciation for the many gifts from our Creator. An avid lifetime bird watcher, during the previous half century I had actively and consistently remained on the lookout for possible magpie sightings. These miraculous birds never appeared at or near my former mountain hideaway in Dixie Valley in the high Sierra. In fact, during the early 1990s a University of Nevada professor living in my back cottage, specializing in birds—an "ornithologist"—identified dozens of species that lived in or visited my property; none of those were magpies.

Needless to say, I considered these unexpected sightings of my favorite birds as a sign from above, opening up my burning need to tell you this story.

About the Author

A widely acclaimed artist, graphic designer and marketing expert, Patty Atcheson Melton lives in Reno, Nevada. Her books available at Amazon.com and via all major bookstores in the United States include "Create an Enduring Legacy: The essential, simple guide for creating your book in the self-publishing market."